the Master & the Muses

the Master & the Muses

AMANDA McINTYRE

Spice

Recycling programs
for this product may
not exist in your area.

Spice

THE MASTER & THE MUSES

ISBN-13: 978-0-373-60544-6

For questions and comments about the quality of this book
please contact us at Customer_eCare@Harlequin.ca.

Spice and the Colophon are trademarks used under license and
registered in Australia, New Zealand, Philippines, United States Patent
and Trademark Office and in other countries.

www.Spice-Books.com

Printed in U.S.A.

As always to my supportive family, immediate and extended, for their inspiration, love and patience.

Prologue

I HAVE BEEN CALLED MANY THINGS—RECKLESS, arrogant, perverted, self-absorbed and, my personal favorite, an artist of the "fleshy school." Perhaps these allegations are true; I do not deny them, but to those stifled critics of my work, I turned a deaf ear and listened instead to the beat of my heart, the siren song of my passion.

Had I listened to the naysayers of my work, to the critics who sought to box in my genius, my very soul, I daresay I would not have taken up a single brush.

In truth, I believe the critics are correct in their assessment of my incorrigible behavior. Daring to be different was, and is still, the very essence of my creativity. I am nothing if not tenacious in my beliefs, and proud to be so.

These would-be art connoisseurs know nothing of true art. Their view is monocular, dull and lifeless, linear and plain. It does not see the emotion of a woman's faint blush of arousal, of her cheeks in bloom at seeing her beloved, of her eyes bright and shining in the afterglow of passion. No, to paint such beauty, one must experience it, feel it and grasp it. No classroom, no stack of books can teach these things.

Despite my parents' wishes, I was not destined to be a religious man. Rather, I consider myself a spiritualist, a believer in karma more so than doctrine. My passion lies in the tip of my brush, but my inspiration is women. They are my muses. I ask you, what creature in all the earth epitomizes such beauty and grace? Many artists have tried to capture the beauty of this world. Even so, there are few things more persuasive than the delicate color of a woman's flesh. What could be more inspiring than the soft curve of her shoulder poised to carry the burdens of her world or the pout of her sumptuous mouth determined to carry those burdens with dignity?

Rescued from the mundane existence of their lives, my muses needed no coercion. Fame, independence, appreciation—that is what I gave them in return.

My pulse quickens to think of our conversations, the wine we drank, the free-spirited love we made. I was asked once if I ever loved one more than the other? To that I say, how can a man love only his arm, and not his leg, or his eye, or his mouth? I loved each one for the life she breathed into me, inspiring my work. But I could no more hold them to me forever than I could hold a sunbeam.

Reality and art, in many ways, are one. To my moral censors, I ask how could I *not* fall in love with each of my muses? Each represents a part of my soul. No, to each one I was utterly and completely a devoted slave.

Did they know this? It will not add to my days to know that answer. Life, love—it is what it is. I was both their savior and their sin. I rescued them from the ordinary, redeemed them with the stroke of my brush.

In my quest to capture the perfect image, I may not have been aware of all that my muses had to endure. But I offered them new worlds, new adventures. If that makes me a selfish bastard, then I accept my guilt with open arms.

Do I have regrets? What good Italian does? The bad has given me a better appreciation for the good. The good reminds me that while it is welcome, it is also fleeting. I have tasted the cup of life and offer no apologies.

To you, my muses, I raise my evening port. You have fueled my imagination and lust. Without your inspiration, I would not be the man I am. Helen, my innocent, fervent in your private desires. Sara, my socialite, always reaching for more. And Grace, in saving you, I saved myself.

I am forever slave, mentor and pupil to your inspiration,

Thomas.

Book 1

HELEN

Chapter 1

Leicester Square, 1860

THERE HE WAS, THE SAME MAN AGAIN, WATCHING me as I walked to work. His formal frock coat he wore over an ill-fitting shirt, tucked into rumpled trousers, giving the appearance that he'd just been roused from bed. I assumed he was local by manner of his dress, perhaps not of great wealth, but respectable, except for his deplorable habit of staring. Perched on his head, he wore a too-small brown derby that looked as if it had seen better days. These things I noticed since I've been a milliner's apprentice in one of London's premier hat shops from a young age. It was my job to be acquainted with the most current chapeau styles.

I must admit, I was not at all accustomed to being the subject of a man's interest. It intrigued me, but I chose to ignore my admirer, as any respectable lady would do. He was a persistent fellow, however, and for three days, I passed him standing on the opposite side of the street, daring only to glance at him as I arrived for work at Tozier's hat shop. My overactive imagination, a fault of which I'm reminded often by my mother, soon had me pondering whether he was planning something sinister against my employer.

On the third day just before the noon hour, he entered the shop. I was preparing a hat for display, pretending not to notice the strange thudding in my heart. He hung near the front door for a time, perusing the lady's handkerchiefs and lace gloves, ever so slowly inching his way over to where I stood. Perhaps I had misjudged him and he was simply debating what to buy for his spouse or mistress. Mrs. Tozier kept a private list of the men who often needed a "little something" for the *special* woman in their lives—most often not their wife. Discreet and professional, Mrs. Tozier would take their money, wrap their gift and offer them her smile.

"Pardon, mademoiselle," the mysterious man said in a smooth, baritone voice.

I looked up and met his startling blue-green eyes, clear as the sky and sparked by a mischievous curiosity that sent a shiver through me. His hair was a light brown, slicked behind his ears and dipping just to his collar. The firm line of his jaw, which looked as if it could use a barber's razor, was accentuated by a wicked dimple when he smiled. Perhaps I was mistaken and he was a foreigner? It might explain his hesitancy to approach me if he was unable to speak any English.

"Are you French, sir?" I enunciated my words clearly. He had an aristocratic air about him, a rather regal, pleasant face and, at closer look, he was quite handsome. Had he been dressed more appropriately, he might have passed as a baron or a duke.

"No, I am not French, mademoiselle."

Although I was relieved that I would not need to draw on my minimal skills in the French language, his admission raised a new bevy of questions. "Nor am I, sir. Why then, do you pretend to be something you are not?"

He took off his silly brown derby, and, with a sheepish grin, smoothed his palm over his locks in a vain effort to bring them under control. "My apologies for assuming you might speak French, working at a French hat shop."

"What brings you to our shop, Mr.—?" I waited for his name.

"Rodin. William Rodin. Perhaps you've heard the name?"

I studied him evenly and gave no reply.

He waved his hat. "Well, I am confident that one day you will." His smile would have charmed a snake. "Are you familiar with the world of art, by chance? It is possible you may have heard of my brother, the famous artist, Thomas Rodin." He fingered his derby as he spoke. I noted by the appearance of its tattered edge that if he, too, was in the business of art, it was not doing very well these days—at least not for him.

"No, Mr. Rodin. I am afraid I have not heard of either you or your brother. My time is quite full with my duties here in the shop." I turned the hat stand this way and that, as if studying the display. The truth was, I had but a few times actually engaged in conversation with a male since Mrs. Tozier allowed me to work out front. Certainly not one who seemed interested in my thoughts.

He brought his hand to the collar of his coat, taking on a dignified stance as he tossed me a wide smile.

"Then, dear woman, our meeting is your good fortune, for now you will be able to say, 'I knew Thomas Rodin personally while he was in the prime of his artistic greatness.'"

I dipped my head to hide my smile. I did not wish to offend his pride.

"Are you interested in a hat, Mr. Rodin?"

He placed his bowler on the counter and leaned close. I glanced around the shop and prayed that Mrs. Tozier would not appear. She was a robust woman, with a thick French accent. Not one to tangle with, her grandfather had immigrated to London to open this milliner's shop. I could not afford to lose my job over some strange man and his absurd interest in telling me about his *famous* brother. I held up my hand politely. "Mr. Rodin, my apologies, but I do have work to do. If you are not looking to buy a hat, then I must excuse myself and return to my duties." I turned to leave, and he reached for my arm.

"Let me get right to the point."

"Just as soon as you remove your hand from my arm, sir," I said. However, I could not deny the pleasant warmth of his palm.

His mouth lifted at the corner, as if he knew his touch jarred me. Slowly, he removed his hand.

"I have come to offer you a proposition."

"Excuse me, sir? Perhaps you've forgotten just where you are. If you are here to seek companionship for the evening, the Ten Bells Pub is down the street. I'm sure you'll find what you seek there."

He looked at me in surprise. "No—I mean, of course not. I've come to offer you honest employment. You have the potential to become quite famous."

He liked to use that word with great frequency. "Famous, you say? As *you* are famous, Mr. Rodin?"

His eyes narrowed, studying me before he resumed his amiable expression. "My fame is in knowing the genius of the brotherhood. I am a designer, not an artist in the true sense of the word. However, presently being between projects, I have offered my services to my brother."

"That is quite thoughtful of you, Mr. Rodin. Now if you'll excuse me."

"Wait, I beg you to listen. The artists of the Pre-Raphaelite Brotherhood are looking for new models to pose for them. They have a very specific type of woman in mind and you fit the criteria brilliantly."

"Criteria, for your *'brotherhood'?* Really?" I did not hide my skepticism.

"Indeed. You are what we would call a 'stunner.'"

The word made me sound like the type of woman one would pick up at the Cremorne on a Saturday evening. His eyes raked over me, unashamed.

I pulled a display between us and I busied myself with adjusting the feather on the band of the hat. He continued to stare. No man had ever seen me as a model before.

"Your hands are quite lovely," he said, leaning against the counter.

"Please, you'll smudge the finish. If Mrs. Tozier—"

At that moment, I heard a heavy clomp-clomp coming across the wood floor from the back room.

"There, now you've done it. If I lose my position—"

"I've just offered you another." He straightened and offered a pleasant smile.

"Miz Bridgeton, *eez* there a problem? Are you able to assist the *geentleman?*"

Mrs. Tozier came to my side. She was two inches shorter than I was, but more than made up for her height with her stern demeanor.

I started to explain, but the tenacious Mr. Rodin interrupted me with a slight lift of his hand.

"Madame Tozier." He bowed, taking her hand, placing there a quick kiss. *"Je suis un artiste de design et de poésie,"* he attempted in broken French.

Mrs. Tozier looked at him with a wary eye. She was quite capable of spotting a fake—whether a hat or an accent. She frowned at me, and then at the man. "You are a design artist and a poet. How nice. So, you've come to buy a hat, *oui?*" she stated plainly, tugging her hand from his.

I bowed my head, pretending to be engaged in repositioning the ribbon on the hat in front of me. Mrs. Tozier had little patience for wasting time. And if one had no interest in purchasing a hat then, to her way of thinking, they were wasting her time.

He paused, clearing his throat. *"Madame,* I would like to discuss the possibility of borrowing your fine clerk, Miss Bridgeton, to hire as an artist's model."

Mrs. Tozier's hand flew to her mouth and her expression changed to blatant anger. *"Geet* out, *geet* out of my shop! *You…*you should be ashamed of coming in here and harassing a young girl, so sweet and innocent. *Out,"* she snapped, waving her arms, chasing him to the front door. "You will ruin her reputation! That is what you will do."

I looked down and realized Mr. Rodin had left his hat. Carefully, I tucked it behind the counter. I watched as Mrs. Tozier slammed the door, causing the bell to clatter wildly. With a huff, she pulled down the lace shades that kept out the afternoon sun. She faced me and shook her finger as she stamped back to me.

"Do not speak to such men, Helen. They will only beguile you. Use you like tissue paper and toss you away with as much ease."

I wondered how she knew of such men. "*Merci,* Mrs. Tozier. He has been watching me for several days." Oddly, my heart beat with a fierce and dangerous thrill. In part from her tone, in part from remembering how Mr. Rodin had looked at me. "Do you think he will be back?"

"*Non,* he won't if he knows what *eez* good for him," she huffed, smoothing her hands down the front of her skirt as if ridding his scent from her hands.

I waited until she disappeared beyond the curtains to the back room before daring to hurry to the front window and peer out.

To my strange delight, he was there, leaning against the corner of the building across the street. He caught me looking at him and placed a finger to his brow in salute, stuffed his hands in his trouser pockets and strolled down the street.

Later that night at supper, I spoke to my family about the incident. My papa knew immediately with whom the young man was associated. His words echoed Mrs. Tozier's.

"Bad seeds, the lot of them. They condemn the teachings of the scholars at the Royal Academy, claiming they teach rubbish. Then they carouse the streets, preying on young girls to lure into their studios, promising who knows what and, once there, the poor things cannot defend themselves."

My sisters, fascinated by the conversation, turned their collective wide-eyed gaze to me, waiting for my response.

"But Papa." I carefully chose my words. It had taken a great deal of effort to convince him to let me apprentice at Tozier's, and I did not wish to jeopardize that small bit of freedom I had.

"Mr. Rodin did not appear to be a deceitful man." I popped a dumpling in my mouth, slowly raising my eyes to meet my father's.

"You heard me, Helen Marie. You are to stay away from that riffraff. No good will come of it, I tell you that. Concentrate on your duties and learn the trade. That is what making a real living is—it is not about slapping paint on a canvas and living hand to mouth."

With one last effort to keep the conversation alive, I glanced at my mama, seated across the table from me. Her expressionless face spoke to me in greater volume than if she'd opened her mouth. The conversation was over. It was not to be brought up again.

I was old enough to make my own decisions but, due to my meager wages, was forced to live with my family because I had no husband. My papa and mama were of the belief that a man was the breadwinner and the woman the keeper of the hearth and home. They did not understand that if I met the right man, I would gladly work hard beside him, just as Madame Tozier worked with her husband at the shop. But according to my parents' wishes, until some wealthy gent swept into the shop and asked for my hand in marriage, I was destined to become a spinster with a very good knowledge of making hats. Was this my only opportunity to start a life of my own? Was it a chance to get my poetry in front of another creative soul?

As I helped to clear away the supper dishes, my mother placed her hand on my cheek.

"You are a beautiful girl. You will find a good man, like your father. A man who is not afraid of hard work." She patted my cheek as if that would magically make all my cares disappear.

Later, in the sanctuary of my room, I placed Mr. Rodin's hat inside a round hatbox that I'd found stacked near the refuse bins outside the shop. I tied it with a brown ribbon and tucked it beneath my bed, hoping that I would be able to give it to him on my way to work tomorrow.

For a long time I stared at the pale moonlight on my ceiling, remembering the look in his eyes as he studied me. I imagined reaching out to touch his unshaven cheek, feeling his warm breath on my face as he drew near. Strange sensations made my body tingle. For the first time in my life, I saw myself as a grown woman instead of a child.

Chapter 2

IT WAS ODD TO SEE MY SHADOW AS I WALKED along the cobbled lane to work. Between the constant downpours and the stench from the river that hovered over the city like a hazy specter, the sun was a strange sight. Its warmth lifted my spirits, but the idea of seeing Mr. Rodin had improved my mood long before I set foot outdoors.

I turned the corner, scanning the block before me, disappointed when I saw only the familiar store managers putting out their wares.

"A fine day to you, miss."

I took a step back, taken by surprise at Mr. Rodin's sudden emergence from a closed storefront. "Are you always this forward when in pursuit of potential models, Mr. Rodin?" I squared my shoulders, making sure he thought I did not appreciate him accosting me in this manner. In truth, however, butterflies had taken flight inside me.

He bowed. "Forgive me. I only came to inquire whether you might have seen my hat. I have apparently misplaced it."

My brave response was prompted by my secret delight in seeing him again. "And you did not wish to encounter Mrs. Tozier again, I presume?" It was as close to flirting with a man as I'd ever done.

His eyebrows rose and he gave me a wicked grin. "How astute you are, Miss Bridgeton. I pray you know me all too well."

"Oh, Mr. Rodin, something tells me that I have barely scratched the surface. Nonetheless, I did find your hat before Madame Tozier did." I handed him the round box, which he held high, turning the beribboned container this way and that.

"I can't say when my old chapeau has ever looked better," he remarked.

"I quite agree, Mr. Rodin," I responded with a genuine smile. "If you'll excuse me, I must get to work." I started around him.

"Um…excuse me, Miss Bridgeton. May I inquire of your plans this evening after work?"

I stopped and looked over my shoulder. True it was that I did not belong to an aristocratic circle where gentlemen used calling cards to request a lady's company. Regardless, I was somewhat surprised by his unconventional manner. Then again, what should I expect from a man who had skulked around watching me for days before speaking? I thought of what I would do for one of my sisters. Would I give up easily if I thought they truly needed something? "You must adore your brother very much, Mr. Rodin."

He pried open the hatbox lid, offering a lopsided grin as he plopped the bowler on his head.

"Indeed, I do, but what makes you say so?"

He had not noticed that I had carefully trimmed the frayed edges of his hat. "Because it is clear that you are not to be put off, isn't it? No matter how rude I am."

His blue eyes regarded me with new interest. "Are you being rude?"

"See there, you wouldn't even know!" I replied.

He laughed and the sound of it was so carefree that I daresay I found my mouth twitching to smile.

"Miss Bridgeton, I assure you that my intentions are honorable. Are you not old enough to accept a simple invitation for a walk in the gardens, maybe to enjoy an ice cream with me?"

"For what purpose, Mr. Rodin?" I knew to accept meant I would hear more about this proposal. Moreover, I feared that my interest was not merely in his proposal, but in seeing him again.

"Very well, Mr. Rodin. Shall we meet at the west gate of the Cremorne Gardens, then? Around five?"

"I look forward to it, Miss Bridgeton. You can ask then all the questions that I'm certain are mulling around that beautiful head of yours."

We'd taken our ice cream and walked past the dancing platform to get away from the crowd and the loud music of the outdoor stage. It was a pleasant early evening at the gardens. The lights, hung by lanterns in the trees, flickered in the dusky wane of sunlight. A gentle breeze blew, mercifully keeping the lingering stench of the city at bay, at least for a while. "Tell me about your brother, Mr. Rodin."

I used a spoon to scoop up a bite of the refreshing ice cream infused with lemon. An arched tunnel overgrown with wisteria and vines led to another part of the park. I thought we would be able to talk quietly there.

We walked through the tunnel in silence, the cool shadows as welcome as the treats we ate.

"What would you like to know about him?" Mr. Rodin asked.

I confess my head felt light for no reason I could think of other than the handsome gentleman at my side. Unnerved by my reaction to his proximity, I sought to find a question about his brother that could possibly interest me more than Mr. Rodin. "Why don't you tell me about his work?"

A small blob of ice cream slid off my spoon and landed in the middle of my chest. I grimaced and Mr. Rodin offered to hold my cone while I rummaged through my bag for a handkerchief.

"There now, Miss Bridgeton. I've got it."

He pulled a handkerchief from his pocket and swiftly wiped away the mess. I felt the slight brush of his fingertips over my breast. A gasp tore from my throat. "Please, Mr. Rodin!"

"My apologies, Miss Bridgeton. It seemed simple enough to remove without touching your—"

My brows shot up. "I receive your meaning, Mr. Rodin. You needn't embellish." I took his handkerchief and dabbed at the place where the ice cream had seeped through to my skin. My cheeks burned with embarrassment. "Perhaps we could find a place to sit down?"

"Oh, yes, of course. Here, this looks like a suitable spot."

He waited as I sat, and I shook my head when he offered me the remainder of my cone. He tossed both cones into a receptacle nearby and sat down beside me.

"Please continue, Mr. Rodin. You were telling me about your brother." I took a breath and patted my hair, trying not to look too disheveled.

"About Thomas—" he tapped his long fingers together "—he's a complex fellow, as most men of his position are. His passion is his art and that is what drives him, I suppose."

"Forgive me, but is he any good? Does he exhibit his work publicly?"

He turned to look at me, his expression curious. "You've truly not heard of him?"

I shook my head. "I'm sorry, I have not."

"His earlier works have been on exhibition at the Royal Academy gallery. I believe one or two still hang in a permanent wing at the insistence of one of the academy's wealthy contributors."

"His accomplishments sound most impressive. You must be quite proud."

"I told you, Miss Bridgeton, he is gifted man. Not perfect, mind you, but bright and determined. He is a romantic at heart. His work is largely of women, using poetic imagery, religious stories and legends from which he derives his ideas. Though, in truth, his inspirations are his muses."

"May I ask what you mean by 'his *muses*'?"

"Let me make one thing perfectly clear, Miss Bridgeton. My brother has a deep, abiding love of women. A reverence, I daresay. Thomas regards women with the same awe that other men reserve for the stars, or a sunrise."

"My, what a lovely thing to say, Mr. Rodin." My eye caught the shadowy figures of a couple hurrying into the dense foliage beside the tunnel. There was little doubt in my mind what mischief they were engaging in. I forced my attention back to Mr. Rodin. "Are there many members in this brotherhood, Mr. Rodin? Any other models?"

"There are a handful of us—other artists like Thomas, me, in design…we also have amongst us a poet, a journalist and an author, as well as a few other individuals. You need not take concern, Miss Bridgeton. We are a close-knit group and very watchful of one another."

A woman's lusty sigh came from the other side of the wall. I kept my eyes on Mr. Rodin's face. He continued, despite the distracting animallike sounds coming from nearby.

"There is a certain amount of pride in what we believe in, what we aspire to. Each of us has a purpose, a goal we want to achieve, but we are—"

"Oh, yes…yes, that's lovely, *guvner.*" The woman emitted a loud sigh. "Here now," she said, "let's see what gift you've got for me."

I heard the soft baritone of a man's chuckle. "You are an eager one."

Images of what the couple were engaged in leaped into my imagination and I licked my lips.

"—professional and discreet," Mr. Rodin finished

My face felt flushed, feverish. I fisted my hands in my lap, trying to stay as detached from the events on the other side of the wall as it seemed Mr. Rodin was. I wanted to ask him if we should take our conversation elsewhere, but he appeared to be perfectly content and I did not wish to convey to him that I was as unsettled as I truly was.

"Discreet?" The word squeaked from my throat. "Oh, yes, an admiral trait, certainly."

A deep-throated groan wafted through the flowers and I saw the instant Mr. Rodin recognized it. His mouth curled slightly at one side and he averted his eyes for a moment.

"Did you have any other questions, Miss Bridgeton?" he asked.

"Oh, dear lady! What extraordinary skills you possess!" the man growled from inside the bushes.

I turned my head aside, covering my mouth to hide my smile. I cleared my throat, loud enough, I hoped, to alert the couple they were not alone. It did not seem to deter them.

"There now, hold it still, *guvnor*. You're plenty ready."

"But I paid for an hour," the man remarked with slight agitation in his voice.

"Is that my fault, then? Besides—" she cooed "—there's no sayin' that we can't find us another lovely spot to 'ave a go at it again, if you get my meaning?"

A deep chuckle followed.

I was so entranced by their repartee that I had all but forgotten Mr. Rodin was seated beside me. My eyes flickered to his steady gaze. "Oh, my, what is it that you asked, Mr. Rodin?"

His grin curled upward, deepening that delightful dimple. "If you had any more—"

"Ah…ah, oh, yes…there, that's good, guvnor. *Real* good."

The trellised latticework wall bowed inward with each punctuated sigh coming from the woman.

"—questions," Mr. Rodin finished as he glanced at the heaving wall. He removed his hat and suppressed a grin.

"Perhaps we should leave?" I whispered, as the sounds of the couple's passion escalated. I'd never heard such noises before. A warm, damp feeling formed at the juncture of my thighs. My palms, too, were moist—indeed, my whole body seemed to come alive listening to their lusty cries.

"Are you quite sure? Just when things are getting interesting?" Mr. Rodin smiled openly.

"I think before they get too much more interesting." I stood, finding the backs of my knees weak.

"Very well, I could use a good walk myself."

He offered his arm and we continued to the other end of the breezeway. As we reached the open lawn beyond, I took a deep breath of fresh air. I felt as if all the blood had drained to my toes.

"Are you all right, Miss Bridgeton?" Mr. Rodin patted my hand, still tucked through his arm.

"Yes, I'm—"

A man's loud groan wafted on the breeze along with the music behind us. Few others were in the area as, by now, most people had taken to the dance floor.

I glanced over my shoulder. "I'm well, thank you. Um…might we resume our conversation? I believe you were about to answer my question regarding other models." He cast me a side look.

"Of course. Models… Normally, our artists do not employ more than one model at a time. Once a theme is chosen, the artist begins to look for the face that will complete his vision."

Mr. Rodin eased my arm from his and I felt awkward once more. We strolled together to the pond and watched silently as two swans swam by, gliding effortlessly side by side. I thought about the story of the ugly duckling that my sisters and I were told when we were young, of how the strange little duckling was turned into a beautiful swan. I felt such a complexity of emotions. In the wake of overhearing the couples' tryst, I was more aware than before of my attraction to Mr. Rodin.

"Perhaps you'd like to see some of my brother's work?" he asked, his eyes on the birds. "It might help convince you that my intentions are honorable."

"Oh, Mr. Rodin," I said, not wanting him to think me immature or indecisive. "I do believe you are being truthful. Please understand that I am interested—very interested. It's only that my family is not entirely agreeable to the idea of my modeling for an artist—any artist."

"I could speak with them, if you like," he offered.

I held up my hand. "Oh, no, that would not go over well, I'm afraid. My family's opinion of artists is much worse than even Madame Tozier's."

He frowned. "That is a problem."

He looked away and I feared he was about to end our association. "However, perhaps I could meet you at the gallery sometime and you could show me your brother's work?"

He glanced down, a smile lighting up his face. "Splendid. Yes, that would be most enjoyable."

I breathed a quiet sigh. "Wonderful," I replied, offering him a smile in return.

"Can you meet me on Saturday, then?" he asked, removing his hat. A slight breeze lifted an errant lock of hair, blowing it across his forehead. My fingers twitched to brush it from his eyes.

"Oh? So soon?" I fretted over whether I could quickly devise an adequate excuse to get out of my Saturday chores. "I—I'm not sure I can make arrangements on such short notice."

"Your family?" he asked.

I nodded. He faced me then, and rested his hands on my shoulders. "I cannot deceive you into thinking that the members of the brotherhood are saints. We are flesh and blood, young and sometimes reckless, and we have the same drives as all men."

He searched my face for a moment. "Please go on, Mr. Rodin." I was grateful he held me upright, as my knees threatened to buckle.

"But our passion does not make us unsavory characters to fear. It is embracing that passion that gives the world its beauty. Do you understand?"

"I think so."

"And do you fear me, Miss Bridgeton?

I considered his question. "No, Mr. Rodin. I hardly know you, but in truth, I am far more afraid of how to explain my absence at dinner tonight to my family when I get home."

"Meet with me on Saturday. We can visit the Royal Academy gallery and you can judge for yourself whether you think my brother is worthy of your consideration. Afterward, if you are curious to know more, maybe you'd like to see his studio. I would be most happy to oblige the visit on Thomas's behalf. I think you will find the studio a welcome venue of artistic expression."

"I am rather a bit of an artist myself in that I write poetry," I admitted, precariously considering his offer.

"I knew it." He grinned. "Then I shall see you on Saturday?"

I swallowed, my confidence wavering. "I don't know, Mr. Rodin."

"Come. Let me get you a lemonade while you think on it."

He offered his arm and, for that, I would gladly think on any subject at great length, but I knew that it was getting late and my family would begin to wonder of my whereabouts.

We walked back to the main path near the dance floor where the crowd was thickening as the shops closed for the day and the city dwellers looked for respite from the heat.

I waited as Mr. Rodin approached a vendor, studying from behind how well he carried himself. As he waited in the line of thirsty patrons, a buxom woman with thick blond hair wound haphazardly atop her head touched his shoulder. He whirled in surprise and caught the woman in a great bear hug. They spoke for a moment, and she left. He paid for our drinks and headed back, offering me a broad grin as he handed me the glass. The drink was ice-cold and soothed my parched throat.

"Thank you," I said, and glanced at the woman now engaged in speaking to another man.

"Someone you know?" I asked lightly, sipping my drink.

"Jealous?" William teased.

"Oh, no, I…of course not."

He smiled and sat down beside me. "Please, Miss Bridgeton. Forgive my teasing, I meant no harm." He glanced at the woman and took a long gulp of his lemonade. He made a face as he smiled at me. "And they claim whiskey burns going down." He smacked his lips and blinked. "The woman's name is Grace Farmer. She is an old friend, who occasionally models for the brotherhood.

An excellent cook and a fine woman, though gravely misunderstood, I fear."

"Why is that, and by whom?"

"By virtue that she is a *ladybird,* I suspect. But only those who know her understand her character and the heart of the lady that she truly is." He stared at Grace a moment more before he drained his glass. "Besides, my brother lusts after her hair. It is an artist's dream."

I tried not to let it bother me that the brotherhood kept relations with prostitutes. That would not bode well where my family was concerned. Bad enough that models were already questioned for their promiscuous behavior. But perhaps she was the only woman with a jaded background.

My hand crept to my fiery red tresses as I wondered what his brother would think of *my* hair. I kept it swept up most of the time in a loose coil atop my head. I promptly moved my hand away so I would not reveal my concern to Mr. Rodin. "It's getting late and I should catch one of the ferries back across the river."

"I'll escort you to the dock," he offered.

We walked in silence to where one of the passenger boats lay docked in wait, filling up with weary passengers.

"Thank you, Mr. Rodin. It's been a lovely evening."

"Wait," he stated, and reached for my cheek. His thumb grazed the side of my mouth, sending a shiver down my arms.

"Bit of your ice cream. You want no telltale signs giving you away."

He could have wiped the ice cream on his trousers but instead he licked it from his thumb. I gave him a hesitant smile, wondering how best to explain his part in my detainment to my family.

"You didn't say whether we can meet on Saturday."

"I'll try, Mr. Rodin," I responded. "I'm not sure I'll be able to—"

"I know you'll need to make arrangements. But please try, Miss Bridgeton."

I took the boatman's hand and climbed into the boat.

"I will do my best, I promise." He walked on the dock along-side me as I made my way to the back of the boat.

Squatting down, he peered at me beneath the safety rails. "Say you will try very hard."

"Mr. Rodin."

"Miss Bridgeton, please. What I offer you could well change your life and that of your family."

I looked up, taking notice at that comment. In my world, art was a foreign thing, the value of it linked only with the great masters, not burgeoning new artists breaking the rules of convention. But I had to ask myself if I was willing to settle for *conventional* for the rest of my life. Was going against the wishes of my family in order to satisfy my curiosity worth the risk of possible alienation? My German father could be a stubborn and willful man at times.

In truth, I could not offer Mr. Rodin any certainty I could meet him again. Still, I wanted to see him smile once more. "Oh, very well, then. What time?" I called, my voice sounding almost desperate. I glanced around me, confronting the curious look of a woman and her husband.

"Splendid! Ten o'clock," he volleyed back.

I raised my hand, waving goodbye. "I'll see you then," I shouted. I lost sight of him as he made his way back up the dock toward the garden. I dropped my hand in my lap and felt like a foolish ninny wondering if he ran straight back to Grace Farmer. Of all things to think of! I had a much more important task ahead of me in devising a plan to escape my mother's watchful eye on Saturday.

Chapter 3

MY STOMACH, PRONE TO PANGS OF NERVOUSNESS, had given me trouble throughout the night. When the pain was severe, I was barely able to eat and my mother could tell in an instant if I was worried about something. Mr. Rodin seemed to be going to great lengths to convince me of the validity of this "brotherhood of artists" and the more I pondered my options, limited though they were, the more my stomach gave me issues.

"Did you take your laudanum, Helen?" my mother asked as she cleared away my breakfast bowl, half-full with my porridge. I had waited to come in for breakfast until I knew my sisters and papa were out doing their chores.

"Yes, Mama," I replied, following her into the kitchen. I had not the gumption yet to tell her that I was going to be gone for the day. I knew that I could not simply tell her the truth. She would not permit me to leave. Besides, I was still debating the wisdom of meeting Mr. Rodin alone. But if I was to achieve my independence, I would first need to find out more information. Until I knew more, there was no reason to involve my family.

"I've been invited to…a picnic today." The lie stuck in my throat. I busied myself with washing the dishes.

"That's lovely, dear. I'm glad to see you getting out. Who will be going?" she asked, tucking her rolling pin in the cupboard.

She looked at me with such delight that it made my stomach burn. My mother, I think, saw me as a recluse, though she never said the words aloud.

"Some of the girls from the shop."

"And will there happen to be any gents there?" Her eyes revealed the hope that there might be future marriage prospects involved.

I tried to keep my smile genuine. "It was not my invitation, Mama, I cannot say."

"Where is the picnic?"

My mind went blank. I had been unprepared for further questions. I scolded myself mentally. "Um…the *Cremorne*," I lied again, my stomach protesting my deceit.

She patted my cheek. "Well, it sounds lovely, and it would do you good to get out a bit more. So I shouldn't plan on you for supper, then?" she asked.

I shook my head. "You best not wait on me tonight. I will be sure to catch the ferry by ten o'clock."

"Perhaps I should send your papa down to the dock to fetch you. I don't like the idea of you without a chaperone, especially at that hour."

"I'll be fine, Mama. None of the other girls will have their papas meeting them. I'll be fine." I hastened to gather up a few items before she could think of more questions to ask.

"Helen?"

I heard my name as I headed down the front path and turned to find her holding my parasol out to me.

"Your skin, you know how you burn. Don't forget to use this."

"Thank you, Mum. Stop fretting now. I'll be fine," I assured her.

The morning was brilliant, the sun warm on my face as the boat ferried me across the river. The stench was the only thing marring my delight at having managed to get away from the house with so little inquisition.

I hurried along the cobblestone street wishing I could afford the carriage ride, so I would not be wilted by the time I reached Mr. Rodin. I rounded the corner of the gallery and there he was pacing out front. He stopped and checked his stopwatch. Having no such luxury of my own, I took my time from the toll of Parliament's new clock tower. "Mr. Rodin," I said breathlessly, forcing a smile as I slowed to a respectable pace.

"Miss Bridgeton." The peel of the tower bells sounded. "Splendid, you're right on time."

He offered me his arm and we went inside. The Royal Gallery was quite beautiful, room after room of high-polished floors and great high ceilings. Pictures were hung in ornate gold frames, stacked next to one another on the walls at eye level and upward.

"You want to be able to get the spot at eye level," Mr. Rodin explained. "That's how you know the committee approves of your work."

"And where is your brother's work, Mr. Rodin?" I asked, searching the wall as if I would recognize his work when I saw it.

"Third row from the top…over there. It's a brilliant piece. It should have been lower. But my brother has issues with conforming to the committee's wishes."

He smiled at me when I gave him a questioning look.

"Thomas quit the academy under protest of the teachings here. He's never really quite gotten back on track with the committee. He doesn't have a number of highly influential friends, as I mentioned." He looked at the painting. "Truthfully, Miss Bridgeton, I think deep down he wished the committee would judge his work on its own merit, and not on Thomas's reputation."

I studied the painting as best as I could from my vantage point. It was a lovely portrait of a woman barely covered by a luxurious blue drape. It was the light in her eyes that struck me the most. They seemed so full of life.

"You mustn't let this influence your decision, Miss Bridgeton. Often in life, it is the geniuses who are the least understood."

"Oh, I do understand that." I slanted him a glance and he returned it with a smile. William's solid belief in his brother's work was what made Thomas's painting stand apart from the rest. I knew little about Thomas Rodin, the artist, but the more time I spent with his brother, the more I came to revere him and the more I desired to meet him. I began to realize, too, that wherever there was opportunity to be around William, I was more than willing to take whatever risks were involved.

We came to a statue of a nude male reclining, as though relaxing in a meadow on a pleasant day. Every muscle was intricately carved, portrayed with lifelike precision, and my eyes were immediately drawn to the size of his phallus lying limp against his leg. Having never before been privy to the human male form, I silently wondered if it was realistically proportioned.

"Artistically enhanced," Mr. Rodin's voice issued at my side.

"Oh, I wasn't—" I started.

He raised his eyebrow.

My cheeks warmed and I looked away.

"Dear Miss Bridgeton, when it comes to art, only an intelligent person would have such questions."

"Thank you, Mr. Rodin, but how did you know?" I asked.

"Your face reads like an open book," he replied with a smile.

"I'm sorry, I suppose you find me quite naive."

"On the contrary. I think your innocence suits you beautifully."

"You have a wonderful way of making me feel at ease with myself, Mr. Rodin." I smiled.

He touched my arm. "I want you to feel comfortable in asking me anything. I know already that my brother is going to be as enchanted with you as I am. Your deep-set eyes and that flaming red hair—you're precisely what the brotherhood has been looking for."

"You flatter me."

"Miss Bridgeton, flattery has nothing to do with it. I am trying to convince you to model for us."

"Us? Do you paint also?" My heart raced a little faster at the thought.

"Me? No." He smiled. "I leave the painting to my brother."

As we walked through the remaining rooms, I was impressed by Mr. Rodin's knowledge of art even though he claimed not to be artistically inclined. It seemed he was forever comparing his brother's works to the early works of Michelangelo.

After the tour of the gallery, we took in the gallery's floral gardens. Mr. Rodin plucked a rose from a trellis and handed it to me.

"Thank you," he said, "for coming today."

I held the flower to my nose, breathing deeply of its sweet fragrance. "Thank you for asking me. It's been a lovely day."

"And do you yet have any concerns or questions that you'd care to discuss with me?"

I studied him a moment, hesitating still to agree to his proposition, knowing it would take far greater convincing of my family than of me. "I beg of you one more day to decide." My voice tinged on pleading, afraid that my request for delaying my response might change his mind.

He regarded me with a dubious look.

"Please, Mr. Rodin. I am humbly flattered. However, you must understand I've never received such a proposition before."

He smiled, though it appeared guarded. "Of course."

I offered a sigh of relief and smiled. Looking away, I held my stomach as I attempted to quell my nerves.

"Are you certain all is well, Miss Bridgeton?" he asked

I held up my hand. "It's...I'm fine. Perhaps a little ginger soda would help." I knew that I would need to take my medicine soon.

As he searched for a vendor, I scolded myself for getting so nervous.

Mr. Rodin did not press me further for an answer. We spoke on other topics and later that afternoon, he summoned a carriage and escorted me to the ferry.

At the dock, he handed me a card with his brother's name and address on it.

"If you make your decision, this is where you'll find me."

"Thank you again, Mr. Rodin." I smiled. "I promise to think about it."

The next day at work, a young boy came into the shop, self-consciously removing his cap as he pushed forward to the counter where I stood. In his arms, he carried a bouquet of lovely flowers. "There's a gent outside. He paid me a whole shilling. Says I was to give these to the prettiest girl in the shop." He glanced around and shrugged. "I guess that'd be you, then?"

I took the flowers and thanked the boy, checking the card tucked inside. I held it toward the light so I could read it.

Dear Miss Bridgeton,
Thank you for the lovely afternoon.
W.R.

"Miz Bridgeton, was that a customer at nearly closing time? Remember it is the Sabbath, we must close early, and I have much to do." Madame Tozier's eyes grew wide when she saw the flowers in my arms. "From a secret admirer?"

I tucked the card inside my apron.

"Oh, these? No, a young boy brought these by…for the owner."

"Was there a card?"

"No, Madame. He indicated that the man who sent them wanted to express his thanks." My mind frantically searched for recent sales. "He mentioned something about a traveling hat for his wife." It was as good as I could do on short notice.

She looked puzzled. "No name?" Then her eyes brightened. "Oh, Mr. Smythe!"

Relieved that my lie was validated, I nodded, encouraging the deception further. A sharp pang in my stomach reminded me of the stress I caused myself.

I was glad the shop had closed early. After graciously declining Madame Tozier's invitation to join her Sabbath celebration, I enjoyed the walk through the park for the chance to clear my head.

"Miss Bridgeton!" A familiar voice called from behind. I turned to find Mr. Rodin hurrying toward me. His face was flushed from running.

"I took the chance that you might be closing the shop early due to the Sabbath." He smiled and I felt my knees grow weak. I am not sure at what point I had begun to fantasize about Mr. Rodin and myself. Perhaps it was merely the fact that no man had ever paid so much attention to me before. Yet he seemed genuinely interested.

"I wondered if you'd had a chance yet to consider my proposal."

I appreciate your patience, Mr. Rodin, and your tenacity." My fingers tightened around my parasol's handle.

"My brother says that I am like a dog with a bone once my mind is made up on a matter."

His enchanting grin bolstered my confidence. "I am happy that you have not given up."

He stood before me looking quite dapper in his dark trousers and tan jacket. His wavy hair was brushed back behind his ears, accentuating his chiseled jaw. In his eyes, I saw a palatable hunger.

Although I knew fully that it was not proper for a young woman to accept such a proposal, I had no reason to fear Mr. Rodin. My fear was that his resolve might weaken if I answered no again.

He pulled a long-stemmed rose from behind his back and handed it to me.

Charmed, I took it from him, touching the delicate petals to my mouth as I breathed in its lovely fragrance. Twice, no, three times now, he had given me flowers.

"You received my flowers?" he asked, tipping his head.

I hesitated, trying to find the best way to explain what had happened. "I did, thank you. However, I regret to have to tell you that I gave them away. I am not allowed to accept gifts at the store."

"Duly noted. I could see where a woman of your beauty could cause problems in that area."

I averted my eyes. "Please, Mr. Rodin."

"I mean every word, Miss Bridgeton," he stated.

He studied me for a long moment, tapping his hat against his leg and then smiled.

"Well, it remains whether I can persuade you to visit the studio."

I could not have told him no had my life depended upon it. "Very well. Though you realize it is inappropriate for me to accept your invitation without a chaperone." His eyes raked over me and I admit I quite enjoyed it. There was something daring in the line I was about to cross.

"I believe you have a good head on your shoulders, Miss Bridgeton. I give you my oath, I will be a gentleman."

I took his proffered arm, hoping he would not be too much of one. I had dreamed for the past few nights of what it would be like to have his mouth on mine. I looked away, feeling my face flush again.

Mr. Rodin and I walked leisurely through the park to the line of carriages awaiting passengers. He assisted me into a two-seater, settling in close beside me.

"Cheyne Walk," he told the driver.

The open-air carriage jerked forward and I popped up my parasol to stave off the afternoon sun.

"Will your brother be at the studio?" I asked, keeping my eyes on the road ahead. I dared not look at him. Already I felt brazen at accompanying him without a proper chaperone.

"If he isn't, he will be shortly. He did mention meeting with some of the brotherhood this afternoon."

"Do you live at the studio with your brother?" I gave him a brief side look. He had a handsome profile, and I noted a cleft in his chin that I had not seen before.

"When I'm in London, yes, I stay with Thomas. It was a little hard at first getting used to his quirks." He chuckled. "Thomas paints when the mood strikes him—night or day."

I smiled pleasantly. I had apparently much to learn about the eccentric Thomas Rodin.

The carriage jostled down the cobblestone street, the sun overhead causing me to grow warm. I had bathed and dressed in one of my best gowns, donning a hand-me-down corset I had received as a gift from one of the girls at work. Still, the heat beneath the layers of clothing was suffocating.

At last, the carriage came to a stop in front of a tall, narrow, two-story stone flat. A small balcony looked out over the street from a set of French doors. It was simple, clean and neat, and appeared to be in a good district, putting my mind at ease in that regard.

Mr. Rodin helped me from the carriage and ushered me up a few steps to a painted red door.

"Here we are."

Inside, I allowed my eyes to adjust to the murky foyer. The entry was narrow, with a small room off to the right. I peeked inside, finding the room void of furnishings, but its floor-to-ceiling shelves were filled with books.

"The brotherhood are voracious readers," Mr. Rodin said, leaning over my shoulder. "Come, I'll show you the studio. It's upstairs."

He placed his hand on the small of my back, gently guiding me to the dark mahogany stairwell. Allowing me to go first, we walked up a short flight to a landing and took a sharp right turn to proceed up another set of stairs.

I brushed my palm over the ruby-red wallpaper. It had a raised, velvety texture that I had never seen before. "This design is lovely."

From behind, his hand reached up to rest beside mine. "Do you like it?" he asked.

I tried to ignore his close proximity, how the sound of his rich voice reverberated inside me. "The color is so elegant, like a red wine." I looked over my shoulder and caught his pleased smile.

"That was my inspiration."

"*Your* inspiration?" I asked, surveying the beautiful wall covering.

"This was one of the first designs I sold to a manufacturer right here in London. Granted, it's for a very limited clientele, but it's a start." He chuckled good-naturedly. "Doubtful my designs will ever hang in the academy."

"There are more homes in this world than museums or galleries, Mr. Rodin," I responded without hesitation. He lowered his hand, brushing it against mine in the process.

"Thank you, I've never thought of it that way."

I moved onward, more aware than ever of his presence behind me. At the top of the stairs was a wide hallway. Directly across from me was an open archway leading to a large room. To my right the corridor stretched past four more doors to the end of the hallway and a window festooned with delicate lace curtains. A putrid smell came from the larger room ahead and I lifted my hand to my nose. "Oh, goodness, what is that smell?"

Mr. Rodin laughed. "Thomas would tell you that's the smell of money."

He lightly touched my back, urging me forward.

"You'll get used to it. It's the linseed oil and cleaner for the brushes," he said over my shoulder. "You certainly smell far better."

"Mr. Rodin." A giggle escaped my lips. He eased around me, his chest brushing my side. I held my breath, unnerved at my body's reaction to him.

"Come in."

He waved me into the room and I stood a moment, letting my eyes adjust from the dark hallway to the fused afternoon light in the spacious room. It appeared as though a wall had been removed to create a massive combination studio and study. One end of the room was cluttered with easels, props and a lounge chair draped with beautiful gowns. It looked more like the backstage area of a theater than an artist's haven. At the other end sat a writing desk and another set of shelves holding collectible exotic items and more books. There was an ornate, black marble front fireplace flanked by a grouping of overstuffed chairs. Directly opposite the fireplace, Mr. Rodin had opened the French doors leading to the balcony. Papers pinned to canvasses fluttered in the summer breeze.

"Feel free to look around," Mr. Rodin said as he puttered around the room.

An errant sketch tumbled past me and kissed my toe. I reached down to pick it up at the same time as Mr. Rodin. Our fingers met briefly and my heart faltered. I let go of the paper, not wanting him to see the flush of my cheeks.

"Have you painted before, Miss Bridgeton?" He held the paper loose in his hand, his eyes steady on me.

I suppose his question was not out of the ordinary. Most well-bred women in London included painting, poetry and music in their list of abilities. "I've only written a little poetry. Dreadfully novice, I'm afraid." My eyes drifted to the sketch in his hand. Done in charcoal, it was the picture of a nearly nude woman reclined on a chaise. A drape thrown haphazardly over her legs. I looked away, scanning the pictures stacked against the wall, and wondered if I would be asked to pose nude.

Without comment, he placed the sketch on a stack of others on the desk, weighing them down with a thick book.

"Who do you read?" he asked, watching me as I inspected the stacks of paintings leaning along the wall. In one group alone, there were as many as a dozen paintings with various backgrounds, but the same woman's face. "I read most anything, Mr. Rodin. But I have a particular fondness for Dickens."

He chuckled. "A fine fellow, Charles." He glanced at the floor. "A bit zealous, but he means well."

"You know him?" I asked, wide-eyed.

He shrugged. "We had him over to dine one evening. He has some definite ideas on social reform."

I searched his face wondering whether or not to believe him. I'd begun to think that perhaps Mr. Rodin had not been embellishing on his brother's notoriety. "Did your brother paint these?" I asked. Mr. Rodin walked up beside me. "They all look like the same woman."

"Yes, these are the same woman. Thomas can be a bit possessive once he chooses a subject."

There was an underlying tone in his voice, though I could not pinpoint it exactly. Sadness? Frustration? His breath tickled the back of my neck. The woman in the paintings was undeniably beautiful. How could I compare to such beauty? "Do you think he will find me suitable?" I touched the collar of my blouse nervously.

I became aware in an instant of my ardent feelings for Mr. Rodin. While it was one thing to dream in the privacy of my room, it was quite another to deal with my desire while standing in a room alone, next to him. He had kept his word, remaining the perfect host, the consummate gentleman, and the realization of what I had agreed to illuminated my thoughts. I had hoped for, perhaps secretly wished, this would happen, that we might find ourselves alone, able to address the growing admiration I felt for him and I was nearly certain he felt for me.

It was both exhilarating and frightening to realize that I had just made the first big decision of my adult life.

Chapter 4

HIS FINGERS WERE WARM AS HE LACED THEM through mine. It would have been wiser for me to run. There was danger that he would snatch my virtue; perhaps more that I would allow it. I closed my eyes to the divine sensation of his thumb brushing back and forth over my wrist, aware of the desire rising inside me.

"What are you doing, Mr. Rodin?" I said breathlessly.

"How could my brother not find you absolutely perfect, Miss Bridgeton? He would have to be blind."

My heart thudded as I turned to meet his smoldering eyes. Unable to move, I fought to collect my thoughts, searched for a reason to deny what my body craved. I had spent days thinking of nothing but William.

"My father cautioned me that men, especially men who want something, will stop at nothing to achieve their purpose. Is that what you're doing, Mr. Rodin?" His eyes drifted to my mouth and I knew his curiosity matched mine.

"I confess, Miss Bridgeton, that since we first met, you have pervaded my thoughts." His crystalline blue eyes met my gaze.

"I pray, do not tease me, sir." I could not tell if my stomach was misbehaving or if more was happening to me. I had a dull ache deep inside—a yearning that I could not explain.

His grip tightened as he leaned toward me. The struggle for restraint was evident in his eyes and in the tick of his set jaw. A gust of hot air blew through the open balcony doors, sending a rustle of papers to join the pleasant buzz beginning in my head.

"And you, Miss Bridgeton, do you not know how you've bewitched me?"

He moved closer, afraid, I think, to frighten me. His warm, musky scent overtook my senses as he searched my eyes, asking silent permission. The mere brush of his lips to mine snatched my breath away, unleashing a primal need.

I boldly met his mouth, secretly thrilled by his deep-throated growl as he backed me against the wall. I curved my body to his hard muscled warmth, sensing his arousal through the layers of clothing between us.

Sweat trickled between my breasts, skittering over my heated flesh. The images conjured by the couple in the gardens leaped into my mind. I gave in to the lustful sounds in my memory, causing a ravenous fire to course through me.

I savored William's mouth slanting over mine, seducing, pulling me deeper under his spell, and whimpered softly when his greedy tongue plunged between my lips. He smelled of the warm summer wind, tasted of honeyed tea and cinnamon.

"God, but you are lovely," he said, his lips nibbling the sensitive flesh beneath my ear. "Tell me you've thought of this," he whispered. "That you've wanted this as much as I have dreamt of it."

His hand glided upward, over my waist, pushing higher until his palm closed gently over my covered breast. I squirmed beneath his fervent kisses, succumbing to the rapture of his intimate caress.

"I need to…I must touch you."

He looked at me with those mesmerizing eyes, demanding more. Despite the warring factions in my head cautioning me to end this, I could not refuse him—I did not *want* to refuse him.

I turned my back to him, lifting my hair to allow ease in unbuttoning my dress. His lips pressed to my exposed flesh, sending a cascade of shivers down my spine and straight to my core. Half-dressed now, I laid my cheek against the cool plaster wall, enjoying the brush of his hands as he peeled the dress slowly down over my body.

He kissed my shoulder, turning me to face him and, for a moment, we stared at each other. Frozen, I stood still as his eyes raked over me, assessing, deciding, it seemed, whether to continue. Before now, I'd never compared myself to another woman. I worried my lip, a nervous habit I deplored, but I feared he was having second thoughts.

My body trembled, alive with anticipation. He set to the task of unhooking the closures down the front of my corset, stopping intermittently to capture my face in a spine-tingling kiss. "Hurry," I whispered, anxious to be rid of my confinements.

I braced against the wall, grateful when he slid the stiff corset from around me. My breasts bobbed free, straining against my whisper-thin camisole. He dipped his head, closing his mouth over the fabric, drawing the rosy tip of my breast between his lips, teasing, taunting me.

My fingers tangled in his hair, kneading with luxurious euphoria, desire pulsing hot inside me. Through hooded lids, I watched how his mouth mastered my body, summoning new sensations.

Between scalding kisses, he tugged the wispy fabric over my head, binding my hands in the cloth, holding them above as he captured my mouth in a fierce kiss. William pulled back, took a deep breath and leaned his forehead to mine.

"It is the last thing I want, Helen, to deceive you or to make you think that your father is right. I did not plan this, and if you tell me to stop, I will, without question. But I pray you do not." He swallowed hard, searching my eyes.

I reached for his face, my fingertips—tentative, unsure—touching the roughness of his shadowy beard, fueling the fire already in my blood.

"I will not stop you, Mr. Rodin. I have thought of little else these past days." I met his mouth, coaxing him back to me, my hands awkwardly working at the buttons of his shirt between my fervent need to taste his mouth.

He took my hands and kissed them, stepping away to peel off his shirt and drop it in haste to the floor. My breath caught at the breadth of his shoulders, the soft dusting of hair on his sculpted chest. He was every bit as well formed as the statues I had seen at the museum.

The intensity of my fleshly appetite surprised me. It was as though another woman had been awakened in me. The sheen of his hard muscled flesh left me languid, craving his touch.

He slipped his hands beneath the waistband of my drawers, his eyes locked to mine as he drew them over my hips and waited for me to step from them. I pressed my palms against the wall, wearing nothing now but my old high-top boots.

"I am about to burst looking at you," he said. "See what you do to me."

My eyes lowered to the raised definition in his trousers, then flickered back to his heated gaze. The fact that I had caused his arousal, something that I'd never done for a man, delighted me. Still, I was not sure precisely what to do next. I did not have to ask.

He dropped to his knees, circling my waist with his hands, drawing my body to his mouth. He lavished attention on one breast and then the other.

"You are a virgin, aren't you?" he whispered.

His breath caused the gooseflesh to rise on my exposed skin. I nodded, my eyes fluttering shut as his kisses descended to my hip, his mouth kissing the tops of my thighs.

He lifted my leg over his shoulder, parting my feminine folds. I let out a small gasp as he slid his calloused thumb along my warm, wet maidenhood. My back arched forward and I covered my mouth to quell the soft sounds coming from my throat. His finger slid deeper and my hands flew to his head, in an effort to keep my weak knees from buckling.

"Don't be afraid, Helen. I'll take care of you," he soothed.

Sweat formed on my upper lip; my throat was parched. I was a stranger to this bliss, following blindly, my mind spinning in carnal bliss.

"I want you to remember this, Helen. Remember that it was me."

His hot breath on the inside of my thigh preceded the slow stroke of his tongue inside my drenched cleft. Brought entirely under this wanton turbulent need, I welcomed his intrusion and rocked my hips gently, inviting more from his rapturous tongue.

His tongue flicked a spot that brought me to my toes. I was like a glass teetering on the edge of a shelf, about to break. I held his face in my hands as he looked up at me.

"Tell me what you want, Helen," he said. His breathing was shallow, his eyes glittering with desperate urgency. "Be certain."

"Do not stop, not now." I brushed my hand over his hair and he offered a wicked smile.

He stood and swiftly unfastened his trousers, shoving them to his feet. I stared in rapt fascination at his swollen member jutting toward me. Fear flashed in my mind, but I wanted this as I had never wanted anything before in my life. My eyes rose to his heated gaze.

I'd never felt so reckless, so deliciously wicked. It was a powerful aphrodisiac. I wrapped my arms around his neck and he cupped my bottom, lifting me around his waist. His eyes held mine as he braced his hands against the wall and slowly entered me, hesitating when a gasp tore from my throat. The short pain gave way to a greater bliss and I welcomed the slick friction of our fused bodies.

"Are you all right?" he whispered, raking his mouth across the top of my shoulder.

"*Yes,*" I sighed, beginning to move with his rhythmic thrusts. I held his face to my neck, pushing my mother's scowling face from my mind, instead delighting in these new, wondrous sensations.

He straightened, repositioning himself, and thrust deeper, a possessive glint darkening his eyes.

"Look at me, Helen," he said, his voice rasping from his throat.

Sweat dripped from his brow, his breath hissing with each lunge. My body wound tight, my every sense sharpened. The thick scent of linseed and paint mingled with the drugging heat of the sultry summer evening. The flesh on my back stung where it rubbed against the plastered wall.

My control shattered and I gasped, quaking with unspeakable delight. I gripped his shoulders, hooking my legs firm around his waist. William panted hard with each thrust, driving impossibly deep—

He shifted, and the movement increased the wave of tremors rolling through my body, unraveling me. His muscles bunched beneath my clinging fingers.

My name wrenched from his lips as he pushed into me thrice more, and with a shuddering sigh dropped his forehead to my shoulder.

A breeze wafted through the balcony doors, cooling our sweat-drenched bodies. I turned my eyes to the waning light outside, surprised by how different things looked. How my body was satisfied, but my heart was still uncertain. I did not expect false promises, or a proposal of marriage to amend our wanton lust. However, I was not prepared for the stark emptiness inside of me at their absence. My eyes were blurred with unshed tears. He leaned back, his eyes soft with concern.

"Did I hurt you?" he asked, kissing my forehead.

The juncture betwixt my thighs was sore. I offered a wobbly smile, memorizing the sensation of him still nestled deep inside me. "No," I answered shyly. How could I tell him that I would marry him this instant if he asked?

He eased away, holding me like a delicate vase.

"Careful," he said with a quiet dignity. "You're all right, you're sure?"

My flesh grew cold, and I wrapped my arms around myself, searching the floor for my clothes.

Without comment, he handed me my undergarments. I sensed his discomfiture through his formality.

"Yes, thank you. I'm fine." My words sounded strange. I smiled, afraid to allow my true emotions to show.

His eyes met mine, and where I had seconds earlier seen concern, I saw little more than guilt. We dressed silently as if embarrassed by our impetuous actions. This behavior was new to me, as I suspected it may have been to him. He'd called me Helen in the throes of passion, I realized. How should I address him now? The socially expected protocol of *Mr. Rodin* hardly seemed necessary now.

He was a quiet man—caring and attentive. A confident man, in my view, having no need for constant reassurance. Still, I could not understand his silence. Had my silly heart chosen to see only what it wanted, rather than what was real? Dear heavens, had my father been right all along?

William finished dressing and walked out to the balcony. I followed, pausing for a moment at the open double doors. He leaned against the railing looking out over the city, far away in his thoughts.

The stench of the Thames settled over the city at this late hour.

"He cannot know," William said suddenly, his back still turned to me.

Certain that I had not heard him correctly, I moved to his side, curling my arm through the crook of his elbow. He picked up my hand and pressed it to his lips.

"Who do you mean?" I asked. "My papa? My family does not need to know." I studied his stern profile.

"No, Helen, not your father. You are old enough to make your own choices." His eyes raked over me briefly before he looked away.

"No, *Thomas.* It would make him furious if he knew we'd been together. If it had been anyone else but me, it would not matter. I do not know how best I can explain it, Helen. It's…how it is between us."

I stared at him, not believing what I had heard. Had he refused my immediate insistence to marry him, or even to make a true commitment only to me, *that* I would have understood. "Are you saying we must pretend that what happened between us did not? Why, William? Doesn't he want you to be happy?" My words tumbled from my mouth before I could think.

He kissed my hand again, this time facing me. His expression was firm, determined.

"This is not about *my* happiness, Helen. It is about *his* life, *his* work, his way of doing things," William stated, showing no emotion in those eyes that I'd just seen overflowing with passion. I saw instead the plea of a man begging me to understand, asking me to forget possibly the most wonderful thing that had ever happened to me. How could I ignore my feelings when my virtue was at stake?

"We cannot take this any further. I should have had more control." He shook his head as if scolding himself.

"Then I won't be his model, William," I said, grabbing his hand. "That is all there is to it."

"That would not be fair to you nor to Thomas."

My mouth gaped open, unable to find a response to his absurd comment. I squeezed shut my eyes, concentrating on putting together the pieces of this jumbled mess. "You cannot deny what has happened. I—I don't understand." I reached for his face and he backed away. He turned, shoving his hand through his hair.

"I am nothing like him, Helen. You will see once you've met him, once you get to know him. His presence alone commands those around him. He dominates everyone in his world. Not in an abusive way, please do not misunderstand." He braced his hands against the balcony railing as he stared out over the street. "He is a kind man and a good man."

"As you are, William." My arms ached to hold him again. I wanted him to tell me he was as happy as I was.

"You say that now." He offered a short laugh and tossed me a side look.

"What do you mean? Do you find me that shallow? So easily won by any man's charm?"

His eyes drifted shut and he offered a weary sigh. "It isn't you, Helen." He smiled. "It's him. I have never known a man so suited to his own skin, so confident in his opinion, so sure of his skill and his future. He is nearly perfect in all he does."

"You love him, of course." I touched his arm. Beneath his shirtsleeve, I felt the muscle that I had grasped moments before grow tense, unyielding.

"I would rather die than disappoint him." He stared straight ahead, his focus and his response unwavering.

"And so if I choose to model for the brotherhood, he would find it disappointing that we care for one another?" The idea that the sweetest freedom I had ever known was being snatched away boggled my mind.

"If he finds out what has happened between us, you will not be asked to model. *That* is exactly my point. Until he is finished, we cannot allow ourselves the luxury of having any sort of relationship, other than business." He slapped his hand against the railing.

"You're serious?" I asked. "Look at me, William. Tell me that you don't care for me." I stood firm, challenging him with a hard gaze.

Finally, he faced me, grabbing my shoulders. His eyes bored into mine, hard and cold.

"I owe him everything, Helen. He deserves my support and respect. His mind is brilliant, his gift rare. I would not usurp his goals in trade for mine."

Dazed by his words, I stepped away and batted at his hands when he tried to hold them. My stomach roiled uneasily.

"Helen, if what you say is true, then these feelings you believe are real will be there when you are done with your work here. Know this above all else—I do not regret what has happened. It is just…ill timed, I'm afraid."

His eyes implored me to take him at his word. I didn't know what to believe.

"Until his paintings are finished, he must have your undivided attention. That is just the way it has to be." He walked inside the door and held his hand out to me, waiting for my response.

Tears choked my throat and, despite his words, I pushed myself into his embrace. He held me close and I pressed my cheek to the warmth of his chest.

"I'm sorry, but if you agree to pose for the brotherhood, you become my brother's muse and I, your most willing servant in every way, save one."

The front door banged open and a loud voice called from below. "Will, are you up there? Come here, man, I need your help!"

William eased me away, searching my face before he gave me a brief nod. "It's time to meet Thomas." He smiled and walked across the studio.

A person holding a stack of wobbly wood crates appeared on the landing, his arms shaking as he struggled to balance the boxes.

"I'm about to make a god-awful mess, Will. Where the devil are you?" A deep, rich laugh followed, one filled with an energy that was infectious. Despite the ache in my heart, I found the camaraderie between the two brothers much like that between my sisters and me. I suddenly understood William's standpoint, though I did not like it.

"You buffoon!" William called out loudly in response. "Why on earth do you insist on dragging these crates home?" he scolded, stepping forward to help his brother.

Without William at my side, I was suddenly the shy introvert he'd met that day in the hat shop.

"These are far cheaper than palettes, my brother. Say, while I was picking these up at the tavern, I saw that McGivney's is having an oyster special tonight. What do you say we go down and toss back a few with some pints? I've just sold another of my paintings to John."

"That's wonderful, Thomas," William replied, dropping the crates to the floor. "First, there's someone I'd like you to meet."

I stood transfixed, motionless at the threshold of the balcony's doors, trying to process all that had happened. A surreal sticky substance trickled down my leg, reminding me of what I had done. William held out his hand to me, motioning me to his side. Unable to arrange my hair properly, I quickly pulled it over my shoulder, twisting it in a loose braid. I did not take William's hand.

He smiled, dropped his hand to his side and turned to his brother. "This is the woman I spoke to you about. Helen Bridgeton, I would like you to meet my brother, the extraordinary and gifted artist, Thomas Rodin."

I was mesmerized by how accurate William's assessment of his brother was. It was, I determined, the reason I could not find my tongue. His manner and his odd clothing made him seem larger than life. The air fairly crackled in his presence. I found myself curtsying as if about to dance.

His eyes came alive and, as though I was the only one in the room, he walked toward me, silently assessing me from head to toe. He wore the trousers of a proper gentleman, and so, too, the shoes. That, however, is where all semblance of the current era stopped. His coat, dark blue velvet and showing wear on the shoulder, was festooned with ornate blue seed pearls and stiff piping, reminding me of the old-fashioned, aristocratic clothes I'd seen in the paintings at the gallery. He wore a shirt, too, adorned with lace cuffs, and on his fingers beautiful rings of gold, one bearing a black stone the size of a small bird's egg. The eclectic array of clothing and color enhanced his exotic olive skin, making him look like a painting come to life. Were it not for the shadow of his beard, the swagger of his walk and the obvious gleam of sensuality in his eye, I would have taken him for a dandy. Instead, I found myself curiously drawn to him.

Yes, I had gravely underestimated the impact of his brother's effect on me. I felt like a ripe apple being eyed for its tart sweetness.

"Turn," he stated bluntly.

I blinked, pressing my lips together in uncertainty that I would pass muster. My eyes met William's unreadable gaze. He nodded and I turned slowly, my fingers locked together, holding on to my braid.

Thomas reached for my hands and I relinquished my grasp as he inspected them closely, turning them back and forth. I grew uncomfortable at how long he studied them, praying he would not care how unkempt my nails were, how dry my skin was.

At last, Thomas drew my hands to his lips and kissed them with lingering reverence. His lip curled provocatively, highlighting the slight cleft in his chin, giving character to his handsome face. His hair, an unruly mop, produced a shock of chestnut curls that dipped low over his forehead. I noticed a thin white scar slicing across the outer edge of one eyebrow.

"My brother is to blame for that," he said, cocking his eyebrow as though reading my mind. His eyes narrowed, joining his easy, predatory grin. "Your hair is glorious. That deep russet—those mahogany undertones are positively scandalous! Dante's delight, you are a lovely gift to be certain. By all that is decadent, woman, your eyes alone have utterly captured me." He strode over to William, grabbing him in a fierce embrace. "Well done, William, you have found us a 'stunner.'"

"Now we *must* celebrate. Our cups—as our dear mother would say most devotedly—do runneth over, and so shall ours, down at McGivney's."

In two steps, he had returned, grabbing me around the waist, holding me close as he spun me around. The delight on his face reminded me of a child on Christmas morning. I clung to his broad shoulders, looking down at a face so closely resembling William's, but with eyes that sparked mischievously. I caught William's guarded expression as Thomas placed my feet to the floor.

"Shall I call you my muse?" He narrowed his eyes, studying me. I admit I was so smitten immediately by his zest for life that I quite forgot the obstacles facing me with taking on this position.

"My apologies, Mr. Rodin, but I have not yet accepted this position."

He drew back in surprise and laughed aloud. "I like her, Will. She has a feisty spirit. Perhaps, we should consider paying her more?"

"I would prefer that you stop talking about me as if I cannot hear," I said with a boldness that surprised me.

Thomas took my chin between his fingers. His grin was positively wicked. "Yes, you and I will get on quite well. I like a woman who knows her mind, who knows what she wants and has no fear in obtaining it."

I glanced at William, who had busied himself with stacking the crates against the wall. My mind flashed with the image of our bodies entwined, braced against that very wall…

"The details," he stated bluntly. "You'll get a half shilling a week. I will need you here every day—"

"I'm sorry sir, but I am employed during the day."

"But I cannot paint without light." He shrugged. "We shall have to see what can be done. Now—" he clapped his hands together "—what's next?" He searched the room and spotted William finishing with the crates. "Oh, thank you, Will."

"Perhaps, Mr. Rodin, you should call me a carriage. It is getting late and my family will be wondering where I am."

Thomas pursed his lips together, a scowl darkening his face. "No. No, my dear. You will dine with us this evening. Besides, I want you to meet a few of our close friends in the brotherhood. I will send word to your family that you are spending the night in town. Besides, it is far too dangerous for a woman to be traveling across the roads at this hour. I'm sure they will understand and appreciate the wisdom of it."

He obviously had never met my papa. "I am hesitant to agree, Mr. Rodin. My papa can be quite set in his ways in, well, most matters concerning his daughters." I checked William's face for his reaction. He found interest in his shoes suddenly.

"A bit forward, interesting for one who appears so innocent. Quite a provocative blend," Thomas responded, offering his brother a quick side glance. "Yet never let it be said that I don't like a good challenge."

He gave me a wink

"Your papa will have to understand. I am about to make his daughter part of artistic history—surely he would not deny you that. Besides, and you should know this about me before we begin any sort of affair together, I usually get what I want. Now, is it my understanding, or was I mistaken, that you *are* interested in this position?"

My eyes darted from Thomas to William. "Of course, but I need to make arrangements—"

"Good. I hope you do not have an aversion to oysters?" He raised his dark eyebrows, awaiting my answer.

His arrogance, I suppose, was part of his charm. I wondered if all artists were like him, or if he was a rare breed unto himself. "I've never had them, Mr. Rodin."

He leaned down, his fingers grasping my upper arm, and placed his unshaven cheek against mine.

"I insist you call me Thomas. Mr. Rodin is the name given to a gentleman and my father. I am neither. Do we understand each other, Helen?"

His breath tickled my ear. My gaze flickered to his. "Yes, Thomas."

"Splendid!"

He laughed as he hooked one arm through mine and grabbed William with the other. "We're starting afresh, with a new project! Yes, I can see it now. It will be a boot in the rear of the Royal Academy!" He laughed. "But tonight, I want to enjoy this moment with my two favorite people in the entire world!"

Chapter 5

FROM THE MOMENT I AGREED TO MODEL FOR
Thomas, my life began to move at a rapid pace. I was thrilled that
he assumed responsibility for contacting my family, yet concerned
at the same time about what he would tell them.

The carriage that Thomas secured rolled up in front of Mc-
Givney's pub. The loud din of voices, some raised in song, filtered
through to the outside. I'd never been in a real pub before.

Thomas helped me from the carriage and nodded to William,
who took me by the elbow and escorted me to the establishment's
front door.

"What will he tell my family?" I asked William. He'd already
begun to distance himself in a cordial manner.

"Hard to say, but Thomas is quick on his feet," William responded, not looking at me.

I did not understand how William could so easily dismiss what
had happened between us. It was not how I believed it should be.
I wanted to speak more to him about it, but it would have to
wait—Thomas, smiling triumphantly, walked toward us.

"There we go. I've taken care of that." He gave me a wink.

"May I ask what you stated in your message, Mr. Rodin?"

He tucked his arm around my waist and leaned in close. Again, I was assaulted by his exotic, earthy scent.

"Call me Thomas," he whispered, and placed a hasty kiss on my temple. "I insist." He wagged his finger at me.

"Very well…Thomas. Again, may I ask what message you sent?" For all of his charismatic charm, I needed to know what he had told my family so I could uphold the lie when I returned home. It was not something I was looking forward to.

He shrugged. "Simple, really. I told them you were staying in town to help a friend."

"A friend?" I repeated, seeing my father's face in my mind as he read the note.

He opened the pub door and the boisterous sound from inside came spilling out onto the street.

"Yes, you do have friends, don't you, Helen?" he called to me above the din, ushering William and me ahead of him.

"Yes, of course—" I started, but the noise drowned out my words. The thick smoky haze caused me to squint. The acrid scent of ale and sweat permeated the air. I held my hand to my nose as I was pushed forward, the crowd catching me in its current. I lost sight of both William and Thomas. I tried not to panic as I stood in the midst of the sea of men, most of them drunk. A hand snaked around my waist and instinctively I batted at it.

"It's only me, Helen." Thomas pressed his mouth near my ear. "Hold tight and stay close. I'll get us to our table." He did not let go as we weaved through the crowd. Ahead I saw one of the barmaids, gripping two tankards in one hand. She bumped into Thomas, causing him to stop. He acted surprised at first, then threw his head back and laughed.

"Annie, you little trollop. How are you?" He released my hand and grabbed her face, kissing her hard on the mouth. With a sly smile, he discreetly tucked a shilling down the front of her low-cut bodice, then he tugged me to his side, clamping his arm around my waist.

"Annie." He grinned with pride. "I want you to meet my newest pupil, Helen."

The woman looked me over from head to toe, her dark brown eyes snapping in challenge.

"'Pupil' is what you call it now? Be mindful, Helen. Thomas surely enjoys his role as teacher." She kissed his cheek and eyed me again.

"Do you think she has what it takes, Thomas, to be one of us?" she said, as if I did not hear what she was saying, or didn't care if I did. Regardless, if she was the example of an artist's model, I did not intend to become like her. Although it seemed my new employer found her most agreeable.

Thomas's laughter melded into the roar of the crowd. "Bring us a round, Annie, and some of those oysters. Come, Helen. Pay this wicked wench no mind. She'll be lucky if she ever sits for me again," he shouted, but his smile revealed he was teasing.

"Watch out for that one, Helen," Annie called over her shoulder as she handed the pitchers to the barkeep. "Be sure you know what Thomas will have you sittin' on!" Thomas reached over and smacked her bum. Her surprise turned to glee as she faced him, plucked her fingers down her cleavage and retrieved his monetary gift. She gave him a sly wink and kept her eye on me as Thomas pulled me toward the back of the pub.

"Thomas! Will here says we've got us a new stunner," exclaimed a ruddy-faced man with spectacles perched on his rose-tipped nose. He stood as I squeezed between two large chaps, lost my footing and careened headlong toward the floor.

William appeared seemingly from nowhere and caught me before I landed flat on my face.

"Don't be frightened, Helen. The boys are friendly."

"Thank you," I responded, quickly releasing myself from his grasp.

The man with the glasses offered me his seat. William ushered me to the chair. I tried to offer the men a friendly smile, wondering if I would have to spend much time with them collectively.

I had a sudden change of heart and turned to find William to ask him to take me home, but he had disappeared and apparently so, too, had Thomas.

Annie sauntered up to the table and slammed two pitchers of ale on the table, sending the contents splashing over the side.

"Let's see what she's got," she called out to the men around the table.

My heart stopped. *What on earth?* I frantically scanned the faces of the men, whose eyes had all turned to me. I was grateful to spot Thomas making his way over to my side. He held out his hand.

"They're perfectly harmless, I assure you." He looked down at me, his cerulean-blue eyes sparkling wickedly.

"I—I don't understand." I looked again at the men seated around the table. They did not seem as friendly anymore. One of them, a stately looking chap with a shaggy blond beard, smacked the table once with his hand. He looked at his peers, giving them a grin, and they, too, began to slap the table.

"These are my brothers, Helen. Their approval is vital. It would not bode well to keep them waiting," Thomas said. "Besides, it's all in good fun."

I cautiously took his hand and stood. The drumming grew louder. My gaze landed on Annie, who'd precipitated this demonstration. She gave me a smug look, amusement dancing in her eyes. "What am I to do?" I asked Thomas, averting my eyes from hers.

"Get up on the table," he responded with an easy grin.

"You want me to stand on the table in front of all these people?" I stared at him with wide eyes.

"Your face is going to be seen by far greater numbers, my muse. Come on now, up you go."

"But I—" I started, but my protests dissolved when his hands circled my waist and he lifted me to the tabletop.

Raucous laughter and applause followed as I looked down at the gallery of approving male faces. Thomas held my hand, displaying a sense of ownership that I found comforting.

The brotherhood men nodded, waving their hands, motioning for me to turn. A couple of them lifted my skirt to view my ankles. Thomas slapped away their hands but laughed good-naturedly. After a moment or two, I offered a smile, dipping in a short curtsy. I no longer felt like that ugly duckling. I looked down at Thomas, his fingers locked with mine, his smile encouraging, and I believed I'd become a beautiful swan. The catcalls and whistles continued, drawing curious onlookers into the private circle.

"Very well, gentlemen, that's enough," Thomas ordered, reaching up for me.

I inched to the edge of the table and leaned forward. He grabbed me around the waist, his hands sliding precariously close to my breasts as he lifted me to the ground. He held my gaze possessively, letting my body slide slowly down the front of his.

My feet touched the floor, but he continued to hold me close, his arm encircling my waist.

"You've got your balance, then?"

Pressed against his solid frame, I could barely think, my heart still beating from the rush of my initiation. Balance? Doubtful.

"I do, Mr.—Thomas," I answered, pleased when I saw Annie scowl and turn back into the crowd.

Thomas kissed my forehead and drew back, his eyes resting for a heartbeat on my mouth before he returned his eyes to mine.

"Welcome to the brotherhood, Miss Bridgeton."

"Do call me Helen," I said bravely.

"As you wish." He grinned.

I was living a lie, but to whose benefit? For two months, I had been telling Madame Tozier that my stomach was the cause of the many afternoons that I had asked to leave the shop early. However, as my acting skills grew weaker, the actual pains in my stomach increased. I found myself losing track of the days, and on more than one occasion I had nearly taken too much of my medicine, forgetting when I last took it. I could not sleep.

William's aloof behavior pervaded my mind. Since our liaison, he had not attempted to speak with me except in passing and was usually absent when I was at the studio. At night my mind would creep back to that summer afternoon, how the soft warm breeze had wafted over our fevered bodies. I lay on my bed, mesmerized by the flickering flame of the oil lamp beside my bed. I remembered his tongue, the roughness of his hands gliding over me, plucking my nipples until I begged for more. Desperate to recapture that euphoric feeling, I used my hands to imitate his, brushing my fingers through my soft curls and spreading my sweet crevice, mimicking the exquisite pleasure he'd given me. I licked my dry lips, arching my back to the memory of him heavy inside me, his body pressed to mine. In my mind, I saw the sweet determination in his gentle eyes, our bodies fused in delicious, slick friction. Then my body broke free, my muscles caressing, squeezing around him.

I stared at the flame, drawing my hand over my stomach, my physical need now satiated. Nevertheless, I held on to the desperate longing for his affection, realizing with chilling clarity that perhaps he did not feel the same. I'd even written a poem for us called, *Another Time, Another Place,* and slipped it into William's coat pocket hoping he might respond, but if he found it, he made no mention of it.

It was of little surprise to me when William entered the studio one afternoon and announced his departure.

"Well, I'm off soon. My train leaves within the hour."

"You're leaving?" I rubbed the back of my neck, stiff and sore from sitting too long. I bowed my head so he would not see the disappointment in my eyes. "Thomas didn't mention it."

"It's just a short trip to Rome. I plan to tour a few cathedrals and perhaps a garden or two in search of inspiration."

"Be cautious of those beautiful gardens, Will. Some of their caretakers do not appreciate foreigners plucking them," Thomas said with a smirk.

It was evident he was speaking metaphorically of women. I

brushed his comment from my mind, rubbing my arms under the sleeves of the itchy damask gown that Thomas insisted I wear. The two brothers embraced and William gave me a tight smile. "Miss Bridgeton." He nodded.

"Mr. Rodin." I continued the appearance that we'd never been intimate with each other. If he could perform the task so well, I could, too. After William left, I followed Thomas out to the balcony. We stood watching his carriage amble down the cobblestone street.

"I miss him like the devil when he's gone," Thomas said quietly.

He sighed and wrapped his arms around my shoulders, resting his chin on my head.

"It's just you and me now, Helen. He's gone and left us behind while he trots off on a new adventure."

"Does he take these trips often?" I asked. The warmth of Thomas's arms made me feel secure. It was his nature to be physical—he was prone to giving hugs and pecks on the cheek, even to the other men in the brotherhood.

He lifted aside my unbridled hair and nuzzled the sensitive spot beneath my ear.

"When the spirit moves him. I prefer to find my inspiration closer to home." The smell of wine wafted beneath my nose as his palm moved over my right breast, squeezing gently.

"Are you inspired, my muse?" he whispered against the curve of my neck.

I slipped from his grasp. "The light is waning, Mr. Rodin."

"I have asked that you call me Thomas," he said with quiet firmness.

"All right, Thomas. Still, if you wish to do more this afternoon before I leave—"

"Oh, yes, my muse. I would *love* to do more."

"I've no doubt you would, Thomas. Do you think I am so innocent that I do not know your reputation?"

He looked at me curiously. "I think you pretend not to know how you affect me, Helen."

"I do think, Thomas, that you have found your inspiration much too easily in the past."

His smile grew wide. "Aha! My innocent little muse has a cunning side, as well."

"I am not worldly, it is true, but I do know a rogue when I see one."

"A rogue?" He held his hand to his heart. "Woman, you wound me with your words far too romantic for a man like me. A man, as you say, of my reputation."

"Perhaps I should take my leave for the afternoon." I turned away and he grabbed my arm.

"My apologies, Helen. I had no idea that my affections would be repulsive to you."

"You are not repulsive to me, Thomas, nor are your affections. But do not think that because I am here, you may take advantage of the situation."

"I see. You are a woman who prefers to be wooed, is that it?" He stepped around me, blocking my escape back into the studio.

"I am a woman with needs, innocent though you think me to be." I faced him.

His gaze narrowed and he took my chin between his fingers.

"Those dark circles—your complexion is pale. Helen, what is the matter? What ails you?"

His immediate change in topic and manner scattered my thoughts.

"I am not sleeping well," I admitted.

He pulled me into his embrace and laid his cheek on the top of my head.

"You must learn to trust me, Helen. When you are unhappy, I am unhappy."

"I don't see myself through your eyes, Thomas."

"Then I will have to do better at showing you how important you are to me."

He smoothed his hands up and down my spine, and I welcomed this tender gesture. "You have been good to me, Thomas."

"I could be much more, Helen, if you'd allow."

His concern for my health prompted me to admit my worry regarding my employer. "I cannot keep lying, Thomas. I fear I will lose my job, or worse, Madame Tozier will go to my mother and ask her about my health."

He frowned. "Neither she nor your family realize that you've been posing for me?"

I sighed. "Not everyone is as enamored of the brotherhood as you may like to think."

He chuckled. "You needn't remind me." His eyes drifted over my shoulder as if deep in thought. "Then we shall go see this Madame Tozier and teach her to adore the brotherhood," he said finally.

I laughed softly. "Do you honestly think that *you* can make a difference?"

"Go get dressed. I'll order us a carriage." He smiled. "Oh, wait, do you need any help?" he called after me.

"I can manage getting dressed on my own, Thomas, thank you," I tossed back, but the smoky color of his eyes, the intimate way that he had touched me, lingered in my mind. As I dressed in his bedroom, I looked around, trying to get a clearer picture of my mysterious employer. He lived in an unkempt state and I often wondered if he hired a maid to come in and tidy up after him, but I had never seen one when I was there. I assumed that he ate out, as I'd not seen a cook either. He seemed, however, to have an endless supply of tea, wine and raspberry scones on hand. His bed was unmade, the sheets rumpled, and my mind flashed with the image of Thomas sprawled across it, his nude body draped with a careless covering. Need welled inside me. Having once tasted the precious honeyed bliss, my body craved it. I hurried to finish dressing and remove myself from the temptation of my imagination.

"Thank you, Madame Tozier, for your contribution to the arts," Thomas said. "We'll be certain to credit the lovely hat that Helen holds in the painting to your generosity."

As he had predicted, Thomas had managed to charm my employer, reducing her to a blushing admirer.

Thomas placed his delicate teacup on the plate he held.

"I will be visiting Miss Bridgeton's family as soon as we have a painting to give them. I must say it is refreshing to find a noted person in the community who appreciates the importance of the arts. Art is what differentiates us from the animals, don't you agree, Madame Tozier?"

"Oh, yes, I do agree, Mr. *Rodeen.*" Her smile was demure. "We must educate the unfortunate souls who do not understand such things."

I glanced away, covering my smile with my napkin. Thomas was openly charming, a shrewd businessman and, as he made no qualms in saying, he usually got what he wanted. A shiver ran through me, remembering his hand on my breast. What more did Thomas want from me? I chose to set those questions aside for the moment and simply be grateful that some of my guilt had been lifted from my shoulders. I had him to thank for that.

"Thomas, did you mean what you said about giving my family a portrait of me?" I asked later as we rode back to the ferry where I would catch my ride home.

He took my hand, patted it and rested it on the top of his thigh. "I needed to gain Madame Tozier's trust, Helen. I had to make certain she would not trot off to tell your family all about us herself. By entrusting her to keep it our little surprise, she will keep our confidence."

"So, in short, you lied?" I asked.

He shrugged. "I prefer to think of it as stretching the truth, quite harmlessly. Perhaps we can take them a portrait someday. Would that be so awful?"

The image of my papa raising his gun to the sky and giving a single warning shot emerged in my head. "Perhaps we should wait a little longer before we tell my family," I said, as my stomach began to bother me again.

"Tilt your chin down. Now lift your eyes…good…there. Hold that look—perfect."

I held my gaze steady on a spot of light shimmering over Thomas's shoulder. Being his muse was a much more daunting task than I had imagined. When he noticed my stress, he would break into song and dance me about the studio until I was in better spirits. On occasion, he would take me to the pub to dine with others in the brotherhood, but although I tried to fit in, I found myself preferring to be alone with Thomas at the studio.

Several letters had arrived from William, always addressed to Thomas. He indicated that he was having a splendid time in Rome and hoped all was well back home. Never once did he ask about me, specifically. That single afternoon with William began to fade, replaced by the colorful moments I spent with his brother.

"Do you wish to discuss something with me, Helen?" Thomas asked, wiping his fingers on his paint rag.

"I'm sorry, Thomas, I'll do better." I shifted, straightening my spine.

"Is it your monthly?"

I suppose that by now, I should have been more used to his frank manner, but today it surprised me. I'd never spoken to anyone other than my mother on that subject. "No," I uttered in haste, averting my eyes and feeling foolish.

Thomas knelt before me, taking my hands in his. The warmth of his concern flowed through me. There was kindness in his eyes that put me at ease.

"It is natural, Helen. What kind of man would I be if I were not sensitive to these things? Many women have posed for me. I would be a thickheaded boob if I did not understand."

"I have not been sleeping well. I have bouts of insomnia, but it will pass."

He studied me and then slapped his knee. "You need the fresh air and sunshine of the country."

He smiled up at me, his eyes twinkling. I thought that he

meant we should visit my family at last, and now, faced with the reality of it, I wasn't sure if I was ready just yet. "Oh, I could not face my family today, Thomas. Perhaps next week when I'm better rested."

He nodded. "Very well, we won't go to see your family, as you wish. We'll take a ride. I know! We'll have a picnic! It's a lovely day for it. We need to get some color in your face."

He pulled me to my feet.

"Go change and meet me out front."

Although I considered asking whether I might instead lie down for a while, I knew that once Thomas made up his mind he was not easily deterred.

The carriage ride was indeed relaxing. We spoke little, enjoying the view, silent in our private thoughts. Once or twice I caught Thomas looking at me and we would share a friendly smile. Since our conversation on the balcony, he'd not made any further advances. I often wondered, knowing the healthiness of his sexual appetite, how he was satisfying his cravings.

Thomas tapped the driver with his cane and we came to a stop by a small grove of willow and oak trees.

"You're welcome to go up to the house, good man. You'll find a well there to water your horses. I'll fetch you when we're ready."

He grabbed a small basket and stepped down, holding his hand out to me. "Come on, I want to show you the grounds."

"Will the owners mind us traipsing around the property?" I asked, noting a small cottage in the distance.

"It belongs to the brotherhood." He offered his hand to help me down.

Thomas continued to hold my hand, guiding me through the knee-length grass. Overhead, the sun shone in a brilliant blue sky. I breathed deeply. The setting was beautiful and it reminded me of the places I had played as a child. "The brotherhood? What would the brotherhood need with all of this land?" I asked, ducking beneath the low-hanging branches of the willow trees as best I could. One snagged my bonnet, pulling it away from my head.

Thomas laughed and reached up, loosening my coppery hair and causing it to spill over my shoulders. He stopped, holding my hat in his hand, and fingered my hair. "Breathtaking," he said, taking a strand and brushing it over his cheek. "You have a natural beauty that few women can boast of, Helen. You should embrace it with great confidence."

We sat beneath a willow, lunching on fresh peaches and cheese, bread and wine. He tore a loaf of bread and offered me a taste.

"We've talked about building a communal studio." He stood and shook off his coat.

"What?" I asked, swallowing the bread without properly chewing it. I washed it down with a large gulp of wine. "Why would you want to leave the studio? Would you all live here together?"

Thomas stretched out on his side, crossing his long legs, and propped himself up on his elbow. "It's the perfect solution, really. Sharing props, easels, paints—"

"Models?" I asked, feeling a tinge of jealousy.

He leveled his gaze on me. "That has always been the way of it. From the formation of the brotherhood—we share and share alike."

"I do not think I like the idea, Thomas." I tipped back my glass and finished off the wine. I sensed it warring with my medicine, causing my tongue to loosen.

"Because you are uncomfortable around the brotherhood?" he asked quietly.

"I don't think they like me, Thomas. I hear their whispers when I don't laugh at their lewd jokes."

"Lewd? Why, Helen, I never took you for a stick-in-the-mud."

I paused from filling my cup, my ire rankled. "I am no such thing, I assure you. I simply prefer different company." I took another sip of wine and bit into a ripe peach. The juice dribbled past my lips and trickled down my chin before I could catch it with my fingers. Tiny droplets landed on the flesh exposed above my bodice.

I watched his eyes follow the liquid. A slow throbbing tugged betwixt my legs.

"And whose company do you prefer, Helen, if not that of the brotherhood?"

His gaze flicked up to mine and I swallowed. Beyond the sound of my breathing was the din of nature—the buzzing, the chirping and the chattering.

"I prefer when it is only you and me, Thomas," I confessed, unable to take my eyes from his.

"And why on earth would you have the desire to be alone with the likes of me?" His grin was tempting, as he intended it to be, I am certain.

"Do not think I am like Annie, Thomas," I warned, pointing my finger at him.

He caught my hand, turning it so that the peach dropped to the ground. Then one by one, he drew my fingertips into his mouth, sucking off the juice.

"Believe me, Helen. You and Annie are nothing alike."

"Do not mock, me, Thomas. True, I am not as free and easy as Annie is. I have not perfected the art of flirting with a man." I pushed to my feet, humiliated…no, insulted that he did not know me well enough to understand. I pressed my hands against the tree, shielding my face from his view. He touched my shoulder.

"Helen, I wasn't mocking you," he said. "Turn around and talk to me."

I faced him, my heart pounding with my wounded pride, determined that I would speak my mind. "I admit that in many ways I *am* innocent. Surely by comparison to your other muses, you must think me but a country nitwit."

"Helen, of course not." He smoothed his hand over my cheek. "You misunderstood what I said." He smiled down at me. "No, my sweet Helen. You—"

He kissed my forehead.

"—are so much more—"

His mouth drifted to my eyelid, to my cheek, and hovered over my mouth.

"—fascinating." He brushed my lips, teasing, until I leaned forward to meet his mouth. I tasted the wine on his lips, his tongue, as they melded with mine.

I was glad for the firm support of the tree against my spine. My fingers dug into the bark as he left a trail of warm, wet kisses down my throat.

"On the contrary, Helen—" his hot breath seared my flesh "—I find you utterly beguiling."

My eyes floated shut and William briefly crossed my mind. But Thomas's kisses, deep and thorough, left me breathless, dissolving what was left of his brother in my heart.

"William was right in choosing you," he whispered. "He knew I would be infatuated."

He held my face, his thumbs stroking the tender spot beneath my jaw.

"Is it wrong for me to feel this wicked, Thomas?" I reveled in how it felt to have someone desire me, to know that I was capable of giving back pleasure.

"Do you wish to feel wicked, Helen?" he asked.

"Yes, Thomas. Teach me." I surrendered to his arduous attention, tired of carrying around my burdensome concerns. He reached around me, working at the buttons of my gown. I smoothed my hands along his strong forearms, my fingers sliding through his as I drew his hands between us. I looked up at him. "Teach me how to please you."

He searched my eyes. "Very well, muse. As you wish."

He held my curious, hungry gaze, as he peeled off his cravat and proceeded to unbutton his shirt.

My heart thrummed unsteadily as piece by piece he took off his clothing until he stood fully naked before me. He took my hands and pressed them against his muscled torso.

"Touch me, Helen. Satisfy your curiosity."

He remained statuesque as I walked around him, stopping to

rake my fingers over the sinewy muscle of his shoulders. His firm buttocks clenched as my fingers lightly trailed over his hips. I leaned my cheek to his sturdy back, bringing my arms around him. He was a beautiful man, if men can be described in such terms.

I smoothed my hands over his hard stomach, smiling as he stiffened to my curious touch, then wrapped my fingers lightly around his rigid cock.

He drew in a sharp breath.

"Does this please you?" I asked, skimming my palms over his body, taking luxurious time with my exploration.

He whirled to face me, pushing his hands under my breasts, sliding his mouth roughly over mine. Then he covered my hand with his and guided me back to his erection, capturing my mouth again in a heated kiss.

I moved my fingers over the hard ridges of his phallus, my thumb delicately skimming across the velvety tip.

"Do you wish to please me even more?" he asked, lifting my chin to meet his heated gaze.

I licked my lips and nodded.

He held my shoulders, easing me down to my knees in front of him. His erect cock jutted proudly from a soft patch of dark hair.

I looked up and received his nod. I eased my hand along his warm length, watching as his eyes drifted shut. Empowered, I leaned forward to kiss the glistening tip.

"That's it, my muse."

He stroked my neck, his fingers deftly skipping over my chin. "You are good to me." His guttural moans spurned me on. Something inside me yearned to harness the power of this man, his authority, his leadership in the brotherhood, and to watch him unravel before my eyes.

His hand covered mine, guiding my stroke, showing me the secret spot at the base of his cock that made him cry out with pleasure.

A sharp, bitter taste appeared on my tongue and I drew back, standing as I wiped my mouth. Thomas turned away, his hand working rapidly, his breath catching as he cast his face heavenward and emptied his seed on the grass. The firm muscles of his buttocks clenched and unclenched with the fierceness of his release.

I stared at his backside, mesmerized by the hard, angled plane of his body. He looked over his shoulder and I averted my eyes, ashamed to intrude on his privacy.

He came to me and took my hand, bringing it to his lips.

"You should see your face, blushed with color, with yearning."

"Yearning?" Of course, I knew what he meant. I took a deep breath and moistened my lips. My body teetered on the precipice, ready to fall apart.

"Oh, yes," he whispered, bending down to grab my skirts, lifting them higher as he backed me against a tree. His eyes sparked with arousal. "Your turn."

Without pretense he slipped his hand down the front of my thin cotton drawers, his long fingers parting my drenched folds.

My breath caught as he parted me, dipping into my warm crevice, stroking long and slow as I held his sinful gaze. I grasped his shoulders as my body tightened, his smiling face hovering over mine.

"There now, let go, my muse," he whispered against my mouth.

I shut my eyes to the exquisite pleasure that coursed through my veins, awakening every nerve ending. Thomas kissed me, his masterful fingers summoning each delicious spasm from me.

"Live with me," he said, releasing my skirts. He raised his hand to his mouth, tasting my juices. "I do not want to be away from you ever."

I was smitten with his request, but I knew to say yes to him would mean banishment from my family.

"As lovers?" I did not expect anything more from Thomas.

"As my muse," he responded, kissing me passionately.

"What will people say?" I asked.

He shrugged. "If they must pry, then I shall simply tell them that you are my new pupil."

He dropped to his knees and drew me into his embrace.

"Do not make me wait another moment for your answer, Helen. It is sheer torture!"

I laughed, something I hadn't done in weeks, it seemed. "Very well, but I warn you, my skills in the kitchen are limited."

He looked up at me and grinned. "My sweet muse, it is not your skill in the kitchen that interests me."

I held his face and smiled. It was a heady thing to have the devoted attention of a man like Thomas. I wondered if he'd ever had a model living at the studio before, and I considered how William might respond to the news. Could I wait forever to find the happiness I deserved? With Thomas at my side, I had no need for anyone else.

Chapter 6

THOMAS DUCKED AS MY PAPA HURLED THE painting across the room, barely missing the top of his head. My mama shoved my sisters into the back bedroom and closed the door. My portrait lay splintered on the floor and I knew it would soon be firewood.

"You have scarred my little girl—" Papa started, his face turning purple with rage.

"Papa, I am no longer a little girl—"

His eyes, full of anger, turned to me and he raised his finger, shaking it with fury. "You have lied to your family, Helen. Your deception is not a small matter—it is unforgivable."

"Papa, please—" He cut me off with his upturned hand. I turned to Mama, pleading for her to make him understand.

She stood to the side, wringing her hands with worry, but she did not come to my defense.

"Mr. Bridgeton, I assure you that Helen has been treated very well…"

"Do not," Papa bellowed, "speak in my house!"

"Papa, *please* try to at least be decent to our guest," I said.

"Decent?" His voice rose and my mama covered her mouth

with her apron. "Do not talk to me about decency." He glared at me and then at Thomas, and headed for the door, his jaw set firm. He stopped long enough to grab his hat. "I am going to the barn. I don't wish to find either of you here when I return."

A quiet, strangled sob tore from my mama's throat. Her eyes shimmered with unshed tears. Papa did not look back as the door slammed behind him.

Had I truly believed they would understand or support my decision? There was nothing more to be said. I stood and brushed past Mama as I went into my room to collect a few of my things.

My sisters, Beth and Rosalind, peeked out of their room and I stopped to hug them both. I handed my bag to Thomas who waited by the front door.

"I'll wait outside," he said.

I gave Mama a brief hug, not knowing when or if I would see her again.

"Be well, Helen. Take your medicine." She stroked my cheek, and I burned her leathery skin into my memory. As I walked to the carriage, I saw the light was on in the barn, which meant Papa was inside brushing the mare. It was what he always did when he wanted to think. I debated whether I should tell him goodbye.

Thomas seemed to read my mind.

"Do you need a moment?" he asked, holding open the carriage door.

I took one last look over my shoulder, drinking in the tiny cottage with its slanted roof and peeling paint, the sagging porch that Papa kept meaning to fix. "No, let's go," I said, getting into the carriage.

I leaned back against the soft, cushioned seat and stared out the window at the familiar rolling landscape. I hoped against hope that my parents would have a change of heart, knowing I would not make a decision of such consequence without careful thought. However, in my family's world, women were still considered inferior in many ways, expected to be content serving the men in their lives, and I knew deep down that they would never understand.

Thomas took my hand and brought it to his lips. "I will take care of you, my muse. I don't want you to worry. We are your family now, the brotherhood and me."

I looked at him and wondered if I was really gaining my freedom or simply trading the men that I served.

Thomas took me to his bed that night, soothing my pain with his tenderness, turning my concerns to pleasured sighs. I surrendered myself body and soul to him, something I'd been reticent to do before. If this was servitude, then I welcomed it for the luxurious power that I felt in my decadence.

My fingers curled around the bedrail and I welcomed the pain of my knuckles tapping against the wall with the increased motion of Thomas's fervent thrusts. His long hair swayed, brushing over my flesh, and his eyes penetrated my soul, claiming my body, making me want to give back, to meet his challenge. I arched toward him and he caught my mouth in a searing, possessive kiss, demanding my climax—my loyalty. Crying out his name, I gave him everything and, in return, he gave me all that he *could* give. It was enough…for now.

In the days that followed, we existed in a state of marital bliss, without benefit of the legal and moral paperwork. We lived with the smug belief that conventionality was misguided, and my security was founded on the idea that what we had was pure and true.

It was early morning; the heavy fog of London still blanketed the rooftops. After awakening me with a frenzied bout of lovemaking, Thomas was in the mood to paint.

He had dragged me into the studio, him in his shirt and me wearing nothing but a blue silk drape that he handed me in haste.

"On the lounge," he ordered as he set to the task of arranging colors on his palette. I had grown used to his impulsive bursts of inspiration, quite often occurring in the afterglow of passion.

We nibbled on fruit and a little cheese. It was all that we had in the kitchen.

Thomas stood over me, eyeing the drape. He held out his apple for me to take a bite, as he experimented with the cloth, trying to find what pleased him.

I squealed when his hand playfully squeezed one of my breasts.

"Forgive me. I thought that was the drape." He grinned.

"You insatiable rogue," I teased.

"Merely appreciative of your beauty, madam, and if I may say, your breasts are a true gift of nature." He bent his head, pushing back the cloth to reveal my breast, and left a tender kiss on my flesh.

"As plump as a succulent peach." He glided his paintbrush across my skin, circling it deliciously slowly around my nipple.

"I grow hungry just to look at you," he whispered, leaning forward, his soft lips touching mine. "How will I ever get this painting done, you naughty muse?"

"Perhaps you need my inspiration?" I held his smoky gaze, feeling brazen. He had a way of making me feel my body was a work of art, created for his pleasure alone.

"Perhaps," he said quietly, sweeping the brush along the underside of my breast, the soft bristles teasing my senses. I discovered to what degree Thomas was skilled with a paintbrush as he delicately stroked the sensitive flesh of my inner thighs.

The corners of his mouth lifted when he parted me like a flower and tickled me with his brush, causing me to squirm with need.

"So exquisitely beautiful it is, my muse, to see your arousal."

I covered my face with my hands, lost in his taunting stroke. Thomas was an exquisite lover, showing me pleasure in ways I'd never dreamed. I'd come to ignore the niggling in my head that he'd never once used the word *love* in any of our conversations—never once whispered it when he took me to his bed. I also ignored the fact that his friends rarely stopped by anymore since I'd moved in.

My thoughts dissipated as his tongue replaced the brush, his creative mastery summoning a shuddering, toe-curling climax from me.

A sound from behind brought Thomas's head up and he casually pulled the drape over my naked body.

"Will, you're back. You should have sent word. I'd have met you at the station." Thomas rose to greet his brother.

I sat upright, holding the drape over me as best I could, bolstering the courage to look at William, wondering how long he had been standing there before Thomas noticed him.

"William," I stated quickly, slanting a quick glance at him.

"Helen," he responded evenly.

"We've got news to share, Will. Helen has moved into the studio on a permanent basis."

If William was shocked by the news, he kept it concealed well.

"Then you two are…together now, I surmise," he said, averting his eyes from mine.

Thomas chuckled and slapped his brother's shoulder. "As if that wasn't evident, eh, Will?"

My face burned and, finding a large throw, I quickly wrapped it around me. "I'll go get dressed and fix us some tea." I hurried from the room, wondering how after all this time I should be uncomfortable in William's presence.

The two brothers could not be more opposite. They possessed equal charm, but while Thomas seemed content in his bold approach to life, William was quiet, as though he was still searching for what it was he wanted.

Since Thomas had taken me under his wing, he'd become so much more than just my lover—he was also my friend and my teacher. He was on time with my weekly sum for posing, took me to museums, plays and to grand mansions where we dined with writers and other artists. He'd made me a part of his life, embracing me in every way that a suitor intending marriage would. He created a desire in me, encouraged my passion and nurtured it. No one had ever treated me like this. I felt like a goddess when I was with him.

I brought tea into the studio, pouring for William first, and then Thomas who, I noted, liberally laced his with whiskey.

"I suppose I should start looking for a place to move," William said. I looked at Thomas.

"Nonsense, your room is your own—this place is your home, as well. There is plenty of room here, William. Besides, you are gone half the time on one of your bloody research adventures. No, I will not hear talk about moving. Don't you agree, my dear?" He curled his arm around my waist, drawing me down to sit beside him on the arm of the chair.

"Of course, William. We are family—you, Thomas and I. We wouldn't dream of you living anywhere else," I said, putting my arm around Thomas's shoulder.

I could not say what I saw flash in William's eyes, but I looked away quickly, feigning a bright smile at Thomas. He slipped his hand around my neck and drew me close, kissing me tenderly.

For any other man, it would have been a gesture of warning to another male—a sign of possession. But for Thomas, it was simply his way of saying he wanted me again.

"Very well, then. I'll try not to be underfoot too much." William raised his cup, and as his eyes met mine over the rim, that summer afternoon flashed again in my thoughts.

"I have a proposal for you, my muse," Thomas stated as we lay in bed after one of our late-day trysts.

I had been living with him for nearly three months and I'd discovered that his sexual appetite was insatiable, innovative and addictive. There was nothing I denied him.

He untied the silk bindings from around my wrists and kissed my tender flesh, settling himself comfortably beneath my arm, his head on my breast. The mere thought of the word "proposal" brought to mind a hope that I continued to harbor deep inside. I waited, mentally telling myself to remain calm, to let him get out the words before I cried for joy.

"I've been thinking, since I am between projects and still deciding what to do next, that I may consent to let John borrow you for his current project."

This was not at all what I was expecting.

"John? But I rather like being your exclusive muse, Thomas."

He leaned up on his elbow, looking down at me as he twirled a strand of my hair around his finger. "I feel we both might benefit from a fresh perspective."

Fresh perspective? I had taken part in nearly every fantasy Thomas had ever designed in his head, proving without a doubt he had an endless imagination.

"Is this your way of saying you are…tired of me?"

"Oh, muse, of course not." He kissed my nose. "But it will be good for you to find out what it is like to pose for another artist. It's a professional courtesy to share one's model."

"A professional courtesy, nothing more?" I asked.

He tipped his head, studying me. "Do you doubt my intent?"

"No." I looked away and his hand caught my chin, forcing me to look at him.

"Do not ever doubt me," he said with a calm sternness. I'd never seen that look in his eye before, almost as if I had betrayed him by questioning his decision. He smiled then, and his expression softened as he lowered his head to kiss me.

"It would be inhospitable of me not to share you. He has already asked and I told him that you wouldn't mind."

"Of course not," I replied quietly, my thoughts caught between disappointment and my desire to please him.

"Perhaps you need convincing, my muse."

He kissed me again lightly, teasing this time as he eased his palm over my stomach, sliding his fingers between my thighs.

"John is quite an interesting fellow. Well traveled. I'm certain he'll keep you amused with his stories."

He kissed me again and I knew he was luring more than my body to be at one with him.

"What will happen to our—" I swallowed hard, pulling his face to mine in a fierce kiss as my body trembled with pleasure "—our afternoon *tea?*"

Thomas grinned, bracing his arms as he moved over me and nudged my legs apart.

"You mean our afternoon fuck?" he whispered in my ear.

Lately, he'd begun slipping naughty words into our lovemaking and he knew how they aroused me. His cock teased my opening. I couldn't resist him and he knew it. I wrapped my arms around his waist, smoothing my hands over his firm buttocks, and pulled his hips toward mine, urging him to fill me. Satisfaction sparked in his eyes and he knew he'd gotten his way.

"I'll simply make sure—"

He slid into my slick heat with a shuddering sigh.

"—that John has you home," he said, kissing me once more as he withdrew partway, "before afternoon tea."

He lunged deeper, emitting a lusty sigh. He was a scoundrel. A wicked, wanton scoundrel and I could not say no to him.

I wrapped my legs around his hips, holding his body to mine, caught up in our frenzied coupling, and as we came together, I scolded myself for having doubted his suggestion.

Later, as he dozed with me curled beneath his arm, I watched the light of day turn to murky shadows of twilight and thought about how my life had changed. It had been months since I'd last seen my family. In that time, Mama had had another birthday, as had one of my sisters. I was now living out of wedlock, with a man who loved me with his body, yet thought nothing of offering me as a prop to another man, with the belief that it would improve our relationship.

I shut my eyes, overwhelmed with my thoughts, softly fingering the curls on Thomas's chest. Perhaps he was right. Perhaps my absence would leave a hole in his daily life and by so doing, he would be spurred to commit to more than just living together. I looked up at his handsome face, thinking how easily he slept at my side. I hoped desperately that this would prompt a proposal of a different kind, as I had missed my monthly and wondered if I might be carrying his child.

My flesh was numb. The portrait was supposed to be of a young woman lying in a river. The background had been painted and I, dressed in a gown that I understood was found in a second-hand shop, was to lie in repose partially submerged in a warm bath for hours, while John painted me. I was able to forgive John for the horridly musty stench of the wretched gown, but less forgivable was his failure to keep the water warm, as he had promised. Daily, for over a month and a half, I'd spent four to six hours in tepid water. I'd watched for my monthly and, when it did not come again, was pressed to tell Thomas, but chose to wait until I was sure.

The painting was at a critical point. John was as immersed in what he was doing as I was in the water. Though the water had grown cold, I lay there thinking that I could endure it a few moments more. However, those few moments turned to minutes and those minutes to even longer. He did not break for a meal, nor offer me anything to drink. I sensed myself growing numb and bent my fingers to encourage the blood flow.

John cleared his throat in way of reprimand, indicating that I should not move.

"Your eyes, shut your eyes," he said from behind his canvass wall.

I took a deep breath, clasped my hands over my chest and fought the urge not to ask him how much longer he would be. Instead, I tried to think of other things.

My thoughts turned to Thomas, wondering what time it was and if he would fetch me soon. I thought of my family. I thought of Mama and what her reaction would be to the possibility I was with child. The image of her face swam in my mind as I remembered how we laughed while hanging laundry on a warm summer's day. My mind wandered to when I was young, playing hard all day and falling asleep on my bed—totally, utterly exhausted…

I could not remember right away what had happened. One moment I was in the studio and the next I was lying in a white bed, surrounded by four white walls. I struggled to keep my eyes open. I was aware of people's voices, but my strength was gone, and every time I tried to answer a question, the darkness would suck me back into blackness.

Then I felt a hand holding mine.

"Stay with me, my muse."

It was Thomas's voice. The harder I tried to respond the more the blackness held me tight, trying to drag me down.

"I swear I'll never do such a thing again." It was Thomas. *Where was I? How long had I been here?*

"If you can hear me, Helen, squeeze my hand."

I tried as hard as I could, but the effort was too much.

"She moved her hand." Thomas's voice was excited, returning the faint squeeze. He urged me to move my hand again.

"Thank God," another man stated, although I did not recognize his voice. The blackness was tugging at me again, draining my energy, pulling me back to sleep.

My body was listless, but when I was finally able to hold my eyes open, I realized I was in a hospital room, a sheer curtain surrounding my bed.

Thomas, seated at my bedside, held my hands. He smiled and the look of relief on his face warmed my heart.

"You've returned to me, my muse," he said, his blue gaze steady.

"I feel so weak," I said, trying to smile. "How long have I been here?"

"A little over a week," he responded.

There was no one else in the room, but I remembered the voices. "My family, did you send for them? Did they come?"

He rubbed his fingers over my knuckles. "No, I didn't send for them, Helen. The doctors didn't want a lot of visitors until they could assess your situation."

I let the sting of wondering if they would have come even if they'd known drift from my mind. "What is my situation? What happened, Thomas?"

"The doctor says you succumbed to exhaustion, brought on by lack of sleep, proper nutrition…and your pregnancy."

There was my confirmation. My gaze darted to Thomas. "How is…the baby?" I whispered through a dry throat. My voice cracked and it hurt to swallow.

"Unharmed." He lifted my hand to his cheek. "Why didn't you tell me?"

I shook my head. "I didn't know for sure, until now."

He shook his head. "Well, there is no question now, you must marry me."

I blinked, unsure of what I heard. "This is not the time for frivolity, Thomas."

"Who here is being frivolous? I meant what I said."

Still drowsy, I answered, "You don't mean it, Thomas. You don't even believe in the sacrament of marriage."

"Preposterous. I've decided that we should be married and at the earliest possible date, provided you don't mind that it won't be lavish."

"Because of the baby?" I asked, needing to know that it was more than guilt prompting his sudden decision.

"Helen. I care deeply for you. We get on well together. You are my muse. You're carrying my child." He grinned at me with that charming smile. "Does a man need any more reason than that to marry?"

What about love?

Then the thought struck me that perhaps where others required those words to convey their feelings, Thomas showed his love in less conventional ways. He had not given me any false promises, and he was showing how much he cared for me and for his child. What more could I ask for from anyone? "If you are sure this is what you want," I replied, taking his hand.

He stood and leaned down to kiss my forehead. "Of course it's what I want."

A few weeks later, after I'd gained some of my strength back, we were married in a small country church with only the groundskeeper and his wife as witnesses to the union. I had to sit for much of the ceremony, still too weak to stand for extended periods. I wondered how I was going to manage carrying a child.

Thomas preferred the wedding to be private, telling William there was no need to cut his latest research trip short to come home for it. Thomas was still not talking to John after all that had happened.

It was not the ceremony of my dreams. No reception, no celebratory dinner surrounded by friends and family. Thomas took me to Brighton, at the suggestion of the doctor, where we stayed in a beach cottage owned by a friend. He never mentioned whom, but I suspect, by virtue of some of the belongings in the house, that it belonged to John's family.

Though I had lost a great deal of weight, which raised concerns about my ability to carry the baby to term, the warmth of the sun did wonders for my spirit and I felt my strength returning daily.

Thomas's confidence was encouraging, as well. He would sketch constantly. His favorite subjects were the bay, the sailboats dotting the horizon, and me. We laughed and made love, took walks and, while he spoke little of the future, I felt our marriage was secure and that the arrival of the child would serve to create the bond between us as a family.

In the weeks following, after we had returned to London, Thomas stopped sketching and turned to reading. He took an avid interest in photography, a new form of artistic expression breaking ground in France. He spent long hours in the bookshops at *Holywell,* bringing home postcards and books depicting exotic pictures of men and women engaged in various forms of sex.

As my body grew round and soft, Thomas's appetite for these exotic images increased. I could see him becoming restless and, while I tried to show my contentment in sitting by the fire and knitting things for the baby, I could not help but worry that we had not spent much time together in recent weeks.

"Thomas," I asked, noting his absorption in the book he was reading. "Have you thought of any names?"

His focus remained on his book. "Names? Names for what?"

I lay my knitting in my lap and stared at him, perplexed. "Why, for your son or daughter." I chuckled quietly. "That must be a very interesting book if you've forgotten that I am carrying your child."

Thomas slammed the book shut, laid it on his lap and stretched his hands over his head. He gave me a lopsided grin. "I'm no good with names, my muse. I will let you decide."

He tapped his fingers on the hard leather cover of the book, staring down at it as if pondering whether to return to his reading.

"Perhaps we could name him after your father, if it's a boy."

"No," he said decisively, slapping the book.

"Your mother perhaps, if it's a girl?"

His eyes rose and held steady on mine. "Perhaps we should come up with something unique, instead of hanging a used name on him."

"Or her." I smiled.

"Yes." He yawned. "Of course… Would you mind awfully if I ran down to McGivney's? Some of the brothers are meeting for a game of darts."

"Oh, that sounds like fun," I said as I put my knitting aside. "Let me get my shawl. I'd like to get out."

He rose and came to my side, placing his hand on my shoulder. "It's dreadfully loud and smoky down there, my muse. And odds are that the brothers will have been drinking and you know how they get. You can barely stomach their antics when they're sober." He laughed and kissed the top of my head. "I won't be long, but you needn't wait up. You need your rest."

"Then I guess we're through with discussing names?" I asked, watching as he put on his heavy jacket to walk the few blocks down the street. He plopped his hat atop his head and smiled over his shoulder.

"I have no doubt you will find the perfect name for the child." With that, he hurried down the steps and out the front door.

I glanced at the book he'd left behind and prayed that Annie was not working tonight.

Chapter 7

I COULD NOT TELL IF THOMAS WAS CONTINUING to grow more distant, or if I was growing distant from him. He was once again ecstatic about painting. However, when I asked him to tell me about his new project, he refused, saying only that it was going to set those bastards at the academy on their ears.

He would rise early, summon a carriage and would often be gone until after dark. When I'd offer to fix him dinner, he'd respond by saying he'd "gotten a bite at the gardens," or "run into an old friend who owed him a meal." I had no viable reason to mistrust what he told me. Nevertheless, I grew more despondent, knowing that my figure was not what it once was. My concern was furthered when Thomas, claiming the bed was no longer big enough for us both, resorted to sleeping in the guest room.

I was grateful for the days when the cold London rain would keep him captive at home. On those days, it seemed there was nothing amiss between us. We would chat as we sat near the fire— him with his book and me with my knitting. And I would scold myself for my needless worry.

"Helen, my dear, what would you think of hiring a house-keeper? Someone who could help tidy up the studio, maybe do the cooking? They wouldn't live here, unless you wanted them to, of course." He glanced at me over his book. We'd never had a servant in the house; Thomas thought it to be a sign of the blasé wealthy.

With him having not sold a painting in a while and with a child on the way, I wondered how we would afford it.

An idea popped into my head. "I could send for one of my sisters. I'm sure that Mama could talk sense into Papa, once they learned of my condition. Her compensation could be room and board," I offered, quite enthusiastic over the idea of having a sibling to keep me company while Thomas was away.

Thomas nodded and then shut his book soundly. "Good, I'm glad you're receptive to the idea. However, that won't be necessary. I have already acquired a suitable candidate. She is a fine woman. I've known her for some time. She's a good friend to the brotherhood and familiar with the studio. I won't have to teach her what not to touch, how to clean brushes."

My heart sank. "I see that you've put much thought into this. Are you planning to tell me who this woman is that you've decided on?"

"Of course. Her name is Grace Farmer."

"From the Cremorne?" I gaped at him in surprise. He looked at me.

"You've met her?"

"Not really. Your brother ran into her one night at the gardens. He told me about her."

"William took you to the gardens, did he?" Thomas smiled and raised his eyebrows.

"That was when he was trying to convince me to model for you, and that's not really the point of this conversation, is it?"

He shrugged. "What did he tell you about Grace?"

"That she was a friend to the brotherhood, misjudged by people because of her profession," I said.

"And what do you think of her?" he pressed.

"She's a prostitute."

"People have to eat, Helen. I'm quite certain Grace has the protocol not to bring her clients here." He chuckled.

I felt he was mocking me. "I'm glad you feel comfortable enough to trust her, Thomas. And how exactly did you happen to find that Miss Farmer was available for this position?" I turned the small baby blanket I was knitting between my hands, trying to stay calm.

"Well, strange as it seems, it was William who suggested it when I told him I was looking for someone to help out around the house."

"Oh, really, William? How thoughtful." I sighed, averting my eyes from his.

"Is there a problem between you and Will?" Thomas asked.

I swung my gaze back to his. "I haven't seen William in ages. I haven't seen anyone. If you remember, I have been confined to this house like a bird in a cage," I cried.

He wore the expression of a man at his wit's end with what to do with his pregnant wife.

"I'm sorry, Thomas, I have these episodes." I sounded foolish, perhaps petty, but I did not care. I was over four months with child and feeling bloated as a sick cow. "Tell me that you aren't the least bit attracted to her."

He smiled. "Is *that* what this is about?"

He set aside his book, knelt at my feet and rested his hands on mine.

"Your concerns are unnecessary, Helen. I have hired her to clean the studio because she knows what to do and I trust her implicitly with the task."

I stared at him, realizing that he had never asked me to clean the studio. I shoved aside my concerns, reminding myself that he was doing this to help me.

"I thought," he said, "that perhaps it would be good to have someone here to help you as your time draws near."

I looked down at our interlaced fingers and realized that it had been ages since he'd shown me any sort of intimacy. "I miss you,

Thomas," I said, quietly brushing my hand through his unkempt hair that I so loved. He raised my hands to his lips, placing there a lingering kiss.

"It won't be much longer, my muse, and we can be together again." He patted my hand and rose to go back to his chair.

"When does *she* start?" I asked, trying to snatch him back from the distance I already felt.

"Tomorrow," he replied, opening his book and settling into his chair. "I thought it best not to wait."

Part of me wanted to strangle William for his suggestion. What in blazes was he thinking sending that harlot into my home?

How could Thomas not notice her? She was breathtakingly beautiful and wore her vivid golden hair secured loose, so that wispy tendrils lay against her swanlike neck. Her clothing was far more refined than I would have thought for a woman of her profession. Instead of plain clothes, she wore brightly colored skirts with matching waistcoats. Each day she wore a different hat, nothing as mundane as a bonnet, but expensive traveling hats like those that I once sold at the shop to the private and wealthy clientele.

Three days a week, Grace would arrive in a black polished hansom carriage, and her driver would wait until she was finished with her duties to sweep her away. I had no idea of where she lived, or how she acquired such luxuries. And selfishly, I admit that I was just as happy that Thomas was gone on his research trips when she was around.

Grace found me reading in the front parlor downstairs one morning. Thomas had just kissed me goodbye and said he was off again with some of the brothers to do more sketches in the woods. They'd probably be at the farm. He cupped my cheek before he left and reminded me that his research wouldn't take up too much more time.

"You don't get out very often, do you?" Grace asked politely, as she ran her rag absentmindedly over a shelf.

"In my condition, I prefer to be at home," I replied, not looking up from my book.

"Is Thomas happy about the child?"

"I don't see how that is any of your affair," I offered curtly, hoping to send her back upstairs.

Her blue eyes glittered with knowledge, the kind foreign to me, and yet, in spite of my distaste for her, I wanted to know how well she knew my Thomas. My pride stopped me, however.

"He'll come around, I wouldn't worry."

A shiver skittered up my spine at how well she could read me. "What makes you think I'm concerned?" Was I that readable, that predictable?

She shrugged. "You stay around here all day, waiting for him to come home. Don't you have family that is interested in your condition? Have they been here to visit?"

I stared at the book in my hands, not knowing what to say. I'd been following Thomas's suggestion to wait until the baby was born to tell my family. However, I was growing desperate to have my mother know that I was with child, so she could be here with me when my time came. Still, Grace's remark and her sticking her nose in where it did not belong did not sit well with me. "I'm going to go lie down awhile. I'm suddenly quite tired." I waltzed past her and up the stairs, holding my belly with the book in my hand. I made it my single purpose to discuss the idea of an afternoon visit to my family with Thomas tonight after supper.

"That was a sumptuous meal," Thomas sighed, leaning his head back against the comfortable wingback chair. He took a swallow of his port and closed his eyes. Grace had left us a leg of lamb, cooked to perfection, and roasted potatoes and carrots for our supper that evening.

He had come home quite enthused about his tromp through the woods, saying he was inspired about a new project. I waited patiently for the right time to approach him with my request.

"Thomas, I've been thinking I would like to have someone I trust with me when my time comes," I reasoned.

"Fine, I'll send for my mother," he stated, his eyes still closed.

"Thomas, you've barely acknowledged your mother for the entire time I've known you. Does she even know that I exist, much less that you are giving her a grandchild?"

He opened one eye. "Of course she does."

I was admittedly startled at this revelation. "And what was her reaction?"

"William didn't say."

"William? You let William tell your family that you married and were having a child?" I didn't know whether to laugh or cry.

He frowned, pushed up from the chair and drew me into his arms. "Please, Helen, you need to stay calm—the baby."

Thomas stroked my back while I fumed inside at his lackadaisical attitude about our marriage, our family.

"I haven't spoken much about them as I am not exactly the apple of my family's eye. My father thinks I am wasting my time with my art, and my mother—well, let's just say she didn't get the priestly son that she'd hoped for."

He rested his chin on my head. "William, on the other hand, has always been my mother's darling boy."

"Thomas—" I began, but my thought was snatched in my next breath. I gripped his arm, unsure what was happening.

"Helen, what is it?" he asked.

There was a flutter deep inside me. Everything else paled in comparison to the wonder of this strange little flip. I grabbed Thomas's hand and held it to my belly. "There, can you feel her?"

"Her?" he asked. "How do you know?" His eyes searched mine.

I held my hand over his, searching calmly for the movement again, but the child had quieted. "I don't know. It's just a feeling." Calmer now that I had his attention, I held his hand in mine. We waited a moment more and when nothing happened, I turned to him, determined to state my case. "Thomas, I want to go visit my mother. I can't stand the thought that she doesn't know I'm having a child."

He squeezed my hands between his and looked at the floor.

"Helen, I have something I need to tell you." He paused a moment, as if formulating his words. "I'd hoped to wait until the baby was born. I didn't want to upset you." He raked a hand through his hair, his gaze uncertain.

"Thomas, for God's sake, what is the matter?"

"I've been to see your parents."

He held my hands tight when I tried to tug them away, the massive onyx ring he wore on his index finger pressing uncomfortably against my flesh.

"I went to see them when you were ill. After I discovered you were having the baby, well, I couldn't have that on my mind, too, if something would've happened to you. You were weak for a time and none of us knew what to expect. I was frantic. We all were, even John."

"If he'd kept the bathwater warm, none of this would have happened," I spewed out hatefully.

"Helen, John was not to blame entirely. You hadn't been taking proper care of yourself, either."

I nodded, pulling my confused thoughts back to the present. All I could think about was that my family knew I was ill and still did not come to see me. I took a deep breath, blinking back my tears.

"Go on, Thomas, tell me what happened."

"I told them you were in good hands, at a good institution. I told them about the child, how I planned to marry you and make a good home for you both. I tried to reassure them about the brotherhood, the family we belonged to here and how well we care for each other. I told them that I would see to it that our child would receive an education in the fine arts and that we'd send him to university."

I stared at him, wondering why he'd not comforted me with

these words before now. It was the first time he'd ever spoken about our child's future. "What did they say? Were they happy for us?"

He released a weary sigh and my hope dissipated.

"I wish that I could bring you better news, Helen. Your mama was distraught, and though your sisters and I tried to comfort her, she would not be consoled. Perhaps if your papa had been more understanding—"

I looked up. "Papa? What did he do?"

Thomas cleared his throat. "He said that he would neither bless our union nor claim the bastard child existed."

My heart twisted brutally in my chest. Bile rose in my throat and I covered my mouth, choking back the tears.

"I am sorry, Helen."

He rested his head in my lap, as would a child who wanted to be comforted. "Why didn't you tell me before?"

"Because of this." He lifted his head to look at me. "I didn't want to upset you. I wanted to wait until you were stronger, until we had a healthy beautiful child to show them. Was I wrong?"

He stroked my cheek. "Please tell me you forgive me. I did mean well." His lips found mine, tears mingling with the joining of our mouths. I could not remember the last time he had kissed me other than to say goodbye.

"Of course, my dearest, of course you would be thinking of my health and our child. I would not have expected otherwise."

Thomas wrapped his warm hands around my face. Anticipation flooded my heart, certain he was about to say the words I had longed to hear from his mouth.

"I promise you, after the child is born and you are strong again, we will go to visit your family and proudly show them their grandchild. How will they be able to refuse such a gift?"

I bowed my head and nodded, not allowing him to see the fresh tears welling in my eyes. I had hoped to hear how much he loved me, how we would get through these trying times together. But what I heard was him telling me to sit here and take care of myself while he went out gallivanting with his brethren. I couldn't believe that my family had no more care for me than that, my mama especially. I had to find out for myself.

After an early breakfast the next day, Thomas left to go sketching with the brothers. I looked out of the window and saw Grace's carriage parked below, her driver munching on an apple. "Grace?"

I wandered into the studio and she met me at the kitchen door. She wiped her hands on a towel. "Yes?"

"I wonder if I might borrow your carriage and driver for a few hours. It's a lovely day and I've been cooped up inside far too long."

She eyed me for a moment and shrugged. "Supper is around seven, as usual, provided the two of you return on time." She said no more and asked no further questions as I had hoped.

An hour later, I could see the rooftop of our barn and the grove of apple trees where we used to pick apples at this time of year.

To my delight, Mama was hanging the washing on the clothesline. My sister Beth was working in the garden, and Rosalind sat on the steps with a bowl of beans in her lap. My heart squeezed at the familiar sight. I leaned out of the window as the carriage swayed, rolling over the uneven ground, and saw the look of joy on my mama's face.

"Helen?" she called, lifting up a sheet to walk beneath it.

The carriage had barely come to a stop, and I did not wait for the driver to open the door. "Mama!" I waved to her as I stepped from the carriage. My feet hit the ground and, like in the days of my youth, I picked up my skirts and began to run toward her, though with more of a waddle than a brisk gait. I spied a patch of bright yellow flowers, knowing that in a few weeks they'd be replaced with great, fat pumpkins. Plucking the pumpkins, preparing them for pies was a treasured memory I held dear. I wasn't paying heed to the tangled vines trailing across the path in front of me, and my foot snagged on one of them causing me to fall forward, unable to catch myself before I landed flat on my face. I lay still, fearing the worst, realizing that the baby had cushioned

my fall. Beth reached her arm under mine and I pushed to my
knees. Rosalind grabbed my other arm and brought me to my
feet.

"How far along are you?" Mama asked, concern filling her
eyes.

"Four months, maybe five."

"Let's get you inside to lie down for a bit."

They helped me to my old bed and I lay flat on my back, my
mother and two sisters fussing over me. "I'm sure I'll be fine. The
doctor says that the womb is a strong, safe place."

Mama looked down at me. "I've a mind to send for Gretchen
Collins down the road. She's a good midwife—delivered all three
of you, right here in this house."

"Where's Papa?" I asked, ignoring her suggestion. She whispered something to Beth, who glanced at me and took off like a
bolt from the room.

"I don't want to cause any trouble, Mama," I stated. "I just
needed to see you. I needed to know that you weren't angry at
me for not coming here and letting you know about the baby."

She sat on the edge of the bed and hugged me. "How could I
be angry with you? I am so glad you are here. How long can you
stay?"

"I can't stay long. I've borrowed the carriage from our housekeeper."

"Your housekeeper?" She looked impressed.

"It's far too complicated. I just wanted to see you. I want
you—and Beth and Rosalind—to come when the baby is born.
We have plenty of room and we would welcome your help."

"I'll have to wait and see, Helen. It's your father. He's a
stubborn old German and I don't know if I can leave him here
alone for too long."

"He's still angry with me, then?" I asked.

"He'll come around. It's just going to take time."

"Where is he?" I asked again. "I'm going to have to get back
soon."

"He's in the fields, but perhaps now is not the best time to see him, Helen. I think, though, that you ought to let Gretchen take a look at you."

I swung my legs over the side of the bed. There was no pain, no spotting. I stood and felt no dizziness. "There, you see? Good as new." I hid the queasy feeling in my stomach from her. There was no need to concern her. I would rest on the carriage ride back home.

My mother studied me a moment, and then her eyes came alive with a thought. "Wait, there is something I want to give you." She hurried to the chest in the corner of my bedroom. My father had made it for me on my ninth birthday. She handed me a small package wrapped in old paper. Inside was a worn blanket, a bonnet and a pair of tiny knit booties.

"These were yours. I thought that my granddaughter might be able to use them." Unshed tears shimmered in her eyes. I hugged her tight, then my sister. "I will put them on her the first day. Tell Beth I'll see her soon."

They walked me to the carriage and, while I hated not seeing my father, perhaps, in this case, Thomas was right.

"I'll see you soon." The carriage jerked forward as it started down the lane, taking me from my old life back to my new one.

Chapter 8

THE DIRT ROAD BACK TO TOWN WAS ROUGHER than it had seemed when we'd traveled it earlier. I bit my lip, fighting the nausea making my stomach roil. No doubt the stress of the fall, coupled with sneaking away to see my mother against Thomas's wishes, did not bode well for my nervous stomach. I leaned my head back against the seat and tried to rest to no avail. When I saw the outskirts of London, I sighed with relief, never more glad to see our familiar cobblestone street. I thanked the driver and trudged slowly up the stairs, bone weary and too tired to find Grace. I decided to lie down for a few moments, and later I would thank her for the use of her carriage.

With barely the strength to remove my hat and coat, I peeled back the bed linens and, fully clothed, crawled beneath the comforting quilt and drifted off to sleep.

I awoke feeling groggy and feverish. My stomach was still unsettled. I noted an uncomfortable cramping low in my belly, but put aside the niggling fear that it had anything to do with my mishap. I decided to make myself a cup of tea and wait for Thomas to come home.

I tossed off the covers, finding it easier to turn on my side and push myself upright as I swung my legs over the bed. A wave of nausea hit me quick and I thought I might lose my stomach. I waited, breathing slow, closing my eyes, willing the nausea to ease, and after a moment it faded away.

Bracing my hand on the nightstand, I stood and almost instantly felt a gush of something wet between my legs. I grabbed my skirts, tugging them over my knees, my thighs, knowing that it was far too early for the baby to be coming.

My heart stopped when I saw the bloodstained fabric of my drawers. Panic gripped my heart. I stumbled to the doorway. Was Grace still here? Had Thomas returned?

"Thomas!" The shadows of the dusky hallway teased my muddled thoughts. Was it evening or early morning? "Thomas!" I called again and heard no response. My head was light, as if the life was being sucked from my body. I sank to the floor, resting my cheek on the cool wood of the door frame.

My mind was a haze and I fought to discern the sounds around me. I heard a door slam shut and the sound of footsteps on the stairs, although they seemed far away, somewhere in a dream. "Thomas." I moved my lips, but they felt strangely detached from my body. My head seemed too heavy for my neck and it flopped forward to my chest, where I saw a large, dark spot forming on my skirt. The thought crossed my mind that I was going to die.

"Helen? Oh, Jesus, Helen!"

I peered toward the voice, searching for a familiar face, but the image was watery. I recognized the faint scent of bay rum. *William.*

I felt myself being lifted into his arms. "William," I whispered. My body seemed to be floating in midair. I was disoriented, my eyes fluttered shut and I just wanted to sleep. I remembered telling Papa I was sorry and leaning my head on a solid shoulder. If I could rest for a few minutes, I would be fine.

"Stay with me, Helen." William's voice grew distant. I wasn't able to answer him before the black sleep took me.

★ ★ ★

Twice now, I'd awakened in a hospital room. This time, however, both Thomas and William were there. Thomas sat at my side, his hands holding mine. William, off to the side, looked on.

My husband's face was drawn and dark circles rimmed his eyes, red from crying. He managed a smile and squeezed my hand, but he did not speak.

Instinctively, I moved my hand over my belly, expecting to feel the tight little ball that I'd come to accept as part of me. My eyes darted to Thomas then, and I could see him fighting with his emotions.

My heart felt as if someone squeezed it, strangling the life out of me. My thoughts searched for a reason, my eyes filling with unshed tears. I blinked and looked at William, who averted his eyes, placing his hand over his mouth.

Thomas spoke first. "We almost lost you, Helen. If William hadn't found you when he did—"

I looked again at William, his image swimming through my tears. "It was you." He didn't look up, he simply nodded.

"I'm sorry. I'm sorry I couldn't get you here fast enough," he said, his voice cracking.

"No, William, it wasn't your fault. If I hadn't gone to see my mother—"

Thomas's startled gaze turned to mine. "What did you say?"

There was a bitter taste in my mouth and my chin quivered as I tried to force the truth from my lips. "I borrowed Grace's carriage and went to see my mother. I needed to see her."

He bowed his head, resting his face on our hands. For a moment, I thought he was crying. William started for the door. "Wait, William, please stay." I focused on Thomas. "I tripped. It was an accident. I thought I was fine. I thought if I rested I would feel better."

"I asked you to wait." His words were muffled, but his authoritative tone was clear.

"I needed to see her," I insisted, feeling as if I had to defend my actions to him when what I needed was his understanding, his compassion for the loss I had suffered—that we had both suffered.

He looked up, anger infused in his steely eyes. "If you hadn't—"

"Thomas, stop. There is no one that can be blamed." William placed his hand on his brother's shoulder. "Especially not Helen."

Thomas jerked his shoulder away from William's grasp. I could see the torment in his eyes. He wanted to blame someone, something.

I yanked my hand from his and batted at his head, tired of his selfish behavior. "Don't you dare be rude to him, or to me. I lost this child, too, Thomas."

Thomas pushed from the chair, toppling it over as he strode from the room.

"I'll go see to him, Helen," William said, following his brother out the door.

For the first time, I'd seen Thomas at his most vulnerable, and I realized that he was not comfortable with any reality other than his own. However, I could not tell if his anger was due to his grief or simply because I had defied his wishes.

Exhausted, I purged my body of its pain, giving in to my heart-racking sobs.

Thomas was unusually quiet. For more than two weeks, since my release from the hospital, his schedule had been full of appointments and meetings with the brotherhood that kept him out late most evenings. When he didn't have a meeting, he went for long walks at night, sometimes not returning until after I was in bed.

Though I tried, he didn't want to talk about what had happened. It was as if he wanted to forget the episode entirely. We existed in the same house, on occasion sleeping beside each other but never touching. Other times, I would find him in his reading chair in the studio, a blanket pulled up beneath his chin, his hair and clothing disheveled. While the doctor encouraged me and said that I should be able to carry my next child to term, under the present circumstances, I doubted there would ever be another child.

William put his next trip on hold, staying on at the studio and becoming an intermediary between Thomas and me. Moreover, with Thomas gone so much of the time, I'd come to rely on William's strength as a confidant and companion. I feared my despondency, more evident some days than others, was an awful burden for him to bear, but he didn't seem to mind. Perhaps more disconcerting was that I began to dwell more and more on the days before I met Thomas, remembering how captivated I had been with his brother. It was dangerous water to wade into, but I was desperately lonely.

"You are looking better, Helen." William smiled. Admiration shone on his face as he took the teacup I offered. My hand trembled as our fingers met, tipping the cup precariously in my hand. William caught it and righted it without a word.

"The doctor says my stamina is improving," I said, easing onto one of the dining-table chairs. Thomas preferred the table placed at the end of the studio, where there was plenty of room for the brothers to dine together on occasion.

"I saw Thomas going out for a walk as I came in. He seemed in good spirits."

I didn't bother to hide my surprise. "Then you've apparently seen a different Thomas than the man I'm married to." I had seen little of him in recent days and tried not to think about where he went at night or who might be giving him comfort. I did not like sounding like a haggard wife, but the truth was that I was growing restless, hoping to find a glimpse of the old Thomas who had swept me off my feet and into his bed.

"I confess I'm worried, William. He is not painting. He refuses to talk to me about anything. I don't know who is more the ghost around here—him or me."

William looked at his cup. "Time heals wounds, Helen. He just needs more of it."

"And what shall I do in the meantime? I carry around this guilt, remembering what he said to me in the hospital, the implication that if I had listened to him, this wouldn't have happened."

"He was angry and hurting, Helen. He didn't mean what he said."

"And I wasn't?" I challenged his loyalty to his brother.

William studied me with his calm, clear blue eyes. "Helen—" he narrowed his gaze "—what you don't need is to keep torment- ing yourself. What happened…happened. It was just fate." He stared at his cup. "Somehow we find a way to move on."

I considered his words, spoken while he traced the rim of his cup, lost in his private thoughts. In my twisted, selfish brain, I wondered if the loss he was referring to was not mine, but his. Was it possible he still harbored more than sisterly affection for me? The thought, however remote, sparked an adulterous curi- osity in me. "Do you suppose then, that it was fate, William, that you instead of your brother found me?"

He sat back, ramrod straight against the chair. What a handsome man he was, with many physical similarities to Thomas but none of his attitude. I looked away briefly, afraid he would see my torrid thoughts.

"Helen, don't." He shifted in his chair. "It's not the same."

"Why shouldn't I be grateful that you were there, even as you are now here instead of him?" I left it unsaid that it should have been—should now be—Thomas offering me comfort. But he was far too busy in his quest to "set the academy on its ear!"

The muscle of William's square jaw ticked as he stared intently at the floor. His humility was part of his charm, as had been the case from the first day we met. I tried not to think of his unsel- fish kindness, how he held my hand when we walked in the park and how his eyes burned for me that fateful summer's day.

"I am not trying to make you feel uncomfortable," I said quietly, though in truth my thoughts were driving me to distraction.

He cleared his throat, his eyes carefully watching me. The air between us crackled with awareness.

"Let's talk about something else." He placed his cup on the table. "Have you considered going back to your writing, at least until my brother has you modeling again?"

I easily waved off his suggestion. "I'm not sure I'll ever model again for Thomas. I'm sure my appearance is not the stuff of a stunner any longer." I shrugged, giving the impression I didn't care, although the uncertainty of my future weighed heavily on my mind. "I tried to do some writing after coming home, but I couldn't stay focused."

He shrugged. "Perhaps you will pick it up again. It might be good therapy. I still carry the poem you gave me, you know."

I stared at him wide-eyed, unable to believe that after all this time he would still have it. The thought made me smile—something I had not done in weeks. "You are a true friend, William." I laid my hand on his forearm and he smiled stiffly, taking a sip of his tea, effectively moving my hand away without a word.

I found his reaction rather strange but chose to ignore it, instead changing the subject. "Well, then," I asked with as much brightness as I could muster, "tell me about you. What have you been doing? Are you working on your designs?" I was grateful for his company, to be able to visit with someone. I think that I was so desperate for human contact that I might even have welcomed Grace's company, but she'd not been present since my return from the hospital.

"I've been back to Italy. I spent a few days in India. I've been studying patterns in ancient architecture and artwork," he replied.

"That's wonderful, but the expense must be enormous. Forgive my curiosity, but however do you manage it?"

He shrugged. "It is a goodly sum. That much is true." He took another sip of tea.

"I'm sorry, I didn't mean to pry," I said. "I'm certain that someone of your talent has a generous sponsor."

He released a deep sigh. "He's never told you?"

"Who? Thomas? Never told me what?" I asked.

"Thomas funds my expeditions. Mostly from the sales of his earlier works. He set up a trust for me when I was younger. The idea being that after I achieve my success, I can take care of him in his old age."

I had to chuckle. "That sounds like a plan Thomas would come up with." I took a sip of my tea and shook my head in wonder. "I had no idea."

"As I once told you when you and I first met, he is a generous man."

I nodded. "Yes, I do remember and please do not misunderstand. I don't deny his generosity, William. Thomas is a good man—complicated—but truly a good man, as I believe you are. It's just that…well—" I flashed him a smile "—you're here and he isn't, and there is very little I can do about it."

William's eyes bored into my soul, making me think things I shouldn't. I fiddled with my cup and we sat for a moment in tension-filled silence, cordially drinking our tea.

I pushed past the awkward silence in an effort to change the topic, shift it away from Thomas and my loneliness. "So tell me, what lovely lady has caught your eye these days?"

He responded with a halfhearted laugh. "I'm afraid there's no one. I'm gone so much of the time…" He stopped as if about to say more, and shrugged. "My work is enough," he added as an afterthought.

"Well, I hope that you won't always feel that way," I said. "You deserve more." He looked at me, his gaze steady, curious.

"Why is it so important to you, Helen? My life is my affair, isn't it? If I choose to share my life with someone, then it will be my choice, not directed by someone who is clearly—" He set his cup on his saucer. "I'm sorry, Helen. I said too much, I should leave."

He pushed up from his chair and hesitated as he looked down at me. Finally, he leaned down and placed a chaste kiss on my cheek. "Wait." I grabbed his hand. "You meant to say someone who is clearly *unhappy,* didn't you?"

I heard his tense sigh. "I reacted badly," he said. "I apologize."

I clung to his hand as I stood. "Isn't that what friends do, William? Don't they speak openly with each other? Don't they wish the best for each other?"

"Yes, I suppose, Helen." He patted my hand, gently tugging his from my grasp. I held on firmly, desperate to hear what I hoped was true.

"We used to talk about so many things. Do you remember our walks in the park, our trip to the gallery?" It was a selfish display, begging him for attention like this. But looking at him reminded me of easier days—days when the future looked brighter.

"Helen, I am sorry, but I would rather not talk about this."

"Of course, what's in the past is in the past." I gave a short laugh. "It can't be resurrected, nor should we wish that it could be, right, William?"

He stared at the floor but did not respond. I pressed further, needing to understand how he'd been able to walk away from me so easily, never once showing that he cared. "Is that the reason you travel so much? To get away from here?" *To get away from me?* He glared at me.

"You think you know me? You think you know how I feel?"

"No, of course not," I said. "I only wanted to know—"

"You want to know the truth, Helen?" His gaze narrowed as he squeezed my hand tight. "I'll tell you, then. It nearly killed me to find you on the floor, nearly gone...to realize how close I came—" He shut his eyes. "We came, to losing you."

My fingers ached, but no worse than did my heart. We stood looking at each other, the challenge to walk away or follow through on our emotions, hanging with tantalizing fascination between us. "I'm glad it was you that found me."

"You might have died," he said, searching my eyes.

"But I didn't," I tossed back. "I just want you to be happy, William. You're the kind of man every woman wants."

"Everyone except you, is that what you mean?" he snapped back.

My lips parted to respond, but the shock of his words barred my voice. It was not me who had walked away that day—or was it? I finally found my tongue and my spine at once. "That was your choice, William."

His laugh was cynical. "And later, when you had the choice to marry?"

I tugged at my hand, my frustration growing. "You're hurting me."

"You made the choice, Helen."

He yanked me closer, capturing my hand against his chest. "You said nothing, and I thought it was because you didn't care, that you were being loyal to Thomas."

"Of course, good old dependable William. Steadfast and true, predictable as the sunrise. Just give him a pat on the head every now and again? Is that the picture you've painted of me, Helen?"

I was shocked at his perception. "N-no, of course not," I stammered.

"Do you think it was easy for me to watch you carrying *his* child, wishing it were mine? Do you think it was easy coming back from a trip and finding out that you'd married him?"

He grabbed my shoulders, squeezing them painfully.

"I—I didn't think—"

"That's right, Helen. You didn't, not that it would have mattered, because I've always thought of Thomas first, before my own happiness. I took care of him, saw to his needs, consoled him, celebrated his successes—then you came along and took that job away from me. Yet, here is the ironic twist. What I first thought was best for Thomas was really what was best for *me*. And I have had to stand by and watch him squander that." He touched my cheek and I nearly burst into flame. "I've had to watch him squander the gift that I gave up." His eyes shimmered as he leaned his forehead to mine. "If I had the chance to do it all again, I would never have stepped aside."

His thumb brushed my cheek. I dared not look at him, his mouth so temptingly close, his confession igniting a fire that coursed through my blood. His finger touched my chin, coaxing me to meet his gaze, and there I saw the torment and passion I had seen once on a summer afternoon long ago.

His lips captured mine, claiming me in blinding, selfish lust. He pressed his body against mine, pinning me to the table and sending one of the teacups shattering to the floor. I welcomed his heated kisses, trailing down the slope of my neck, succumbing to his urgency to find my mouth again, appeasing this vicious hunger that consumed us both.

"I should burn in hell for what I want to do to you, Helen," he whispered, his breath hot against my cheek.

I swallowed hard, my fingers stiff from gripping the front of his shirt, but I did not want to let him go. "Tell me, William. Tell me what you'd do," I pleaded shamelessly, my loneliness nearly swallowing me whole.

"No, Helen. I'm sorry, I can't."

He held my face, searching my eyes for an answer that I could not give him.

"William," I whispered, leaning up to capture his mouth in another soul-searing kiss.

"We can't," he said, squeezing his eyes, blinking them as if trying to clear the haze of desire between us. If fate had anything to do with my life, it had just dealt the cruelest hand to me yet.

"Can't, or won't?" I asked with bravado, his taste lingering on my lips.

He closed his eyes for a moment and drew me close, rubbing his cheek over my hair.

"God, I envy him," William said quietly. "Like an open wound, and it is a torture that I live with every day, knowing that it is him who has every right to be in your bed."

He stepped away, holding me at arm's length, and then turned from me, raking a hand through his hair. "I'll go mad if I dwell on this. You are not just a model anymore, Helen, but his wife. What I feel is wrong in so many ways."

He reached for my face, stopping short, and curled his fingers, drawing his hand to his side. "I have no right, not after all Thomas has done for both of us." He pressed his lips to my forehead in a tender kiss. "I have to find a way to forget, Helen, and I need you to forget, too. It's the only way." He dropped his arms to his sides as if touching me was poison, forbidden, and the next moment, he was gone.

I sat staring blindly before me long after he'd gone. The man I had married had no time for me; the man who desired me more than I could conceive was noble to the point of martyrdom. My loneliness consumed me. I had to have time to think, to get away from here and go back to where I once remembered feeling safe and secure—home. I prayed that Papa would accept me.

The next morning I spoke to Thomas about going home for an extended visit. He agreed that the fresh air and sunshine would be good for me. "You're sure that you will be well?" I asked, a part of me hoping that Thomas would try to talk me out of leaving. We stood on the front stoop, my bags already in the carriage.

"It's only for a short time, Helen. Between William and Grace, I'm sure I can manage adequately. I was once a self-reliant bachelor, if you recall."

I tried to dismiss the sense that he wished he was that again. Thomas gave me a peck on my cheek. William drew me into a quick, brotherly hug but I knew it was nothing more than a show to mask his true feelings.

"Enjoy your stay," Thomas called.

I rested my head against the seat and closed my eyes, letting the gentle rocking motion of the carriage lull me. It seemed I had lost everything—my child, Thomas *and* William. I had to ask myself if it was worth the lying and heartache that I'd put my family through to attain my independence, only to have nowhere else to go but home with my bag of broken dreams.

Chapter 9

"ARE YOU GOING BACK SOON?" MAMA ASKED AS she grabbed another bed linen from the basket, snapping it before she hung it on the line.

"Have you tired of me already?" I covered my eyes from the sun as I looked up at her. Beth and I sat on the back step shelling peas. Papa, sullen at the tragic news of losing his grandchild, had drawn me into his arms, forgiving my trespasses, yet no doubt feeling even more justified in his feelings about Thomas and the brotherhood. He told me I never had to go back if I didn't want to, that I could live with them.

Mama, on the other hand, believed that because a priest married us in the sight of God, my place was at my husband's side, regardless of how he felt about me. She did not ask how I felt about Thomas, and I wouldn't have been able to answer her anyway.

"Helen, of course I don't want you to go, but you do have a husband and there is the matter of your marriage vows," she said, hanging another shirt.

"Do you think he and Thomas could ever see eye to eye?" I asked, clinging to a small thread of hope that if Papa could forgive me, perhaps he could accept Thomas, too, and learn to love him as a son.

"One step at a time." She smiled. "Beth, run on inside and see to the meat on the stove. I want to talk to your sister alone."

Beth did as instructed and Mama sat beside me on the step. "What troubles you, Mama?" I asked, sneaking a couple of fresh sweet peas. It had been wise to come home. The crisp, clean air, digging in the garden, the homegrown food—it had all done wonders for me physically and emotionally. I felt stronger, but I was not sure that I was able to face Thomas yet.

"You do feel it was wise for me to come here, don't you?" I asked.

"My children are always welcome. I do not want you to forget that, but you have started a new home, as well. One that will soon be filled with children of your own." She looked at me with a hopeful smile.

"Maybe," I replied, searching her eyes. Could I bring myself to tell her about William? Did it matter anymore? My heart was still raw from all that had happened. I'd lain awake more than one night remembering our last scalding kiss, the torment of passion in William's eyes. What could I do to put the same fire in my husband's eyes again?

"Oh, of course you will." She patted my arm.

"Mama? Can I ask you something?"

"Anything."

"Was there ever a time when you weren't sure how Papa felt about you?"

"Ah," she replied. "He's still in mourning, then?"

I shrugged. "I'm not sure. Thomas is…he's distant. I don't know how to get his attention."

"Most men just want to know that you *want* their attention and that what you *need* more than anything is them."

I tucked her words in my heart. "What if you aren't sure if what *they* need is you?"

She smiled, pressing her hand to my cheek. I smelled the laundry soap on her skin.

"You listen to me, Helen. The reason he proposed to you does not matter. The point is that he did and at that moment, you became all that he needed, all that he wanted."

"But I fear he blames me for losing his child."

"Neither you nor Thomas are to blame. These things happen. They are no one's fault. He will come around," she said, "in time. But you must be the one to guide him past the pain, Helen. Men are funny that way. Sometimes we have to show them how strong they really are. That's what it means to be a good wife."

"Sometimes I ache, Mama, desperately trying to remember how that child felt inside me. How can I show someone strength when I have so little to give?"

"That is where most women are misguided, Helen. Men think they are the ones who are strong, but they see only physical strength. Women often bear far greater burdens and those burdens make us resilient—stronger."

She brushed back my hair, her eyes brimming with love.

"When your father declared he had no eldest daughter, I was torn between the choice you made and his—my heart was breaking. Yet, I believed that he would eventually come around, and he has, Helen. The two of you don't agree on everything, but he has accepted your choices and your husband to the extent that he is able."

She took my hands, pressing them between hers.

"I know that your heart has been through so much. But you've got to be strong. Thomas will come around."

For a woman with no education beyond the farm, my mama was the wisest woman I knew. I hugged her tight. It had been almost a month and I decided it was time for me to go home to my husband.

I felt amazingly calm. Perhaps my time away had done more good than I realized. I felt stronger, more ready to do what it took to try to piece together my splintering marriage.

The carriage pulled up in front of the studio, and the driver helped me down and carried my bag to the door. I handed him my fare.

"Will that be all, miss?" he asked.

I glanced up at the balcony and saw that the doors to the studio were open, giving way to a faint glow, indicating the likelihood that Thomas was having his nightly port in front of the fire. I was anxious to talk with him, to tell him how well things had gone at home and how my papa had decided that if I thought Thomas was a good man, then he did, too. I wondered if William would be at the studio.

"That will be all, thank you." I opened the door to the flat and quietly placed my bag inside. With Mama's words bolstering me, I hurried up the steps, hoping that my return would be a pleasant surprise for Thomas. That maybe our being apart would have secured what we felt for each other. I wanted desperately to be held in his arms again.

I heard voices coming from the studio as I mounted the second tier of stairs and I slowed, realizing with a sick feeling that one of them was female. I paused at the top of the steps, afraid of what I was about to stumble in on. Sheer will drove me forward into the studio and I stood in the shadows, my eyes seeing what my heart feared. Curled up in front of the fire, cradling a glass of port and dressed in one of Thomas's shirts was Grace. Thomas was kneeling in front of her, his hands braced on the arms of her chair. Based on her soft expression, their conversation was quite intimate.

I felt nauseous at first, and then angry. I forced myself to step farther into the room. "Thomas?"

Thomas shot to his feet and whirled to face me. "Helen?"

"Surprise." I gave him a tight smile.

Grace rose from the chair and placed her glass on the mantel.

"Oh, please don't feel you must leave on my account," I said to her, all the while looking directly at my husband.

At that moment, the front door slammed and the sound of someone bounding up the steps followed.

"Thomas, there's a bag downstairs, I thought that perhaps Helen—"

"Hello, William," I said politely. How much did he know about Grace and my husband? He was the one who had suggested she come to clean for us, after all.

"Helen." His gaze darted from Thomas to Grace and her lack of proper clothing.

"Will, be good and go hold that carriage for me," Grace said. He nodded and tore off down the steps.

I held my gaze firm as she walked up to me.

"Your husband came to my rescue tonight, Helen. Don't be too hard on him." She looked at Thomas. "I'll get my clothes."

"Grace," Thomas said, "there's no need for you to leave, not after what you've been through."

"I'm fine, Thomas. I'm sure that you and Helen have a lot to discuss."

I glanced at Thomas and followed Grace out into the hall, waiting until she'd collected her things from our bedroom.

William nearly bowled me over as he raced back up the steps, my bag that I'd left at the front door in his hand.

"I'll put this in your room," he said, stepping around me, hesitating but a moment as he looked over his shoulder. "It's nice to have you home," he said, quietly ducking into the bedroom to deposit my bag, then going across the hall to shut himself in his room.

I waited at the bedroom window, feeling like a spy watching my own husband from behind the window curtain. I saw Grace lean forward and give Thomas a light peck on the cheek. Guilt mixed with my rage as I thought of the episode with William just before I left. But I had to reason whether I would have been driven to such things had I not already felt insecure about our marriage. That was the very reason, in fact, that I left; to gain a clear perspective of what I wanted—what I hoped Thomas still wanted.

I came away from the window when I heard the front door

slam. Thomas appeared a moment later in the doorway, smiling as if nothing at all had happened.

"You look positively radiant," he said.

I assessed his dress trousers and shirt. "Why was Grace here, dressed in your shirt? Where did you go tonight?"

"It's good to have you home, as well," he responded drily.

"Is it?" I asked, removing my hat and gloves.

He placed my bag on the bed. "If you are referring to what just happened in there…"

I cocked my head. "I'm sorry, Thomas. *Was* something happening in there?"

He rubbed his hand over his forehead. "It appears that you may well have misinterpreted the situation."

"Misinterpreted?" I asked. "You're dressed for an evening out and I come home to find you kneeling, quite intimately by the way, in front of a whore who is wearing one of your shirts. What's there to misinterpret?"

"Helen, my muse. Let's not quarrel. It's your first night home."

He reached for my coat and I moved away. "Tell me where you went tonight, Thomas. Did you escort Grace somewhere?"

"I went to a charity art event and no, I did not escort Miss Farmer," he stated.

"Yet she wound up here. Would she have spent the night had I not returned?"

He shrugged. "Perhaps," he said. "She'd been through quite an ordeal. I was being a good friend."

"As if she hasn't flirted with dangerous men before," I said acidly, my anger spewing from the bitterness of his apathetic response to our marriage over the past few months. "It is rather a hazard of the trade, isn't it?"

"Don't be a bitch, Helen," he stated flatly. His eyes were cold, his mouth pressed in a firm line. "I'm going to assume that you are weary from your journey and so not entirely in charge of your senses." He slid me a look. "I'll go fix you something to eat."

"I'm not hungry," I replied. Already my stomach had started

to roil. A sob clogged my throat. This was not the homecoming I had planned.

He stopped, his hand resting on the door frame. "Fine, I'm going to fix myself a port. I'll be in the study." The door closed with a final click.

My marriage was unraveling before my eyes. I paced the room, my fists clenched at my sides, considering my options, which were few.

If I broke down now, if I gave up, I would wind up living at home or trying to live on my own. Not an easy thing to do these days in London, harder yet after being an artist's model, whereby society readily labeled you as tainted—a sinner by choice, not by need. The thought of living in a ramshackle flat somewhere, with a dozen other women—it was enough to give me pause and not act in haste.

I hung my coat on the back of the door and freshened my face and hair in the oval dressing mirror propped in the corner of our room. In the reflection, I saw the unmade bed over my shoulder and my heart stopped at the sight of the tangled sheets. I found it surprisingly easy to suspect that it had been recently used. I walked over and laid my hand on the sheet to check for warmth, then lifted it to my nose to check for the scent of a woman. I sat down, holding the sheet to my face, breathing deeply of Thomas's familiar musky male-and-spice scent.

Catching my reflection in the mirror, I remembered the day Thomas brought it home from an auction.

"To add luster to our bedroom," he'd said with a wicked smile.

My thoughts drifted to the number of times that I'd gazed upon our reflection, aroused by our entwined limbs, the languid movement, hard flesh against soft. I thought the passion would last a lifetime. But, neither one of us was the same; at least, I wasn't. Where tragedy serves to strengthen some marriages, I was afraid it had done the opposite for us. Perhaps there were already problems that we ignored and this just brought clarity to them. I rose from the bed, straightened the sheets and decided I needed to talk to him, if only to clear the air between us and to find out where we stood.

I walked into the study, determined to make him listen this time. He was going to see me, his wife—not a lover, not his muse. His wife. "Thomas, I wanted to talk to you about earlier this evening." My thoughts were cut off when I saw William standing next to his brother. As always, the resemblance between them was a bit startling. "I didn't realize that…" I fumbled whether to stay or return to my room. "I'll come back later."

"I was just saying good-night," William said.

He paused at my side and handed me a folded note.

"You look rested, Helen," he said quietly, pressing the paper against my palm as he wrapped his fingers around my hand. It was brief, but the warmth he offered with his gentle eyes and his hand distracted me for a moment.

"Thank you, William." I slanted him a curious glance.

"Good night," he said to both of us as he slipped out of the room.

Thomas stood in front of the fireplace, nursing a glass of port. He had not yet acknowledged my presence.

I stepped into the light, quietly unfolded the note and began to read.

Dear Miss Bridgeton,
It is my pleasure to inform you that your poem, Another Time, Another Place *has been selected winner of our annual poetry competition. Yours was chosen from over two hundred submissions and was our judges' unanimous favorite. It is the guild's sole purpose to foster new talent and, as such, we invite you to submit a portfolio of your work for consideration in future publications. In addition, you will receive, via private courier, the contest purse winnings of five hundred pounds. We thank you for such a poignant submission and look forward to seeing more of your work, as well as to oversee the advancement of your career.*
Most sincerely,
Cecil B. Thomas, Esq.
England Poetry Guild

"What is that?"

Thomas's voice startled me. "Oh, just a note that Mama stuck in my pocket, reminding me to take my stomach medicine." It was a bald-faced lie. My stomach had not bothered me in weeks.

I noted a new canvas on his easel. "You're painting again?" I'd not seen him pick up a brush in a long time. He stood, staring into the fireplace, as he sipped his port.

"Merely dabbling, mostly."

He continued to stare into the fire. "Has Grace been posing for you?" I asked as delicately as I could, hoping it would not set off any of his tirades. I heard his frustrated sigh from across the room.

"Does it matter, Helen? Even if she were, which she isn't, would it matter? *I* am an artist, *she* is a model. *You* were not here."

I rubbed my hand over the back of my neck, feeling the tension rise. "I suppose it shouldn't, Thomas, but you must admit, after being gone for nearly a month, it was rather awkward to come home and find another woman seated before my husband with barely a stitch on."

"She was nearly raped tonight, Helen. You have no idea what a monster this man turned out to be. Her dress was torn. I gave her some clothes to wear." He leaned on the mantel.

"It's fortunate that you were there," I said, my voice steady.

He glanced at me, shoved his shirtsleeves up his forearms and knelt in front of the fire, sifting the embers with the iron poker.

"I wanted to apologize." I took a deep breath. "I may have misinterpreted what I saw earlier."

"Thank you, Helen. While I appreciate your apology, there is something I feel you may have forgotten, or perhaps have never fully understood. I am a connoisseur of women. The variety of them astounds me, excites me—it is the very essence of my artistic success," he said as he shoved at the burning coals. "You had to have known this before you agreed to marry me. Why would you think that I would, by virtue of a piece of paper, suddenly cast aside all that I am, all that I need to inspire me?"

An awkward silence stretched between us. A million different responses resided on the tip of my tongue, but I could not speak.

"There's a new era coming, Helen. We're on the cusp of it, even now. An era when artists and poets will embrace the decadent and deviant, harnessing its beauty, creating an art form so unique it will shame those who have tried to suppress freethinking for so long. And we who understand this raw beauty must embrace it, encourage it, live it ourselves in order to let our voices be heard above the din of mediocrity. The movement is young, in its tender beginnings, but it's coming," he said, poking at the logs. "It's coming as sure as a glorious climax! You mark my words!"

"Well, thank you for enlightening me." I stared at him, the eyes of my heart wide-open. He was on one of his tirades again. The critics were no doubt being particularly vicious to him right now and I fought the guilt of asking too much of him.

My chest felt tight; I had to breathe. I stepped out onto the balcony and gulped in the night air. The air was stale, far different from the country, with a lingering odor of sewage from the Thames.

I thought about what Thomas had said—that I had to have known what he was like when I agreed to marry him. And in truth, wasn't his persona—his rakish, devil-may-care attitude— what drew me to him in the first place? The realization surprised me. Yet I had never felt a part of the brotherhood, never understood their rebellious mission to make the world see things their way.

I jumped, startled as Thomas's hands curved over my shoulders. He wrapped his arms around me, rubbing his unshaven cheek to mine.

"I have missed you, my muse," he whispered softly, nuzzling the side of my neck. "I don't like it when we squabble. I much prefer to have you in my bed or in front of a canvas where you spark my inspiration."

He knew he'd gone too far. He knew *this* was the Thomas that I craved—attentive, loving, devoted. My body responded from habit, desirous as always for his magnificent body. I brought my hand to his cheek and he turned his face, kissing my palm.

His hands drifted upward, moving over my breasts, rubbing the rough lace of my corset over them, building a tormenting need between my legs. Desperate for his touch, I grabbed his hand and pushed it between my legs, needing to appease my yearning. He required no further encouragement and, grasping my skirts in one hand, he slipped his hand down the front of my drawers and plunged his finger into my warmth, stroking until I was drenched.

"Tell me, Helen. Let me hear you say that you want me to fuck you."

His face pressed against the shell of my ear, his blunt desire was like a delectable aphrodisiac. I leaned my head to his shoulder and nodded. He knew me well. He knew I wanted to feel his body close, connected to mine. Yet, I knew that to accept him fully, I must also accept the brotherhood's ideals, if not Thomas's own, that were susceptible to change at whim. Once more, I tried to make him understand. "Thomas. I am not like the rest of the brotherhood. I need more than decadent and deviant behavior in our—"

The momentum of his fingers intensified. A gasp escaped my lips as my body trembled on the verge of release.

"You are more like them than you know, my muse. You are decadence come to life, Helen. You were born to inspire."

The scent of port on his breath wafted over me. I allowed his intrusion into my body, surrendering to his hand, and lost in a euphoric haze, I believed I was something more—a goddess, a muse.

I slid my hands around his neck; his hardened length pressed against my skirts, his hand between my legs, performing exquisite magic.

"Yes, my muse." He kissed my cheek. "You remember now, how perfectly we fit together, don't you?" he whispered.

Aroused to near delirium, I drew one hand over my covered breast, my hips meeting with his rhythmic motion. "I want us to be everything to each other," I said, turning my face to his, seeking his mouth. He clamped his arm across my chest, his chin digging almost painfully into my shoulder. He drove two fingers deep and I squirmed against his hold. "I love you, Thomas," I said in a strangled plea, my body mastered by him.

"Come for me, Helen," he growled with a menacing tone in his voice. "I want you slick for me."

The thought that our marriage was about his needs and not mine became clear in my mind. I struggled from his grasp, shoving away his hand as I pushed down my skirts. My body quaked between arousal and revelation. I turned to face him, steadying myself against the balcony railing.

His expression was dark, his steely blue eyes holding steady on mine. He was the epitome of smooth-talking seduction and reckless lust.

"What the hell are you doing?" He stared at me a moment longer and then a devilish grin emerged on his handsome face. "I think I could begin to like this game, my muse," he said, taking a step toward me.

I held up my hand to stop his advance. "This is no game, Thomas."

He sighed heavily, casting a gaze heavenward. "What, Helen? What is it *now?*"

I searched his face, watching the free-spirited love that was there moments earlier dissipate into impatient tolerance. And at that moment, I realized that no matter what I agreed to, no matter how much I tried to love and please him, it would never be enough for him to reciprocate. My touch, my love, would never be as special to him as his was to me. "I don't think you'd understand, Thomas. It is me. I'm only just beginning to understand who I am, what I need."

His face contorted with a mocking frown. "What you need? Haven't I given you everything you need? Perhaps you're right. Yes, perhaps the problem is with *you,* Helen." He jabbed his finger at me. "You aren't the same woman I married. Maybe you need more time to think about what you have, instead of what you haven't." He turned on his heel and left the room. "I'm going to the pub. Don't bother waiting up."

I slumped against the balcony rail and listened as he slammed the front door, the tap-tap of his walking stick echoing in the empty street.

As I watched him disappear into the shadows, it occurred to me that he was right. I was not the same woman. I was the woman—for better or for worse—that he had created. I reached in my pocket for the note William had given me and stared at it. Here was my future, my independence. And I realized that there was only one man I had to thank for that—the only man who could have sent in that poem.

After a moment, I walked back inside and closed the balcony door behind me, preparing to face the man who had always been there for me.

Chapter 10

MY HEART WAS AT BATTLE WITH MY HEAD. I thought too much, it had always been a problem with me.

I had made the decision to speak to William, to thank him for his kindness in submitting the poem, for having faith in my work, for being there at nearly every low point in my life, supporting me in his own quiet way. However, lingering cobwebs of doubt hung in my mind, guilt that perhaps I'd acted too rashly, that I hadn't given Thomas enough time to come around. Was he right? Was I being selfish by wanting more from him? Deep down, I knew that to stay with him was going to bring me more heartache than I could tolerate. My health, my heart, my pride would not allow it. I now had the opportunity to stand on my own, not compromising myself for anyone else's life, but living my own, as I wanted, under my terms.

Then there was William—as loyal a brother as there ever could be. A true friend, he'd served as my guardian angel, watching out for me. How could I ask William, whose kisses had reduced my bones to ash, to turn against his brother—for me?

A small laugh bubbled from my throat and I considered how utterly presumptuous I sounded. I paced the studio, nervous as the day I had arrived at this place, sensing the anticipation and excitement of the unknown. Here I was again, standing at the same crossroads, but this time I was not as innocent. I unfolded the note and reread it. I knew now I could survive on my own, that I had a future and I did not have to rely on any man *to care for* me. But I desperately needed to find out if there was a man who still cared *about* me.

There was a dim light shining from beneath William's door. I swallowed, trying to quell the rapid beat of my heart as I raised my fist to knock.

I hesitated at first, changing my mind and changing it again as I turned on my heel, summoned my courage and returned to the door. I was coming to thank him. I was coming to let him know what had happened between his brother and me. Not for any other reason, I told myself. Just because Thomas and I were about to go our separate ways did not guarantee that William would be any less loyal to his brother, despite what he'd said to me in the heat of passion.

I pressed my knuckles to my lips, contemplating the wisdom of what I was about to do, not knowing where it might lead. However, I could not leave without thanking him. I tapped on the door and fingered the note in my hand as I waited.

"One moment," William called from inside.

I brushed my skirts and patted my hair, waiting for him to open the door, my gaze diverting to the stairwell out of guilt. The note slipped from my grasp and fell to my feet. I stooped to pick it up and the door opened.

"Helen?"

I saw his bare feet first. "Oh, William…um, hello." My brain slowed as I straightened, my gaze following the fit of his trousers to the exposed muscles of the undershirt he wore. His suspenders hung loose on his hips.

His mouth curled up at one corner. "Hello."

My mouth had suddenly gone dry and I licked my lips to try to moisten them.

"Oh, beg pardon," he said, quickly drawing his suspenders over his shoulders as if it would make a difference to his state of undress. "I wasn't expecting company."

He braced his arm on the door casually, waiting for me to speak. When I didn't, he leaned out and looked down the hallway.

"Where's Thomas?" he asked.

"He…went to the pub," I said, trying to force my gaze from how the thin cotton shirt molded to his chest.

He studied me a moment. "Did you want me to go fetch him?"

"Oh, no…it's actually you I wanted to speak to, if I may?"

"Of course, uh…just let me get a shirt on and I'll meet you—"

"Here is fine." I walked past him into the room, taking in the exotic decor. I'd always given him his privacy, never venturing into his room. I was entranced.

"Certainly, come in," he said and started to close the door, then smiled over his shoulder and eased it back open.

I looked around for a place to sit.

William stepped around me and picked up his jacket and dress shirt from the back of his reading chair. A lamp on the table beside it burned bright, lending a soft glow to the room. "What did you need to speak to me about?"

"This." I held out the note to him. "Have you read it?"

"No." He shrugged. "It was addressed to you."

I smiled, quickly unfolding the paper. "Here, read it."

He took the paper from me and moved closer to the light. A book lay on the arm of the chair and I leaned over to see if I could read the title.

"Romanesque design," he offered, not looking up from the note.

"Oh," I stated, feeling a bit like I had intruded. I straightened, clasping my hands behind my back as I glanced around the room. His bed was nothing more than a large square mattress lying on the floor, but it was covered with a rich brown coverlet with a gold pattern and piled high with exotic-looking pillows of reds, gold and greens. To one side was a dark dressing screen made of intricately carved wood and beside that, a table topped with an array of miniature wood carvings. I saw the well-traveled man and his tastes that he rarely showed in front of Thomas or the brotherhood, and my admiration for him grew. He was quietly forging his own way in this world.

"Helen, this is wonderful news!" He looked up with a genuine smile. "Of course you plan to send them more."

I covered my mouth, quelling a wobbly grin. My heart leaped with his jubilant reaction. "Perhaps," I said, sniffing, keeping my tears at bay. "I don't know. I'm still trying to believe they got the right person."

"Come here, sit down." He moved the book and held my hand as I perched on the end of the chair. He knelt in front of me and, with a soft smile, leaned forward and used his thumb to brush away an errant tear.

"Of course they got the right person," he said. "Tell me, what did Thomas say?"

I hesitated and took a breath before I spoke. "He doesn't know."

"Why not?" he asked, narrowing his gaze.

"It wouldn't matter to him."

"Helen, I don't think—"

I pressed my fingers to his lips, my heart thudding in my chest. "William, you know I'm right about this. You once told me that you and I could not pursue a relationship because Thomas didn't want me to have a divided focus. Do you think it would be any different if he had to share me with the further pursuit of my poetry?"

His tranquil eyes were steady on mine and I pressed on.

"We had a talk tonight, your brother and I." I looked down at my lap. "Well, I tried to talk with him. He was not as willing." I squeezed his hand, hoping to make William understand. "He told me I'd changed and I realized he was right—I have changed, for the better, I think. I have come to see that the very things Thomas and I don't see eye to eye on are the very things that make him he creative genius that he is. Nevertheless, I cannot be viewed as his statue on a pedestal anymore, William, and ignore my own needs. I have to know that I am loved for who *I am,* not for someone else's belief of who I am."

William sat back, bracing his hands on his knees. "Helen—"

"Please, William." I stood and walked toward the door. "I'm not asking you to change how you feel about Thomas. I understand, really, I do. But I can no longer be his idea of a goddess, limitless in my giving without need of receiving something back."

William rose to his feet, walked over and took my hands. "He's a fool, then." He regarded me with gentle eyes. "Because he doesn't realize the treasure he's let slip through his hands."

I shook my head, tears clogging my throat. It was difficult to leave Thomas, but twice as hard in some ways to leave William, because he had always been there when I needed him most.

"I thought that being his muse would be enough, then I thought the idea of having our child would be enough, and then…that losing that child would be enough to make him see…to make him want me enough."

He drew me close and I put my arms around him, clinging to him, never wanting to let go. But there was no way I could stay. "I'll be leaving, William, just as soon as I can arrange for a place to live. I don't want anything from Thomas. And I wish him well, but I cannot stay with him."

His hand stroked my back soothingly, the reliable William I had come to know.

"You cannot leave, not like this," he said.

I leaned back to look up at his face. "I cannot stay, I've told you why. Thomas was more in love with the idea of a muse than having a wife. He never even said he loved me. Doesn't a wife deserve to hear that?"

"No, Helen, you don't understand."

"I've tried to understand him, William, and I appreciate why you love him so—"

William's mouth came down hard on mine, obliterating my words, and then my thoughts. He held my face, his kisses desperate, hungry, stealing every last bit of reason in my head. He leaned back, searching my eyes, and when I did not move, he reached around me and slammed the door shut, causing me to jump.

He slid his hands around my neck, lifting my chin to look at him. "My brother may not have said the words, Helen, but I will." His gentle blue eyes held mine.

"I love you. *I love you.* I have from the first day and have tried to be noble, tried to stay away, tried not to think about you every day."

He touched my face, rubbing the pad of his thumb across my lower lip.

"How many times have I lain on this bed and thought of you?" He shut his eyes. "You were right about that night. I chose to leave, I had to, I couldn't be here. I thought if I could be away from you, I'd forget."

"William," I said softly, letting the uncertainty of coming to see him tonight fall away. I drew him into my embrace, holding him close. "Love me, William," I said, turning my face to kiss the warmth of his exposed flesh.

In a frenzy of kisses and sighs, we helped each other undress until our clothes were strewn across the floor. I sat on the bed, inching back until I lay propped on the pillows. He unfastened his trousers, dropping them to his feet. I took him in fully, my flesh heating as I gazed upon the wonder of his body. His skin was dark from his travels, his muscles firm and sculpted. My heart raced at seeing his impressive cock jutting between his thighs. But what stole my breath was the look in his eyes. There was the unbridled hunger that I'd longed to see.

William knelt on the bed, the warmth of his breath soft on my calves, causing gooseflesh to rise on my skin. He nudged apart my thighs, brushing his thumb across my delicate folds, and dipped his head, his masterful tongue causing me to lift my hips off the bed. I watched through a euphoric haze, propped up by pillows as he nibbled and teased, driving me to a desperate need.

"William," I sighed. My body was on fire.

"Not yet, my love," he whispered, trailing warm, wet kisses over my stomach. The feel of his exquisitely callused hands jogged my memory of how much I loved them caressing my flesh. I held his head as he suckled each breast and I leaned down to kiss his disheveled hair. Rising to his knees and lifting my hips, he slowly pushed into me, a low-timbre growl rolling deep from his throat as he quickened his thrusts.

Encased in his arms, I kept my eyes to his, wanting to see his face when he came inside me. We were companions in deceit, lovers lost in ecstasy.

My body shattered, unraveling in delicious waves as my legs tightened around him. He buried his face in my shoulder, finishing his own release. I kissed his shoulder, tasting the salty sheen on his muscled flesh.

The erotic haze in my brain lifted and my eyes opened to the view of the door. There stood Thomas, his hand on the doorknob.

"Oh, God," I whispered, gently pushing William from me while trying to cover my nakedness. William's gaze followed mine, seeing his brother's stricken look.

"Stay with me, Helen," William whispered as he got up from the bed and dressed casually as if nothing had happened. He faced his brother, who continued to stare at me. I was leaving him, I knew, but I didn't want it to end like this.

Thomas gave a sarcastic chuckle. "How ironic."

My cheeks burned with shame.

"I suppose you'd like an explanation?" William offered.

Thomas's livid gaze raked over me, then his brother.

"If you think that you possibly have one," he said. The door slammed behind him and we heard the sound of glass breaking and objects being thrown against the wall.

I leaped from the bed and drew on my chemise as William stuffed his arms into his shirt. "I'm going to talk to him." He paused at the door and came back to me, taking my face, giving me a soul-searing kiss. "I don't want you to regret anything. I don't, nor do I believe that what I feel for you is a sin, Helen. I love my brother, but he is no more a husband to you than I have been, and it's time one of us happily accepts that responsibility, that honor—if you'll have me when all is said and done?"

Tears trailed from the corners of my eyes as I looked up at him. "Yes, William, I want that more than anything."

"Get dressed, then, and meet me in the studio."

I paused at the door, hearing my name.

"It's not as though I didn't know that things weren't good between Helen and me. We've both sensed it and it wasn't just losing the child, William, though I swear, I don't know if a man ever fully recovers from such an ordeal."

I swallowed the tears threatening to break lose again.

"The god-awful truth, William, is that I am afraid I married Helen because I wanted to save her. Lord help me, I do care for her. I swear I do, but, it's not the way she wants, nor is it the kind of love a woman like Helen deserves. I leap into things that I shouldn't, I become obsessed with my work and I loathe interruption. When I want to go out, I go out. When I decide to travel, I do it."

"You pompous ass," William hurled at his brother.

"Excuse me?" Thomas launched back with as much vinegar in his tone.

"You've used her, just like you've done with all your models. But Helen is different, Thomas. She is more delicate than the women you are used to. She deserves better."

"And you think you're better?"

I stepped into the room then. "Yes, Thomas, he is. From the very beginning, William was my friend first, my confidant." I walked over and took William's hand.

"How long has this affair between you been going on?"

"Only today," I replied.

"Two years," William stated, and kissed my hand. "No, from

the first day I saw you, Helen, you captured my heart." He looked back at Thomas. "But I knew you wouldn't take her as a model if you knew how I felt."

Thomas plopped into his chair, wringing his hands in thought, then rested his chin on his fists.

"And did you harbor these same feelings for William, Helen? All this time?"

I glanced from one brother to the other. "I thought I loved you once, Thomas. I hoped that when you asked me to marry you, things would change. I thought you would want to settle down and start a family—have a home."

Thomas stared at the floor.

"William loves me, Thomas," I said, kneeling at his side. "I knew there was an attraction, but not until today did I know how he truly felt. He has always been loyal to you, in spite of those feelings."

Thomas studied my face with an inquisitive look, as if some new light had illuminated his mind. He looked up at William. "I understand his loyalty, Helen."

"I don't want that to change because of me," I said.

Thomas leaned back in his chair, staring straight ahead, lost in his thoughts. When he finally spoke, he sounded like the old Thomas.

"Thank you, Helen. I know being married to me has not been easy." He looked at his brother. "For either of you."

"Thomas, I need you to know that what happened would not have, had I not already—" I paused, summoning the courage to say the words to his face. "Had I not already said goodbye to you in my heart."

He looked at me for a moment and nodded.

"Thomas, I need to understand something. The other night…with Grace…"

"It was nothing, Helen. Not like what you think. Grace and I, well, I can tell her anything. We have a very special bond."

He was wrong—it was definitely more than that. But I would

not be the one to tell him. I had, however, seen the look on her face as he knelt before her.

I could not read the look on his face. He seemed neither angry nor sad. I took William's hand in mine. "I know that we have committed a terrible sin, but I assure you that what I feel for William is pure and true."

"I've no doubt of that, but I am not your judge, Helen. I have no wish to create a scandal for any of us. Although I hope you understand why I would think it best if both of you were to leave."

He went to his supply cupboard and fished out an envelope from an old crockery jar. He handed the envelope to William. "There is plenty there to begin a new life together."

"No, Thomas, I can't take this." William held out the envelope, giving it back to his brother.

He refused to take it. "Think of it as an early wedding gift. You have lived in my shadow far too long, Will. It's high time you started putting those dreams of yours together. It's time to show this world the talent of another Rodin."

I clasped my hands in my lap. "Thomas, I want you to know that I never meant to hurt you. Not today…not with the baby."

He looked out of the window as though gathering his thoughts. "Nor did I intend to be such a piss-poor excuse for a husband. My brother is quite right about you, Helen. You were not what I am used to. I don't frankly know if there is a single woman on this earth made for me. Perhaps it is my fate to be a perpetual bachelor." Thomas shrugged. "The truth of the matter is that I know William is going to make you happy, Helen. He will be the man you deserve. God knows he has hung around here too long taking care of me."

"I don't know what to say. I'm sorry." I rounded the table and embraced him.

Thomas hugged me tight then held me at arm's length. "I will miss you both. I hope one day we may sit down together again as family." He steadied his gaze on William. "You'll be all right, then?"

William wiped his hand over his face and nodded.

"I hope you know, Will, there is no need of forgiveness, either of you, and I wish you both nothing but happiness. Please take care of Helen where I failed to do so."

He pulled William into a quick embrace. "If you'll excuse me, I have an appointment I must be ready for."

The carriage was waiting downstairs. William had taken our large bags down to pack them. I had not seen Thomas the rest of the day as we readied to leave. I walked through the rooms one last time, checking for anything I may have forgotten. When at last all the bags were packed, I stood in the studio alone, brushing my hand over Thomas's easel, taking in the piles of sketches stacked atop boxes and the silly crates. I spotted a sketch Thomas had done of me while I was reading, and I pondered whether to tuck it amongst my belongings.

"He won't miss one. I have several that he doesn't know about."

I turned to find Grace watching me. "It was too much responsibility for me, I think…being his muse," I said as I rolled up the small piece of parchment. "May I ask you something?"

She shrugged.

"You've known Thomas for some time—"

"Some days it seems like a lifetime, others, I am not sure I know him at all," she said.

"At what point did you know you loved him?"

She looked at me with a puzzled expression, and then laughed. She dropped her hat on the hall table beneath the mirror.

"You have a misguided notion, Helen."

"Do I?"

Her gaze narrowed on me. "A man like Thomas has many models—many women he calls 'muse.' I was never your rival, nor were any of the other women who model for him. His mistress is the ever-changing, ever-demanding passionate affair he has with his art, his work."

I frowned. To me, it sounded like an excuse. I saw her smile as though she knew what I was thinking.

"I have spent a lifetime in the company of men—many, many men. I see the same problem over and over. Women struggle to compete with a man's passion, instead of allowing him the freedom to explore his mistress. The secret is being available when he grows tired of her and turns his eye your way."

"Is that enough for you, Grace? Don't you want more from someone than that?" I asked, feeling a bit sorry for her and yet, here she was dressed in the finest clothes, traveling in a beautiful coach, able to do what she wanted. I thought of the men who adored her, and couldn't understand why I should feel sorry for her.

"To be utterly worshipped, treated like a goddess for a few moments with no strings, no false promises. Who would want more than that?"

Perhaps she and Thomas were better suited to one another than I realized.

William came into the study and nodded at Grace. He took my arm gently and kissed my temple. "The carriage is ready. How about you?"

I was taking him home to meet my family. "Yes, I'm ready. Goodbye, Grace."

After William helped me climb into the carriage, he kissed my hand and said, "I've got to check on one last thing, love."

I watched him rush back inside the studio. It was hard to believe two years of my life had passed behind these brick walls.

A few moments later, I glanced up and saw Grace come out on the balcony. She shook out a small rug as she watched us.

My gaze followed hers a short distance down the street where a polished black carriage was parked. Thomas, dressed in his finest dark blue velvet jacket and black beaver top hat, stood next to the carriage engaged in conversation with a beautiful dark-haired young woman. No doubt his next muse. He glanced up and tipped his hat as we drove by.

William took my hand, wrapping it securely in his.

Book 2

SARA

Chapter 1

Oxford, London, May 1863

"I AM THE GRAND DUCHESS," I USED TO CRY WHEN I was young. My cousin Amelia and I would sit in one of the grand carriages needing repair in my uncle's stable and pretend we were of affluence and wealth. That we had the freedom to do whatever we wished and to travel anywhere we wanted.

Dreaming is easy when you're young. Nearly ten years later, life had taken on a sobering truth.

"Sara!" My uncle Marcus stepped from the barn and called for me. "Step light and help with the stables this morning. Poor Deven has all he can handle with the new foal about to come." Reality brought me back to my twenty years of age, still helping to muck the stables and spread dung around my aunt's roses.

I covered my eyes, shading them from the brilliant morning sun attempting to break the haze of morning. "Coming," I replied, trying to hold my breath from the stench. I wrenched off my gloves, grateful to leave the putrid scent behind. Uncle Marcus called it the salt of the earth. Horse dung, of all things!

I lifted my hem and tiptoed through the grass still wet with dew.

This was my favorite time of day, with the silence of the mist-covered pasture. I imagined that this was my country estate, setting aside for a moment that it was a small cottage with a barn. My uncle had bought it from a man going to America, using the meager inheritance left to me at the time of my parents' death.

I nodded to Deven as I stepped into the cool shade of the barn. He was not more than a few years older than me, and a handsome lad, with sandy-brown hair and a wicked smile that had me thinking things I ought not. "Good day, Mr. Mooreland." I smiled, noting how he watched me walk by. I was still a virgin, though Mr. Mooreland was determined to change that status. I did not fear him. I knew he would never do anything that I was not prepared to offer freely…and *had* on one or two occasions.

"Miss Cartwright—" he tipped his worn tweed cap "—lovely morning, wouldn't you say?"

"Perfect for mucking horse dung, Mr. Mooreland," I replied, grabbing one of the pitchforks off the nail on the whitewashed wall. I heard his chuckle as I walked to the far end of the barn.

"Or a dip in the pond later on?" he called after me.

I looked over my shoulder. "I have plans this evening, Mr. Mooreland. I don't wish to ruin my hair. Perhaps another day." I stepped into the stall and began my task. The truth was I would need a bath before my cousin and I attended the theater tonight. I'd made a promise to the stock boy at the farmers' market that I would go riding with him one afternoon in exchange for two tickets he stole from his uncle who works the box office window. I heard a sigh and turned to find Deven Mooreland stepping into the stall behind me. I'd do just about anything to gain seats to the theater.

"To the theater again, Miss Cartwright? I suppose that means you'll need a rig and a driver?"

I stopped sifting through the hay and met the gleam in his eye. "I suppose I shall. Would you be offering your services, then?"

He smiled and leaned against the archway. A lazy smile crept up his face. I had met few men that I had much interest in. Deven

Mooreland and, more recently, the stock boy, were the extent of my social education with the male gender.

For the moment, Deven Mooreland, with his sparkling green Irish eyes and his wicked smile, was my tutor to the passions of the flesh. He had broad shoulders and could, with ease, toss two bales of hay at one time. Yet he had a gentle side, especially with me. Being the age given to musing upon such things, I'd on occasion snuck down to the pond and spied on him as he bathed. And I must admit that what I saw sent peculiar sensations over me. More than once whilst in bed at night, I'd dreamed of joining him in the pond.

"Oh, now, Miss Cartwright, you know my services dunna come for free."

"You mean, of course, our agreement not to tell my uncle that Amelia has come with me to the theater."

He raised a sandy eyebrow and shrugged.

"I doubt he'd be pleased ta hear his young daughter—she's what, a mere seventeen?—is sneaking off under false pretences with his lovely, not-as-innocent-as-she-looks niece."

I stabbed the pitchfork into the hay, squaring my shoulders, and watched as his gaze dropped a few inches below my chin. "What is it you want, Mr. Mooreland? And please remember that I am a lady."

"A lady now you are?" He took a step inside the stall. "I see a young girl in front of me. But I am well aware of the potential."

"What will it take to retain your confidence, Mr. Mooreland?" I could be stubborn when I wanted. Being on my own after my parents' death, I'd learned quickly how to get what I wanted. He took another step toward me, checking over his shoulder for my uncle. "I thought you were watching over the mare in her time?" I smiled, certain that he would retreat at my reminder.

"She's resting now, and your uncle has gone inside for his mid-morning coffee and a bit of making hay with your aunt." He grinned.

Deven was close enough now that I could smell the odd mix of leather and hay on him. His earthy presence did strange things to my lower belly. He traced a finger down my cheek, smoothing the tip of his callused thumb over my lower lip. Heat darkened his gaze as he looked down at me.

"I dunna want anything, Sara girl, that you are not willing and happy to give."

He lowered his face, his eyes searching mine, watching for some resistance. His palm came around my waist, resting on the small of my back.

"Dunna tease me so, Sara," he whispered, leaning to my ear to speak. "Surely you remember that night just last week? When you said we'd continue our...*visit* another time?"

His breath fanned over my temple and the pitchfork fell from my hand. I had only to glance up at him before his mouth found mine in a frenzied rush. My senses heightened with the warmth of his mouth upon my neck, traveling lower still over the curve of my shoulder.

Frightened, but more curious, I cautiously slid my hand between our bodies. My hand trembled as I found the firm elongation beneath his trousers.

"We...must be cautious, Mr. M-Mooreland," I sighed. He quickly undid the buttons on the front of my blouse, shoving aside the flimsy fabric. My day corset, a hand-me-down and ill fitting, hung loose, providing easy access for his determined hands to tug on the binding until my breasts lay exposed.

I swallowed, finding my breath and glancing at how expertly his fingers caressed and squeezed my soft globes. My mind grew hazy, drifting into the delicious sensation.

"You've grown into a fine woman, Sara, one that could bring a man to his knees." He knelt before me, drawing me close, his mouth moving over my flesh, warm and wet, teasing.

A hot, throbbing urgency, one I had felt before with Deven, began again between my thighs. I grew precariously close to begging him to do whatever it would take to relieve me of the torture.

His hands clamped over my bottom, his fingers pressing the skirt between my legs, stroking me through the fabric, causing me to grasp his shoulders to keep my knees from buckling.

There would be a strap in my future were we found out, and likely Deven's, too, before he was let go. I was not yet prepared to take such a risk, no matter how much I wanted him to finish, no matter how much he wanted to appease me.

"Stop," I muttered weakly, tossing his silly tweed cap aside to thread my fingers through his haphazard curls.

A low groan rumbled from deep in his throat as he drew one pert nipple between his teeth and tugged on it.

About to lose my senses entirely, I twisted my fingers in his hair, forcing him to look at me. I swallowed, captivated by the passion I saw in those eyes. "We must not go further. My uncle could return at any moment."

His breathing labored, he stared at me, as if debating whether to heed my request.

"You owe me, Sara" he finally said. There was anger laced in his disappointment.

He stood, chewing at the corner of his lip as he watched me right my clothes. In a swift movement, he grabbed my waist and hauled me to his chest. "Next time, I will not stop. Not for the hounds of hell."

He released me and grabbed my pitchfork, shoving it into my hand before he strode out of the stall. Weak in the knees, I wondered if this was a normal reaction or if I truly had some sort of true affection for Deven Mooreland. The feeling of being desired by such a man, a man so powerfully sure of what he wanted, was overwhelming. How any sensible woman would choose to remain untouched before she married was a puzzling thing to me.

I stared at where he'd stood, letting my hand brush over my still-sensitive breasts, remembering how they'd fit in his palm, how he'd teased them with his teeth and tongue. The thought alone was an aphrodisiac to my senses. I licked my lips. If what had transpired just now had such a profound effect on my body, what in heaven, if heaven did indeed exist, would happen if I allowed Deven the freedom he so tenaciously sought? Something damp trickled down the inside of my thigh as I forced my thoughts back to my task. I was not at all sure how or if I wanted to deny him any longer.

"One day, Amelia, I'll be able to afford the best seats in the theater for us," I said as I hurried her to the carriage waiting at the side of the house.

"Mama and Papa think we are going to Miss Andrea's to see her new piano." She giggled as she scrambled into the hansom.

"Miss Cartwright? A word with you, if I might?"

I turned to the voice at the back of the carriage and found Deven standing in its shadow, preparing to board into the driver's seat. "Excuse me, Amelia. The driver wishes a word with me. Oh…" I paused and stuck my head back into the carriage. "You are certain that Miss Andrea's family owns a piano?"

Amelia nodded, holding her gloved hand up to try to hide her smile.

"She has been sworn to secrecy, Sara. She even crossed her heart in oath!"

I smiled at the innocence of my cousin and hoped her friend provided an alibi if pressed. To our good fortune, Miss Andrea and her family were so new, my aunt and uncle did not know them. With any luck, I would soon find gainful employment on my own and prove my maturity and independence, thereby no longer being forced to sneak away, just to enjoy a simple social outing. "I'll only be a heartbeat."

Careful not to soil my dress, I rounded the back of the hansom and stopped short. I admitted to a slight flutter in my heart. Mr. Mooreland was dressed in the fine uniform that my uncle used only for special paying clients.

His eyes took me in from head to toe and perhaps it was the result of my lacing being drawn a bit too tight, but my breath caught in my throat. I forced a smile, careful not to look with too much yearning at his delectable mouth and remember where it had been a few hours earlier.

He offered a gentleman's bow as he removed his tweed cap, the only piece of attire that was out of line with an otherwise perfect appearance. "May I give you my compliments, Miss Sara, on how you look this evening? Blue silk definitely suits you."

My cheeks heated and I am certain a warm blush covered every inch of my flesh, even the parts of me that did not show. "Thank you, Mr. Mooreland. You look quite dapper yourself this fine evening." I kept my voice low. There was no need for Amelia to be privy to the special arrangement that Mr. Mooreland and I shared. "Was there something you wished to speak with me about?" I grew anxious at how he looked at me, as if I were a feast set before a starving man.

"Were it up to me, Miss Sara, I would prefer to be engaged in more than talk just now. What I would give to peel away your layers and—"

I held up my hand to stop him, offering him a stern look. "Mr. Mooreland, if you please. Now is not the time."

He tossed me his devil-may-care smile and plopped his hat over his shaggy brown hair. "Understood, miss. Until tomorrow, then? I shall be content for now to provide you with *only* my hired services."

I swallowed. "Mr. Mooreland, may I remind you that I never fully agreed to—"

He placed a leather-covered finger to my lips. "Neither did you deny my suggestion. You have teased me long enough, Sara Cartwright. It is time you became the woman you pretend to be." He narrowed his gaze on me. "Unless, of course, you are afraid."

I didn't answer him right away, partly because the arrow of his challenge pierced me with the truth. He knew me well and he knew I would not back down. "Very well, Mr. Mooreland. Now, we must be on our way or we shall miss the opening act." His perfect white smile shone in the twilight as he offered me his hand and I climbed in beside Amelia.

"Is all well with you, Sara? Mr. Mooreland is agreeable to helping us, isn't he?" Amelia asked, concern flashing in her large brown eyes.

I smiled and looked away, hoping it was dark enough that she could not see the heat of my blushed cheeks. "Of course, he was just confirming what to say should he be asked." The carriage lurched forward and we rolled down the lane.

Amelia grabbed my hand and squeezed it.

"Aren't you positively excited, Sara? The theater is such a lively place." Her expression clouded. "You don't think that anyone who knows Mama and Papa will be there, do you?"

I considered how best to explain to the dear child that her parents, though rich in many ways, were considered among the dirt poor of London's social circles. It was unlikely that we would run into anyone who knew them. I patted her hand. "You needn't worry, Amelia. I've taken care of everything."

She grinned. "I have a secret, Sara. Do you promise not to tell?"

I fought to focus on her innocent musings, while I grappled with giving up my virginity to the Irish stable groom. "Yes, what is it?" I replied, blinking away the thought of Deven cupping my breasts.

"It's about Mr. Mooreland," she whispered, her eyes bright.

I glanced at her. "What about Mr. Mooreland?" *Oh, please let Deven not have already begun flirting with Amelia!*

"I find him rather cute, don't you?"

"Shh, now. Do you want him to hear you?" I scolded. I eyed her, uncertain whether to pursue the topic. My curiosity bade me to speak. "Has…Mr. Mooreland ever made advances toward you, Amelia?"

Her mouth gaped open and she pressed her hands to her cheeks. "Oh, my heavens, no! Oh, I—I wouldn't know what to do."

The tension in my stomach subsided most happily. "It's all well, then, Amelia. You want to give yourself plenty of time to explore the strange world of men. There is much to be learned." I patted her hand as if I knew one farthing about the subject. I offered her a smile and turned my eyes to the road.

Chapter 2

"SARA, SHALL MR. MOORELAND BE ABLE TO GET us to the theater on time?" Amelia gave me a fearful glance. It was opening night for the new theater and it was suggested that one should arrive at least a half hour before the doors opened to ensure a good seat in the gallery.

"I am quite sure, my dear cousin, that when he puts his mind to it, Mr. Mooreland can accomplish much." More than once, I had replayed the memory of his face as he presented his challenge to meet him at the pond.

"You have our tickets?" she asked, shifting forward on the edge of the buggy seat, straining to see farther ahead.

"Yes, Amelia. I have them here in my bag." I followed her gaze, noting the number of carriages dropping off passengers at the side entrance. The crowd awaiting entry seemed to be growing, stretching closer to us as we sat in the carriage.

"Do you think it's nearly big enough, Sara? Look at all the people."

"They said the Globe holds over fifteen hundred seats, Amelia."

Scores of couples hurried down the street, swerving around our hansom to meld into the crowd. I took note of their attire, watching the feathered touring hats of the elite bobbing up and down as though alive in their pecking. Taking one last look at my blue silk skirt, jacket and matching blouse, I tapped Amelia on the knee. "Here we are. Hold tight to my arm, and try not to get separated."

After graciously helping us from the carriage, Mr. Mooreland tipped his hat and gave me a wink, then told me that he'd be at the pub down the street until after the show.

I squeezed my cousin's arm as we were pulled into the throng of anxious theatergoers buzzing about the Wych Street entrance. Many were already taking nips of refreshments brought from home, a combination, I suspect, of ale and ginger beer. Like giant butterflies, women fluttered their fans as they waited in the stifling heat. When at last the doors opened, we were jostled about like cattle being steered in a chute. I fought to hold on to Amelia's arm. Caught off balance, I lost my footing when a chap rushed forward, shoving me aside in his haste to meet his chum.

"There now, I've got you, miss."

Two arms hooked beneath mine, preventing my fall. "My sincere thanks…" I struggled to glance over my shoulder to see my savior's face and could see only that it was a man. He lifted me upright and I was immediately swept into the current, moving me toward the narrow stairs to the gallery above. I searched for Amelia, at the same time unable to dispel the mesmerizing scent of sandalwood and the soothing voice of the man who'd come to my aid.

"Sara!" Amelia called and, finding my hand in the throng, grabbed me around the waist and pressed close. "I feel like I am being herded into a stall."

We reached the top and stood, briefly scanning the rows of seats. People were scrambling to find the best seats, in some instances, pushing one another aside to claim their spot.

Amelia spotted two seats down in front. "There's two, hurry!"

She grabbed my hand and steered me through the crowd. Two men stood between our goal and us. "Excuse me." I glanced at them, and smiled. "Are these seats occupied?"

The man facing me peered around his companion's shoulder and smiled. "I'm afraid they are, miss." His face was friendly, with bright eyes and a wide smile.

"My apologies," I stated, and reached for Amelia's hand.

"Wait," the other man said quietly. The sound caught between my shoulder blades. I'd heard that voice before…in my ear.

"Please, why don't you and your companion take these seats? We have decided we would prefer to sit higher."

His voice suited him. An austere-looking man, he was dressed elegantly in a brocade frock coat and pristine white cravat and shirt. Ruffled cuffs peeked out from beneath his coat, and his ringed fingers perched on a walking cane.

He was an imposing figure in height, with a presence that was difficult to ignore. His eyes were intense, glistening with a spark of challenge. A firm jaw and equally firm mouth with a bare shadow of beard held me captivated.

"Sara?" Amelia nudged me. "What shall we do?"

I blinked from my reverie. "I'm sorry, that's terribly kind, but we couldn't—

"I insist." He waved his hand toward the seats. "John, go find us seats there in the fourth row," he said to the man he was with.

"Thank you, Mr…?" I stated, gently prodding Amelia to her seat. I followed behind and he stood his ground, offering a charming smile as we met face-to-face.

"The name is Thomas Rodin. I hope you didn't turn that lovely ankle of yours with that nasty fall." His smile was easy, un-complicated, as if he had all the time in the world to speak with me.

"So you are the man I should thank." I pretended that I had not already recognized him from the shaving cologne he wore.

"My pleasure." He bowed. "I love saving beautiful women." The corner of his mouth quirked.

My knees felt odd. "Perhaps I should sit. The show is about to begin."

He took my hand as I sat, offering a gentleman's kiss to the back.

"I don't believe I caught your name?"

"That's because she didn't give it to you," Amelia blurted.

"Amelia! Mr. Rodin just gave us his seat."

"No harm, the young lady is quite right. I'll bid you good-night and enjoy the show." He gave a nod and a hint of a smile before he made his way to the seats farther up in the gallery.

"Imagine, asking a woman's name and in a theater of all places," Amelia whispered.

"Imagine," I mocked with a smile and nabbed a quick glance over my shoulder, finding the mysterious and handsome Mr. Rodin looking at me from his seat.

Before the first act was finished, there were people standing in their seats, whilst others craned their necks to see over those who stood up to stretch their legs. The benches were narrow and most without backs, except for the last row against the wall. I did not complain, as there were so few opportunities for the theater. And for a shilling, we could not be choosy.

The air was stagnant in the upper gallery, although the sunlight roof did offer a bit of ventilation. The city had, in the past few days, been caught in the ruthless jaws of an early heat wave, causing the usual stench near the river to worsen and permeate the air.

I hoped that Amelia did not regret her choice to accompany me.

"Does this performance have an intermission, Sara? My throat is parched. Do we have any of Mama's lemonade left?"

I checked the one jar that we'd both been sipping from during the first act. If we were to have anything for the second we would have to pace ourselves. "Just a sip, Amelia," I cautioned, holding the jar out to her. She reached for it and it slipped from her gloved fingers, crashing to the floor.

I watched in horror as the liquid trickled through the floor-board cracks to the patrons below. I knew by the screams when it had found its mark. I was humiliated beyond reproach. "Come on, we must find Mr. Mooreland." I grabbed her hand and carefully stepped over the dozens of pairs of legs as we picked our way to the exit at the top of the stairs.

Poor Amelia was in tears.

"All will be well, Amelia. It was an accident. I am sure it happens frequently," I consoled her.

"I assure you the audience below has seen much worse."

I turned and found Mr. Rodin and his companion coming toward us. A cloud of faceless "Shh's" rose from the audience seated nearby.

"Let's get to the stairwell, Miss Cartwright."

Mr. Rodin placed his hand on the small of my back, urging me toward the stairs. We paused at the top step.

"It's a shame for you to miss the show. Perhaps if you wait here a moment the chaos will die down," he said. "However, between you and me, that was the most excitement I've seen all night—on- or offstage." He grinned.

I found myself smiling back in response. "Thank you for your kindness, Mr. Rodin. It is getting late and we must be on our way."

"Perhaps I can offer you a ride in my coach?"

"Thank you again, Mr. Rodin, but we'll just find our driver and—"

"And where would he be?" he asked.

I chewed the corner of my lip. "In one of the pubs. He was meeting us after the show."

"Well, then, I shall help you find him. The pubs are not safe places for two beautiful young women to be at this hour."

"But you'll miss the rest of the play," I stated, curious why he would go to such lengths to help us.

"You would save me, Miss Cartwright, from dying of utter boredom." He held out his arm to me.

It seemed my choices were to continue to argue with him or simply accept his gallantry. "Very well, Mr. Rodin." I smiled, tucking my hand in the crook of his arm. "I appreciate your assistance."

"And now, since I have saved you both from an embarrassing fate worse than death—"

Irate voices wafted up the stairs as a woman and her companion stomped up the stairs to the street level. The woman sobbed uncontrollably into her gloved hand, her sodden blond hair sagging around her shoulders.

Mr. Rodin tugged my arm gently, pulling us into the shadows of the upper stairwell.

"The theater will see to the cleaning of your wife's fur, monsieur," the manager tried to calm down the angry man. "It was an accident."

"You can be certain that you will be hearing from my lawyers. I will see this theater closed within the week. That commoner's gallery has no more scruples than a pack of hounds. I want the culprits who did this to my wife found and restitution made for her humiliation," the man bellowed.

I heard Amelia's gasp from over my shoulder.

I held my breath, hoping that our departure was not ill timed. We could not afford a scandal. Neither of us would be allowed away from the farm again.

"Breathe, my dear," Rodin whispered.

In the half-darkness of the stairwell, I was aware that he'd turned to face me, shielding us from the view below. Perched a step above him, our noses nearly touched. His eyes were penetrating, as if able to see the struggle warring inside me. Here I was skulking in the shadows with a complete stranger and all I could think of was doing things with Mr. Rodin that I'd only ever allowed Deven Mooreland to do. What kind of woman did that make me?

"How much longer must we stay here, Mr. Rodin?" I asked, forcing myself to peek over his shoulder. His hand came to rest at my waist. I brought my eyes to his. He brushed his thumb back and forth over the fabric and I admit to entertaining the naughty thought of his making the same gesture a few inches higher.

"Just a moment longer. They'll move on." He offered that calm smile. "Are you uncomfortable?"

"No! Quite well, thank you," I responded, my breath hitching as his hand drifted higher.

"Excellent. Now, young woman, tell me your name or I shall be forced to bring the manager here." His hand now rested on my ribs. Just a simple extension of his thumb and—

"You tease, Mr. Rodin," I responded breathlessly.

"Really? So you are calling my bluff?" He raised his eyebrow.

I could barely force my mind to think beyond his hand poised just beneath my breast. My cheeks warmed. I was lured by the ease with which his harmless flirtation had turned to subtle seduction. Surprised even more how I welcomed it.

"My name is Sara Cartwright," I said, fighting the urge to press into his palm.

"Sara, what a lovely name. It suits you, as does this color," he said softly, studying my face. "You are in fact, Sara, what men in my world call a 'stunner.'"

"Is that a compliment, Mr. Rodin?" I asked.

"The highest, I assure you." He smiled, then glanced over his shoulder. "I think it is clear to leave."

He took my arm and led me down the remaining steps. I dared not look back at Amelia, knowing she had to have disapproved of everything she'd heard. I had blatantly broken every rule of etiquette tonight and I was grateful she was behind me, unable to see Mr. Rodin's hand.

We stepped out into the evening air, as thick and stifling as it was inside and heavy with the stench of filth.

"Perhaps you would be safer to wait here and let us go search for your driver," he offered. "What is his name?"

"Mr. Mooreland, Deven Mooreland. He's wearing a plaid cap," I called as he and his friend walked down the street toward the pubs. My gaze was drawn to Mr. Rodin's confident gait with his broad shoulders, his erect stance and long-legged stride.

We waited for what seemed a long time when finally we saw Deven, with Mr. Rodin and his companion, striding toward us.

"Your driver, Miss Sara?" Mr. Rodin asked.

I peered at Deven's face, saw the unmistakable sheen to his nose, and knew he'd been drinking. "That's Mr. Mooreland, to be sure. Thank you again for your kindness."

"I'll go get the hansom." Deven held up his finger. "It's just down the street."

"Go on with him, John. I'll wait here with the ladies."

He gave Amelia a smile. She raised an eyebrow and turned her attention to her playbill.

"Miss Cartwright, I would like to ask you something."

Mr. Rodin turned so that he stood between Amelia and me. In the murky light of the gaslamps, his eyes glittered with excitement.

I nodded, captured by something I could not name. It was a feeling of anticipation and adventure. A slow thudding began in my heart.

"Have you ever considered being a model?"

Shocked by his statement, then realizing that he was likely only teasing me again, I shook my head and gave him my friendliest smile. "By that I presume you mean for an artist?" I'd never before been to a museum, but I would sometimes sneak my uncle's news sheets and had read about a small band of artists who were stirring up trouble within the Royal Academy. Could this man be involved with them somehow? The mere thought of standing in the presence of such a prominent figure in London's society prompted me to prod him further. "Are you an artist, Mr. Rodin?"

He removed his hat, revealing a mass of brown curly hair. "Master artist Thomas Rodin at your service, madam."

"Master? Then you are a graduate of the Royal Academy?" I asked, even more intrigued at his offer.

He glanced at the sidewalk and faced me with a humble grin that produced a delightful dimple alongside one cheek.

"I began there, and many of my brothers, my peers, graduated from there." He cleared his throat. "However, I chose to leave the academy. I felt their methods were too confining."

I was not certain I understood his meaning, and my silence prompted a misunderstanding on his part.

"I understand entirely if you are not comfortable working with anyone other than an accredited academy-trained artist. Thank you, Miss Cartwright, I am sorry to have detained you."

He turned and started to walk away, and I saw my future

dimming with his every step. "Wait, I meant no disrespect. It's just that I've read some of the news—"

"You read?"

He sauntered back to me and, from the corner of my eye, I saw Amelia shaking her head.

"I am a voracious reader, but that would not be a prerequisite for what you seek, correct?" I hurried on before I lost my nerve. "Are you asking me to model for you, Mr. Rodin?"

His pleased grin sent a jolt through my system. I'd never met anyone like him. It was as if he could barely contain his enthusiasm—or whatever it was that drove him.

"I would be deeply honored if you would consent to coming by my studio. At least to satisfy any questions you might have." He fumbled in his pocket and pulled out a card. "Here is the address. Thursday, around two, if that suits your schedule?"

I took the card from him and blinked a couple of times to read the scrolled writing. Was it fate that I should meet him? Did he know that what he offered me was a chance to make something of myself? To not have to muck stables for the rest of my life? "Does it pay, Mr. Rodin? This position of modeling?"

His eyebrows rose slightly. "A shilling a week, lodging when the project demands it, and meals. The plumbing is modern."

That alone piqued my interest. I'd never seen a real bathing tub. "Very well." I glanced at Amelia, who stared at me with wide eyes. "I shall be there—" I held up his card "—day after tomorrow."

"I am looking forward to it, Miss Cartwright." He bowed low. I was enchanted. The hansom pulled up next to us.

Amelia crawled in on her own despite John's futile attempt to assist her.

Mr. Rodin took my elbow and gently guided me as I stepped into the carriage. I gave Amelia a quick look and knew that I was going to have to explain a great deal. I would need her help if I was to get what I wanted—what I needed.

"Until Thursday," Mr. Rodin said, and I turned to face the two men tipping their hats.

The carriage rolled forward and I placed my hand on my stomach, finally able to breathe as the carriage rumbled over the dimly lit cobblestone streets.

"Surely, Sara, you are not considering the very idea of going to that stranger's home?"

Amelia's voice jarred me from my scattered thoughts. "I'm sorry I wasn't—I didn't hear all of what you asked." My skin felt flushed and my heart was beating fast. "Do you know what this could mean, Amelia?"

"Besides trouble with Mum and Dad?"

She looked at me as if I was not quite right in the head. Nevertheless, the truth was that my mind, though jumbled, was clear with purpose. My heart, now there was another matter. "I could save up for an education. It could mean so many possibilities for me. I want to do more than stay on the farm until I should marry yet another farmer. I want to see things, go places where I've not been before. I'm not meant to marry a commoner, Amelia. I want a man who's adventurous and passionate and has a thirst for knowledge."

"But you will have to convince Mama and Papa to let you go," she responded.

"I will take care of it, Amelia." I turned toward her, taking her hands in mine. "Don't you want me to be happy?"

She scowled at me and sighed. "Of course I do, Sara, but sometimes we must learn to be happy where God has placed us." She squeezed my hand.

"And what if it takes more than what God has given me to make me happy?" I asked, searching her face. "I am going to need your help, Amelia. I am going to have to ask you to pretend to know nothing of my whereabouts."

My comment drew a look of concern from her.

"Sara, whatever you're thinking, please, I beg you, reconsider."

I knew in my heart that I had to go to the studio, if only to satisfy my own curiosity. I also knew that asking for my cousin's silence put her at great risk. I did not want her to get in trouble.

"I do not like this, Sara. Truly I do not, but perhaps you will see his true colors by going to visit him."

"Thank you. You are the only *sister* I have ever known." I hugged her close, taking a cleansing breath as I faced forward. I had much to think about before my meeting with my future employer.

"How will you get to town to meet Mr. Rodin?" Amelia asked.

"I will have to find a reason for Mr. Mooreland to take me." I searched the horizon hoping to find an answer in the starry night.

"Do you think you can convince him to keep his silence, Sara?"

Her question drove straight into the heart of my greatest challenge and deepest fear. If my plans, still in the making, unfolded as I hoped they would, I might not be returning home. My new life might well begin as a model for a famous artist, as long as my whereabouts were kept secret from my aunt and uncle. Deven Mooreland's issuance came back to me, taunting my mind. Perhaps there was a way to gain his silence in exchange for something he wanted, and wanted very badly. "You leave Mr. Mooreland to me, Amelia. He and I have often been able to reach an understanding on difficult matters."

"Dare I ask any more?" She stated her question quietly.

"The less you know the better, Amelia," I said, offering her a quick smile.

Chapter 3

I LOOKED ACROSS THE BREAKFAST TABLE AT MY aunt and uncle, wondering if this was the last time I would do so. Last night, I had packed two small bags and hidden them beneath my bed, and I'd written a note, leaving it in Mr. Mooreland's private storage box in the barn. I urged that it was imperative we meet that day at the pond, no later than noon.

I stirred my porridge, dodging glances from Amelia. There was an odd tension at the table this morning and I wondered if my cousin had broken her vow of silence. I'd been careful to splash cold water on my face before coming downstairs, hoping to mask the dark circles beneath my eyes from having lain awake half the night considering what I was about to do. Certainly, once I made my way well enough, I could return and help the family that had taken me in when my parents died.

"What are your plans for the day, Sara?" my aunt asked, taking a sip of her tea.

Amelia took a sudden interest in her breakfast bowl.

"After I check the roses, I thought I might do some reading and perhaps take a walk." I fiddled with my food, my stomach beginning to knot. I glanced at the people who'd served as surrogate parents for the past ten years of my life. How could I leave them this way? Would they understand my desire to want more than what their lives could afford me? "Was there something you needed me for?" I asked. My aunt, born of a German background, had wed my Irish uncle in a scandalous union that threatened to split our family apart. From that day, she'd spent all of her energy trying to fit in with my uncle's and father's family, to no avail. My grandparents were hard people, set in their ways, and Aunt Perdita was never able to please them. It was sometime during my midnight ponderings that I decided if anyone could understand following your dreams, Aunt Perdy would. She had made certain we were raised in a strict household with the proper instructions of a lady. Even though the chances were that we would never marry above our social position, Aunt Perdy was determined to make it look like we should.

I noted the side glance she gave my uncle and his slight nod, urging her to continue with whatever it was she had to say.

"Sara, you're reaching an age when a lady begins to consider her future. Since you have no suitors and since we cannot, as you know, afford to send you to a women's university for proper training, it's time to consider how you might make a good wage helping others. Acts of kindness are never wasted."

My porridge clumped in my throat and I had to force myself to swallow. "W-what exactly do you mean, Aunt Perdy?" I tried to remain calm, realizing that this discussion was bound to happen one day—yet today of all days? It could not be more ill timed.

"The Lord and Lady Barrington came by yesterday. Your uncle was checking on a new piece for their coach. We were conversing, Lady Barrington and I, about the weather and how lovely my roses were in bloom…"

I stared at her, the sound of her voice like that of a bee buzzing about his prey before he stings.

"It would just so happen that she has experienced a terrible spin of bad luck—well, bad luck for the poor housekeeper, I

suspect, but I question what tomfoolery might have been trans-
piring between Lord Barrington and—"

"Perdy, God in heaven, get on with it," my uncle sighed.

"Well, the poor woman has four children as it is. All under the
age of ten and she's with child again, maybe two, the doctor says.
And so far all girls! It seems that Lord Barrington is determined
to sire a boy—"

"Perdy," came my Uncle Marcus's quiet warning. He was a patient man unless rankled, and then he was a force to be reckoned
with.

She dismissed him with a short wave of her hand and I stared
at the two of them engaged in a dialogue that didn't include me,
but would change my life entirely and seal my fate. I saw my hope
of fame and fortune dwindling with each passing moment.

"Well, she says that because there may be twins, the doctor may
have to prescribe bed rest for the last three months of her pregnancy. Already the poor dear is as big as a barn. I don't know how
she'll last another month."

I was about to explode. To what end had my aunt committed?

"The point is that she is looking for another housekeeper, as
well as someone to govern the children. I told her that you were
quiet proficient in reading and writing and fair in numbers, as
well. Oh, you should have seen her face! The poor woman nearly
wept with joy. Had you been here, I'm certain she would have
offered you the position on the spot."

If I was going to make my way on my own, I was going to
have to make my stand. "Aunt Perdita, I—"

"Of course, you'll have your own quarters—food and uniforms
are provided. And the salary, though modest to begin with, is
competitive for a young woman in that position."

I found I could not say the words. I did not want to appear un-
grateful and what if Mr. Rodin was not truly who or what he
said he was? What then? And if the bargain had been struck and
agreed to, I would have little other choice but to concede to their
wishes.

"What do you think, Sara?" Aunt Perdy asked, her eyes sparkling with delight.

"What do *I* think?" I asked, my heart lifting a notch. Then nothing had been settled? "May I have a few days to think it over?" I asked.

My aunt blinked, not bothering to mask her surprise at my response.

"Well, I suppose that would be the suitable thing to do, but I caution you not to hesitate very long. Such opportunities to better one's situation are a rare gift and do not come along every day."

I felt a great burden lifted from my shoulders. My appetite returned and I nodded quickly, finishing my breakfast. "May I be excused? I have much to think about," I asked, pushing back my chair. Amelia looked up at me and I smiled, though I could barely stand to see the sadness in her eyes.

Perhaps Deven had forgotten about my request, or my uncle had found him another job to do. The late afternoon sky above was mottled with dark clouds, previewing a bout of rain before morning. The heat from the day lingered like a haze as a cool breeze stirred the trees. I lay on my back and listened to the symphony of sounds around me.

"I was afraid that maybe you'd have gone back home."

I sat upright and found Deven, smiling, as he plopped down at my side. He struggled with his shoes, wriggling out of his socks and leaning back with a great sigh of relief.

"Your uncle went into town with your aunt to check on a part from the mercantile," he said, staring out across the pond, its dark gray surface reflecting the sky above.

"Deven, I'd like to think we are friends. You and I, we've known each other a good while now and—"

He leaned on one hand and trailed the other along the back of my neck, twisting an errant curl around his finger.

I hunched my shoulders, smiling as I tried to find a way to explain that I was going to need his help. "I need—"

"I need, too, Sara," he said quietly, leaning over and placing a kiss on the back of my neck. His fingers stroked my throat, slipping lower to the top of my simple gown. I'd purposely worn my long chemise and pantaloons in the event I might take a dip in the pond.

"This is important, Mr. Mooreland," I said through a sigh, as his fingers dipped down into my bodice.

"It is important to me, as well, Sara. I know this is your first time and I want it to be good for you. I promise to be gentle."

I faced him then, his eyes a few inches from mine. "And what if I say no, Mr. Mooreland? Will you stop?" I searched his eyes, licking my lips that had gone dry.

He brought his mouth to mine, tempting me with nothing more than a slow peck, his mouth hovering over mine, waiting for me to make the next move.

"You won't," he whispered, looking up at me.

He was right; I didn't want to stop. Far too long, I had imagined what being with a man would be like. If I was about to embark on a journey of independence, I needed to understand what this magical pleasure between a man and a woman was all about.

I reached for his face, cupping his cheek as I pressed my lips against his mouth. His hand found the back of my head, holding my face to his, his mouth growing eager, his tongue seeking entrance to my mouth. Parting my lips, he took advantage, slanting his mouth, commanding the kiss and my mind.

"Do you like that, Sara?"

He kissed my eyes, then where the pulse beat fierce beneath my cheek before he found my mouth again. He was slow and methodical, driving me to a point of needing more. "More," I whispered, intoxicated with lust.

He stood and shrugged from his coat, watching me as he drew his shirt over his head.

I swallowed as his muscled torso came into view, sleek and tan, as fine as any stallion I'd seen. His breeches hung low, and a line of dark hair trailed to where a large bulge strained against the suede cloth.

"You needn't be afraid, Sara. I promise we will fit together perfectly. I've known so for a long time now."

Fit? The term alone caused a slight spasm in my lower belly. "I—I don't know."

He reached for my hand. "Let's go for a swim."

I nodded and, standing before him, quickly discarded my gown and stood there in my transparent underpinnings.

"You are beautiful, Sara."

He took my face in his hands, kissed me thoroughly, then led me toward the water. "Your breeches, won't they get wet?"

"I didn't want to frighten you." He paused, the water lapping at his ankles.

"I won't be, Mr. Mooreland." I tried to state with a confidence that I clearly did not possess.

"Call me Deven, Sara. Mr. Mooreland makes me sound so old. I'm only a year or two your senior."

He unfastened his waistband and shoved his breeches down his finely honed legs. His muscles bunched as he struggled to get them off. With one final look telling me this was my last chance to change my mind, he tossed the pants away and stood facing me.

His member looked much larger than I remembered, then again I *had* been peeking through the bushes at a distance. Strong and thick, it protruded from his body at a sharp angle. I could not tear my eyes from the sight of him naked. I had seen pictures of Greek art before, but none of it had prepared me for Deven's girth.

I reached blindly for his hand and followed him into the water, letting it cool my heated body. The fabric of my underclothes clung to my every curve and I was aware of the power I had by the look of pure hunger in Deven's eyes.

"I cannot help myself, Sara." He came to me then, fumbling with my chemise until he was able to draw the dripping cloth over my head. My dark hair tumbled from my combs, lost now in the pond.

His mouth moved over the tips of my wet breasts, his fingers teasing and taunting, pinching my raw buds and sending a line of fire straight between my legs.

"Are you wet?" He kissed my mouth, brushing my hair over my shoulders.

"I'm standing in the water, Deven, of course I'm wet."

His hand smoothed over my flesh, briefly pausing above the band of my drawers before dipping lower, his palm resting over the fabric that covered my dark curls.

"I mean here." He kept his eyes on mine, as his fingers slid to my nether lips, parting them, pushing the thin, soaked fabric farther inside. "Do you trust me?"

I nodded, my body teetering on the precipice of the unknown. He slid his hands over my hips, easing down the last barrier between us. A rush of cool water kissed the opening between my legs. With gentle reverence, he kissed my torso as I held his shoulders and stepped free of obstruction. He rolled up my drawers and tossed them onto the grassy bank.

"Come here, Sara, let me hold you," he said, drawing me deeper into the water, until I nearly floated into his embrace.

The water lapped against my breasts, my toes barely touching the rocky bottom. He reached down and grabbed my hips, his rigid staff brushing against my opening.

"Don't be afraid. I promise you will enjoy it as much as I."

He captured my mouth, drugging me with his kisses, unaware until I felt the sharp sting of my maidenhood tearing that he'd entered me. My fingers dug into his back flesh as he pushed deeper and I leaned back, arching against his mouth upon my breast. "This is what you meant by fit, then?" I asked, moving my hips awkwardly trying to meet his rhythmic thrusts.

"Aye, Sara, isn't it like I told you it would be? Perfect." The muscles in his neck strained, and I sensed the tightening of my own body in anticipation of something far greater than I had ever known.

Determined now, he looked at me, a fierceness glazing his eyes. His hands pressed my backside tightly against him.

"Come Sara, let go, it will be all right, you'll see." He clenched his teeth and odd, strangled noises came from his throat with each fervent thrust of his cock.

My body was not my own. I was filled with tension and yet I felt myself soaring, spinning higher. I shook my head as if to make the sensation cease, yet I wanted more. Sore as I was, the water aided the friction of his cock that I found quite pleasant. I didn't want the feeling to end. I had the definite idea that Deven pressed for that very thing. "Does…it…have to…end just yet?" I said, my words punctuated by his driving force.

"It is the way it works, Sara. I am about to…oh, Jesus." He pressed his teeth over his lower lip. He took a deep breath and stared at me.

"Kiss me, Sara. Kiss me hard and do not stop."

I cupped his face, bringing my mouth to his, forgetting all else save the wetness of his flesh and the taste of his tongue mating with mine. A sensation coursed through me, surprising me, nearly knocking me out of his arms. I turned my face to the heavens, unable to breathe as my body was rocked over and over.

"Aye, there's my girl" he breathed, and shoved hard, his face contorted in sweet agony.

It had lasted only a few moments from start to finish.

He licked his lips and smiled. "You are no longer a virgin, Sara. How do you feel?"

I slid from his arms, my muscles aching as I tried to navigate my way back to the bank. I had suspected I would feel something more, some twist of emotion, of joy or guilt—something.

There was none of that.

"Sara?" He trudged through the water after me, sitting down beside me, his member semi-limp against his leg. "Did I hurt you?"

The event had been pleasurable enough—certainly the journey to the conclusion, at any rate. "Should I feel strange? Because I don't."

His gaze on me narrowed, a frown creasing his brow.

"Oh, no, I mean it was fine, perfectly fine, Deven. I—I…it…well…it doesn't last very long now, does it?"

He grinned and shook his head as he stared at the ground. "I'm afraid I've been ready since I received your note, Sara. I'm sorry it was not more of a pleasure for you. But I tell you it was heaven for me."

"I did enjoy myself, Deven. Perhaps I expected more…you know, before." I felt no shame or discomfort seated beside him which, in itself, I found a bit odd, but perhaps it was my newfound independence helping me to place things in perspective. After all, when one is learning, the idea is to study the subject from as many angles as possible, isn't it?

"Might we try it again, only here on the ground this time? And then after, I would like to enlist your partnership in a matter most grave."

"Grave, you say?" He smiled wickedly and pushed me to my back. "More secrets for me to keep, Sara?"

Chapter 4

DEVEN KISSED ME THOUGHTFULLY, BEING MORE thorough than before. I could envision a lifetime of his attention. He'd make a fine husband for any deserving woman. Kind, handsomely built, unafraid of hard work, determined in his way, and confident.

He moved his hands over me, caressing, slow in his reverent worship of my body. I was lost in his adoration, floating without a care, accepting without reservation the pleasure he offered.

"Sara," he sighed. "I want to make you happy." He left a trail of kisses down my belly, causing gooseflesh to pop up over my skin. I wondered, as I stared at the sky through the leaves above, whether I could make Deven happy. Was it possible to make another person happy by sheer want of it?

He kissed the tops of my thighs, running his hands over my hips, down the length of my calves. I threaded the fingers of one hand through his tousled, sandy-colored curls as he nibbled playfully at my flesh. His thumb brushed softly over my nether lips, parting my flower. With a glint in his eyes, he glanced at me, bent his head and slid his tongue along my silky folds. The sensation brought me upright, my legs spread-eagled before him. "What

are you doing?" I stared at him in wide-eyed shock. I knew a little
of what transpired between a woman and a man, but this had to
be something no lady would ever allow.

Perched on his knees, settled between mine, his cock projected
proudly in his lap.

"'Tis just another means of pleasure, Sara. Did I hurt you?"
He frowned.

I thought a moment. "Well, no, not entirely."

"Then, you rather enjoyed it?" He studied me.

I chewed at the corner of my lip, a nervous habit. "It was not
altogether unpleasant, I guess. It was…well, a surprise."

He smiled. "I will let you know from now on what I'm going to do to you." Leaning forward, he took my shoulders and
kissed me gently.

I glanced down at his ample phallus. "Do men like to be
touched…there?"

"Aye, Sara. If you'd like to touch me, I would not mind a bit.
In fact, I would like it very much if you would."

He took my hand, placing a kiss in my palm. "Do you want
to?"

My lips pressed together as I studied the pale pink glistening
head. "All right, yes."

He kept his hand over mine, moving my fingers down his
length. It was smoother than I thought it would be. I drew my
hand slowly back to the velvet knob. He held my hand as a guide,
his eyes glazed over, his breathing growing erratic.

"Not q-quite so hard, gentle. Yes…that's it," he sighed, his
hands taking my face and kissing me as I continued.

I was intrigued by this strange power I had over him. His eyes
drifted shut as a low moan escaped his lips. "This offers you enormous pleasure, doesn't it?" I asked in rapt fascination, watching
his expression turn to one of ecstasy. Wanting to see what more
I could elicit from him, I slid my thumb over the tip and saw a
glistening drop appear. "And what should happen were I to put
my mouth here?" I placed my mouth over him, teasing the soft

flesh with my tongue, tasting the salty tang of the miniature pearl.

His eyes glittered with a dangerous passion. He swallowed hard. "Too much more of that and you'll have me in your hand."

"And that is not where you wish to be, is it?" I smiled, proud of my accomplishment. Brazen, I took him deeper this time, stroking with my hand. I discovered that in giving him pleasure, my body, too, reacted with pleasant sensations.

"Do you want me to do this to you?" he asked.

I nodded, licking my lips from the taste lingering on my tongue. Deven proceeded to show me that sex between a man and a woman could be more than a quick poke.

My fingers dug into the mossy grass as the mastery of his mouth brought me to the edge of release. "Please." The word stole from my lips. He settled between my legs, capturing my mouth in a searing kiss.

This time I needed no prompting for I was more than ready. He pushed deep and I lifted my legs around his waist, pinning him to me. Would this be what it was like every night were I to marry Deven? With such a voracious appetite, it would be no time before we had little ones running about. Then all my time would be spent at a scrubbing board, hanging clothes in the sunshine while my dutiful, hardworking husband tended to our land.

Deven panted hotly against my cheek, his elbows digging into the soft grass on either side of me. Fluidly, we moved, as if timed to one another in perfect union. The sweet motion of his cock was delightful, heating me to the core. My breath caught as a sensation that threatened to tear me apart tore through my body. He uttered a groan and his body tensed once before he pushed deep again and shuddered. Then his hard body, slick with exertion, lay atop me and I could feel his rapid heartbeat against my chest. At that moment, I understood how easy it would be to lose my heart to this man. "I cannot breathe," I whispered, disappointed when he moved off me.

Neither of us spoke. What more was there to say? I could not determine what had changed between us, but something had shifted—I sensed it. I knew that while I could be content living a life with Deven, I could not be truly happy married to him. I wanted more to my life.

He slanted me a strange look as he stood and began to dress. "We should be getting back to the house. Amelia may begin to suspect your absence."

I wanted to tell him that she already was a co-conspirator in my recent plans, but something niggled at me. I had to find a way to ask for his help without compromising the friendship—the very intimate friendship—that we'd forged. I did not want to wound his pride.

We walked silently, Deven following me on the worn narrow path that led to the back of the barn. Was I different now, truly a woman? Not in my own eyes, but in the eyes of society, I had stained my virtue. Something that I could never take back. Unexpected tears threatened to weaken my resolve.

"You've not said much, Sara. Are you well?" Deven asked. His concern was so like him. I felt his hand touch mine, urging me to slow down and address him.

"Sara?"

I faced him boldly, trying to show my newfound sense of womanhood. "What is it, Deven? What do you want me to say?"

His eyebrow twitched as he stared blankly at me.

"Whatever it is that you said you needed to speak to me about. Let's start there. We have a lot to talk about, I think."

Frustrated, I turned around and continued to walk. I didn't want to hurt him, nor did I wish to make him think that there was more to our relationship than what had just happened between us.

"You really haven't the courage to tell me the truth, have you?"

I stopped short, looking up at the dark rain clouds. "Tell you what?" I pivoted on my heel and faced him. He'd stopped a few feet behind, his arms loose at his sides. I shut my eyes, refusing to look at the hurt and anger I saw in his.

"You don't have the courage to tell me that I'm not good enough for you."

"Don't be absurd, Deven." I walked on.

"Tell me the truth. By God, Sara, I've a right to know," he bellowed, quickly closing the short distance between us. He grabbed my shoulder, forcing me to face him.

I was frozen, pinned by the fierce look on his face. I fought back in my poor defense. "This is not entirely my doing, Deven Mooreland," I warned, pointing my finger at him. He grabbed my shoulders and I tried to wrench away, but he held tight.

"Tell me you feel *nothing* for me," he demanded.

"Don't, Deven." I tried to break free. He was right. I was a coward.

"Say it, Sara. You owe me that much. For the past year or better, you have teased and taunted me, pretending to be interested when all you wanted was someone to help you keep your lies a secret."

I ceased my struggling, the sting of his words making their mark on my heart. His handsome face pleaded with me to tell him what I knew…what he deserved to hear. Was I no better than a common whore? I needed his help, but now, more than that, I needed him to understand. I didn't want to hurt him. I never meant for that to happen.

I plopped down on an old tree trunk at the side of the path, ready to confess my secret. "I need your help," I said wearily, kneading the dull ache throbbing between my eyes.

A short disgusted laugh pushed from his throat. "So you gave yourself to me thinking that it would win my cooperation? Poor Sara. I'm sorry you felt the need to go to such measures. I'd have helped you anyway, don't you understand that?"

I felt nauseous. Not because what he said was true, but because he knew me better than I knew myself. "I didn't mean to hurt you, Deven. You must believe me."

He walked a few feet, facing away, and leaned his hand on a tree.

"Oh, you didn't, Sara, but I'd like to know what is worthy of giving me your virginity." He glared at me over his shoulder. "That must be some secret."

"Don't, Deven," I said quietly.

"Don't? Don't what, Sara? Speak the truth?"

I sighed, a lump forming in my throat. "I'm leaving."

He whirled to me, pinning me with a fiery hatred in his eye. "What do you mean, you're leaving?"

"I've been offered a job. A position in town."

He raised his brows. "A governess? House servant?"

"No, I won't be serving others. I'll be gainfully employed as a...performer." I chose my words carefully, knowing Deven was not going to approve. But I needed his help, not his approval.

"A performer, you say? For whom?" he asked warily.

"Thomas Rodin." A moment ticked by.

"I've never heard of the gent. Who is he? What does he do? Is he one of those American playwrights come over to make his fortune? Bloody money grubbers," he muttered.

I shook my head. "You met him, the other night. He was the man who fetched you from the pub and no, he is not a playwright, nor American, but a British artist and known within the circles of the Royal Academy." I chose not to share on what terms he was known, finding it inconsequential to my purpose in needing Deven's help.

"That bloke is an artist?" he repeated with unmasked skepticism. "What does he want you to do for him, Sara, clean his brushes?" He smirked.

"Of course not," I said, my frustration growing measurably. Wasn't he able to see the natural beauty in me, as had Mr. Rodin? Wasn't it perfectly clear that an artist would only see me as a potential model?

"He wants me to model for him, you ninny."

Deven stared at me a moment before answering. "And you *believed* him?"

My intelligence bruised, I glared back at him. "Yes, he thinks that I have what it takes to be a…what did he call it…oh, yes, a 'stunner.'"

"Is that so?" Deven snorted.

"It's the truth, I swear."

"Be careful Sara, 'tis a cloudy day. Don't tempt God with a lightning bolt."

"Well, I—"

"Did this artist fellow happen to mention that you might have to take off your clothes for him?"

"Enough. I thought I could speak honestly to you about this—"

"Honest? Now you want to talk honesty?" he tossed back.

I leaped to my feet, hands fisted. I could have continued to argue until my face turned blue. It wouldn't have mattered. He wasn't going to understand, because he didn't want to understand. I walked away, deciding to allow him to wallow in his bitterness. How could I be held responsible for his mistaken perceptions?

"Don't you dare walk away from me, Sara Cartwright."

I stopped but refused to turn around. In my next breath I was spun around to face him, looking up mere seconds before his mouth descended hard on mine. It was a desperate kiss, neither passionate nor welcome. I turned my head, breaking the kiss and he leaned his forehead to my temple.

"Deven, you will forget me. Someone more worthy of you will capture your heart."

"Sara, I beg you, don't go. This Rodin…this man who claims to be an artist. He will never feel for you what I do," he whispered. "What kind of a life is that?"

I pulled from his embrace and placed my hand on his unshaven cheek. I was going to miss him and I knew one day that I would realize it fully. "I don't know what kind of a life it will be, Deven. But I want an education, I want to see and do so many things before I settle down—if ever I choose to settle down." I studied his face. "You deserve someone who can return those feelings.

You cannot give me what I want. I'm sorry, but that is the truth. You hold a very special place in my heart—"

He jerked his face from my hand and scowled.

"You made me a woman, Deven, and I am grateful that you were my first. But I do not feel the same for you as you apparently feel for me."

"Grateful?" he spit out the word bitterly.

"Please don't say it like that." I averted my eyes from his gaze. Taking a deep breath, I faced him straight on. "Will you help me?"

He gave a short laugh and shook his head as he stared at the ground. "I shouldn't."

His eyes met mine. There was pain and loathing reflected in them. "You're right, of course. You have no obligation." The thought of walking to town, carrying my bags, having to leave in the dead of night with no light to guide my way, flitted through my head. It was my life and my choice. It was up to me to find a way. "Then I'll say goodbye here, Deven," I said with as much courage as I could muster. I had wanted my independence—well, here it was. I had expected it to feel more exhilarating than this, instead I felt unsettled, unsure.

"Wait."

His voice caught me as I walked away.

"I will see that you get to where you're going. I want him to know I'm keeping my eye on him. But if he's not who he says he is, I'm putting you over my shoulder and hauling you back home."

Tears leaked from my eyes as I squeezed them shut and bolted back to him, hugging his neck tight.

He quickly pried my arms away and held me at a distance.

"When do we leave?"

"I'm to meet him at his studio tomorrow at two in the afternoon," I said.

"I'll have the hansom ready at one-fifteen. I'll leave it up to you what story you plan to fabricate this time. Good day, Miss Cartwright."

I watched him walk away, his long-legged, determined stride putting distance between us as quickly as possible. And as I saw him disappear inside the barn, I prayed that I would not regret my choice.

I finished my chores as swiftly as I could the next day, and managed to get my bags out to the hansom where Deven waited. A tearful Amelia joined us a few moments later.

"Here, I want you to have this." My cousin pressed a white lace doily into my hand. Along the edges were delicate yellow flowers with blue stitching. In the center, the same color ribbon wrapped around a bouquet of flowers.

"It's beautiful, Amelia, thank you," I said, holding back the niggling concern that I should reconsider what I was doing.

"Look here, I've stitched both of our initials. So you will remember our friendship. You know what they say, that daisies never forget."

She hugged me tight and I purposely avoided looking at Deven as I held her, comforting her. "I'll not be away forever, Amelia. When I've saved enough, made something of myself, we'll go to the theater again."

"If Mama and Papa allow it, Sara. Where will I write to you? How will I know where to find you?"

I gave her a slip of paper with the same address that was on Mr. Rodin's card. "Here is where you can reach me. If you need me, send for me and I will come without delay."

She sniffed, wiping her shiny red pert nose with her handkerchief, and nodded.

"Now stop crying, your face is mottled and Aunt Perdy will wonder what is troubling you." I hugged her, kissing her cheek quick as I hurried into the carriage. The cab listed slightly as Deven made his way into the driver's seat. With a snap of the reins, the mare in front of me jumped forward and the carriage sprang to life. I'd not told Amelia on purpose what excuse I'd given to my aunt in order to use the carriage, deciding the less she knew, the better.

Deven, on the other hand, was told that he was taking me to where I was to meet Lord Barrington, who would take me to the Barringtons' cottage estate on the other side of town. I'd told Aunt Perdy that I was going to visit them to see how I got on with the children. I could see by his face that Deven was not happy to be part of the fabrication but, without quarrel, he complied, perhaps glad to be rid of me.

The coach pitched and rolled, mimicking the sensations in my stomach, as we entered the busy streets of London. More than once I took out Mr. Rodin's card, checking the address again. *Cheyne Walk*. I scanned the neat row of brick houses along the long and narrow cobblestone street. Deven stopped the carriage a short distance from the front of the building. I peered out the window and saw that blocking the entrance was a large carriage. A handsome man, vaguely resembling Mr. Rodin, was assisting a beautiful woman with stark red hair into her seat. Several bags and a trunk lay on the ground as if they were preparing to travel or in the throes of moving. She wore an elegant traveling hat with a large black ostrich plume, the brim shadowing the details of her face.

A tap on the opposite window startled me and I turned to find Mr. Rodin, his charming smile greeting me. I unlatched the window, drawing it aside.

"Mr. Rodin, my apologies, I didn't see you."

"Good day, Miss Cartwright. I'm afraid I have some rather poor news of my own. As it turns out, today is not the best of days to meet. My cleaning lady is working today in the studio and—" he glanced over his shoulder "—my brother and his fiancée are leaving today."

His gaze lingered on them for a moment, and I wondered if the woman had been a model. He cleared his throat and looked at me with a bright smile.

"Can you meet me at the Globe, say tomorrow night, around seven? I have something I wish to show you."

"Mr. Rodin, I…"

"Of course, I understand if you've changed your mind."

"No, no, I haven't. I will be there…yes, I will be there." I repeated with greater conviction, though not at all sure how I was going to sneak out a second time.

"Wonderful, until then, milady." He bowed, tipping his hat.

As I watched him hurry back across the street, a movement from a small balcony above caught my eye, and I saw a woman lean over the ledge, a rug in her hands, shaking out the dirt. She had a mass of blond hair she'd swept up into a loose coil atop her head and from the way her bust shook, with each snap of the rug, it appeared she wore no under-bindings of any sort.

She paused and looked down at the carriage for a moment, before she turned her head as if to answer someone and disappeared back inside.

"Shall I return home, Miss Cartwright?" From above, Deven called down to me.

"Yes, Mr. Mooreland. There has been a slight change in plans."

I heard a snort of laughter, or perhaps it was the horse.

Chapter 5

I WAS NOT WELL. SINCE LEAVING TOWN, MY STOMACH had been churning to think what would happen if Mr. Rodin changed his mind. By the time we rolled up the farm's lane, I thought I might lose my stomach.

Aunt Perdita opened the door and stepped onto the front porch. She peered into the cab, a look of concern marring her face. "Sara, my dear. What happened? Your face is positively ashen. I hope you didn't receive bad news from the Barringtons?"

She helped me from the carriage and my hand moved to my stomach. "I did not make it as far as the Barringtons." At least that much was the truth. "I am not feeling well. Perhaps if I rest awhile, I shall be well enough to return tomorrow?"

"Of course, dear girl," she clucked, placing her arm around my shoulder as we walked together to the house.

"Shall I fetch your bags, then, miss?"

Only I detected the subtle mocking tone in Deven's voice.

"No thank you, Mr. Mooreland, I am confident that by to-morrow I will be able to travel again." I looked over my shoulder and caught his irritated expression.

"Tell me, what is he like, Sara?" Amelia sat on the edge of my bed, having just brought me a cup of tea that Aunt Perdy ordered me to drink. She said the herbs would ease the stomach pain I was having. Pains she suspected were of a womanly nature. I'd never had them before with my monthly, but the thought of my time with Deven pervaded my thoughts and I hoped the two were not related. I put it out of my mind. "Who...Mr. Rodin? Well, I barely know him." I sipped my tea, breathing deep the honey scent of the chamomile.

"No, not Mr. Rodin." She smiled shyly. "Mr. Mooreland."

"Dev—*our* Mr. Mooreland?" I choked on my tea and tried not to let complete shock register on my face. "Isn't he a bit...*old* for you?"

She had a dreamy far-off look in her eye. "He's two years older than you, which would make him only five years older than me." She frowned, her lip protruding in a childlike pout.

I could not readily determine whether my caution was for her sake or mine, but the idea of the two of them seemed absurd at best. "But Amelia—Mr. Mooreland? There are plenty of younger men out there. Don't you wish to meet some of them?"

"Some of my friends are already betrothed, and to men much older than Mr. Mooreland!"

"Wealthy men who will care for them, I suspect?" I posed.

"Yes, that is true, but—" She leaned forward and whispered, "Can you imagine the wedding night?" She gave her shoulders a shimmy.

I could not fault her there. "Still, don't you want to see what's beyond your own backyard?"

She shrugged. "Unlike you, Sara, I like it here in the country. Of course I love the theater and visiting in town, but I like it here. I think I could be happy staying."

"And that is what you want more than anything?" I asked. "To be some man's wife?"

She blinked as though she didn't understand me. "Of course I want to have a house, where I can raise my children."

She offered me a dazzling smile.

"I want to have a big family." She sighed dreamily.

For the first time, I began to see how very different we were in our thinking.

"Well, you may still wish to look around a bit more. I'm not sure Mr. Mooreland is the right man for you."

"Well, then." She looked up at me, her bright brown eyes sparkling with an idea. "Maybe I could come be a model, too?"

"Shh!" I cautioned. The poor girl. What was to become of her when I was gone? Aunt Perdy and Uncle Marcus couldn't afford a formal education. Still there were apprentice positions in town and there was always Lady Barrington's brood. Though in truth, I would not wish such a fate on someone of Amelia's delicate constitution. She cried far too easily and was better suited to her dreams than to the reality of governing unruly children. "Oh, Amelia, I'm sure everything is going to work out for the best. Just don't be too quick to make plans just yet. You are still young."

"But I'm not a child any longer," she retorted.

"No," I assured her. "You are quite the young woman and deserving of a wonderful man who will treat you with respect and cherish you."

As I patted her hand, I wondered if I would ever arrive at the point where I wanted the same. Did it make me odd, or any less of a woman that I did not yet aspire to such a life? Perhaps I was deluding myself that there was more to experience than only being a wife or mother. But something still niggled at the back of my brain, telling me there was more to life. Either that or I had not yet met the man who would make me want to settle down.

As the carriage pulled up beside the crowd gathering for the Friday evening show at the Globe, I thought of the confident look on Aunt Perdy's face as she hugged me goodbye. She thought I was on my way to Lady Barrington's for a few days to see how I fared with her children, when, in truth, I had no idea of where I would lay my head this night if things did not turn out as I'd hoped with Mr. Rodin. I wanted my aunt and uncle to be happy with me, and I did not like manufacturing stories to achieve my purpose, but I simply saw no other way. All I could hope was that once I'd established my fortune and place in society, they would understand my unconventional thinking and welcome me back home.

Deven pulled my two small bags—all that I had in the world—down from the carriage and stood beside me as I searched the crowd for Mr. Rodin.

"Are you certain he'll show?" Deven asked, his eyes scanning the crowd. "I hope you remember him, because his face is a blur in my mind."

I rose on tiptoe, checking over the heads of the dozens of people milling about the theater doors. "There he is," I stated, watching as Thomas Rodin wove around the edge of the crowd. I took a deep breath. At least he had not forgotten.

He removed his bowler the minute he found me, his eyes darting toward Deven and the bags he was holding.

"You can put those bags in my carriage if you like." He spoke directly to me. "I see you've decided to accept my offer." His smile was most charming.

I took Deven's arm and we followed Mr. Rodin down the street where his driver waited. His was a lovely coach with leather seats and high-polished black wood, trimmed with gold. Apparently the art world was doing quite well.

Deven placed my bags in the carriage and waited as I climbed in.

"Is everything to your approval, Miss Sara?" Deven asked. Mr. Rodin had gone to the other side to climb in.

"Absolutely, Mr. Mooreland. Thank you…for everything." I studied his face a moment, wondering when or if I would see him again.

"Good day then, Miss Sara. Mr. Rodin." Deven tipped his tweed cap and turned to leave.

"My love to everyone, Mr. Mooreland. Please let Amelia know I'll write as soon as I am settled. Give her my love."

Deven gave me a tight smile, nodded and disappeared into the crowd.

"May I say, Miss Cartwright, you look stunning in that color." Mr. Rodin sat down beside me, causing me to balance myself to keep from leaning into him. "I think you've inspired our first project…I'll call it Blue Silk. What do you think, my muse?" He smiled and I saw my future.

"Your muse?" I smiled, my stomach feeling as though a cloud of butterflies had taken flight.

"And *you* must call me Thomas," he replied, taking my hand and kissing the back of it. "Let me show you where I will make your face known throughout the world."

"What do you think?" Rodin asked as he lit the kerosene lamps around the room. Beyond the French doors leading to the small balcony, twilight was descending on London. There was the stench of the river mingling with the sharp smell of something in the studio. I wrinkled my nose and heard Thomas's laughter.

"That's turpentine, Sara. A scent that you will get used to. Come, take a look." He ushered me over to an easel. On it stood a wood frame covered in fabric. Beside that was a small table with an array of pots of paint and several crockery jars holding a larger variety of paintbrushes than I'd ever seen in my life. I reached out to touch the canvas and he caught my wrist.

"Nothing touches my canvas except me."

His eyes were steady and it took a moment to realize the gravity of my near mistake. I nodded.

"Otherwise, feel free to explore at will. I have a small library downstairs. I believe you mentioned that you read. Any of the volumes are available at your leisure, when you aren't working." He smiled and continued as if nothing had happened. "There are three bedrooms and a bath down the hall. The kitchen is over there—" he pointed to the corner of the large studio room "—through the butler's pantry." He turned in a circle as if observing his domain. "We took out a wall dividing this room to allow for the light from both sets of balcony doors. I quite often entertain the brotherhood—at strange hours of the night, you should be warned. Do you cook, by chance?"

"A little," I replied, a bit unsure about what I was getting into.

"Scones?"

"Well, yes, as a matter of fact, my aunt…"

"Splendid! I'll make sure that you have everything you need to make those straight away."

"Are you hiring me to cook or to model, Thomas?" I asked. Cooking and cleaning were not what I had in mind.

He cocked his eyebrow in question. "Sara. Perhaps I didn't make myself clear. I entertain my brothers, sometimes with little notice, and as you might guess to hire a full-time cook would seem a waste. The brotherhood thrives on a communal sharing policy. Therefore, your talents in cooking, as well as modeling, will be utilized. Besides, you wouldn't want my cooking, I assure you. You may also, from time to time, be lent to other artists in the group," he stated matter-of-factly as he poured himself a glass of port.

He held the bottle up in silent invitation and I shook my head, offering a polite smile, which didn't seem to bother him a bit.

"I am delighted to see your bags, assuming then, that you will be staying in residence?"

He paused and waited for my response. "I won't take up much room."

He chuckled. "My dear, you'll have your own room. My former model—" he paused to take a sip of port "—as it happens, has left an opening. You'll take her room and share the bath with whomever happens to be here."

"Do you live here?" I blurted out before I realized what I'd said.

"For the most part, yes," he replied.

He was apparently less concerned than I about my forward

question. I took him up on his offer to explore, walking slowly around the perimeter of the room, studying the pictures on the wall and the artifacts from countries far away. "Do you travel much, Thomas?"

"Me? No, I'm rather a homebody, I fear. Most of those trinkets have come as gifts from my brothers and my peers. I have some very well-traveled friends who find their inspiration in learning more about the world beyond these walls. I like my creature comforts, I guess, preferring to stay right here and focus on the person I'm painting to find my inspiration."

I found a stack of canvas sketches leaning against the wall and bent to thumb through them, surprised to discover the sensuality displayed by the models. One sketch was of a woman partially reclined on a chaise longue, with nothing but a throw covering her lower half. She held a feather in her hand and her gaze was fixed on the artist. He'd captured every detail of her full breasts, the slope of her belly, the swell of her hip. I was mesmerized by how her sexuality came through on the canvas. "Who is she?" I asked, sensing him now standing at my side.

"One of my very first models. Her name was Cozette. She was an acquaintance of my aunt. A lovely girl, but she harbored a great many secrets."

"Where is she now?"

He chuckled. "Making some gent enormously happy, I imagine. The woman possessed a fiery passion."

I eyed the portrait, wondering what it was that Thomas Rodin saw in me. "Do I possess such passion, Mr. Rodin? Will you have me pose nude, as well?" I was intrigued, imagining myself in such a decadent pose.

Thomas stood very close, the exotic scent of his skin titillating my senses. I felt his fingers brush my cheek and turned to face him. His eyes darkened as he trailed his fingers along the curve of my neck. My body reacted instantly to his touch, my breasts puckering, rubbing against the rough fabric of my corset.

His penetrating eyes held mine, his fingers traveling lightly over the front of my jacket. He undid the button holding it in place and swept it off my shoulders. With patient ease, he drew it from my arms and placed it aside, taking a step back to study me from head to toe.

"It takes a special woman to sit for an artist, Sara. The trust between an artist and his model is a very intimate bond."

He cupped my face in his hands, his thumbs brushing delicately over my mouth, eyebrows and forehead.

"I can see you are exceptionally beautiful, Sara, and gifted, I think, in the ways of passion, although I daresay you have much you can yet learn. But, I do see a hunger in your eyes, Sara. One that I find most appealing."

He tipped his head, studying me.

"Have you ever considered wearing your hair down?"

His eyes held mine as he slid his fingers into my hair, jostling it from its coil, causing it to sway, threatening to come undone. I placed my hand on his, interfering. "I only wear it down when I retire in the evening, Thomas."

He smiled slowly, with a hint of danger that caused a sinful shiver to rush over my flesh. "Of course. That gives me something to look forward to, my muse."

He stepped away. "Do you like adventure, Sara? What about the theater, does it appeal to you?"

"I adore the theater, Thomas. As to adventure, I've not experienced much, but I am not averse to the idea."

"It's settled, then, to celebrate your new position, I'm going to take you to a special place—one of London's premiere theaters. I promise, it is like nothing you have ever seen." His eyes danced with excitement.

"Now? At his hour?" I was accustomed to an early bedtime and early mornings.

"The night is still young, Sara. Come." He grabbed my jacket and held it for me as I put it back on. I tried to take his sudden whim in stride. After all, I was embarking on a new life, why should I not embrace it?

★ ★ ★

The air was thick with cigar smoke, stinging my eyes, as I followed Rodin through the crowded room. Private tables set within red-curtained alcoves catered to the elite, dressed in their finest clothes. They drank their champagne and toyed with the table servers. I passed by one as she was taking a bottle of wine to a table of men. She was dressed, as all the women servers were, in long stockings, tall ankle boots and short trousers. The ensemble was topped by a tightly cinched red corset that thrust her pale breasts into full view.

Thomas wove me through the tables of boisterous men. At one table, they were passing one of the servers around lap to lap, sampling her kisses and teasing her breasts. It was a different world. Dark, decadent, a place Aunt Perdy would call a "den of sinfulness."

"Over here, Sara." He tugged on my hand just as a drunken sot reached for my waist.

"Sit here," Thomas directed, pulling out a chair for me. Three men seated at the table stood.

"Gentlemen, this is the stunner I told you about. Isn't she a peach?"

I sat with my hands folded in my lap, assuring myself that I'd not just made the worst mistake of my life.

A red-haired gent with a neatly trimmed beard leaned over the table, his hand stuck out in greeting. "Watts, milady. You can call me George. We weren't sure that you weren't a product of Thomas's imagination. Sort of a ghost of the opera house." He shook my hand enthusiastically.

"Woolner's the name. It's a pleasure, Miss Cartwright." A clean-shaven young man with dark shoulder-length hair greeted me.

Thomas flung his arm over the back of my chair, letting his fingers brush lightly against the back of my shoulder.

"Where's Hunt?" he shouted over the din of the crowd. There was no question from the noise level of the mostly male crowd that the drinks flowed freely in this place.

"Can I offer you something?" I turned toward the voice and my gaze locked onto the firm, round breasts of our table server. I heard a low rumble of laughter from the man named Watts seated to my left. Mr. Rodin leaned forward and grinned. I think he rather enjoyed that the situation might challenge my level of comfort.

"Are you thirsty, my muse?" He glanced at the woman's ample offerings. Perhaps because I was from a farm, he thought I would not catch his not-so-subtle innuendo. He was testing me, to see how shocked I might be by his bawdy choice in lifestyle. I would not be run off quite so easily. "A glass of port, please," I replied, eyeing a silver piercing on the woman's dark cherry-colored nipple.

"Did it hurt?" I asked politely.

"This?" She touched herself and I noted the entire table of men went silent, focused intently on our conversation.

"Not so much this one," she said, flipping the ring with a long red fingernail. "But this little imp, he gave me trouble." She turned to face me, pushing her other breast in my face as she leaned down and flicked the other glimmering silver ring.

"This one is still a bit sensitive with the gents. Now and again a chap will get a mite too curious, if you know what I mean?"

She gave me a wink.

"Oh, but not our Mr. Rodin." She wrapped her free arm around Thomas's neck and hugged him to her bosom. "This one's a gentleman, he is." She stood up, thrusting her chest out as she scanned the glasses on the table. "Anything else right now for you gents...and the lady?" She smiled down at me. She was completely unaware how the men at the table were blatantly staring at her. With a nod, she leaned down and kissed Thomas on the cheek, then rubbed off the residual red mark left by her painted lips.

Thomas glanced down at the table, a hint of a smile creating a deep crevice in his angular jaw. Were I to guess, he looked a trifle embarrassed. He slanted me a look, catching my curious expression, and smiled.

"So, Thomas, you brought me to a burlesque theater," I said, trying to show him that his choice of entertainment had not shocked me as much as he'd thought it would. "What were you thinking?"

He laughed good-naturedly and shrugged. "I had no motive other than to show you some of the more interesting sights of London."

"Oh, interesting, indeed. We've covered the female anatomy—when shall we address the male?" I held tight my smile, challenging him that if he thought he could shock me into running back to the farm, he was gravely mistaken.

He leaned toward me, his arm across the back of my chair, and whispered in my ear, "I like your spirit, Sara Cartwright." His breath blew hot against my temple.

I turned to face him, his mouth inches from mine. "What else do you intend to try to shock me with, Thomas?" My gaze dropped to the fullness of his lower lip, imagining how practiced he probably was in seducing women.

"Here's the port for the lady and the whiskey for Mr. Rodin." The server placed the glasses in front of us.

Thomas leaned back slowly, letting a full smile emerge on his face. "I think you will work out fine, Sara, just fine."

He raised his glass. "To a long, sweaty and prosperous union." His brothers in art joined him, raising their glasses in kind.

I smiled and lifted my glass, having passed muster on the first—I had a strange feeling—of many such tests, no longer afraid of Mr. Thomas Rodin, his friends, or the choice I'd made.

Chapter 6

THOMAS WAS HAVING TROUBLE GETTING THE RIGHT shade of pink for my mouth. "Damnation!" He flung another paintbrush over his shoulder—the third one this morning.

It was my third week living at the studio and the second day sitting for his current project. In the first week, he'd taken me to the Royal Academy gallery, noting his one painting and several of his peers'. He introduced me to a number of obscure burlesque theaters, featuring a new art form called "Poses Plastiques," a scandalous form of statue-style posing of mythological deities and stories that left little to the imagination. He was tireless in his quest to try new exotic venues, especially those ridiculed by the upper-crust critics of London's art world. And though I enjoyed the excitement of accompanying him on his adventures into his dark worlds, I much preferred spending time alone with him at the studio, sequestered together in the place where I could experience the totality of his artistic passion.

I'd sat unmoving since first light, maybe four or five hours ago, positioned to his liking on a backless chair, dressed in a blue silk gown that looked as though it had come from the trunk of a Renaissance theater troupe. My back was stiff, and I had no feeling in my calves.

"What in blazes can be so difficult about finding the right shade for a woman's mouth?" he muttered angrily as he scooped up a glob of red paint and slapped it on his palette. His gaze jumped from chopping and mixing the colors to the canvas and back to me.

I'd quickly learned two things about Thomas Rodin. First, he was meticulous when it came to his work, and second, his work was his life. Already he'd shirked from the ornately embellished hunter-green gentleman's jacket that he usually wore. I'd grown used to his flamboyant style with his velvet coats and billowy silk shirts. He rarely wore a cravat, unless going out, and preferred his hair long, although the styles for men were becoming shorter. I would often hear him quoting Shakespeare as he painted.

Today, he'd turned back his sleeves, rolling them to his elbows, revealing the sinewy flesh of his arms and his hands—hands that possessed character, not only in how they held a brush, but by virtue of the skill they possessed.

He paced back and forth, glancing at the canvas, standing at the window, standing across the room and staring for long intervals of time at me.

"Let me try something."

He dropped the palette on the table, walked over and dropped to his knee in front of me. The gesture sent the first tingle up my spine that I'd felt in hours.

"I need to kiss you," he stated simply. "To see how your lips change color."

I raised my eyebrows, trying not to break my pose. "Couldn't I just bite them and achieve the same purpose?"

His eyes sparkled with my subtle teasing, before he pushed his wayward curls over his ears and smiled at me. By God, he was a handsome man, with a smooth-shaven face, a firm jaw and a mouth that was the call to sin. His vest lay open, as did the top of his shirt revealing a tempting smattering of dark hair on his chest. I could not tell if I was merely infatuated with him, or if I was developing stronger feelings for him. I knew only that I had the need to be as close as I could to the passion and zest for life that lay behind those teal-colored eyes.

"I beg you, Sara."

His plea, waxing desperate, was impossible to ignore, even if I'd wanted to, which I did not. "If you think it will help, Thomas," I replied.

I'd no sooner said the words than he grabbed my face and pressed his lips hard against mine. The moment was not at all what I'd envisioned and in the next instant he rocked back on his heels, his eyes scrutinizing my lips.

"Once more," he offered quietly before capturing my mouth again, this time more insistent, hungry.

He broke the kiss but did not move away, his breath coming in short, raspy pants. "Sara," he whispered, teasing, coaxing, sampling my lips until in dizzying surrender, I returned his kiss.

Liquid heat pooled between my thighs. I heard sighs in the back of my brain and realized they were mine. I wanted his hands on me, touching, caressing, stroking. He stopped without warning, leaned back and a slow smile crept across his face.

"There it is." He jumped to his feet, grabbed a brush as he made his way back to the canvas, and began painting with furious glee. "Yes!" he cried, the expression as he turned his face heavenward one of utter joy. "That's what I needed."

I swallowed, feeling the dampness between my legs. I was nowhere close to what I needed. "May I take a break? I need to lie down for a few moments."

He glanced up at me with a patronizing scowl.

"Of course, I've got to work on your mouth. I'll come fetch you when I need you again."

That was what concerned me. On unsteady legs, I held my palm against the flocked hallway wall and found my room. I opened the window to allow in the mid-afternoon breeze. After splashing my face with water from the basin, I stripped down to my thin cotton chemise and pantaloons and stretched out on my bed, letting my eyes drift shut.

I was not certain how long I slept, but I awoke with a start and realized the sun had passed around the other side of the house.

"There's not enough light left in the day, Sara. We'll start fresh tomorrow." Thomas's voice issued from a chair in the corner to my right. I clamped my hand over my heart, pushing myself upright in the bed.

"How long have you been here?" I asked breathlessly.

He looked relaxed, leaning back with his arms draped over the chair, his long legs stretched out before him. He uncrossed his ankles.

"An hour or two, maybe. I think I might have dozed."

His eyes raked over me.

"You are quite fascinating when you sleep." He leaned forward and grinned. "You make these funny little sounds, barely audible, but exquisitely erotic." He leaned his elbows on his knees. "I got hard just listening to you."

I closed my eyes, took a deep breath to steady my nerves and looked back at him.

"Does that shock you?" he asked, easing back into the chair, his gaze fixed on me.

I gathered my wits, determined that if this was another of his tests, I was going to pass. "That seems to be your quest, Thomas, to shock me. Did it occur to you that I might be dreaming?"

His eyebrows rose. "I like that thought. About what? Do you remember?"

"Maybe I dreamed of being in the burlesque, of wearing a corset and carrying a whip. Maybe I dreamed of having my nipples pierced. Would that shock *you*, Thomas?"

"Interestingly, that can be arranged, if you like. For the record, that woman you met has several other piercings. Would you like me to tell you where they are?" He grinned.

I sighed and conceded to his wit. "Very well, Thomas, you've succeeded. I withdraw."

"Oh, no, not when we were just getting started, Sara."

He moved over to sit beside me on the bed, glancing down a where the camisole had slipped off my shoulder.

"So beautiful—a woman's shoulder," he said quietly, tracing hi fingers light along my skin.

My breasts tightened. I twisted the sheeting between m fingers, fighting the desire inside me, not wanting to appear to desperate, though a yearning had been building inside me sinc the moment we'd met at the theater.

His hand touched my chin, lifting my face to meet his eyes My heart thrummed madly in my chest, waiting, hoping.

"You are a lovely woman, Sara. Desirable, determined, a mos lethal combination for any man. You and I both know that kis was not nearly enough."

He leaned forward, teasing his mouth against mine, making me work for the kiss he knew I wanted more than air.

His hand brushed over my covered breast as his lips paid artfu attention to the curve of my neck. I watched the curtains flutter in the evening breeze as he caressed me, drawing a sigh from my lips.

Prompted by his smile, I lifted my arms and allowed him to peel off my top as he eased me to my back. He held my hands captive, pinned above my head as he leaned down, lavishing one breast and then the other until they were tight with arousal.

"You've wanted this, haven't you? You needed me to touch you like this."

One piece at a time, the encumbrance of our clothing was re-moved and we lay wrapped in the sheets, blissfully sampling each other's bodies.

"Haven't you wanted this, as well, Thomas?" I asked, running my palms up his rippled stomach, flicking his taut nipple with my tongue. I knew he expected nothing more from me than the carnal pleasure we shared. The freedom of that, with no strings to tie me down, encouraged my boldness.

"You are exquisite, my muse." He sighed. "From the moment I saw you in that dark theater, I have wanted you. Can you imagine my torture? Watching and worshipping you from afar each day, wanting to please you—wanting you to please me."

His words of adoration were empowering, heady. "I had no idea that I'd tortured you so, Thomas." He handed me his cravat.

"What is this for?" I asked. "You don't wear one."

He lifted his hands to the bed rail and smiled. "They ought to be good for something, then. I am yours, my muse, to do with as you wish."

I held his eyes as I realized what he wanted me to do. Lifting my leg to straddle his hips, I leaned forward and wrapped his wrists, securing them then to the bed railing. He rose up and caught one of my breasts, drawing the tip through his teeth. The short stab of pain sent a delicious jolt to my core.

"To be tortured by a woman of such divine beauty is my pleasure," he uttered as he lay beneath me. I leaned down and cupped his face in a searing kiss, letting my hands glide over him in unabashed exploration. To watch his eyes drift shut and hear the suffering moans from his throat empowered me in a way I'd never known. Desperate need coiled deep inside me and I reached between us, guiding his cock to my drenched opening.

"That's good, my muse," he whispered, and a quiet groan escaped from his throat as I eased onto him.

I braced my hands on his chest, allowing my body to welcome him in glorious fullness.

"The problem most people have with sex is that they don't see the artistic beauty of it." He jerked his hips upward, causing me to gasp openly.

He grinned and repeated the motion. "You should see how beautiful you are with me deep—" he thrust his hips again "—inside you."

I was transported from the limited borders of reality to a state of carnal ecstasy—it was magical, euphoric. Closing my eyes, I leaned back, rocking my hips, feeling my body tighten. I cradled my arms over my head, in full control of my body's pleasure until at last, I came undone and felt my muscles contracting around him. He pushed his hips against mine and emptied his hot seed.

"Untie me," he instructed in a fierce whisper, and as soon as I had he had me on my back, capturing my mouth in a long kiss.

Just as quickly, he leaped from the bed, grabbed his pants and tossed me my dressing robe. "Come with me. This moment is precious."

"But my dress." I pointed to the gown I'd worn before.

"Never mind the dress, Sara. This is kismet. Come, we must hurry."

I had not yet tied my robe before he grabbed my hand and, half-naked, we ran back to the studio down the hall. I prayed no one else was home.

He grabbed a sketchpad as I finished dressing and guided me to the fainting couch. As if arranging a curtain, he positioned me, loosening my robe slightly so only a glimpse of my breast was visible, and then he stood back to observe his work.

"Absolutely perfect," he stated. "You're a goddess." He leaned down and kissed me tenderly.

I rested my cheek in my hand, feeling utterly satisfied, and offered him a smile of pure contentment as he sat in his chair and began furiously sketching.

We were lovers. If he wasn't painting me, he was worshipping me with a passion akin to it. I reveled in this attention, blossomed as a woman beneath his hand, grew in status and acceptance among his closely knit circle of friends—some prominent artists and poets, most with an opinion on everything under the sun. They drew me into their conversations, interested in my thoughts as a woman, as an equal. It was enough to incite my hunger for more. Perhaps I wanted to prove something to myself, or to Deven or my family. Even now, I don't know what it is that drives me, but I have never been completely at ease with myself.

On a rare occasion, Thomas allowed me to be "borrowed" for

a short interval by one of his peers, but he was precise in how long they could keep me.

Thomas loved gathering the boys around him, leaving an open-door policy to the house most of the time. Artists would wander in and out at all hours, seeking his consultation on various matters, or sometimes just to share a drink. When one of them had the good fortune to sell a painting, it was cause for a grand celebration with plenty of food and wine for all.

It was at one of these impromptu soirées that I met a woman named Grace, a former model and longtime friend of Thomas.

I'd discovered, not from Thomas but from Grace herself, that she was currently hired by Thomas to keep the studio clean, although I couldn't remember ever seeing her except that once on the balcony. This evening she was quiet around me, but chatty with the artists she called "her boys."

I sensed a tension between us almost immediately. I suspected it had to do with Thomas, but there was something else—a kind of superiority she held over me, as if she was on the inside and I was not, nor ever would be.

I checked the platter of oysters I'd brought from the pub around the corner. They were Thomas's favorite and he insisted that I buy them for tonight's celebration. He was bringing home a surprise. With a parting glance at the group, engaged fully in conversation with Grace, who looked like a queen holding her court, I took my glass of wine and stepped out onto the balcony. I leaned against the wall and surveyed the autumn sun descending on the horizon. Below, the gaslights began to glimmer, turned by the lamplighter's key. My eye caught the shape of a carriage parked down the street, the silhouette of a driver seated atop the bench in dark silence. I sensed he was watching me, and a shiver ran over my shoulders. The sound of another carriage approaching from the opposite direction drew my attention to where it stopped below. When I looked up again, both the first driver and the phantom carriage were gone. I could not shake the feeling that it had been Deven, perhaps alone, or did he have Amelia with him? I'd heard from her only once since I'd left. She'd written to say that Aunt Perdy and Uncle Marcus would not allow her to have anything more to do with me. For all intents and purposes, they told her, she no longer had a cousin. I wondered why Deven and Amelia would come this far and not contact me. Despite how my relatives felt about me, I hoped that all was well at home.

I heard Thomas's raucous laughter below and took another quick look at the mysterious coach. Determined not to let my imagination ruin Thomas's surprise, I focused on the carriage. A man stood to the side as Thomas paid the driver. "It's about time you arrived," I called down to him. "We've been waiting for you."

He looked up and grinned. "How very much like Shake-speare's Juliet you appear as you lean over the balcony. There is someone I am anxious for you to meet. We'll be up in a few moments."

"I think Sara was considering the idea…wait a minute, let's ask her."

I heard my name and stepped back inside, walking to where the group sat around the fire, lounging with their drinks in hand.

"You wanted to ask me what?" I asked, taking a sip of my port. I did not fear the questions the brotherhood could dredge up, especially under the influence of a good port. Quite often, they included me in their conversations, drawing me in to ask my opinion as a woman.

Watts leaped up and offered me his chair, but I declined, preferring to stand. He returned to his seat and gave me a wicked smile as he patted his lap. "Here then, perhaps?" He wiggled his brows. I shot him a look of friendly warning.

Woolner spoke up, addressing me. "Wasn't it you, Sara, who was so fascinated by the nipple piercing of the woman at the club a few weeks back?"

Everyone's attention turned, awaiting my response. Grace sat on the arm of a chair, sipping from her glass. Her luminous blue eyes drifted up to look at me. "I found them interesting, I suppose," I answered cautiously as I suspected there was more to this topic than mere conversation. I scanned their faces. "Why do you ask, gentlemen?"

"We were curious, if you'd ever consider doing it." Hunt leaned forward in his chair, his dark brown eyes alive with interest. A hush had come over the room. I glanced at Grace, whom I barely knew, but the crook of her eyebrow conveyed a private challenge.

"Is it dangerous, do you think, for your health?" I asked, delaying any sort of commitment to an answer.

Woolner chuckled, raising his glass. "It seems every woman at the club has them and, by God, they all look in splendid health to me!" Rousing laughter followed on the heels of his comment.

I took a long swallow on my second glass of port for the evening and set the empty glass on the table. Summoning my courage, I slanted Grace a side look. "Well, gentlemen, I suppose it is not entirely out of the realm of possibility," I answered with a careless shrug.

Woolner let out a whoop and slapped his leg. He held out his palm to Watts and grinned as money was exchanged between them.

"See there, I told you that you underestimate our little Sara!" Woolner said.

I was aware, then, that it had been a ruse, a mere bet between brothers about how open-minded I was. I laughed along with them but wished that Thomas would hurry upstairs. I started for the door to see the reason for his delay.

"I will do it," Grace stated boldly.

That got the attention of every man in the room, as it did mine.

"That's right. I'll do it right now, if Sara agrees to perform the task."

My eyes widened. Had she really suggested such an absurd idea?

"Ouch," I heard one of the men mutter under his breath.

She shrugged. "How bad can it be? Come on, Sara, I understand you're good with a needle and thread."

"That won't be necessary, Grace, and you might want to watch how much more of that port you have tonight." Thomas stepped into the room behind me, his hand patting the small of my back.

"Good God, Grace, as if we don't have enough tongues wagging against us as it is! Can you imagine if something went awry and you wound up in the infirmary, what those bastard critics would do to us in the papers?" He walked to her, smoothed his hand over her cheek and looked at me.

"Now if my two favorite women are done with this nonsense, I suggest that if anything should be allowed to touch either of you lovely creatures it should be me."

He smiled as he drew me into his arms and kissed my cheek.

"Let it go, my muse," he whispered in my ear. "Now give me that beautiful smile of yours and meet our new brother."

Chapter 7

"EVERYONE, I'D LIKE YOU TO MEET MR. EDWARD Rhys, the newest member of our little den of creativity."

I looked behind me, having quite forgotten that Thomas said he had someone with him. The gentleman stepped from the shadows into the glow of the firelight. He was on the thin side, and his face showed more than a week's beard, not allowing for any possibility of seeing what his face truly looked like. He wore his hair long, and it appeared he'd not bathed in a few days. His eyes were his most striking feature, a pale gray-green that held your gaze. I knew immediately that Thomas saw in them great potential.

"Mr. Rhys comes from Wales. He's been traveling, doing research, selling his paintings in the manner most artists do, doing portraits for hire down at the Cremorne. I finally convinced him to join us and soak up some of our creative genius."

"Mr. Rhys, welcome. I'm Sara."

He held out his hand, taking mine in a gentle grasp and offering a smile that was just as charming. "Thank you," he said quietly.

He followed Thomas around the room, greeting each of the brothers. Grace stood, offering her hand to him. "Mr. Rhys, it's nice to see Thomas took my advice."

"Thank you, Grace." Rhys took Grace's hand and kissed it.

"As if you wouldn't shove your advice down my throat, woman, if I didn't," Thomas laughed. "Still, I'm grateful to you this time. This one has real talent."

"Yes, I'm very aware that Mr. Rhys is something special," she remarked, slanting him a smile.

An uncomfortable silence followed and Grace chuckled quietly. She boldly walked up to Thomas and started to give him a kiss. He turned, offering his cheek instead. They grinned at each other and Grace smacked him on the shoulder then went back to her seat.

The rest of the group didn't seem to notice the interaction nor the fact that Mr. Rhys seemed lost. It looked like the poor man hadn't eaten in days. "Come, Mr. Rhys, get yourself a plate. We have all this food and barely anyone has touched a bite." I took Mr. Rhys's arm, guided him to the banquet table and offered him a plate.

It did not take him long to fill his plate, with no hand to carry his drink.

"Let me bring your drink," I said, pouring a glass of red table wine. He glanced up at me, nodded and scanned the room, choosing the spot at the end of the large table apart from the cluster of chairs near the fire.

"There you go," I placed the glass in front of him, waiting a moment for a response. There was something different about him. He seemed more down-to-earth in his manner.

I looked up at Thomas as he joined his new protégé at the table. He reached for my hand and drew me to his side.

"Thank you, my dear, for preparing such a grand feast and for making Mr. Rhys feel welcome here." He reached over and slapped Rhys on the back. "You'll not find a woman any better than Sara." Our guest looked up, his eyes lingering on mine until at last I looked away.

I caught Thomas's expression of concern, the compassion in his eyes for Mr. Rhys. He shook his head as if to tell me it would be well.

"We'll get you a nice place to lay your head, Edward. After a stout breakfast, we'll get started setting up a spot for you here in the studio." Thomas smiled.

While Thomas and the others visited, I snuck out of the studio and readied Mr. Rhys's bedroom. The room had formerly belonged to Thomas's flesh-and-blood brother. I'd never met him, but Thomas had nothing but praise for him. It was in passing conversation with one of the other artists one day that I found out that the woman Thomas's brother left to marry was Thomas's first wife. That alone explained why Thomas was not yet ready to commit to a relationship, perhaps. Lately he'd taken to spending several nights a week in my bed, but I wondered if his nightly visits would slow with a new guest in the house? I was unsure that I truly wanted to be tied down to Thomas, anyway. I was making good money and had been building a nice nest egg to further my adventures. I was supplied with everything that I needed and I had great admiration and a healthy respect for my employer. What more did I need than that? The goals that I'd set out for myself were slowly coming to fruition. Still, while I was open to the possibilities with Thomas, I had to consider, too, the other influences in his life—one of them being his mysterious bond with Grace Farmer.

I'd just laid out fresh towels on the end of the bed and turned to leave when I abruptly ran into Mr. Rhys's chest. A gasp flew from my throat as he grasped my arms to prevent me from toppling backward. His light green eyes held my gaze intently. I cleared my throat, looking for my voice. "I left toiletries by your basin," I stated, unsure how to read his expression. "And the loo is right next door."

He let his arms fall to his sides as he stepped around me and picked up a fresh towel, burying his face in the fabric.

I paused at the door, looking back over my shoulder, and watched as he leaned down and slowly rubbed his hand over the bedcovering. I wondered what he'd been through before Grace found him. I suspected I would learn the answer with time. "If you need anything, Mr. Rhys, I'll just be in the studio."

"Thank you, Mrs. Rodin. You've been more than kind, both you and your husband."

I opened my mouth to correct his misjudgment, instead offering him a smile. "Please call me, Sara."

"Aye, then…thank you, Sara," he said.

The sound of my name rolled off his tongue like a sweet confection. It was lovely, his voice and his manner. A vast change from the brotherhood, who were always so loud and boisterous, constantly teasing and joking about.

"Good night then, Mr. Rhys," I said, closing the door behind me.

"You were very kind to our guest tonight, thank you." Thomas lay on his side, twirling a strand of my hair around his finger.

"I don't mind, Thomas. I find it interesting that Mr. Rhys thought we were husband and wife." I tossed the idea out to see what his response would be.

"Our relationship is a healthy one, don't you agree?" He leaned down to give me a tender kiss. "What Mr. Rhys thinks of our relationship is of no concern to us, now is it?"

It was clear he didn't wish to discuss his marriage with me. Instead, he'd led me to think that bachelorhood was his preference. And whatever his reason, perhaps it was. That suited me just fine, so long as I was the only one he was sleeping with.

"Is *Grace's* view of our relationship of any importance to you, Thomas?" I asked, needing to know what underlying bond they shared.

"Sara, you shouldn't fret over Grace. She and I have known each other a long time."

"Yes, it seems she makes that point clear every time she sees me. Perhaps she's jealous?"

The moonlight from beyond the window streamed in across the bedsheets. I curled in close to Thomas, feeling a sudden chill. His arm came around me, holding me to his chest.

"Grace? Jealous? I think you misjudge the woman. Grace is a free spirit. We've always had an understanding, she and I. I don't try to hold her down and she is free to come and go as she pleases. I think what you see is her natural protectiveness of me."

"Free as in she is able to sleep with whomever she pleases?" I asked, wanting to ask if he shared the same free-spirited ideals.

A long silence stretched out before he answered. "Is she sleeping with one of the brothers?" he asked.

His question in answer to mine caused me to lean back, searching his handsome face. I understood that there were likely some residual wounds left from his first marriage, in light of the fact he did not speak of his wife, yet he seemed even more defensive about Grace. "I have no idea, Thomas, who she might be sleeping with, nor do I care." I kissed the warm, firm plane of his chest, feeling his body come alive at my touch. "With the exception of you, of course." I smiled, leaving a trail of kisses down the midline of his torso. I suppose it was egotistical to think that could be all it took to awaken his passion. Still, I didn't want him to think about Grace, even as a friend.

A sound in the hall startled us both, neither of us being used to anyone else staying overnight in the two-story flat. He chuckled low and drew my face up to meet his.

"There's a favor I want to ask of you, Sara," he said, turning to his side to face me.

I tucked a shock of his hair over his ear and kissed him slowly. "What is it, my love?" It was a term of endearment, nothing more. We both knew it.

"I would like you to pose for Edward. I'm not working on anything at the moment."

I slid my hand down between us, encircling the warmth of his hardening shaft. "I wouldn't say that's entirely true, Master Rodin."

Thomas chuckled. "You are a wicked little muse."

He playfully smacked my bottom and I buried my face in his chest, joining his quiet laughter.

"Yes, you are," he whispered turning me to my back. "But I think you rather like it." He nudged my knees apart and, on one swift movement, entered me with a pleased sigh.

He rolled his hips, rocking gently until I arched against him in a silent plea.

"Wicked muse," he laughed quietly, withdrawing partway and lifting one of my legs over his shoulder. He pushed in again, emitting a groan that caused me to unravel beneath him.

An explosive climax overtook me and I shoved the sheeting against my mouth as he continued his insistent thrusts, prolonging my pleasure. He bent my knee, changing his angle, setting off another climax. This time he joined me, uttering a sensuous groan deep in his throat.

Lifting my calf, he kissed my ankle, gliding his hand over my heated flesh. I did not want to ask where he had acquired his lovemaking skills, but I was grateful for them just the same.

"I need my sleep now, you wanton woman." He let out a short laugh as he stretched out at my side, covering us both with the sheets. "Then it's settled?" Thomas yawned, jabbing at his pillow to fluff it.

"You mean sitting for Mr. Rhys?"

"Mmm-hmm, yes." His voice was drifting.

"If you want me to, Thomas, I will."

He reached for me, patting my hip.

"I cannot hold you forever, Sara, can I? You all leave me, you always do."

I turned on my side to face him, tucking my hand under my cheek as I watched him sleep. "I wouldn't leave, Thomas," I barely whispered, too afraid to admit to the words. "Not if you asked me to stay."

I awoke to the sun warming my face. I turned with a smile to wake Thomas and found the bed beside me empty. In his stead, a note lay on the pillow.

*I couldn't wake you; you look so beautiful when you sleep. Will be
out for the day most likely. Millais has called me to his house for a
meeting, something to do with the Spring Exhibition. Please see to
it that Edward finds a good place in the studio to set up his things.
Will see you later tonight,
Thomas*

It did not bother me to pose for Mr. Rhys, but what unnerved
me was Thomas leaving me to settle in our new guest. His silent
demeanor was difficult to read.

I drew on my dressing robe to go to the loo, not wishing to
run into Mr. Rhys in my altogether. I opened the door and the
lavatory door opened at the same time, revealing a fine-looking
sculpted torso and trousers that hung on lean hips. A towel
covered Mr. Rhys's face. "Good day to you, Mr. Rhys," I chirped,
setting aside the fact that I found myself staring at his body.

He dropped the towel and my eyes were immediately drawn
upward to his handsome, rugged face. He had shaved off the
beard, leaving behind a smooth, chiseled jaw. His dark golden hair
hung to his ample shoulders in enticing wet ringlets. He flashed
me a smile that had me reaching for the door frame.

"G'day, I am sorry if you had to wait. I thought I should try
to make myself a bit more presentable."

"Indeed," I said, staring blatantly at him, the sound of his
voice like an instrument.

"You have a lovely accent, Mr. Rhys." I hadn't moved from
my spot in the doorway.

He grinned shyly and looked down, raking his hand through
his hair. "I'm sorry. My brogue gets a bit thick, I'm afraid."

"Oh, no, it's…*lovely*. Interesting," I remarked, pulling my robe
closer around me. His shoulders were well toned, his skin bronzed
from being outdoors. I hurried inside the loo before he could see
the warmth staining my cheeks.

"Let me get dressed and I'll make us some tea," I said.

He nodded with a brief smile and headed to his room.

"Oh, I was wondering if you might have time to do a wee bit of posing for me, Mrs. Rodin."

"Yes, Thomas asked me to help you get your things set up in the studio. I'd be happy to pose if you'd like to get started."

"Wonderful, thank you, Mrs. Rodin."

I paused, trying to find the right words to convey that Thomas and I were not married. "Mr. Rhys, it is sufficient to call me Sara, since we are, after all, going to be working together."

"Very well, Sara," he said with a twinkle in his eye. "If you're sure that Thomas won't mind the familiarity."

"Mr. Rodin and I…well, we aren't…" I stammered, looking for the right words.

"Ah, I see, now," he said, "you're lovers, then?"

I stared at him, surprised by his bluntness. When I did not respond, he stopped and looked at me, his eyebrows lifted in question.

"I'm not sure that is any of your affair, Mr. Rhys."

A smile curled up the side of his face.

"I'll take that as a yes, then, Sara, and no, it probably isn't my affair…but it surely makes life interesting."

For the better part of the next month, I sat on a wood box, dressed in a long, sufferingly hot vestment of dark blue, a sheet draped over my head to resemble a wimple. My duty was to hold my hands up in prayerful pose, as if speaking to God. The days were long and tedious. Unlike Thomas, who often spoke aloud and paced when he worked, Mr. Rhys uttered few words and rarely strayed from his task.

To add to my concerns, Thomas seemed to be getting more and more involved in his own world, a world where he was researching venues of public attack on his critics, while also trying to come up with a project that would elevate his talent in the public eye. The adventure that I'd originally sought was confined to the four walls of this studio. Fortunately, Mr. Rhys was not difficult on the eyes, once he removed the shaggy beard, and although he spoke little, he did have an appetite for my cooking, which was more attention than I'd received from Thomas.

"This is amazin' stew, Sara." He held his bowl up for his third helping.

"My aunt taught me well, Mr. Rhys. I have a well-rounded education and hope to travel one day to broaden it."

He eyed me with a humorous glint in his eye.

"Do you find that an unreasonable goal?" I asked.

He shrugged. "Not if that's the life you want."

I shifted in my seat, his words unsettling me. "Would you mind explaining your thoughts?"

He glanced up, surprised that I would ask, apparently.

"No disrespect, Sara, but most women these days aspire to one thing only and that is to find a good husband—preferably a wealthy one with title—and settle down to the task of making babies."

"Well, perhaps I am not like the women you know, Mr. Rhys."

He slanted me a look. "That much is true, Sara, and would you please call me Edward? I'm a simple man and find that these silly English social niceties are a waste of time."

"We like to call it etiquette, Mr. Rhys...Edward." I ducked my eyes before he could pin me with a look, though I felt his gaze as much.

I must have hit a nerve for he did not respond then, nor did he speak to me until several days later when I was pining about the beautiful late fall afternoon, imagining taking a turn in the park, going to the gardens with Thomas, seeing a play. It had been ages, it seemed, since I'd had any social life at all.

"Mr. Rhys, do you think we might stop long enough to have tea? My back is aching frightfully." He looked at me, then the canvas, then toward the balcony doors, which we'd opened at my insistence. He heaved a great sigh.

"Very well, I can wait," I conceded not so graciously.

"No, that's fine. We'll break for a few moments."

He dropped his palette on the table next to him and, stuffing his hands in his pockets, strode across the room to stand in front of the fireplace.

The heavy robe weighted me down. I had to try twice before I could get to my feet. I stretched, lifting my face to the ceiling to work out the soreness in my neck.

"Wait, that's it…that's what I've been looking for…stay right there." He ran back to his easel and began to paint

I heard his brush gently slapping against the canvas.

"May I shut my eyes?"

"Yes, yes of course. Just hold still."

Concerns about where Thomas had run off to this morning swirled in my mind. I heard a carriage stop out front. "Wait, Mr. Rhys," I pleaded, excited that Thomas was home early. I lifted my skirts, ran to the balcony wall and peered over it to the street below, barely hearing Mr. Rhys's litany of curses following close behind. I beheld the sight below and felt as if someone had slapped me.

Thomas was climbing out of the carriage and seated, holding her hand out for him to kiss, was Grace. I took a step back, knowing neither of them had seen me. Was this how he was spending his time when he said he was with clients? Granted, we had an open relationship, but I always thought…at least I thought it was understood that we were exclusive to one another for the time being.

I shuffled back into the studio, confused.

"Do you think you can pose exactly as you were?" Mr. Rhys asked.

I yanked off the gown, not caring that all I wore beneath was my camisole and pantaloons. "That's all for me today, Mr. Rhys. I must lie down," I said, looking back over my shoulder. He stood there, palette in hand, staring blankly at me. "I do not wish to be disturbed."

Downstairs, I heard the front door slam as I eased my bedroom door shut and turned the key. I was in no mood to be in the presence of the brotherhood just now, especially not Thomas.

Sometime later, there was a soft tap on my door, a pause, and then another tap. I lay on my bed, cocooned in darkness.

I can't keep you forever, Sara.

His words came back to haunt me and hot tears fell down the sides of my face, soaking my pillow. *He never made any promises, you ninny.* I felt angry that I'd allowed myself to think there was more between us than heavenly sex. After all, hadn't I come to the studio seeking my independence? To build enough of a nest egg to be able to support myself? I had managed to set aside a good sum of money, one that would see me through until I could find gainful employment.

I wiped my face and blew my nose, sniffing as I turned on my side and began to weigh my options. There was the possibility I'd misjudged the situation. Perhaps Thomas had been walking home and Grace had passed by in the carriage, offering him a ride. It was possible.

Tomorrow, I would confront him with the circumstances and gauge his reaction. Then I would know what I needed to do.

Chapter 8

"HE LEFT YOU THIS." MR. RHYS HANDED ME THE
slip of paper. "He told me to make sure you received it first thing."

I held it in my hand, turning it over several times and finally
unfolded it. As I suspected, once again he had another meeting
that would likely last the whole day. He would see me as soon as
he could. In recent days, he'd taken to sleeping again in his own
room. I would hear him come in in the wee hours of the morning
and wait for him to come to me, but he hadn't for many weeks.
I stuffed the note in my pocket, catching Mr. Rhys's side glance.

"Can I get you a cup of tea?" he asked.

"Yes, that would be nice," I replied. My thoughts were
muddled by my restless night.

"Is everything all right?" He handed me a cup.

I took a sip of the strong brew and let it soothe my troubled
nerves. "I will be fine. Thomas is gone all day, another meeting."
I wasn't about to let it bother me as I had in the past.

"Here, I bought these down the street while on my morning
walk."

He passed me a plate of fresh-baked scones. I broke off a piece
of one and placed it in my mouth although I had no appetite. Its

buttery flakiness melted on my tongue, reminding me of Aunt Perdy's scones and the fact that I was not welcome there anymore. Still, I had the greatest urge to be back home—a once familiar place where people knew me, accepted and loved me. I thought of Deven and how he'd wanted me to stay. Twice, since Mr. Rhys's arrival, I'd seen my uncle's carriage sitting down the street. The second time, I'd run outside to try to speak to the driver, whom I strongly suspected to be Deven, but he either didn't hear me or refused to stop.

"Miss Sara?"

His voice jerked me out of my reverie. "I nearly forgot. This came for you yesterday after you'd taken ill."

I licked biscuit crumbs from my finger and gingerly took the envelope from his hand. "Excuse me," I said, walking to the far end of the great room to Thomas's writing desk. I sat down and flipped the note over, recognizing the red wax seal stamped with an *A*. It was from a writing kit I'd given to Amelia on her last birthday. I slid my thumb beneath the seal, muttering a silent prayer that everyone was well back home. I forced my mind to focus on the delicate handwriting, something that Amelia prided herself in, even though her penmanship was often difficult to read.

> *I hope this letter finds you happy and well, Sara. By now, I suspect you may have spoken to Mr. Mooreland—Deven, I suppose I shall have to get used to calling him. He insisted that he would deliver my note to you personally to see how you were getting on. I have missed you terribly as you might have guessed and, especially now, I wish more than ever you were here.*

I was puzzled as to how and when the letter was delivered. "Mr. Rhys, did you see the person who delivered this? Did he wish to speak with me?" I asked.

He looked at me with a puzzled expression. "Yes, Miss Sara. He did. However, you made it clear that you did not wish to be disturbed."

My mouth gaped, but I could not find any words. Deven had wanted to speak to me? Why would he insist? I glanced back down at the letter.

Oh, my dearest sister, I hope you will understand my reason for wanting to write you myself, despite what Deven may have already told you. It's just that I never anticipated, not in my wildest dreams, that this would happen to me.

I looked up, a cold dread beginning to form in my stomach. If this were about her family's health, she would have spoken of it by now. She was skirting the issue. My heart was convinced of it. I searched for where I'd left off.

…at Christmas. We both hope that you'll be able to come.

Both? Why would I suddenly be invited back for the holidays? I reread the paragraph and flipped over the letter, searching for the part I must have missed. I scanned through the page until my eyes settled on one word.

Married.

I blinked a number of times, apprising my brain of what I thought she was saying and started over, reading the entire paragraph once more—slowly.

Deven and I have discovered that among our mutual love of the country and Da's business, we share a special fondness for each other. I suspect that for me it is more of an infatuation, having long admired the man from afar, as you know. Those feelings, I hope, will deepen in time. I so look forward to filling a house with children. Right now, I still get butterflies when Deven looks at me. It is such a glorious feeling, Sara. I cannot imagine what our wedding night will be like. It frightens me and yet I am breathless with anticipation of it.

Deven and Da have formed a partnership in the livery business

*and Deven has promised to build us a cozy little cottage on the banks
of the pond at the edge of the wood. Do you remember how we used
to swim there in the summers?*

Fat tears fell on the page, splotching the ink, and I quickly
turned away and brushed my cheek, holding the paper upright,
swallowing the lump in my throat, determined to finish.

*We cannot afford both the house and a honeymoon, so that will
have to wait. But the exciting news is that I have spoken to Mum
and Da, and they have given me permission to invite you home for
the ceremony on Christmas and we both hope—*

I let the letter fall to the desktop and leaned my forehead
against the heel of my hand. Deven and Amelia getting married? The thought was surreal. I dropped my chin in my hand
and stared out at the gray autumn morning. I could not go back
now and without Thomas, I had no idea where my future
would lead.

"My apologies, Miss Sara—"

"It's Sara, Mr. Rhys. Just…Sara." I gritted my teeth to hold back
the dam of emotions that threatened to break loose at any
moment.

"Then I insist you call me Edward."

More tears stole from my eyes, trickling down my cheek, and
I offered a short laugh in response to the irony of my situation.
Perhaps, in truth, I had no reason to feel lost or rejected. Hadn't
I gotten exactly what I'd wished for? If so, why did my heart feel
as though it was breaking?

Edward stood on the other side of the desk looking down at
me.

"Is it bad news? If you'd rather not discuss it…" he said quietly.

I tossed the letter on the desk. "No, actually its wonderful news.
These are tears of joy."

Startled, I looked up and met his tranquil jade-colored gaze.

"Yes, Edward, of course. I'm sorry, it's just everything is…well, it's all a bit overwhelming at the moment."

"Family?" he asked,

I nodded. "My cousin, more like my sister, really. You see, my parents were killed when I was young and I moved in with my da's brother and his family. Amelia is three years younger than I am. We grew up together, went everywhere together. We had wicked, vivid imaginations—oh, my, the trouble we could muster." I smiled at the memory.

"I'm sorry about your parents. I am an orphan, as well, but spent my youth in an orphanage. It sounds like the two of you are very close." He tucked his hands in his trouser pockets and smiled.

I glanced up at him, finding it a bit odd that we were discussing our intimate lives. Edward was not known for his stimulating dialogue. "We are. I am very happy for her. She's marrying a wonderful man who will—" I paused to let the emotion pass "—adore her." Pain squeezed at my heart and I closed my eyes against it.

"He is a fool, you know."

I opened my eyes, puzzled by his statement. "I don't understand what you mean."

"Sara, I took the note from his hand. I saw his face. He was a fool to let you go so easily. A woman such as you is a rare find."

I shook my head. "You're wrong, it's not like that. He's no fool. On the contrary, he's marrying a woman who will make him a wonderful wife."

"I'm a man, Sara. I saw the look on his face when he asked for you."

"Don't…just don't." I held up my hand. "I no longer wish to discuss this."

He scratched his chin. "Fine, if that's what you want."

"It is. In fact, I've made a decision about something and need your help, if you are willing. Since I won't be attending the wedding, I'd like to send them a nice gift."

"Are you sure, Sara? I would be more than happy to accompany you to the ceremony, if you wish."

"Oh, no, Edward, I couldn't ask you to do that." I gazed at him with wide eyes, holding back my tears. I knew my reasons were shallow, that it was spineless of me not to attend, but although I was happy for both of them, it only made my situation all the more dire. I was pitiful and selfish, and it was easy for Edward to see through me, I was sure.

He waited a moment as if he understood. "Then how can I help?"

"I wish to send a monetary gift, to be used for their honeymoon."

Edward's eyes narrowed intently on me. "That's very generous of you, Sara."

I leaped to my feet, hoping that my generosity would somehow appease my own fears and sadness. Fear that I would grow old without someone to care for me as Deven had. I consoled myself that as a model there would be more work, if not with the brotherhood, then perhaps with other artists. I could build up my funds again and, in the meantime, plan my future travels. "Shall we get started, Edward?" I asked.

"You're sure you're feeling up to it?"

I rounded the edge of the table. "I'm fine, truly…at least, I will be. Let's not speak of this again, agreed?" I stuck my hand out, hoping we could shake on it, be done with it. Edward's grip was strong and my hand felt small in his. Then he did something I didn't expect—he kissed my hand.

I pulled it away. "I do not want nor need your pity," I warned.

"That's not what I meant…" he started.

"No, marriage is not meant for women like me. I want more. I need more. There are places I want to see, things I want to learn." Tears choked my throat. "How can I expect you to understand?"

"Sara, you don't need to explain yourself," he stated quietly.

I waved away my concern. "I just need some time to put it all in perspective. Just give me time, I'll be fine." Perhaps if I repeated the words enough I would truly believe them. "I'll be fine."

"Of course," he said, offering me a smile, but his expressive green eyes gave away his true thoughts on the matter.

Two weeks before the holidays, Edward sold his painting of the Madonna, for which I'd posed, to a private buyer that Woolner had arranged. Thomas was not happy, however, stating that he should have saved it for the Spring Exhibition where he would have gotten top dollar for it. All the same, the sale had given Edward validation for his work and a boost to his artistic self-esteem.

Frustrated that his protégé did not consult him and notably agitated with his inability to come up with his next project, Thomas announced that he was leaving London for the holidays and going on a trip with his friend, John Millais.

"It will be a grand time, Edward. You should come with us. View the old churches, carouse the streets of Rome. I hear they are filled with stunning women."

I stood on the balcony watching the first few flakes of snow beginning to fall on the city. Thomas thought I couldn't hear him since the doors were closed, but he was mistaken. I heard every word.

"I have another project I'd like to start, Thomas. One I have in mind for the exhibition," Edward said.

"Well, fine then, but don't say I didn't offer."

"What about Sara?" Edward asked. "I wager she'd love Rome."

"Sara, traveling in Rome with a group of men?" Thomas laughed. "No, not this time. Besides, if you're going to have another project by deadline, you two will be working night and day."

I was grateful that Edward had tried to persuade Thomas to take me with him. I hadn't yet had the opportunity to tell Thomas about Amelia's wedding, but it was apparent that he wouldn't have gone even if I'd decided to attend.

"Sara?" Thomas bellowed.

I wrapped my coat tight around me and hurried inside, my face chilled from the cold. "Yes, Thomas?" I said, pretending I hadn't heard their conversation.

"I'm off to Rome, my dear. I'll write of course, and I don't want you to worry. If you need anything, just put it on my tab at the store."

"May I ask who else is going?" I flung my coat across a chair.

Thomas glanced up as he continued to stuff a few books into a small bag. "Oh, Millais, Hunt…"

"Grace?" I looked away. I felt cheap, as if I'd been discarded for the next best thing.

He lifted my chin. "There are no women joining us, Sara, or I would have asked you first." He glanced over his shoulder at Edward. "As it is, it appears that you and the great artist have much to accomplish." He placed a kiss on my forehead. "I'm off, you two. Stay out of trouble. You're a lunatic, of course, for starting a project this late," he said to Edward. "Happy Christmas!" He tromped down the stairs and the front door slammed.

"Happy Christmas," I muttered.

I dug into the bottom of my dresser and found the stocking where I'd been hoarding my life savings. I carefully counted out half of the total and wrapped it in the brown paper that the art canvases came wrapped in. Spotting a fancy hair ribbon, I tied it around the packet and wrote a quick note to Amelia. Edward hired a carriage and took it himself to the farm. He told me later that he'd left it with a delightful woman with sparkling brown eyes.

I was pleased by his description. "She was happy, then? You stayed with her while she opened it?" I asked.

He cocked his eyebrows in question. "Those were your instructions, were they not?"

"Yes, thank you." He grinned openly and I felt a small flip in my stomach.

"Over-the-moon would be a better way to describe her reaction, Sara."

I sighed. "Good, I'm glad."

"She asked me to thank you." He leaned down and kissed my cheek.

I gave him a dubious look. "She told you to kiss my cheek?"

He stared at me a moment, stuffed his hands in his trouser pockets and strode to his easel setting to the task of mounting a new canvas.

"I've got a new project in mind."

There were times when I sensed there was much more to Edward Rhys than he let on. Perhaps I was simply fearful of getting too close to him, afraid of what I might find. He exuded an odd blend of masculinity and compassion, which I found intriguing. As he worked at mixing his paints, I sauntered to the corner where the props were stored. The brotherhood—Thomas in particular—took pride in their ability to bring a theatrical element to their work. Thomas had managed to acquire many interesting items while speaking to stage players over a drink, after a show.

"Is it mythological?" I looked over my shoulder and held up a gold urn, twice the size of a good melon.

He shook his head.

"Someone from the holy book, then? Rebecca, perhaps? Her story is a good one."

"Could you face me, Sara?"

The insistence in his voice surprised me. I turned around. "You needn't get nasty, Edward."

His hand worked feverishly over the canvas and he swore under his breath every time a piece of his charcoal snapped off. This was his elusive side—serious, focused and obsessed. He was admittedly a handsome man, even with the scowl he had on his face at this moment. The thought caused gooseflesh to rise on my arms. We'd been cooped up too long in this studio. Part of my problem was that I was still angry with Thomas for going to Rome without me, and my only consolation was that Grace hadn't gone with them.

"Edward, I think you and I should treat ourselves to a night out. Perhaps go to the theater. It is almost Christmas and we have not been out in weeks. We could go down to McGivney's and see who's there."

He attacked his work with greater intensity. I waited patiently for his response, folding my hands in front of me. "Did you hear me?"

"Yes," he replied, not looking up. "They're all in Rome."

"Maybe Grace will be there."

"I have a deadline, Sara. Please be patient."

The reprimand, however gentle, took me aback. "Fine. Do I need to stand?" I huffed.

"No, you can sit." He peered over the edge of the canvas. "I didn't think you liked Grace."

I had pulled over a chair and started to sit, when Edward pointed to the couch. "I would prefer you sit over there."

The memories of Thomas and that couch were too painful to dismiss. "I would rather not," I said.

He peered over the edge of the canvas, his eyes steady on me.

"I'll just sit here. It would be helpful if I had *some* idea of what your project involved."

"Dammit to hell," he muttered, clamping his hand over the edge of the canvas. "You," he stated with a final bluntness.

"Yes, I know, and I'll do my best, Edward. Just tell me what you want." I was growing exasperated with his elusiveness.

"I…" He sighed and raked his hands through his wavy hair.

"Edward, calm down. Let's just start at the beginning. What is your concept? What is it you wish to convey?" I folded my hands in my lap.

"Sex," he bellowed.

"I see," I stated quietly, and reached for the buttons on the front of my dress.

"No." He tapped the top of the frame and looked out the French doors.

I waited for him to make up his mind. "Do you wish me to undress, Edward?"

"Yes."

I undid a few more buttons.

"No."

I stopped.

"I can't do this, Sara. I can't paint you. I feel like I'm losing my mind."

I was inclined, at the moment, to agree. Then again, I'd just given away over half my savings and where would that leave me if I quit now? I'd be without an income and with no prospects of one in sight over a very long and cold winter. I searched how best to encourage him. "It's only temporary, Edward. All artists have their moments."

"Dammit, this isn't going to go away so easily, Sara."

He grabbed the canvas and flung it across the room. I watched in surprise as it flew across the room, sailing over the writing desk and sending a crystal vase shattering to the floor. He paced back and forth, like a tiger I'd once seen at the zoo. I'd never seen him behave so violently. My heart pounded as I cautiously walked over and began to pick up the shards of glass.

"I'm sorry, Sara," he said. "I don't mean to frighten you."

I found my tongue. "Well, I'm afraid you're not going about it very well, Edward," I said. "Maybe you could find me a dustpan?" He stalked to the kitchen and returned with one.

I started to sweep up the mess. "You're a fine artist, Edward. I'm sure we can find you another model, better suited—"

"Where did you get that idea?"

I continued to sweep up the glass, dumping it in the wastebasket.

"You said you didn't want me," I tossed back.

"As…my…model," he enunciated each word.

"Yes, I understand. I think I should go see if I can find something for us to eat, perhaps that would help." I'd only taken two steps before he caught my arm and backed me up against the desk.

"What are you doing?" He held my wrist, his stormy eyes piercing.

"I know you miss Thomas," he said.

I grappled with the truth. "No, not that much, really." I swallowed, my skin feeling flushed.

His gaze fell to my mouth "You're certain of that?"

I licked my lips. "Why do you ask?"

"Because I am going to kiss you, Sara. It's been eating me alive."

"How do you know *I* want *you* to kiss me?" I swallowed.

The corner of his tempting mouth curled into a half smile. "I don't, lass. But I'm willing to find out."

I curled my fingers on the edge of the desk in anticipation.

"Sara, I am no good with flowery words. I had to be sure you were over Thomas, that nothing would come between us. I wouldn't want to hurt either of you."

His meaning now became clear. Good Lord, was I over Thomas? I looked into Edward's eyes, thrilled by the hunger I saw, knowing it was for me. "What exactly are you trying to say?" I searched his face, needing to understand whether he imagined a quick affair or something else. Though in my present state, an affair would have sufficed.

"I'm trying to say that I don't want you as my model anymore. I want *you* and quite desperately, but I won't come between you and Thomas."

His hand cupped my cheek and his fingers slid around my neck, drawing me to his mouth. "I have been in love with you for weeks—painting you, watching you day after day. I've rejoiced when you smiled and ached inside from your pain. You are a good woman, Sara—kind and generous. Is it any wonder that I would fall in love with you?" His thumb softly brushed the underside of my jaw.

His mouth followed the path of his thumb, causing my blood to course through my veins as he nibbled the sensitive spot beneath my ear.

"You can tell me to stop, Sara," he whispered, heating my flesh.

He traced the low collar of my gown, his fingers skimming the swells of my breasts. My eyes drifted shut and I tipped my head to allow his tender exploration, my pulse pounding furiously.

His hands covered mine as he leaned forward to meld his mouth to mine in a slow and thorough kiss that caused my head to spin.

"God in heaven, don't ask me to stop," he said quietly. "This gown has got to go, Sara, I've got to have my hands on you."

I lifted my arms and he drew the dress over my head. His eyes glittered with wicked hunger, seeing that I wore only my chemise beneath. He captured my mouth in a searing kiss, pressing against me to preview what I could have if I so desired.

"I mean to take you, Sara. Unless you have no desire for me." He lowered his head and latched his mouth over my right breast, sucking hard and sending a current of pleasure to my center. I couldn't believe this was Edward. He reached around me, shoving away everything on the desk, sending it flying in all directions as he hoisted me to the table. He eased me onto my back, gliding his large hand down my body, and lifted the hem of my chemise as he nudged apart my legs. The smooth wood was cool against the pads of my bare feet, braced on the edge of the table.

His breath played against my inner thigh as he parted my quim with his gentle fingers. A lusty sigh escaped my mouth and I lifted my hips to meet the insistence of his velvet tongue doing wicked things to my drenched clit. It had been so long since I'd felt these decadent sensations.

My hands roamed over my body, delighting at the luxurious pleasure. Between the delicious stroke of his finger and his ardent tongue, my body was driven to a frantic need. I heard the sound of my own cry as my body broke free. Edward yanked me upright, kissing me hard and rolled me to my stomach against the table.

"My turn," he whispered, bending down to tease my ear with his tongue. He brushed my gown high over my hips and pushed into my slick heat with a guttural sigh. My breath caught as he began his slow and steady thrusts.

The hard tabletop caressed my breasts with each lunge, causing my body to grow tight. My reason grew dim as I surrendered to the euphoric bliss. He stopped suddenly, filling me to the hilt as he placed tender kisses at my neck.

His tenderness, combined with the fierce thrusts that followed brought my body to a dizzying need. "P-please, Edward."

"That's what I wanted to hear, Sara."

His large hands were warm. I leaned my cheek against the desk, relinquishing my body to the pleasure building inside me. The low-timbre sounds he made heightened my arousal. His magnificent cock made me want to forget about Thomas and how he'd hurt me by not asking me to Rome. If I'd gone with him, I may have never experienced this. In a blinding moment, a strangled gasp tore from my throat and I felt my muscles clench around him. With a deep growl, he finished in a wild driving force, his fingertips digging into my flesh as his body jerked against me, emptying his hot seed.

He pulled me into his warm embrace, softly whispering words in a language I didn't understand. His hands rubbed my back, gently caressing as I listened to the steady thrum of his heart against my cheek. There was a sense of security, something I was not sure I'd ever felt with Thomas and would never have expected with Edward.

"Marry me, Sara," he said quietly. "I'll see to it that we go all the places you've always wanted to go."

I molded my body to his, holding him tight, wanting to believe him, wanting to believe that it was possible to have a man to care for me and encourage my dreams, as well.

"I don't want to wait, Sara. There's a little chapel just over the border in my country. We can be married right away."

"I don't know what to say, Edward." I leaned back in his arms and searched his face. Had I suddenly found the man who was everything I needed? It would be a surprise to many if I accepted his offer, especially to Thomas—and I realized I did love Edward in many ways. Companionship, trust and loyalty were as good as any building blocks to any happy marriage, weren't they?

"How far away is the chapel?" I asked, feeling reckless.

He grinned with a confident, sensuous smile that promised a lifetime of carnal delights.

"We can leave tonight and be there by morning." He picked me up and kissed me again. "Do you wish to wait until you've had a chance to speak to Thomas?" he asked, searching my eyes.

"I think he will be pleased for us, Edward. I shan't worry about him, nor should you. The decision is mine." I wrapped my arms around his neck and kissed him lightly, the kiss quickly turning heated.

"Sara, you've made me a very happy man," Edward said against my lips between kisses.

I smiled and hugged his neck. "Do you mean to take me again, Mr. Rhys?"

He offered a roguish grin as he stepped free of his trousers and scooped me into his arms. "Aye, lass, and this time in my bed."

I curled into his chest, hoping this feeling would never end.

Chapter 9

EDWARD BUILT ME A HOUSE. A COZY COTTAGE filled with plenty of light for his studio, out in the country, so I could have my own garden. He told me that Thomas had given him the land and the old farmhouse, and that it was to be used for the brotherhood. However, the way things were going within the brotherhood, Thomas had decided it would never be used for a studio. So he gave it to Edward, telling him to consider it a wedding gift and maybe allow him to come take walks in the woods out back from time to time.

Edward was determined to make us a beautiful home, but it was costing more than we had, and soon worries over finances began to take their toll on our marriage.

My husband was a proud man and his concerns over how to complete his vision for the house and take me on the travels he'd promised caused his creativity to suffer, rendering him unable to paint, unable to regain his passion. Eventually his despondency affected our intimate life.

Our lovemaking turned stilted, less spontaneous. It made me feel less attractive. I tried everything to encourage him. "It's only temporary, Edward. You'll get your spark back soon enough."

"How do you know, Sara?" he asked me one night. "Maybe I'll never get that spark back. I don't know where things have gone wrong."

"You have me." I smiled, curling my hand over his naked thigh.

He brushed my hand away. "Do not mock me, Sara, this is serious. If I cannot paint soon we may lose everything. There'll be no money left. Then what kind of husband would I be?"

"It will be all right, Edward." I snuggled close to his back, but lay awake wondering if I should try to find employment. I could not speak to Edward about such things. It would wound his pride. Despite my efforts, he grew more distant each day.

One morning as we ate breakfast in the sunroom, he announced that he'd been invited to go to India with a few members of the brotherhood.

"Well, I suppose that would be fun. Perhaps we should try to have someone stay here while we're away," I said, silently wondering where we would find the funds to pay for such an exotic venture.

"It's just me going, Sara. They agreed to pay my way as long as I agree to pay them back after my next sale."

"Oh, I see."

He continued. "I think this is what I need. It will help me to be amongst other artists right now. I am hopeful I will gain back my creativity, my perspective."

"Of course. And what shall I do while you're off searching for your perspective?" I asked, staring at the garden.

"I have thought of that." He gently put his teacup down.

"I'm listening." I kept my eyes on the garden.

"Look at me, Sara," he said quietly.

I looked at him, seeing a man that stress had aged.

"I don't like the idea of you out here alone while I'm away." He hesitated as if choosing his words carefully. "I've heard from some of the brothers that Thomas is despondent. Grace says that—"

"You've seen Grace?" I asked, wondering when…or, God forbid, how long he'd been seeing her. "Edward, I don't understand any of this—"

"I went to see Thomas at the studio, to see how he was faring in view of the backlash from the critics. Grace happened to be there, cleaning. She's been cooking for him. He doesn't look good, Sara."

"Thomas will find a way," I said. "There are few obstacles that stop him when he wants something badly enough."

Edward stared at me briefly before he continued. "I invited Thomas to come stay here while I'm away. It would provide you with companionship and, maybe out here, he could get the rest he needs, go for his walks—maybe he could get *his* inspiration back."

"Why doesn't he just go to India with you?" I asked, finding this whole conversation strangely surreal.

"The newer members don't want him along this time. They say he's gotten too rebellious, even for the brotherhood." Edward buttered his toast. "I owe him a great deal, Sara. I don't have much, but I can offer him clean air and sunshine. You know how he loves to stomp about in the woods."

I stared at him. "So, you've already invited him?"

He smiled and took my hand.

"I've not been a very good husband to you, Sara. I realize this. But it doesn't mean that I wouldn't do whatever it takes to make you happy."

"What are you saying, Edward? That I would be happier with Thomas?"

He shook his head, brushing his thumb back and forth across my knuckles.

"No, my love. But I know that you were happy when you were posing for him. Perhaps he can offer you right now what I can't."

"Can't, Edward? Or won't?" I stood and pulled my hand away.

His eyes remained on his plate. "You cannot give, Sara, what you do not have. That is what I am hoping to recapture." He touched his napkin to his mouth. "It's settled. Thomas will be here tomorrow. Now I must go and get my things packed."

The next morning, I stood in the foyer as Edward arranged his bags and waited for the carriage that the brotherhood had sent to fetch him.

"Are you certain about this?" I asked. "You could stay. We could take walks, maybe go to town and take in the theater. You'd find your inspiration, surely."

He offered me a smile but his eyes were filled with sadness. "I'll miss you very much, Sara. However, I think it's best for both of us. Something is off-kilter, and I suspect it is me, and not you. You are as curious and insatiable as ever. I'm not entirely sure I have given as much in this marriage as you have given to me."

I hugged his neck as the carriage came up the lane. "Don't say that, Edward. I love you, I do."

He eased me away from him, opened the door and bent to pick up his bags, only to set them down again.

On the other side of the door stood Thomas. I barely recognized him. His face was gaunt, and dark shadows rimmed his eyes. Nevertheless, he offered us a weary grin. "Splendid, I was afraid I'd miss saying goodbye." The two men embraced. We'd not seen Thomas since we settled the deed on the property just after his return from Rome.

"Thomas, my old friend," Edward said, reaching out to him. "I'm glad you came. You'll be a good man and watch out for Sara while I'm away?" He picked up his bags and carried them to the waiting coach. "Get a lot of painting done. The exhibition looms, as you know."

Thomas raised his hand briefly. "You have a wonderful time and don't worry about Sara."

I ran to the coach and held my husband's hand. "Edward, are you sure?" I pleaded once more.

"Take care, Sara. I'll be home before you know it."

I watched his smile, the one I'd come to cherish, disappear as the carriage took him away.

"So," Thomas said, coming to stand beside me.

"So," I replied, staring after Edward's coach. A pointed and uncomfortable silence followed. I had not been keen on the idea of inviting Thomas to the house for reasons I was too uncomfortable to face. "Tell me what have you been working on?" I smiled brightly. I realized the absurdity of my query. Was he not invited here to rekindle his passion for painting? I cleared my throat. "Forgive me, Thomas, I have not spoken to you in some time."

He studied the ground. "I haven't spoken to anyone in the brotherhood these past few months. Watts and Woolner are busy with their work. Grace tolerates me as much as possible, helping me with cooking and cleaning, but I'm not good company of late. In fact, before I came here we had yet another squabble, damn if I can remember now what it was about."

I smiled. Despite his appearance, his voice was calm, self-assured as always. "Of course, Thomas. We'll get you back to your old self again, and maybe it will inspire you to paint."

I glanced at the speck on the horizon that was my husband. I knew how Thomas could be when he painted and I was keenly aware of my vulnerability just now. Edward's loyalty to Thomas was a bond that reached perhaps beyond our marriage.

"Are you well, Sara?" Thomas's hand lightly touched my shoulder, startling me. He pulled it away and my eyes snapped to his.

"You seemed so far away just now."

"I miss my husband." *I miss the sex between us.* I reprimanded myself silently and started inside. He followed me into the house.

Thomas stood in the foyer of the cottage, his brown curls cropped shorter than I remembered. His face was unshaven and he appeared a bit older, a bit thinner, but at that moment, with how I felt inside, he looked wonderful.

"Do you prefer Mrs. Rhys or Sara?" he asked, shifting his bags to his other hand.

I searched his eyes, looking for some semblance of the passion I'd once seen in them, but they held no gleam of wickedness, of vivid imagination. It was as if his fire had been snuffed out.

"Call me Sara, as you always have, Thomas. Now, Edward mentioned the exhibition. Is that what I'll be sitting for?"

He offered a mediocre laugh. "You don't really expect me to answer that now, do you? I've only just arrived and I want to hear how married life is treating the two of you. Imagine my shock at returning from Rome to find you already married!"

I smiled. "Very well, Thomas. I'll have Bertie bring us tea in the library. In the meantime, you can take your bags to your room. It's up those stairs, the second door to the right."

He regarded me for a moment. "You are still as beautiful as the day I met you."

I clasped my hands tightly and smiled, choosing not to respond to his comment. "I'll see you in the library."

I sat as far from him as space in the library would allow, trying not to think of the fact that we were alone in this house for the next few weeks. Thomas took his cup and leaned against the windowsill.

"How is Grace? You mentioned a disagreement." It was a mindless conversation. I sipped my tea and stared out the window, reminiscing about the rainy afternoons when Thomas and I would break for tea. Then he would sit beside, nudging and teasing me until tea turned into a passionate tryst. "It eases my tension," Thomas would say, "and I daresay it puts color in your face, Miss Sara." He would laugh and then paint like a mad man.

"I'm afraid Grace acts rather overprotective of me at times. Probably because we've known each other for so long." He shrugged. "She'll be angry with me for a while, but eventually she'll forgive me."

"I hope the tension with her hasn't affected your creativity."

"No, it's not Grace. I haven't painted in weeks." He glanced outside.

"What do you suppose the problem is?" I asked. As I watched him leaning against the windowsill, my marriage vows warred with my loneliness. God help me, I could still remember the first time that Thomas touched me...

His eyes met mine. Here was a man who made his living putting souls on canvas for all to see. I pondered not being able to use the gift God gave you, the torment he must feel.

"I suppose I'm getting older. I cannot lie though, Sara, the critics hound me incessantly. They seem to revel in slamming everything that I do. It has become exhausting. I fear I am losing the fight."

It hurt me to see his confidence reduced to average. He'd once been so passionate about his calling, ready to set the world on its heels. Thomas Rodin was anything but average.

"You've always had critics, Thomas. They've not bothered you as much before." I stood and filled his teacup. He touched my arm.

"Come sit here beside me, Sara. I have missed these conversations between us. You always helped me put things into perspective. We are still friends, aren't we? That hasn't changed because of your marriage." He patted the cushion.

I was reticent but conceded. Holding my teacup primly in front of me, I perched on the edge of the seat. He still smelled of sandalwood and soap, which I found comforting. "Yes, we are friends, Thomas." I smiled at him and went back to my tea.

He quietly cleared his throat as if about to approach a sensitive subject, or perhaps my nerves were simply on end. "You and Edward seem quite content." He looked around the room. "You have a lovely home."

"Thank you, Thomas. It wouldn't be possible without you."

"It sounds like it wouldn't be possible without your husband's backbreaking work." He smiled.

"True, I am a very lucky woman."

"I'm sorry I wasn't able to help with the design. I've been struggling with my creativity, battling with the critics as always."

"Edward got on well on his own." I prattled on telling him that my husband had graciously sacrificed a full month of painting to finish the cottage so we could move in. "Then he focused on the details inside and, unfortunately, he became absorbed with that instead of balancing his painting with the construction. I hope that this trip will rejuvenate his creativity."

"Always the perfectionist, that Edward," Thomas commented. "Careful eye to detail…at least in most things," he added, glancing at me over the rim of his cup.

Edward's attention to detail was something I'd long admired about him, but today Thomas's comment made it sound more personal. My cup rattled as I set it on the plate. I didn't realize how my hand trembled, nor did I understand why I felt the need to defend Edward, especially to Thomas.

"So you are happy, then?" he asked, walking to the window once more.

"Yes, Thomas, we are."

He glanced over his shoulder. "No, I asked if *you* were happy, Sara."

I stared at him, knowing to lie was pointless. By now, Thomas had to understand how strange it all looked. "My husband has just left for a four-week trip to a foreign country."

"And he didn't ask you to join him, did he?"

The direction of his questioning left me feeling unsettled. "I'd rather talk about your painting, Thomas. Did you bring your supplies? Your easel?"

I stood, carefully placing my cup on the tray. Thomas set his next to mine. I sensed Thomas standing close and images of the carnal passion we once shared, before Edward, before my marriage vows, flashed in my mind. Did Edward truly love me, or was I just a prize to be won from Thomas?

"I am certain he was thinking only of your welfare, Sara. Now if you'll show me where it is, I can set up my studio. I find myself anxious to baptize this house with the scent of linseed and turpentine."

"Of course. Edward felt the sunroom would suit you best. He said it should offer you plenty of light." I walked ahead of him, waiting as he gathered his belongings. "Edward said, 'You know how Thomas is about his light.'" My focus fell to his broad shoulders and lean hips as he stooped to pick up his bags.

His eyes met mine and as if he knew where my focus had been, he offered a slight smile. "In here." I hurried on ahead, making my way in haste through the parlor and the dining room to an archway at the other end of the house. Three of the walls were windows and beyond was my precious garden, where I spent much of my time. "The ceiling, I'm afraid, is lower than what you are used to, but I think you'll find the room suitable for your needs."

He hadn't spoken. I turned around to face him. "Will this do, Thomas?" He stared at me, his eyes glittering... *Were those tears?* I couldn't think of a time when I'd ever seen him weep.

"Thomas?" I took a step and forced myself to stop. "What is it?"

His eyes drifted shut and he breathed deeply, as though absorbing his surroundings. "I am eternally grateful to the both of you. I have no idea how I shall ever repay you."

I tried not to let shock register on my face. This was a different Thomas Rodin—vulnerable, exposed. He was not the brash and reckless man with an effervescent charm I was used to. "Thomas, it is Edward and I who should be thanking you for your generosity. Whatever we can do to help, we're here for you." I wrapped my arms around him and he laid his head on my shoulder like a child and quietly sobbed.

After a time, he whispered against my neck, "Thank you." A kiss followed on my cheek as he brought his hands to my face. He placed another kiss on my forehead.

"You have no need to fear me, Sara. I am here only to reclaim my joy in painting and to care for you in the absence of my dear friend."

I nodded, keeping my eyes downcast, not trusting myself to look at him, to get any closer to that mouth.

"Thomas—"

He lifted my chin, his eyes searching mine.

"You do believe me, don't you? I would do nothing to jeopardize your marriage."

My gaze dropped to his lips, the same that I had kissed many times before. How would I be able to resist him under the same roof? I knew it was wrong to dwell on it, but my own husband had planted the seeds in my head. I stepped away, straightening my hair. "I must see to dinner, Thomas. Please make yourself at home." I hurried off before the simple act of friendship turned into something more.

Chapter 10

THREE-AND-A-HALF WEEKS. I WAS BEGINNING TO feel skittish, worried that I'd not yet heard back from my husband and tempted more and more by the way Thomas looked at me when he didn't think that I noticed. His appearance was improving each day and the fire that had once burned in his eyes had reappeared. My traitorous memory could not forget the passion of his touch, his avid attention to all things carnal, the way he once made me feel alive.

I had purposely avoided his presence as much as possible, keeping occupied with sewing and reading—relieved that Thomas had not yet required me to sit for him.

"Any word from Edward?" Thomas came into the library, his hair damp and tousled from his morning bath. He wore a shirt loose over his trousers, and his feet were bare.

"Not yet. You don't think anything has happened, do you?" I glanced at him as I walked to the window. I wrung my hands, trying not to imagine why I hadn't heard from Edward. Was he thinking of me as much? Did he miss me? Thomas seemed to sense my concern.

"It's not easy to get mail out in some of those remote areas," Thomas offered. "Try not to worry."

I shook my head. "I am certain he is capable of taking care of himself, Thomas. It's just that—"

"Just that what, Sara?"

I saw his reflection in the windowpane as he moved to my side. "I shouldn't burden you with my troubles."

"Posh, Sara. I am the burden here, if anyone."

He placed his hands on my shoulders and I leaned my cheek against his hand. "I confess, I am glad you're here, Thomas."

"What can I do, Sara?" He spoke quietly, his thumbs brushing along the nape of my neck. The fresh scent of his soap wrapped around me, offering me an odd sense of familiar comfort.

I closed my eyes, allowing my shoulders to relax, unaware until now how tense I'd become. Thomas had always had a knack for being able to calm my nerves. "Edward and I…" I was hesitant whether to share my intimate problems with Thomas. Then again, who else knew us as well? "In truth, we did not part on good terms."

"It will be well, you'll see. Absence is a wonderful aphrodisiac." He traced the slope of my neck. "Women are perfect creatures of passion. There is no need to lie to yourself about that, nor try to keep it from me. Edward is a good man, but when he asked me to come here, I sensed that he was carrying a weight on his shoulders that, frankly, only he would be able to resolve. Unfortunately, in his quest to face his demons, he has ignored your needs, hasn't he?"

I felt the tension slide from me as he massaged my shoulders. I could not deny what he said. My efforts in trying to infuse passion into our bed had been met with apathy and frustration, causing greater anxiety in me. I had tasted Edward's passion and to have it denied without benefit of understanding left me feeling hopeless, yet at the same time wanting. Whether it was wise or not, Thomas's companionship had filled that void and for whatever reason, I felt my husband knew that when he asked him to stay on at the cottage. Did I dare call his bluff and embark on finding out if I was still capable of passion?

"You have a way about you, Thomas. I wonder if you realize what you do to women."

He chuckled low, wrapped his arms around my waist and tucked his face next to mine.

"And here I thought I'd lost my charm."

My hand found the smooth, muscular hip beneath his trousers. I remembered the sinewy strength of his legs and the prize that I'd once been privy to thrust proudly between his legs.

I mentally told myself to stop, that no matter what problems Edward and I were having, this wouldn't solve them.

"Perhaps Thomas can give you what I cannot right now, Sara."

Edward's words came floating back to me in gentle approval. Perhaps he was right.

"Oh, Thomas, you're still a rogue—" I smiled "—but that is what I've always liked about you."

"I can give you passion, Sara, if that is what you desire." His breath whispered hot against my temple.

I felt his hands circle my waist, resting scant inches below my breasts. He nuzzled his face in the warm curve of my neck. It was a simple breach of fidelity, a mindless moment shared between two former lovers—if I were to stop it now. But the delicious sensation was far too enticing. I was aware of my buttons coming undone, my blouse dropping to the floor, a chill rushing over my exposed flesh.

"You are so exquisite, Sara. How am I expected to keep my hands off you?"

Thomas cupped my breasts in his hands, easing the white swells upward until my pink nipples peeked over the ribboned edging of my corset. He slid his hand down my throat, dipping inside my corset, pinching and rolling my tender nubs until I ached to have the damn obstruction off me.

I stood the torment for as long as I could and turned toward him, drawing his face to mine in a furious kiss. His fingers worked at the strings of my corset, a chuckle slipping from his mouth as the knots gave way. He spread the lacings, removing the corset and freeing my breasts. Between kisses, he drew off my blouse and camisole, tossing them aside, his hands quick to return, pushing up my breasts, taking of his carnal feast.

My palms squeaked against the windowpane as Thomas suckled and taunted each breast. His quiet moans mixed with the heady pleasure consuming me. It had been so long since I'd felt anything like this, since I'd wanted this.

The juncture of my thighs grew soft and moist. "Thomas," I sighed. He knew so well how to mold me, to touch me in a way that made it impossible to stop.

"God, Sara, I want to be buried inside you. Do you remember how fine we were together?"

I nodded, biting my lip as I fought the guilt that tried to creep into my thoughts.

"I want to fuck you, Sara. Slow and easy, like it used to be, but you have to want it as much," he whispered against my cheek.

"Thomas," I said softly, brushing my hand over his hair. "It has been so long."

He slipped off my drawers and pressed my back to the window, his face inches from mine as his hand slid over my damp curls and between my legs. A glorious moan of pleasure escaped my throat.

"That's it, my muse," he breathed out on a sigh as he pressed his palm over my breast.

"I cannot." I swallowed, shaking my head gently. "What about Edward?"

Thomas took my hand and led me to the settee.

"Come here, Sara. Sit." He motioned to his lap and I sat facing away from him. Through the confines of his trousers, his erection pushed unashamedly against my bare bottom.

"If Edward was here, he would find you as irresistible as I do. He'd want to see you happy, just as I do," he whispered, kissing the back of my neck. He spread his knees, so, too, moving mine apart, his hands sensuously rubbing my inner thighs.

"Relax, Sara. I will see to your pleasure. I will make you come as I suspect you have not in too long. You are much too beautiful, too deserving, to go without passion."

I succumbed to the magic of his stroke, lying back and closing my eyes, placing his hand over my breast, lost in the utter delight of my body awakening as if after a very long sleep. *"If only—"* the misty words repeated in my mind *"—if only Edward would love me like this."*

"Sara." I knew his scent before his mouth covered mine, not allowing me to speak. Through my hooded lids I saw my husband kissing me, his tongue splendidly mating with mine. They were *his* callused fingers caressing my breasts, his mouth drawing my tips gently between his teeth. All the while, Thomas continued to stroke me, captivating my mind in a euphoric bliss.

"Thomas…" My words were cut off by another sensuous kiss. Was I dreaming? Had Edward really come back early? Was it because he missed me?

"You are so lovely," Edward whispered between intermittent kisses. "I just want to see you happy, Sara. I'll do anything for you." His mouth captured mine, erasing all my thoughts, all my fears. In my joy, I threaded my fingers through my husband's hair, verifying it was him. His lips moved over my body, drawing my hips forward, nibbling on the tender juncture of my thighs.

A sigh tore from my throat and pure heat coursed like a slow-burning fire through my veins, my hips responding gently with the delight of his tongue.

"There, my muse, your pleasure is all we want," Thomas whispered in my ear.

Thomas's hands, warm and caressing, slid over my breasts. I pressed into them, engulfed in sensual, ravenous need, taking my fill of what they offered. It was decadent and so unlike my before-now staid husband to partake in such a venture. I lifted my arms over my head and allowed their exquisite worship of my body. I didn't think about whether it was right or wrong, or what would happen after.

My breath caught each time Edward's tongue teased my clit.

My body coiled tighter and I heard my sighs echo in the silent room. The warmth of the afternoon sun shone through the windows, illuminating the dark sheen of Edward's hair against my pale flesh.

I came in a powerful rush, crying out my husband's name, "Oh, Edward, sweet Edward." He rose, capturing my mouth, my juices mingling with his fiery kiss, drawing out the rolling waves of my shuddering climax until I was utterly spent. My body collapsed against Edward's shoulder and he held me close, stroking my hair.

I opened my eyes, the sensual haze dissipating now and the reality of what had happened taking shape in my mind. "I love you," I whispered against the curve of Edward's shoulder.

He gently eased me back and searched my face, swallowing hard, as if he, too, was realizing what had just happened.

"I—I need to think, Sara…if I am what's best for you."

I grabbed his hand as he turned to leave. "Of course, you are, Edward."

He glanced over my shoulder at Thomas and drew my hand to his lips for a soft kiss.

I jumped from my lover's lap and ran to the window, watching as my husband climbed into the carriage he hadn't released yet.

I turned to meet Thomas's unflappable gaze.

"You love him," he stated, closing his eyes. A smile lifted the corner of his mouth. "He loves you, Sara. He just needs to sort things out." He rose and handed me my dress. "If you'll excuse me, I think I will go pack my things. For once, I'm not going to think about what's best for me."

He leaned forward and kissed the back of my head.

"Be happy, Mrs. Rhys."

It was late. I'd chosen not to eat supper; I had no appetite. Instead, I'd taken a long soak in the tub and lain down, hoping to find the answers that would not come to me. Now I sat at my vanity in my robe, brushing my hair as was part of my nightly routine. The soft glow of the kerosene lamp cast odd shadows on the wall, amplifying the loneliness I felt inside. Would Edward return? God, I prayed that he would. We had so much to talk about, so much of our marriage yet to be lived, and with the same passion he'd shown this afternoon, if he so desired.

Even now my body tingled at the heat in his eyes as he knelt before me, his hands holding my thighs, preventing me from escaping. It had been, without a doubt, a profound experience to have the freedom of such undivided attention and yet, it was knowing that Edward was aroused by me, that he was willing to do whatever it took to please me, that brought me over the edge.

The sound of the door opening caused me to look up. Edward's eyes met mine in the reflection of the mirror. I held my brush suspended in midair as I waited for him to speak.

"I've missed you in a most desperate way," he whispered, drawing the brush from my hand and dropping it to the floor.

I stood, bending over to pick up the brush, and felt his hands come around my waist. His hands slid beneath my robe, over my thighs, as he gently nudged me forward. The fire in his eyes was all I needed, as I leaned on the vanity and welcomed him inside me. He filled me to the hilt with his glorious length, bringing me to my toes.

"Open your eyes, Sara," he said softly. "Look at me."

My fingers dug into the edge of the table as my eyes rose to his. My breasts, showing through the gap of my robe, swayed with each slow, methodical thrust and my core tightened in a furious spiral. I teetered on the delicate edge of release, my gaze holding to his to be sure that I was not dreaming. This was Edward, needing me, desiring me. My body clenched in glorious release around him as he followed with a guttural sound, matching the pleasure of my sigh.

He drew me up, the warmth of his body shielding my back as we looked at each other in the mirror. "I do not want to live my life without you, Sara." He kissed the crown of my head. "I don't know how to make up for all that I've put you through."

I turned into his embrace, pressing my cheek against his broad chest. "I just wanted back the man who seduced me that day in the studio," I said. "I needed to feel that you still desire me, Edward."

"More than you know, my love. All the while I was away, every night you invaded my dreams. Everything I saw, everything I experienced—I thought about what you would think. I yearned to have you at my side, sharing every moment with me. That is why I came back—" he brushed his hand over my hair "—to tell you that I am miserable without you."

He leaned away from me, holding me at arm's length. "But I want you to be happy, Sara. And I meant what I said earlier. In some cultures, it is permitted to have more than one lover. I can learn to live with that, if it is what you want, but I think part of me had to know whether you were mine entirely, or if you still harbored feelings for Thomas. I didn't realize until I left that it was likely a big part of why I invited him to stay here." He searched my eyes. "I was aware of the risk involved, but I had to leave so that you would be able to decide for yourself what you needed, what you wanted."

I held my hand to his cheek, feeling the familiar roughness of his unshaven face beneath my palm. "I will always have affection for Thomas, Edward. However, not in the same way I have for you. Thomas only loved me with his body—it is all he knows, at least for now. But I hope one day he will feel what I feel for you— something built to last, to weather the storms that will come. You, Edward, have my heart, my soul and my body, if you so desire it."

"I've missed you so much," he breathed against my neck, his fingers slowly drawing my robe from my shoulders. His warm lips touched my flesh as he eased the gown over my arms and let it pool at my feet.

"You are so soft…so beautiful."

He nuzzled my ear, drawing my hair aside to place tender kisses across the back of my neck. Languid curls of dark desire began to form deep inside me. I turned in his arms, my hands working fast to undo the buttons of his shirt, peeling it back to smooth my fingers over his warm skin. I pressed my lips to his flesh, finding where his pulse beat fiercely at the base of his neck. Impatient to have him inside me, I struggled with his trousers as his hands moved over me.

"My sweet Sara," he said, lifting me into his arms and carrying me the short distance to the bed. He laid me down and I watched him make haste to finish undressing, his beautiful body emerging and setting fire to my blood. He lay down beside me and I drew him close, delighting in having my husband home again, in my bed where he belonged. "I've missed seeing how you used to look at me. I didn't realize how much," I said softly, slipping an unruly curl over his ear.

He kissed me slowly, fanning the need inside of me so long denied. I surrendered to the mastery of his hands and parted my legs, welcoming him, breathing in deeply as he filled me until our bodies fused as one.

He held my eyes with his stormy gaze, leaning above me on his elbows and rocking his hips, moving in a sensuous rhythm and building me up again. Tears pricked the backs of my eyes as I clamped my legs around him, gripping his back, feeling his muscles bunch beneath my fingers.

"Come—with me—Sara," he said, his words broken by his fervent thrusts. I rose to meet him in perfect rhythm. Thomas had been right—people did lose sight of the beauty created by the union of a man and a woman. My world began to spiral out of control as another climax shattered me apart. I clung to Edward's body, drenched with the heat of arousal as he followed with a primal groan, reclaiming all that was his—all that was *ours*.

Breathless, he rolled to his back and stared a moment at the mirror I'd insisted he hang above the bed. He drew me under his arm, his hand skimming tenderly over my heated flesh. There was no need for words. As I drifted to sleep, I felt him lean over and kiss my temple.

"Sleep well, my love—" he leaned over to kiss me "—we've only just begun to catch up."

The muffled clip-clop of horses coming up the hard dirt drive woke me. My body was sore from being awakened in the middle of the night for another round of lovemaking that drove us into a near frenzy and disheveled the bed linens until they hung off the corner of the mattress. Careful not to wake Edward, I scooted off the bed and wrapped a sheet around me. It was early yet, the sky barely showing signs of daybreak. I pushed my hair back from my face and looked to the entrance below, seeing Thomas handing his bags to the coachman. No longer did I feel disconnected, heart and body, as before. Both were now devoted entirely to Edward, and I knew he was mutually devoted to me.

Thomas opened the carriage door and I saw a woman, dressed in fine clothes. *Grace.* I wondered if she would ever admit how deeply she felt for him.

"Sara?" my husband called out sleepily.

"Over here," I replied, smiling as he swaggered hurriedly toward me in the frigid room. He peeled the sheet from around me and moved in behind me, wrapping us both snugly inside.

"Why are you up? You ought to still be in bed on such a chilly morning." He bent to kiss my cheek.

"He's leaving," I said, pressing my hand against the cold glass. Edward rested his chin on the top of my head and, covering my hand with his, drew it back beneath the sheeting and enveloped me in his tight embrace.

"Let's go back to bed, my love," he whispered in my ear. "I have much I want to share with you that I learned while in India." He nuzzled my ear and I turned into his arms, finding there all the adventure I'd ever need.

Book 3

GRACE

Chapter 1

Cremorne Gardens, 1858

IT WAS A BEAUTIFUL SUMMER EVENING AT THE Cremorne. Most of my usual clients were at the opera, indulging their wives in a night out, showing them off to London society. It is common knowledge, of course, that most of them keep at least one mistress. And, I think for some, their wives approve if only to keep from having to perform themselves. I suppose you could say I may have held more marriages together than been reason for their end. Tonight, however, I was free to spend an evening of leisure, enjoying the music, the lights and the festive gaiety of the gardens. Here I could lose myself. I could forget the small room above the pub where I had lived for the past ten years since escaping from hell.

To look at me now you would not see, unless you were very astute, the horror of what I've been through. I was just twelve when I was ripped from my family's bosom, kidnapped by a brothel madam's thugs while at market with my mother. There are times I can still hear her screaming my name, the burlap sack over my head unable to drown out the sound. I was told that I was to be sold to the highest bidder in a private auction. I was not to make a scene, for no one would come for me. It would be easy to end the life of someone whose whereabouts no one knew.

So it was that I was placed on a block with several other girls of about the same age, in the middle of a large, dark building. I could see nothing beyond the lamps framing the platform. I could hear the sound of an auctioneer, the intermittent baritone voices of men calling out their bids. I never knew the face of the man I was sold to, but he kept me in a small room, with no windows. He fed and clothed me, gave me books to read, and when he needed me—"for medicinal purposes" as he called it—a bag was placed over my head. I had no concept whether it was night or day. Too frightened by the threats to my life and my family, I didn't think about how long I'd been held captive. I began to focus on my opportunity to escape. It came one day after my captor made a routine visit. He'd improperly shut the door, not minding to listen for the latch to drop before he left. Whether it was intentional or a mistake, I took full advantage and slipped out unnoticed.

I was one of the lucky few. It was not until some months after I'd gotten away that I began to hear of others like me. I passed by mothers and fathers wandering the streets, searching for their daughters, desperate for answers. I could only shake my head, not wanting to reveal what I knew for fear of being found by the unsavory characters who'd once nabbed me. I did think of my family, wondering if they remembered me, but I was not their little girl anymore. I was changed and not for the better. As such, I blended into the fray, a ghost on the streets, surviving how I could.

Call me callous, and perhaps my heart is as leathery as an animal's hide, but I am here, some ten years later, alive and breathing, and that is all that matters.

I waved to Deidre, who was on the dance floor with a handsome gent I'd not seen at the gardens before. Deidre and I had met here as I had most of the small circles of women who worked the gardens. We were a close-knit group, watching out for one another. I tapped my foot, enjoying the music and watching the dancers. A shiver crept over my shoulders and I glanced up, looking as you do when you feel you are being watched. Seated on the opposite side of the dancing platform was a young man dressed in clothing depicting an era gone by. The frock coat he wore was made of rich-looking deep green silk brocade with fine beadwork on the collar and cuff. I noted a flutter of white lace protruding from the cuffs and the large white cravat at his neck. His hands rested comfortably on the walking cane he had perched between his legs.

I'd not seen him before and surely he was a gent I would remember. He had the face of a poet, that look about him indicating he was an observer of life and people. His hair was a thick mass of unruly waves, indicative of one who cared little about what was in fashion but who knew what suited him.

I watched him silently scanning the crowd, his piercing, dark blue-green eyes roving across the crowd, perhaps searching for the character of his next poem. Intrigued, I stared at him, safe in the anonymity of the crowd, until finally he turned and met my gaze.

My breath caught. Surprise was not something that I experienced much anymore. It was as if he could see right through me. I felt naked before him.

"Grace?"

A man's voice brought me out of my stupor and I blinked, seeing the smiling face of Jack Adams, one of the stage actors in the Cremorne theatrical troupe.

"You look faraway. Didn't you hear me?"

I smiled, blinking again, feeling strange, as though I'd just looked into the eyes of providence.

"I asked if you would honor me with the next dance," he said, offering a short bow.

I smiled. "Of course, dear. Forgive me."

I took his hand and he swept me into his arms, gliding me across the dance floor. I was aware of the music and of the swirling throng of dancers, but my mind could not forget the mesmerizing look in the stranger's eyes. I searched for him as we glided around to where I'd first seen him, but the bench was empty. My eyes skirted the fringe of onlookers, knowing he would have stood out, but he wasn't there, either.

"Are you well, Grace? You look pale, as if you've seen a ghost." My partner smiled. "Do you need to sit for a spell? Shall I get you a refreshment?"

I nodded. "Perhaps that would help."

He held my arm, guiding me to one of the tables at the edge of the platform. All around me, patrons sat laughing over a pint, indulging in an ice cream.

I pressed my hands to my cheeks, checking for a fever. There was none, yet I could not overcome the strange effect the man had had on me.

"Here we are, Grace. There's little that a pint won't resolve, don't you agree?" Jack guzzled his drink, his eyes scanning the women timidly standing near the platform, hoping to be asked to dance.

"Go on with you, Jack," I said, slapping his arm. "I just need to rest a bit. I'm likely just overcome by the stench from the river. I should be used to it by now." I leaned toward him, nodding in the direction of a lonely young girl. "There, the pretty one with the dark tresses. I saw her looking at you."

"Truthfully?" His eyes darted toward the woman and back to me.

"Yes, go! Skedaddle before another beats you to it. She's a beauty, she is."

"If you're sure," he said, his face turned to keep an eye on the woman.

"Yes, go," I reiterated. He tossed me a smile and sprang from his chair.

"Hopefully she'll say yes," I muttered. I didn't want to see Jack's kind heart squashed.

I watched over the rim of my glass, quietly breathing a sigh of relief when the girl smiled and nodded. Jack glanced back at me and raised his eyebrows, offering me an enthusiastic grin. I raised my glass and wished him well. Feeling better, I scanned the crowd again for my handsome specter. I was about to give up when I spotted him walking along the boardwalk, beside the river.

Curiosity—a fault for some, a virtue for others—pushed me from my seat. I wove through the crowded bay of tables.

When I emerged from the throng, panic struck my heart as it appeared I'd lost him again. I began to wonder, given his unusual dress and elusive manner, if I had not indeed seen a specter, a ghost—a wandering lost soul. Although I did not entirely believe in such things, I knew those who swore to having encountered restless spirits, spirits who had something undone left on earth. But given my body's reaction when our eyes had met, I felt quite certain that this man was flesh and blood.

I squinted into the shadows of the path that led to the boat dock and saw there a man with a cane. "You're a fool, Grace," I said to myself as I lifted my skirts and hurried after him. As I got farther and farther away from the crowd, I became more concerned for my safety. I picked up a handful of pebbles and began to throw them at the stranger's back, one at a time. When he did not stop or turn around, I mentally scolded myself for following him farther. The branches of the trees lining the path seemed to reach out for me and I had to duck in the darkness, keeping my eye on the object of my ridiculous quest. There were very few people now on the path. The man paused, a short distance in front of me. It would have been easy, and probably wise, to slip into the shadows and walk away. But drawn to him for reasons I could not understand, I rolled the last pebble in my palm and debated my options.

He took a step forward and I drew back my arm, sending the pebble on its way—letting *it* decide my fate. In the dark silence, I heard it hit his hat with a dull *thunk*.

He came to an abrupt halt and slowly turned.

I could barely see his face in the darkness, but I remember the steellike intensity of his eyes. "You've not been afraid for a long time, Grace," I told myself quietly. "Now's not the time to start." I walked toward him with an acute awareness of my body. I had never before seen anyone appraise me as he did. Oh, I'd seen lust in a man's eye many a time, but this…this was more intense. It was as if he was studying me from head to toe. I came to a stop a foot or two before him, hesitant to get any closer. I cleared my throat. "Why were you staring at me earlier?"

A smirk played on his delectable mouth.

"I assure you, mademoiselle, I do not make a habit of staring at women." He raised his eyebrows in his defense.

"Are you calling me a liar, sir?"

His smile widened as if enjoying my challenge.

"I would not presume such a thing, mademoiselle."

"My name is Grace, though surely I should not give it so freely to a man who lurks about, ogles women."

He chuckled quietly and then offered me a regal bow.

"Very well, guilty as charged. Thomas Rodin, mademoiselle."

"You can stop calling me *mademoiselle,* sir. Clearly I am about as French as you are."

He placed his hand over his heart.

"You wound my pride, madem—*Miss Grace.* But a lovely lady such as you will surely find it in her heart to forgive an old-fashioned gesture."

I narrowed my eyes on him. "And why is it, Mr. Rodin, that you would practice the 'old-fashioned art' of ogling on me? Surely you are aware of the number of women here at the gardens without escorts?"

He looked away and offered a wry smile. "Yes, I am aware."

"So, you were looking to see what suits your fancy?"

He studied me for a moment. "Not exactly, no. Not for the same reason you believe, at any rate."

"Let me come to the point, sir, for the night wanes. Are you in need of company for the evening?"

He looked surprised.

"Are you propositioning me, Grace?"

I fisted my hand on my hip. "Have we not been through this already, Mr. Rodin? Do you, or do you not, wish to wet your whistle this evening?"

He cleared his throat.

"Um, no, I do not need my whistle wetted," he replied. "Though I must admit it sounds intriguing."

"You prefer to watch, is that it?" I guessed. "Well, I'm afraid that won't be possible tonight. You see I have no clients—"

"Um...no, I think perhaps you have the wrong impression."

"The wrong impression?" I smiled. "Why else would a handsome gent like yourself come to the gardens alone?"

"I am flattered, truly. However, I came as a matter of professional curiosity, Miss Grace."

"Farmer. Grace Farmer. I am pleased to make your acquaintance, Mr. Rodin."

He reached for my hand and I stepped away. An old habit, I suppose.

"I mean you no harm," he said with sincerity in his voice.

I offered my hand, then, and he took it, pressing it gently with his lips.

"Perhaps we can start again on better footing," he suggested. "I am an artist and poet by trade."

I slapped my thigh. "I knew as much! The moment I saw you, dressed as prissy as you are, I pegged you for a poet."

He raised his brow. "Prissy?" He coughed. "I would have thought a woman of your...shall we say, profession, would not be so quick to judge by appearance alone."

"I call them as I see them, Mr. Rodin, as I've a strong suspicion you do. Go ahead then and give it your best. Tell me what you think of me."

His smile was genuine. "Only that I find your hair magnificent and your mouth a saucy delight." He fished inside the breast pocket of his coat. "I'd like very much for you to model for me. I have a project in particular that would suit you perfectly."

Even as handsome as he was and very probably an artist as he claimed, I was wary. "Me? A model? For what, Mr. Rodin? If this is simply a ploy to get me alone—"

"My intentions, Grace, are entirely honorable."

Something in his tone, the way he said my name as if he had known me for years, caused me to stop and listen. "Are any of your paintings in the royal gallery?" I asked. Once or twice, a wealthy client had taken me there on a Sunday afternoon.

"You're familiar with the Royal Academy?"

"Well, not intimately, no. But I *do* know that any respectable artist's work would surely be hung there." I eyed him, watching his expression darken. The muscle of his jaw ticked.

"You are quite right. Many of my peers have works at the gallery and I have one or two, I believe, still hanging there. It is my hope, in fact, that this very project may be accepted into the exhibition next spring."

"Where is your studio, Mr. Rodin?" I asked. He was an odd fellow, but I found myself liking him, I couldn't say why.

"Ah, yes," he said, as if remembering the card he'd taken from his pocket earlier. "Here is the address. Come by tomorrow. Would nine o'clock fit into your schedule?"

I smiled, taking the card from his hand, delighting in the odd combination of his words and dress. Given his build, the lines of his face and the thickness of his hair, I would put him at no more than two and thirty years, if that. Yet his manner indicated a man of greater maturity, stuck in the age of chivalry and knighthood. Either that or I was falling for the grandest performance on earth.

"Very well, Mr. Rodin. I will come by tomorrow and we will discuss your proposition further."

"Splendid. I look forward to it." His eyes darted to my forehead and he reached up, almost by instinct, to brush a wisp of hair from my eyes.

He blinked, aware, it seemed, of being too forward. He drew back his hand.

"Until tomorrow, then?"

I nodded. "Until tomorrow."

I watched as he trudged down the slope to the waiting passenger boat.

"Oh, Mr. Rodin," I called to him. "What shall I wear?"

He turned and hesitated a moment, then lifted his arms.

"Good lady, you may come dressed however you wish, or in
nothing at all! I leave the choice to you."

I chuckled. He was a handsome but cheeky rogue.

Chapter 2

I GLANCED UP AT THE STATELY STONE BUILDING and checked the address again. Not terribly far from the Cremorne, it was situated in one of the districts known for housing various artists and poets.

"Miss Farmer," a voice called from above, and I looked up to find Mr. Rodin, his hand raised in greeting.

"I'll be right down."

I could not count the number of times I'd had to wait for a man. Yet, I had the distinct feeling that this meeting was about to change the course of my life.

The door opened and he stood there in a similar shirt to the one he wore last night, but wearing a vest this time, which fit marginally within the scope of current fashion.

"Miss Farmer." He smiled, opening the door wide.

"Mr. Rodin." I stepped into the foyer, pausing a moment to let my vision adjust to the dim light inside.

"I am glad that you decided to pay me a visit. Come, the studio is upstairs."

I followed him up the two flights of stairs. "Right through here," he said, ushering me through the open door.

The large room which I assumed to be the studio, was like a world unto itself. I glanced over my shoulder and Mr. Rodin smiled.

"It's a bit of a mess. My apologies." He set to picking up papers that were tossed on the floor. "I quite often forget all else when I'm involved in a project. A hazard of the artist at work, I'm afraid."

He grinned and I found his humility utterly charming. "Make no apologies on my account, Mr. Rodin. In general, I've learned that women are the ones who keep a house in order. Men are simply there to provide the means for doing so."

He stopped and looked at me.

"What a pitiful view of romance you have, Miss Farmer."

I looked at him squarely. "I rarely see romance in my line of work, Mr. Rodin."

"Ah, yes, well, I suppose that is true." He looked around, appearing to search for something. "Feel free to look about. If you have any questions, I'll try to answer them as best as I can."

"May I?" I placed my bonnet and bag on a nearby chair. I'd chosen to wear my best dress. One given to me by Deidre when she grew tired of it. It was a pale shade of gray and went well with my fair skin and blond hair. I did not apply paint to my face as a rule, other than a bit of color on my lips from time to time. Unable to afford such luxuries, I carefully rubbed my lips with pomegranate juice, instead.

"If you'll permit me to say, Miss Farmer, you look exceptionally beautiful by the light of day." He stacked a pile of papers, most of which appeared to be sketches, on the corner of the desk.

"Thank you, Mr. Rodin." I stood at his easel, studying the small papers tacked on the corners—intricately drawn leaves and flowers with words too small to read chaotically scribbled off to the side.

"Nature features prominently in most of my work. I believe there is much we can learn by studying its colors and patterns. Don't you agree?" he asked from across the room.

I tried to imagine the process it would take to create something of such beauty. Admittedly, I had trouble conceiving of where to start.

"You are a talented man indeed, Mr. Rodin, if you can look at this blank canvas and imagine a work of art."

"I suppose it takes a person predisposed to seeing the possibilities," he answered.

I ignored his remark, asking instead, "And how do you choose your subjects, Mr. Rodin? Or do your subjects choose you?"

I flipped through a group of painted canvases leaning against a wall. A shadow appeared over the place where I stood. I looked over my shoulder and found him standing close behind me.

"Sometimes I find them, and sometimes…they find me. I believe in fate. Do you?"

I glanced at him, knowing if I allowed, I would again be caught in his piercing eyes.

"I believe in what I can see and what I can touch."

"That is interesting. You impress me as having a more spiritual side," he said.

I folded my arms over my chest and pinned him with a challenging look. "And what, pray tell, Mr. Rodin, ever gave you that idea?"

There it was again. The look I had seen last night—peeling away the layers, splaying me open—looking into my soul.

"Stop it," I said, disturbed by the intensity of his eyes.

"I do not want you to be uncomfortable, Grace. I want you to feel at home. In fact, after some thought, I've decided that if you agree to sit for my project, I'd like you to move in."

"Mr. Rodin!" I brushed past him and picked up my hat and purse. "I am *not* in the habit of taking up residence with men I barely know."

He looked completely baffled. "And yet you would give yourself to any stranger for a single night of *paid* passion?"

"*Sex,* Mr. Rodin. Let's be blunt. The men I accompany are not paying me for passion," I answered coldly as I prepared to walk out. I had determined by the sparseness of his surroundings that

I would not be making much in the way of an income if I were to stay. I was willing to work for a smaller wage, but not for a man who did not, at the very least, respect me.

"My apologies, Miss Farmer…Grace. Please don't leave. Allow me to make up for my blatant wrong." The tone in his voice was apologetic.

I paused at the door. My pride, all in this world that I truly possessed, was bruised. "And how do you think you will manage that, Mr. Rodin?"

"Allow me take you out this evening," he offered. "To a nice dinner, where we can discuss things civilly."

I shook my head. "I'm sorry. I have other plans. Perhaps another time." I hurried down the stairs, not stopping for a carriage until I'd put distance between us.

I cannot say what disturbed me about his offer. Perhaps it was the ease with which he assumed I would accept. It was obvious that Mr. Rodin, try as he might, understood as little about my world as I did his. That alone was reason enough not to proceed any further with this silly notion.

Was I simply afraid of being as intricately scrutinized as the leaf drawing I'd seen?

I'd grown accustomed to being a ghost, to providing a service and then fading into the woodwork. There was something off-putting about Thomas Rodin. He was the type of man who could easily break my heart if I got too close.

Bloody hell, I could not get the man out of my mind.

"Come on, Grace."

Mr. Willoughby was one of my regulars. He smelled like peppermint and cigars. His hands were rough, demanding, as he dropped his trousers in the shadows of the isolated breezeway, shoved up my skirt and lifted my leg around his thick middle.

"Do you like art, Mr. Willoughby?" His hot breath panted against my neck as he pumped his hips against mine with laborious intensity.

"What in God's name are you rambling about, Grace? Art? Hell, I could care less! You're starting to sound like my first wife!"

Why I'd not recognized him sooner for the slob that he was suddenly rankled my ire. *His first wife?* How many did he have?

"I'm sorry, Mr. Willoughby," I said, pushing him from me. "I cannot see you anymore."

He stood before me, his sausage peeking from beneath his protruding potbelly.

"But…you can't! I forbid it, Grace. I paid good money for your cunt tonight."

I handed back his money. "Mr. Willoughby, perhaps you best pull up your drawers and heed my words. Do not pester me again or I shall be forced to visit your good lady. Number three, is she?"

"Five," he muttered, visibly disgruntled as he hiked up his pants.

"Five, then." I brushed my skirts down and looked at him with new eyes. "Mr. Willoughby, if you showed as much fervency with your wife, you may yet be saved from adding a sixth."

He frowned, pressing together his bushy gray eyebrows.

"Do you think so, really?" he asked, adjusting his beaver-fur top hat. "I've always had a fear she would find me perverted. You know, a bit *naughty.*"

Mr. Rodin's offer to model for him, if it took me off the streets, was looking more and more tempting. "Certainly, you could be no worse off for at least making the effort. Who knows, perhaps you will find Lady Willoughby enjoys being a bit 'naughty.'"

It was clear that the possibility had not crossed his mind. "By God, perhaps you're right."

Mr. Willoughby grabbed my hand and pumped it up and down with enthusiasm. He hurried from the alcove where we'd met on several occasions these past few months. He wasn't the only man in London who kept his wife on a glass shelf, when he should be taking her to bed for a good poke. Maybe if they all heeded my advice, the whoring business would not be as thriving a trade.

I took a deep breath, letting out a sigh. I was tired and I wanted something better. Perhaps Mr. Rodin's offer was it.

I went back the next day unannounced. Dark clouds hovered over the city all morning, keeping the sun at bay. It was just my luck that they decided to open up, producing a torrential rain, as I waited in front of Mr. Rodin's studio flat. Worse, I'd told the carriage driver not to wait. I pounded with desperation on the front door, hoping that someone would answer.

"Coming!" I heard a man's voice call from inside. The door swung open and a gent closely resembling Mr. Rodin peered at me through weary eyes. He squinted, trying to see who'd awakened him on a Saturday morning.

"Excuse me. I was hoping to speak to Mr. Rodin."

The man rubbed his fist over his eyes, blinking a couple of times, then looked down at me again. Oh, yes, by the stark color of those eyes, he was related, there was no doubt.

"Was he expecting you?" he asked, stifling a yawn.

"No, not today. I wonder if I may prevail upon your kindness, sir. I am getting soaked to the skin."

He looked up at the sky as if realizing for the first time that it was raining.

"My apologies, miss. Please step inside."

I hurried into the small foyer. There was barely enough room for the two of us. There was a closed door behind me and, with exception of the front door, the only other exit was the stairwell leading upstairs. I brushed the rain off my shawl as best I could.

"I'm William Rodin, Thomas's devastatingly handsome younger brother." He smiled. Apparently, charm ran in the family, too. William took my hand and shook it.

"And you must be?" he asked.

"Grace. Grace Farmer," I replied.

"Oh, yes, Grace. Thomas mentioned something about you the other night."

"Oh, really? I hope it was favorable."

The front door opened then, and the latch plowed William in the stomach before he could move.

"Dammit, Will. Sorry." A soggy Thomas Rodin squeezed into the entryway.

"Did you find scones?" Will asked.

I pressed my back against the wall, trying to make myself as small as possible.

"Blast, Will, can you move out of the way, it's impossible—"

His face came up as his body pushed against mine.

"Miss Farmer?" He grinned and the delight on his face made me glad I'd decided to return. "This is a pleasant surprise."

Indeed, as was the sensation of his body so close to mine. I could imagine how well we would fit together.

And you're here to get a real job, Grace.

"The door…if you could just move a little to the right…" William pushed at the door with one hand and reached for the bag in Thomas's hand with the other.

"Are they still warm?" William asked.

Thomas reacted, as would any brother, reaching up to bat his brother's hand away—and accidentally caught my breast in the exchange.

"Pardon me, Miss Farmer, but as you can see, my brother is a tyrant with few manners. We let him out of the barn every other weekend. It was my turn this week to keep him." He smiled and I found myself enjoying their good-natured banter.

"Mr. Rodin…"

"Please call me Thomas."

His face remained mere inches from mine. My eyes dropped to his tempting mouth, mentally tracing his full lower lip that begged to be nibbled.

"Almost got it."

William shoved the door shut behind his brother's back, projecting him forward. Luckily, my body prevented him from hitting the wall. I turned my head to the side, feeling Thomas's warm breath against my cheek. "Mr. Rodin, I've been considering your proposal."

I took a deep breath as Thomas moved past me. He held up the bag, out of his brother's reach.

"Tea and scones?" He smiled. "Come, Miss Farmer." He reached for my hand and pulled me up the stairs behind him. "Our very lives may be at stake until my brother has his breakfast."

It was the first time I'd ever felt a man could also be my friend.

Six months. At times, it felt like six years. Thomas Rodin could be the most aggravating man on earth. Surly, meticulous in his work, he quite often went hours without saying a word and then suddenly he wanted to do nothing more than talk my ear off.

The topic of my staying at the studio as some type of permanent arrangement never came up again. I came early of a morning and left in the late afternoon, unless one of the members of the brotherhood sold a painting and so created just cause for a dinner celebration. I was often invited to these impromptu, joyful events and was told I was the prettiest of all the brotherhood's previous models, but I suspect their admiration had more to do with my skills in the kitchen. Thomas, however, enjoyed parading me about town, showing me off as the next famous face in the art world.

"The *Mona Lisa*," he said, "has met her rival." I admit the attention was flattering, but my previous experiences made me wary that such fame could last, or that even Thomas's infatuation with me would last. I didn't deceive myself into thinking that I was his first model, or that I would be his last.

There were moments when I was allowed to see a different side to him. One such time occurred on a brisk September evening when I discovered there was more substance to Thomas than he allowed most people to see.

I was clearing the dishes from the table after a party, once again astounded how quickly the studio cleared when everyone was tired and ready for bed. William helped me carry a few plates into the kitchen.

"The meal was delicious, Grace. Thank you. As always, I am not sure that you receive enough credit for these sumptuous delights you create for us."

Embarrassed by his comment, I waved him off and took the stack of dishes in his hands. "I enjoy the company. It's good to see men with such healthy appetites."

He grinned, so much like his brother, and then leaned forward and gave my cheek a peck. "Good night, Gracie."

"Good night," I replied, staring at the door. I heard him say good-night to his brother, as I lifted my hand to my cheek. No one had called me Gracie since I was a child. It was odd that I should think of that after all these years and yet an overwhelming longing for family swept over me and I swallowed a lump in my throat. I shook my head to clear it, wiping my hands as I stepped through the butler's pantry to the studio to make sure the table was clear. Thomas was standing a few feet away at his writing desk, bottle in hand, pouring himself a glass of wine.

"Ah, Grace, you're still here. This is a fine port. Will you join me?"

I'd been watching him all evening. His demeanor didn't quite match the jubilance of the others. "No, thank you. Don't you think you've had enough for one evening?" I asked lightly, fully expecting him to ignore me. I picked up some plates that had been left behind.

"Leave those and come here. I need to talk," he said.

The tone in his voice led me to believe that he'd had more to drink tonight than what I could keep track of. "Just a moment, I don't want to leave the scraps. The insects will have a celebration of their own." I smiled. He was behaving strangely and I realized I should have probably left with the others, or asked William to help me get him to bed. I dipped the dishes quickly into the suds, whisked the plates clean and dried them, setting them on the sideboard.

"Grace!" Thomas bellowed.

I dried my hands and slapped the towel over a chair as I

emerged from the kitchen. "Thomas, it is late. You needn't bellow, I told you I was coming."

"You are not my wife, woman, you are my muse."

"Your muse I may be, but I am not your slave to be ordered about."

He narrowed his gaze on me, looking very much a roguish pirate in the threadbare coat he insisted on wearing. I made a note to see about adding a patch on his left elbow the first chance I could get him out of it.

"I'm in the mood to sketch." He slammed his glass on the desk, and the wine sloshed over the rim, spreading over the lovely dark wood.

Frustrated by his carelessness, I grabbed one of his paint cloths and wiped up the liquid before it could mar the wood. Thomas, oblivious to my endeavors, was preoccupied, searching for his sketching papers and charcoal. I had dealt with my share of drunken sots in my day and drunk, this man was. But why? He was not prone to overindulging in much of anything except flattering his own ego. "Perhaps it should wait until the light of day?" I suggested, mopping up his mess.

He shook his head. "No, *now.* That's what I pay you for, isn't it?"

"You are precariously close to insulting me, Thomas. I've a mind to leave you here and see if you fall off that balcony."

He laughed aloud. I loved the sound, even besotted as he was. Damn, it would be so much the better if he were an ugly drunk. He'd never before put me in a position of compromise, although there had been a time or two I wished he had. That thought prompted my next words. "I should go."

"Oh, Grace, don't be like that." He walked toward me, his arms outstretched, and caught me by my shoulders. "Are you afraid I might persuade you to do something you don't wish to do?"

I pinned him with a look. "I wouldn't try anything," I warned him with a raised eyebrow.

His dimple, an admitted weakness of mine, appeared on his handsome face. "Yet in your eyes I see you cannot resist me."

"Are you in the mood to sketch or flirt, Mr. Rodin? Which is it that you pay me for again?" I held his gaze, hoping he could not see what a tangle he had made of my insides.

"Hmm," he muttered, eyeing me. "Perhaps sketching might be safer."

"Where do you want me?" I asked, as he picked up his drawing papers.

"Oh, good God, woman, watch that tongue of yours, for I surely have thought of it more than once this evening."

"You've thought of my tongue?" I asked as I walked to the corner where he kept the props. "In what respect, Thomas?" I tossed back with a grin.

I heard a growl from behind. I stood and turned around to face him. His eyes had been pinned to my backside. "You've had too much to drink," I stated flatly. "I'm taking you to bed."

He tossed the papers into the air. "That's precisely where I've been trying to get you for the past few moments, my muse! How delightful that you would simply offer."

I cast my eyes heavenward. "Come on, Cassanova." I tucked my arm around his waist and guided him into the hall. Once I had him settled, I decided I would stay in the guest room. I made a mental note to lock the door.

"You are so good to me, Grace," he said, swaying slightly when I let go of him to light the kerosene lamp by his bed. His hands rested on my shoulders, caressing gently. "Thomas," I said quietly. His lips found the back of my neck and I fought the urge to like it. His fingers ran up the curve of my throat, his mouth following.

"I could be your lover, Grace. If only you would allow it," he whispered, touching the tip of his tongue to the sweet spot below my ear. Only one or two men on this earth knew of that spot and it was because I'd told them. Thomas gravitated to it as if I wore a sign. I was barely aware of his hands gliding over my bodice, undoing the buttons of my gown. His fingers slid beneath the fabric, stroking the swollen flesh above my corset.

"Thomas, you shouldn't...." I said halfheartedly.

"But, my muse, you seem to be enjoying my attention." His breath fanned over my cheek. "There, I can feel your heart beating hard against my palm."

His fingers spread, taking a taut nipple between his fingertips and gently rolling it into a tight bud. He turned me into his embrace and I did not protest, at least not aloud, when he lifted my chin and kissed me with slow tenderness.

"Yes, my muse, let me please you," he whispered, leaving soft kisses on my face. "Let me worship your exquisite loveliness." His hands continued their quest to open the fastenings of my corset. He offered kisses more potent than opium and I gave myself over to his magic, lured blindly and willingly so, realizing that come the morning, he would likely not remember much of what happened. I told myself this was not why I was here and made a silent promise to put a stop to this nonsense. After *one* more kiss.

"Grace, you must tell me, as I do not force myself on any woman."

He ran his fingers down the exposed front of my throat, rolling back what part of the corset he'd managed to unhook.

I was lost in his rapturous kiss. *Was that the last one? Yes, it must be...*

"If you only knew what I wanted to do to you," he said softly, rubbing his cheek against my temple.

His hands glided down the curve of my back, grabbing my bottom beneath my skirts, caressing it as he pressed his manhood against me. I swallowed, knowing exactly what he wanted, it was in the getting to that end that intrigued me.

"I want to lay you down on this bed and, with painfully slow precision, remove each piece of your clothing. I want to kiss you from the top of your head to each of your delicate toes, devoting copious amounts of time and attention to the interesting parts along the way."

"You'd be my lover, Thomas?" I said, tipping my head to allow his mouth on my shoulder. "You'd do whatever I asked?"

"Oh, yes, your most devoted slave, designed, created only for your pleasure." He sighed, his mouth leaving searing kisses on my heated flesh.

"Would you love me deeply?" My breath caught.

"Oh, yes, I would, so deep that you would beg for more."

"And would you give me more?" I asked, beginning to realize that he was lost in this drunken rapture. I could have been anyone, perhaps *anything* at this point.

"Yes, oh, my muse, again and again, deeper still."

"My dear lover, before I offer my body to your utter and complete worship, there is one last thing I need to know."

The fiery kiss that came next nearly made me forget that I was about to put an end to this sensual charade.

"Let me be your oracle, my love. I freely offer you my body for your pleasure," he stated, his hands groping with greater freedom. "I offer you my maypole to celebrate the rite of spring," he murmured, the strong scent of port wafting over my face.

Maypole? I held back a smile. "It's September, you drunken sot. Just answer me this one question, and our bliss will have no boundaries." I held his chin between my fingers. His glazed-over eyes, as beautiful in his drunken state as they were when he was sober, glittered with pure lust. "Will you remember any of this by morning?"

He blinked, looking dumbfounded, as I suspected he might be.

"I don't understand." He leaned forward to kiss me. I pressed my hand to his mouth. This was much harder for me to end than I thought it would be.

"Go to bed, Thomas. I'll see you in the morning."

He held my arm as I skirted around him.

"Grace, think about what you're doing."

I paused at the door, putting my clothes aright. "I am, Thomas. I am. Good night." I pulled the door shut, ignoring the pleading look on his face.

Chapter 3

I LAY AWAKE UNTIL THE FIRST FINGERS OF DAWN snuck through the curtains of the guest-room window. I could not quell the memory of how close I came to surrendering to Thomas's seduction. It would have been so easy to succumb. I should have known better, of course. A man like Thomas Rodin, an unabashed romantic when completely sober, would be twice as alluring when his roguish side was unleashed by wine. He was a complex man, and I suppose in some ways that was the reason I found him so intriguing.

I crawled from my bed while the rest of the house was quiet, bathed and washed my hair under the kitchen pump. Taking a cup of hot tea into the studio, I started a fire to ward off the autumn chill and sat down on the rug in front of its warmth to dry my hair. Combing through my tresses was a time-consuming chore, but braiding it at just the right dampness in order achieve the deep waves was well worth the effort for the delight it brought to Thomas's face when I posed for him.

A weary male sigh captured my attention and I turned to the entrance of the studio where stood a bedraggled and bleary-eyed Thomas Rodin.

"Is it entirely possible, do you think, for hair follicles to feel pain?" he asked, wincing as he held the heel of his hand to his forehead.

I smiled, the awkwardness of last night quickly forgotten. "Let me get you something I think will help." I brought him a finger of whiskey and a cup of tea. "The whiskey first." He eyed me uncertainly.

"You're sure of this?"

"Trust me, go on," I prodded.

He closed his eyes and tipped his head back, swallowing the whiskey in one gulp. He handed me the glass and took a long swallow of tea, squeezing his eyes tight. I could almost feel how it would be burning just about now. I winced, watching his face contort.

He drew in a sharp breath, opening his mouth in a loud groan as the liquor infused his system. "This is supposed to help?"

I shrugged. "I've not had to try it personally, but the owner of the pub I worked at swore by it."

"Was he a drinking man?" Thomas squinted up at me with one eye. An unshed tear was poised in his lower lid.

I considered his question. "I never saw him touch a drop, but I'm sure he's mended a few like you."

He threw me a dubious look and shook his head. "Well, if you missed your chance to kill me last night for my behavior, you've gotten a good start on it this morning."

"Do you remember much of last night?" I asked, resuming my spot in front of the fire. He came up and stood behind me.

"Enough, Grace," he stated calmly. "Am I forgiven?"

I nodded, glancing at him over my shoulder. He smiled and sat down beside me, watching as I braided my hair.

"Can you teach me how you do that?"

I grinned. The man was a treasure chest of surprises. "You want to learn to braid hair?"

"I'd like to learn to braid *your* hair."

I was speechless. No man had ever made such a request. "Truly?"

"By heavens, your hair is utterly decadent, Grace. I love to touch it, or hadn't you noticed?"

I chose not to answer his question, instead shifting my body so I could show him how to braid the three strands together. "Over and under, under and over." It took him a couple of frustrated tries, but eventually he had mastered the task. "Now, you just begin up here, at the back of my neck, and work your way down."

He chuckled. "You've no idea how delightfully tempting that sounds, do you?"

"And you've no idea, Thomas, what an absolute rogue you are," I countered with a smile. His expression was intense as he carefully wove the strands together. My body was acutely aware of his fingers, each gentle tug reminding me of those hands on my skin the night before.

We sat in amiable silence for a time with him braiding my hair. Though I'd shared my body with many men, I'd never experienced the intimacy I felt at that moment. It was personal, and the comfort of it invited me to ask him about his family, something I had wondered about for some time.

"Do you have sisters, Thomas?"

He was silent.

"Why did you leave me last night?" he responded, changing the subject altogether.

The question came unexpectedly and yet at the same time I'd been hoping he would ask. "Because I make it a rule not to bed drunken sots."

"Never?" he asked, disbelief in his tone.

He might as well have plunged a dagger between my shoulder blades. "I've kept to it thus far, Thomas."

He continued to braid my hair as I stared silently into the fire. I wondered if the thought had crossed his mind, as it had mine, about what might have happened had he not been drunk.

"Tell me how you came to choose the profession you're in?" he asked quietly.

I chuckled. "You make it sound as though I had a choice. Does all of life appear perfect behind those rose-colored glasses you wear?"

"A hazard of being an incurable romantic, I suppose," he answered.

I smiled at that. "I'm quite certain that the profession I'm in is rarely, if ever, *chosen*. It's a matter of it choosing you."

"Can you explain, Grace? I do want to understand."

While I couldn't comprehend why it was of interest to him, I stared into the fire, searching for the right words. "I suppose the concept might be puzzling to a man. You see, Thomas, there are many different types of women walking the streets—most not by choice. Some of them do it for survival, some to find an escape from a dreary marriage, some to be able to put food in their children's mouths. Very few are out there looking for companionship."

"I didn't realize."

He smoothed his hand over the back of my head. I closed my eyes and pushed away the urge to turn and offer him a kiss. Had he been anyone else, the moment would have felt awkward, but it didn't.

"I assumed that most were unfortunates," he said. "Which were you, then? Did you...have you ever had...children?" he asked cautiously.

I picked at a piece of thread on my nightdress. "I cannot have children."

"Grace, what happened to you?"

I pressed my lips together, reprimanding myself mentally for being too open with him too soon. "It was a long time ago."

"Do you wish to talk about it?"

His hands curled gently on my shoulders, urging me to face him. I did not see pity in his eyes, as I had expected; rather I saw anger, protective and viral. "I think it best left in the past where it belongs."

"I wish I could have saved you from the pain that puts that guarded look in your eye," he said, his gaze intent on mine.

I stared at him, moistening my lips. "No one could have saved me, Thomas. No more than you or anyone could save the countless other girls taken from their families."

"Christ, Grace, I had no idea. Did you ever try to find them—your parents?"

I shook my head. "No, I'd already changed too much. They wouldn't have wanted me. Not the way I'd become. I was no longer their innocent daughter. I felt it was better to spare them of having to live with their pain every time they looked at me."

"I knew a woman like you once. She was remarkable, strong and beautiful."

"Did she pose for you, as well?" I asked, watching him stare off into the memories of his past.

"Her name was Cozette. She was both a model and student, yet looking back, I wonder if I was not *her* student."

"Is that the woman in your earlier sketches?" I asked him.

He nodded, his attention swerving back to me. He scooted so that he could lean his back against one of the reading chairs. "Come, sit here." He held out his arms to me.

"I do not need your pity, Thomas," I replied.

"And you shall not receive it. Think of it as an embrace between friends—*good* friends."

I tucked myself between his legs and snuggled into his warm embrace. Closing my eyes, I felt safe and secure for the first time in ages. He leaned his cheek on the top of my head and we stayed that way for a while, content in the silence, until Thomas spoke.

"What might have happened last night, Grace, had I not been drunk?"

He ran his hand softly down my braid until his fingers touched my shoulder. I wore nothing beneath my bedclothes, although the loose gown covered me entirely.

"I like you, Thomas," I said, fearing I was letting myself get too close, that I was setting myself up for heartache.

His quiet chuckle rumbled from his chest.

"I cannot imagine what a woman like you sees in a chap like me."

I turned my face to his, meeting his soft smile. "Surely you jest? Please don't poke fun at me, Thomas. I couldn't bear it."

"Grace," he said, brushing my cheek with his fingers. "There was no jest in my words. With all you've been through, the horrors you've survived, my character pales in comparison."

My heart stilled as a wave of scenarios—the hopes and dreams of a normal life—rushed like a ghost carriage through my mind.

"Dear Grace," he said quietly.

He leaned down, hesitating a moment, his eyes searching mine. I could barely conceive of what was happening. Was it possible he felt the same as I did? I wanted him to kiss me—I'd thought of little else all night—but this was dawn and he was sober. I felt more vulnerable.

"I want to kiss you," he said softly. "With your permission, and with far fewer libations in my system." He smiled, tipping my chin to align my mouth with his.

"Thomas?" I said, lost in his beautiful poetic gaze.

"Yes?" His breath fanned warm over my cheek.

My body ached for his touch. "I want you to kiss me."

It was the most reverent and chaste kiss I'd ever received, and by far the most potent. I was divinely aware of his hand sliding down my arm, his palm gently covering my breast. Many a man had touched me, but none of them had made me feel as beautiful as I did at that moment.

Through my gown, he brushed the pliant tip of my breast, causing it to pucker. My lips parted in a sigh as his tongue delved deeper, mating with mine. Before I realized it, I was on my back, with Thomas kneeling above me, shrugging his shirt over his head.

"Why me, Grace?" he asked, leaning down into my waiting arms.

Slowly, he fused his mouth to mine as if it were a sumptuous feast to be savored. "Must there be a reason, Thomas?"

He left warm, wet kisses down my throat, nibbling his way to the base of my neck, building a fierce need inside me.

"What about William?" I asked quietly, as I smoothed my hands over the firm width of his muscular shoulders.

Thomas leaned back and looked at me, braced on his elbows. "Are you and William…?"

"No, I meant only, what if…well, this is not very private."

"Ah." His eyes lit with the realization. "It takes a cannon to waken my brother, especially after a celebration."

"Then we've no need to be concerned that we might be interrupted?" I asked, tucking an errant curl behind his ear.

"None at all." His expression softened. "But I want this only if you do, Grace."

"Thomas—" I brushed my hand over his unshaven jaw "—I have imagined this at least a dozen times since last night."

"I am a man most desperately lost to you, Grace. Surely, you must know it."

His eyes raked over me, devouring me, causing my desire to grow all the more. I shifted my gown over my hips, revealing myself to him.

"Sweet heaven," he whispered.

He curled his fingers around my knee, leaving a trail of tender kisses along my inner thigh. A gasp spilled from my throat and I tangled my fingers in his hair as he lavished my cunny, his tongue as masterful as his artistic stroke.

My body floated, swept away by the utter bliss of his loving touch. "Thomas," I sighed. My heart pounded, fierce with the intensity of my arousal. My mind reeled with this new array of emotions spinning out of control. Sex, for me, wasn't about emotions and so, in that, I felt nearly virginal in my feelings.

He gently kissed my bent knee as he freed himself with his other hand.

"Grace, I burn to bury myself inside you."

His admission seared my heart, fueling the fire inside me. Using my legs as a brace, he teased my opening with his swollen cock. He pushed slowly into my slick heat, stretching me, filling me partway, before he withdrew and plunged again, deeper this time. I surrendered to the ecstasy of his cock moving with de-termined control, summoning immense pleasure from my body with each precise lunge. My hands fisted into the fabric of my gown as I held his gaze, staring down at me, his eyes glittering with passion. The frenzy of his thrusts increased, drawing me to a dizzying precipice. I flung my arms over my face, lost in exqui-site oblivion as an explosive climax tore through my body.

"Grace," he sighed, gripping my legs hard against his shoul-ders as he drove into me twice more, shooting his hot seed, before easing his body from mine. "You didn't answer my question," he said breathlessly, carefully pulling my gown into place as he repo-sitioned his trousers.

"What question?" I asked, blinded by the aftershock of our morning tryst. He drew me into his embrace and we held each other as we stared into the fire.

"You're trembling," he said, rubbing his hand up and down my arm.

"Am I?" I said, forcing my mind not to get caught up in an emotional entanglement that I might later regret.

"I asked, what is it that you like about me, Grace? There are so few people, I think, who really like me. Granted, they accept my leadership—"

"And bullheaded stubbornness," I teased quietly. He kissed the top of my head and chuckled. Still, I wasn't sure how to answer. I'd never been asked that question. It was never about what I thought, what I wanted. My life had always been about providing pleasure to others. The fact that he cared enough to ask brought a lump to my throat and yet I felt the need to guard my heart against his poetic charm. "I would have to say that you see me for who I am, Thomas. Not what I am." I looked up at him, feeling more exposed than I'd ever felt before. Though my knowledge of men was vast, Thomas was the exception. I did not know how he would treat my honesty, but I did not blind myself to the risk I took in being so up-front.

"The academy turned down my application, Grace. They said I made a public mockery of the school and its teachings.

Can you imagine? Those buffoons blaming me for *their* lack of competency?"

"Is that the reason you were drinking last night?" I asked, softly tracing the muscled flesh above his heart.

"As good a reason as any," he replied sullenly.

"May I ask you a question?" I laid my palm on his warm flesh, finding his steady heartbeat. This intimacy of conversing after sex was also new to me. Usually, a gent left his money on the table and was out the door without so much as a backward glance. This was far too serene, too comforting, the illusion of security it created.

"Of course you may ask me a question," he replied, stroking my hair.

"Is showing at their exhibition your solitary goal? What I mean to say is, would you paint whether or not there was a venue to display your art?"

He took a deep breath and let out a sigh. "You have a point. Maybe I've been trying too hard to please others, instead of trusting myself." He rubbed his knuckle softly along my jaw. "An old guilt complex, planted by my pious mother, no doubt. I was never good enough for them—my parents." He had a wistful look in his eye.

"Do what you love, Thomas, and one day the world will take notice."

"What a wise woman you are." He kissed my temple. "You've helped me to see things differently."

I pushed from the floor, suddenly ravenous. "I'll fix us a nice breakfast," I said quickly. This newfound intimacy made me nervous. I dared not think about the dangerous waters I treaded with my heart. What Thomas did not know, and what I did not tell him, was that I was beginning to see myself in a different light. He'd stirred up a bevy of new emotions inside me, including the one I feared most…*love.*

It wasn't that Thomas's romantic efforts were in vain. He was more than a friend to me in the next few months. We enjoyed long talks. I taught him tawdry jokes and he taught me about art. Our common ground was in bed, for there we were equals in passion. He tolerated taking me back to my room above the pub each night as I refused to stay at the studio. I was not ready to open myself to such a commitment. Interestingly, it was where I lived that became the source of a bitter disagreement between us.

It had been nearly a full year since I'd begun posing for Thomas. One summer afternoon, I arrived to find a beautiful black covered carriage parked outside the studio. Assuming he had a guest, I tiptoed up the stairwell and peeked into the studio, finding it empty. "Thomas?" I found it strange that he would not have mentioned a guest, since he usually asked me to make a special meal for such occasions.

"Ah, Grace, there you are. Come in here, I have something to show you." He stepped from the guest room into the hallway.

I raised my eyebrows. "Isn't that a worn line, Thomas, even for you?" I smiled.

"You give me no rest," he teased, ushering me in.

"You know what they say about the wicked, don't you?" I volleyed back lightheartedly. I enjoyed the banter we shared. At first I wasn't certain if Thomas would accept my odd sense of humor, but he was quick to laugh and, now and again, let his dry wit show.

"Did you see the carriage outside?" I asked, curious, as I followed him into the room. "I thought you might be entertaining royalty." My gaze was drawn to the beautiful dark blue dress that lay on the bed. The beadwork sparkled in the glow of the lamplight. A fur stole, handbag and feathered hat lay beside it. "This is lovely."

"Do you like it?"

There was a certain amount of pride on his face as he looked from me to the dress. Perhaps it was for his new project.

"Do you know what today is?"

"Thursday, I think. Is this for your new project?"

He brushed his fingers over my hair. "What a fascinating idea, but no, I want you to try it on…see if it fits."

"What are you painting?" I asked, giving him a curious look.

"It looks as though it will fit you."

He was avoiding my question. I lifted the gown, holding it up to me as I turned to look at myself in the oval mirror in the room.

"Let me help you with the fastenings."

"If this is a ploy to remove my clothes…"

"Grace, the dress. Please."

He unfastened all of my buttons and helped me step from one dress to the other. I looked at him in the mirror. "What day is this?"

He grinned. "It is the anniversary of the day, Grace Farmer, that you came into my life. A soggy wench with a sailor's mouth and a passion—second only to mine—for port and warm scones."

It was so unexpected, so thoughtful, that it caused my eyes to well. I dropped my face in my hands, overcome with emotion. His arms came around me and I turned, pressing my face into his chest.

"The dress doesn't suit you? We can find something else."

"You made me cry." I hid my face in the folds of his shirt. "Dammit, Thomas, I can't remember the last time I cried."

"Well, blazes, Grace. Now's not the time to make up for it. It's a dress, not a proposal."

He straightened, holding me at arm's length. "There, now scrub your face and get dressed. I have another surprise. There is one of those…those bustle contraptions. Do you need help with that?"

I shook my head. "I can manage."

"If you're sure. I need to finish dressing. I'll meet you downstairs."

I sat on the edge of the bed. "It's not a proposal, Grace," I muttered, sniffing as I wiped my cheeks. Men like Thomas and women like me weren't the marrying kind, at least not until we were plenty ready. I stood and slipped the gown on and stared again in the mirror. William passed by and whistled low. "It looks like it was made for you." He smiled. "Do you need help with those buttons?"

I nodded and he helped me as I watched him in the mirror. "William, do you have any idea where—"

He kissed the back of my head. "Not a one, but Thomas is probably downstairs, annoying the coachman. Hurry along, if you pity the poor man."

Thomas took me to dinner at an upscale hotel, followed by the opera. It was not one of the bawdy burlesque shows that the brotherhood was so fond of and where I might have felt more at ease than the box seats from which we watched the tragic story unfold. Even so, I was captivated by the grandeur and romance of the opera house and the high-society crowd.

During the intermission, the elaborately dressed crowd mingled over their drinks and jewels. Thomas handed me a flute of sparkling champagne. As long as he was at my side I could pretend to be more than I was.

"Lord Hoffemeyer, so good to see you," Thomas said as a giant of a man and his wife approached us. He accepted his amiable handshake. "I stayed with Lord and Lady Hoffemeyer," he said to me, though his eyes remained on the beautiful woman standing in front of him, "a few years back when traveling in Germany."

"Thomas Rodin, I wouldn't have expected to see you again, especially not in a place like this. I had no idea that you had an interest in opera." The tone in Lord Hoffemeyer's voice was strange.

"There are a great many things you don't know about Mr. Rodin, dear." His wife smiled as her gaze assessed Thomas from head to toe. "How are you, Thomas? My, you are no longer the scrawny, youthful lad that the baron dragged home from the card game, are you?" She tapped his shoulder with her fan.

Thomas gave me a brief, sheepish look and took her proffered hand.

"Lady Hoffemeyer, it is a pleasure to see you again," Thomas remarked, pecking her netted glove.

I caught the tick of her husband's jaw and wondered if Thomas had had an affair with the good lady.

"You promised to come back and see us, you naughty boy." She pouted her ruby lips. "Perhaps we should get together while we are here in London."

Her husband was looking at me with keen interest glittering in his eye.

"Forgive me," Thomas said, suddenly remembering my presence. "Grace Farmer, this is the Baron and Baroness Hoffemeyer of Pomerania. Lord Hoffemeyer was integral in helping to fund the railway system in that part of the world."

I smiled at the austere-looking man and placed my hand in his, allowing his greeting.

"Baron is just a political title, my dear. I much prefer Lord Hoffemeyer. Do you share Mr. Rodin's artistic passion, Miss Farmer?" he asked.

Thomas spoke before I could. "Grace is one of the models for the Pre-Raphaelite Brotherhood, milord."

He regarded me with greater interest. "Ah, yes, I should have guessed as much. You are indeed quite a lovely creature." He turned to his wife. "Look at her, milady, isn't she exquisite? Wherever did Thomas find you, my dear?"

"We met at the Cremorne, milord," I offered with a smile. I noted the way the man glanced at Thomas and then his wife.

Lady Hoffemeyer's penetrating gaze studied me and she licked her lips, before swinging her attention back to Thomas. "When can we meet, Thomas? As you know, we are most anxious to…visit more with you. We will certainly make it worth your while. And why don't you bring your friend along? We could get to know each other better—quite the little foursome in cards, we'd be." Her dark eyebrows slipped upward in question.

Thomas's hand pressed on the small of my back. "If you'll excuse us, I've just remembered there is someone I promised to speak with."

Thomas guided me away from the couple and through the crowd, stopping only long enough to retrieve his hat at the coat check.

"Thomas, what about the rest of the show?"

He said nothing, his jaw firm as he clung to my arm, nearly dragging me down the steps of the opera house. I jerked to a stop and he continued on a few more steps before he realized that I was not with him.

"What in blazes are you doing, Thomas?"

"I thought I made it clear I had someone I needed to speak with." He planted his hands on his hips and stared at the long row of carriages, searching for ours. He motioned to me with his hand. "Come on, there it is. Hurry along."

"Not until you explain to me what is going on," I insisted.

"Now is not the time or place, Grace." He wiggled his fingers.

"I am not leaving until…" The thought stuck me like a bolt. "You are ashamed of me. That's it, isn't it?"

"Don't be absurd." He trotted down the remainder of the steps, glancing over his shoulder toward the door. "I'd like to go now, Grace…please," he added as an afterthought.

Begrudgingly, I followed him down the steps and allowed him to assist me into the carriage. Once settled across from me, he tapped the roof and I waited as the carriage ambled along the cobblestone streets. Thomas's focus was on the window, his mouth in a firm, flat line.

"What is it, Thomas?" I asked finally, unable to stand the wait any longer.

"I'd rather not discuss it just now," he replied.

I wanted to believe that it had nothing to do with me.

"You don't plan to tell me what happened back there?"

"Why did you have to tell them we met at the Cremorne?"

I recoiled in surprise. "Because we did."

He made no response but continued to stare out the window.

"Thomas, if you don't explain your irrational behavior, I'm going to be forced to come to my own conclusions."

He shook his head and gave me a long side glance.

"It is none of your affair. I only wish that you hadn't mentioned the Cremorne."

"Why?" I asked, fearing I knew his answer had something to do with my profession.

"Because they now have the wrong impression."

"The wrong impression?" I asked, stupefied by his remark. "You of all people are worried about impressions?"

"I do have a career that I am, with great opposition, trying to rebuild, Grace."

"Well, then, Thomas, I suppose I should be grateful that you've gone to such lengths to provide me with the finer things in life, although I do not know what you hoped to accomplish with this charitable evening."

He looked at me, his forehead creasing in a frown.

"I don't understand, Grace. Don't you wish to be better than you are? Don't you want to make something more of yourself? Your face now appears in portraits all over Europe. Don't you feel it's about bloody time you learned to act like a lady?"

He might as well have pointed a pistol to my heart. I hit the top of the carriage with my palm and it jerked to a stop. With a quick look outside I recognized the part of town we were in. It was not far from the pub where I lived.

On the corner, a brawl had erupted and patrons spilled out onto the street, taking bets on the outcome. The misty fog of evening mingled with the smoke and noise rolling through the narrow streets. Girls called on gents to see if they needed some company. More important, no one was making anyone feel like they didn't belong.

"I'll walk from here, Thomas."

"You'll do nothing of the sort," he fumed, blocking my arm as I reached for the door. "I can't allow you to traipse through Whitechapel in that gown. Let me take you back to the studio."

"You're worried about your damn dress? Fine, Thomas." I dropped the mink stole in his lap. "I always found you to be a bit on the arrogant side, but I forgave it because I liked you. But not until this moment had I taken you for a snob."

Discarding the pearl-tipped hat pin, which surely dislodged a curl or two, I pulled off the hat and gloves and tossed them on the seat beside him. With a quick work of my skirts, I managed to untie the bustle and shake it to my feet.

"What in blazes…Grace, what do you think you're doing?"

"I am giving back your charity, Thomas. I don't need it."

"Oh, bloody hell. Stop this, Grace."

My pride stung, but I knew it would ease with time. What I did not know was how long it would take for my heart, which I had cautiously opened to this man, to heal. The gown was loose enough that, with a bit of maneuvering, I pulled it off my arms and quickly slid it over my hips. Extracting myself at last, I held it up and dropped the entire sequined mess in his lap. "There you are, Thomas. Now you needn't worry. Perhaps you can find a model that you feel worthy to be seen with you." I reached for the carriage handle and stepped onto the street, clad only in my chemise, corset, drawers and shoes.

"Jesus, Grace, be reasonable."

I stormed down the street, ignoring the prattle of calls and whistles from drunken pub patrons. The carriage rattled to my side with Thomas leaning out of its window.

"Grace, I cannot express how utterly infantile this looks. I am only going to offer one last time. Get in this carriage and let's talk like sensible human beings."

"You are an arse, Thomas Rodin." I jabbed my finger toward him.

"You tell the bloke, little girl," a drunk leaning against the building said, waving his bottle.

"Let me give you a ride home."

I stopped and faced him then, my hands balled against my hips. "In case you've forgotten, Thomas, this is my home!"

His gaze narrowed. Oh, but he was bloody angry with me, which suited me fine as I was more angry with him.

"Fine, be a stubborn wench," he snapped.

"Thank you kindly, sir. At least I know who I am." I spit back. More cheers went up from behind.

"Pigheaded female," he called, smacking the side of the carriage to signal the driver.

"Two-faced toad," I yelled at the departing carriage. I'd shown him that he couldn't treat me like a pet pony, grooming me to show off to his friends. I held in my tears, hurrying along the dank streets, until I reached the safety of my little room above the pub. Only then did I allow the sobs to rack my body, until finally exhausted, I drew my thin blanket over me and fell asleep.

Chapter 4

FOUR MONTHS TURNED TO SIX, SIX MONTHS TO a year, and still I'd received no word from Thomas. I couldn't say I was surprised. I suppose I'd hurt his pride as he had mine. What I had saved from my wages for posing kept me in good standing with the owner of the pub and I offered to help him wait tables and make small talk with the gents one or two nights a week. From time to time, I would go to the Cremorne and found it odd that many of my former clients—having seen my name associated with the brotherhood—did not come around with the same frequency as before. It was not as if I missed the intimacy, though I was lonely. I found Deidre asleep on one of the benches one night. She hadn't eaten in days and she had nowhere to go, so I offered to buy her dinner at the pub.

"Thank you, Grace. You've no idea what this means to me." She stuffed another piece of fish into her mouth, following it with a swallow of ale.

"I understand, Deidre. I've been there before. We need to watch out for each other, don't we? We're all the family we've got."

She looked at me, her deep green eyes filled with too much

knowledge for her young age. "Whatever happened to that artist chap? Did he have his way with ya and cast ya off, then?"

I considered her words, grappling with who had cast off whom. "I posed for a few of his projects. My services were no longer needed after that."

She made a disgusted sound in her throat. "Ain't that just the way of it?"

"I suppose." A twinge of pain, duller now than six months ago, nudged at my heart.

"Excuse me, are you Miss Farmer?"

I looked up at the large man standing next to our table. His thick foreign accent sounded vaguely familiar. He wore a fine coat and derby, and from what I could tell, most of his hair was on the bushy mustache perched above his wide grin.

He held out his hand to me. "Lord Hoffemeyer. I don't suppose I would be so lucky that you would remember me. We met about a year ago at the opera. You were with Mr. Rodin."

"Of course, Lord Hoffemeyer. I didn't recognize you at first. Something is different."

He chuckled. "Perhaps it is the absence of Lady Hoffemeyer?"

I didn't hide my frank surprise. "Perhaps you're right. I remember her as being particularly elegant." I withdrew my hand from his firm grasp. "How is Lady Hoffemeyer?" I glanced at Deidre, who seemed mesmerized by Lord Hoffemeyer's watch-fob chain.

His delighted expression dimmed. "I wonder if it would be too bold to ask that you take a walk with me, Miss Farmer. There is a matter of some importance I would like to discuss with you."

I looked at Deidre, realizing that I hadn't introduced her yet. She raised her brow. "Lord Hoffemeyer, this is Deidre—" I faltered, realizing that I didn't know her last name.

"Just Deidre, guv'ner." She extended her filthy hand to him. To my surprise, he took it and kissed it, causing poor Deidre to turn a shade of crimson.

"Will you be all right if I go for a short walk with Lord Hoffemeyer?" I asked.

"Ah, sure, go on. I'll see ye later."

"A pleasure." Hoffemeyer bowed to Deidre.

I could have kissed him. "You were very kind to my friend, milord. It takes a special man to be so kind."

He offered me a slight smile and we walked side by side in silence for a minute or two. Part of me wondered if he'd spoken to Thomas recently and if that might have anything to do with what he wanted to tell me.

He was a handsome man for his age. There were streaks of silver in his dark mustache and crinkles at the corners of his brown eyes.

"It's my understanding that you are no longer posing for the brotherhood. More specifically, Mr. Rodin."

I glanced up at him with a questioning look. "If Thomas sent you here…"

He shook his head, "No I haven't spoken to him since that night. You two hurried off so quickly."

"I must apologize, milord. I don't know what got into Thomas that night."

"He said nothing to you?"

I shook my head as I looked out across the Thames. "No, I'm afraid we had an argument that night and I haven't seen him since."

"That is unfortunate," he replied, stuffing his hands in his coat pocket. "I hear he has a new model working for him now, a stunning redhead, or so an acquaintance of the brotherhood told me."

I tried not to let it show that the news twisted something deep inside me. With time, I had convinced myself that Thomas and I were never meant to be. "He always thought red hair was exotic," I said, forcing a smile on my face.

He placed his arm on mine to stop me. "If you are receptive to the idea of modeling again, Grace, I would like to ask if you'd pose for my commission."

I wasn't sure how I felt about posing again, but if the money was better than what the pub paid, I was willing to listen. "Do you have an artist in mind?"

"I have commissioned one of the brotherhood artists to paint a very special portrait."

"A special portrait? And what do you mean by that, Lord Hof-femeyer?"

He took a deep breath and let out a long sigh. "It is for my den, Grace. I have a very private collection, painted by some of the most renowned artists of our time."

"And you want to include a portrait of me?"

"Yes, very much. Grace, ever since our meeting that night, I have not been able to get the vision of you in that dress out of my mind."

My cheeks warmed. "Lord Hoffemeyer, pardon me for saying, but you are a very eccentric man."

He shrugged and took my hand, kissing it. "I have been called worse. Still, when I want something, I do not stop until I get it." He smiled.

I had seen that look enough times in my life, usually from the shadows of an alleyway with a gent showing me a pouch, fat with coins. "If you don't mind me asking, milord, what is it you want from me, exactly?"

"A portrait, Grace. One with very specific details."

"Nothing more included in this arrangement?"

"Of course not, Grace. Nothing more than what you are comfortable with." He tipped his hat slightly.

"These details? What are they?" I asked, still leery, suspecting that this wasn't entirely a coincidence.

He smiled sheepishly. "I want a nude, Grace."

"A nude?"

"Yes, I know you might find that odd, perhaps, but my col-lection—"

I stopped him. "You've no need to explain your position, Lord Hoffemeyer." I needed the money if I was going to be able to find a place big enough for Deidre and me to live for the winter. "A nude portrait?" I asked. "That's all?"

"That's it, my dear." He patted my arm. "Oh, and I've made arrangements with the artist to split the fee fifty-fifty."

My eyes widened as I struggled with whether I'd heard him correctly. "Half for me and half for the artist? He agreed to that?"

Lord Hoffemeyer shrugged his burly shoulders. "He seemed fine with the arrangement."

"You must truly want this portrait."

"You've no idea what it means to me, Grace. In addition, while the painting is being completed, I don't want you to have to travel so far to the studio each day. So I'm asking you to move into a small flat nearby the studio I've secured."

"The artist doesn't have his own studio?" I asked, puzzled as to who in the brotherhood wouldn't have his own studio or simply ask Thomas to use his.

"I wanted a place where he wouldn't be disturbed by anyone."

The man obviously had enough money that he could have his pick of beautiful women to pose for him. Why me? "It seems you've thought this out very carefully, Lord Hoffemeyer. Forgive my curiosity, but what is in this for you?"

He smiled and the sparkle went straight to his deep brown eyes. "Now and again when I'm in town for business, I ask that you might consider letting me take you to dinner, perhaps a show. There are times a man simply enjoys the company of a lady."

"And Lady Hoffemeyer would not take offense?" I asked.

"My wife and I have an understanding, Grace."

I nodded. I knew about men and their mistresses. I tipped my head, regarding him. He must have sensed my discomfort as he hurried on.

"Just for companionship, Grace. A friend and nothing more, unless you choose it."

Though I was hesitant to accept his proposal, the truth was that Deidre would have a warm place to stay and meals provided for her if she was willing to work at the pub a few nights in my stead. And I needed the money. With my reputation of being a model now public knowledge, men were hesitant to be seen with me. I reasoned that if I felt things were becoming a problem, I could always leave.

I placed my arm through his. "A nude, then?"

"Tastefully done. I assure you."

"I never doubted it, Lord Hoffemeyer," I replied.

"May I buy you a drink to celebrate our agreement, Grace?"

"I'd be delighted."

Deidre was thrilled to have a warm bed and I introduced her to Barnaby, the pub manager, who started her immediately on serving tables. "You'll call me if you need anything," I said as I hugged her close.

"Don't you worry 'bout me, Grace. I can handle meself." She waved as the carriage Lord Hoffemeyer had sent for me rambled away.

Lord Hoffemeyer insisted on seeing that I was settled into my new apartment before my first day of work. We'd just finished lunch at the apartment, made by the resident cook and house-keeper. The apartment consisted of two bedrooms, a bath with indoor plumbing, a parlor, small kitchen and a pantry. It was filled with furnishings far better than I'd ever had. There was a simple elegance to the flat and I wondered what purpose the nest usually served for Lord Hoffemeyer.

"Do you stay here when in London, Lord Hoffemeyer?" I asked, noting there were indeed two bedrooms. His eyes darted to mine and a smile crept up his face.

"I haven't been here in some time. Lady Hoffemeyer always liked staying here in the past." He looked around at the mementos on the walls and shelves. "But I want you to feel free to make it your own."

He dabbed his napkin to his mouth. "Now, Grace, about your hair. I want it wrapped around your head." He pushed from his chair and stood behind me, working his hands in my hair until it was loosely piled on top of my head.

"I want it exactly as you wore it that night. Wound up around your head like a halo." His hands rested on my shoulders.

"Oh, Baron, surely you have the wrong woman." I laughed.

He chuckled and squeezed my shoulders. "Oh, no, Grace. I have found the only woman who can give me what I want."

I touched my napkin to my mouth and turned to look up at him.

"Are you certain that we've not met before that night at the opera?"

He sat back in his chair and lifted his water glass. "I am quite sure you'd have remembered a big oaf like me."

"You are not a big oaf, milord. I find you more of a snuggly bear," I teased good-naturedly. A man of his power and wealth would be good to have on my side, and besides, he and the baroness were friends of Thomas's.

He held his glass up by way of a toast and smiled. "You flatter me, Grace. I am humbled you think of me in such kind terms. I want us to be friends." He regarded me for a moment. "I trust you have everything you need. If not, ask the cook or the driver and they will see to your needs."

"You're not going with me tomorrow to the studio?" I asked.

"Unfortunately I have some business out of town to attend to. I will, however, notify you when I am back in London."

He rose and kissed my cheek before summoning the driver to take him to meet his ship. I admit it was an odd arrangement, but he had kept his word thus far, with no surprises or uncomfortable requests. I looked around the room and took a deep breath. I needed to get a good night's sleep, so I would look favorable for the first day of my new job.

I was appointed a personal driver and hansom coach. Both were waiting when I emerged from the flat the next morning, prepared to walk the distance. The driver said it was going to rain and said that I should ride, instead.

"Thank you…what shall I call you?" I asked, taking his hand. I was not used to this kind of attentiveness.

"The name's Dobbs, miss. I'll wait for you until you're finished with the studio, as Lord Hoffemeyer has insisted." He bowed. I stared at the man for a moment, wondering when I would awaken from this dream.

There was no one in the hotel-room-turned-studio when I arrived, but there was a note from Lord Hoffemeyer, lying on a lovely deep-rose-colored fainting couch. I sat down and opened the note.

Dearest Grace,

I am most fortunate that fate smiled down upon me that night at the opera. I feel it was destiny that we met again and look forward to cultivating a long and satisfying relationship with you while we partner in this most exciting endeavor.

I have the utmost faith in the artist that I've commissioned. He's a good chap, although he possesses a bit of arrogance, which I think we both realize from experience comes with the mind of a creative genius. Though he has no idea of who I have chosen to model for this piece, I am quite certain that you will handle yourself professionally in your manner and dealings with him. However, should you have any trouble at all, send for me immediately, and as always, I have Dobbs at the ready. I do not anticipate trouble, mind you; do not be alarmed. It is only that with my being out of town, I want your safety and happiness above all.

I will be in touch to see how the portrait is progressing upon my next visit to London. In my absence, I have taken the liberty of setting up accounts in my name for you at the locations listed at the bottom of this note. Until later, my dear, beautiful Grace.
Lord H.

I began to undress behind the dressing screen provided in the corner of the room. My head came up as I heard the door open and someone enter the room. "Hello?" I called out. A silence followed. "Did Lord Hoffemeyer send you? Are you the brotherhood artist he commissioned?"

"Um…yes, madam. I was just checking the lighting in here. He indicated that this was a very special project. He has left me detailed instructions as to his wishes. I assume you have also received similar notification."

Though raspy, his voice was familiar. I wrapped the wide sheath of deep-blue satin fabric around me, as were Lord Hoffemeyer's instructions, and stepped from behind the screen. It fell from my grasp as my eyes slammed into a pair of teal-colored eyes. "Thomas?"

His gaze darted up from his reading of the note. "Bloody hell…Grace?" He stared at me in mutual surprise. "What in the bloody hell…" He looked down at the note.

I took the opportunity to cover myself and hurried behind the screen. It was absurd, of course, to feel so exposed in front of my former lover, but it felt strange. "There must be some sort of mistake, Thomas. Have you or have you not been commissioned by Lord Hoffemeyer to paint a nude of me?"

"Clearly, Hoffemeyer was not of sound mind when he made arrangements for this project."

I frowned. "He is one of the most sound-minded, kind men that I know," I called over the screen.

"Ah, I see, the two of you are on intimate terms, then?" he asked.

I stepped from behind the screen. "Is it any of your business?"

"Then that is a yes?" He tipped his head. I shifted the cloth tighter around me, aware of how his gaze slowly assessed me.

The man was infuriating, if not all the more arrogant than I remembered. "He is a friend, Thomas…a *good* friend."

I took the time to look at him. He wore a jacket similar to the style he so loved, coming across as some sort of Italian libertine with his ruffled cuffs. "I see you've managed to obtain a new jacket. The other was particularly shabby."

He raised his eyebrows. "I don't look shabby." His expression clouded and then he let out a pronounced sigh. "Well, Grace, it looks like we'll have to make do. The money, as I'm sure you've been apprised, is far too good to pass up. He told you of the arrangement?"

"Fifty-fifty," I repeated Lord Hoffemeyer's instructions.

"Yes, an absurd amount," he muttered. "No offense."

"None taken. It will be worth every shilling for every moment I have to spend here."

He raised his eyebrows and began to set up his table. "I suspect he mentioned that I have a new model working for me?"

"I've heard she has glorious red hair. And so, a new muse to titillate you, Thomas?"

He placed his paint box on the table next to the easel. "You say that as if I have an unsavory reputation with women."

I offered a quiet snort. "Oh, no, not unsavory, but definitely a reputation. So she is a red-haired beauty?" I sat down on the edge of the couch, keeping the cloth wrapped tightly around me.

Thomas glanced up at me as he began to arrange his brushes. "She is innocent. Perfect, really, for my current project. She has a fresh face and that look of inexperience in her eyes."

"I see you haven't lost your way with words, Thomas."

He ignored the jab and so did I.

"How is William?"

Thomas shrugged off his jacket and laid it over the back of a chair. "He was the one to find Helen, truth be told. He knew I was looking for a redhead."

"An innocent? How old is she?" I asked, memories of my past creeping into my mind, though I knew Thomas wasn't the depraved sort.

"Not innocent in age, Grace. She is plenty old enough, if that is your meaning."

"Such a nice contrast, an angelic face with hair that the devil calls his own. I'm quite certain that whatever you're planning has to do with creating a controversy for the academy," I commented drily.

"I won't deny that," he responded. After a moment he added, "My schedule these days is erratic at best. I may have to work

nights as I'm in the throes of finishing another project. Are evenings going to prove inconvenient for you, Grace?"

I smiled. "There is no need to be cruel, Thomas. Let's lay our
cards on the table, shall we? You have moved on with your life
and so have I. Evenings are fine with me, daytime, as well, if that
is your preference."

"A lady of leisure you've become, then?" He smiled demurely.

"A lady of learning," I replied calmly.

His eyes glittered with curiosity. "So he takes good care of
you?"

"Let's understand something, Thomas. I'm doing this for Lord
Hoffemeyer." I dropped the cloth and lay on my stomach, drawing
the blue cloth over my bum.

"And here I thought you were doing it for the money."

"Arse," I muttered, propping my chin on my crossed arms.

He chuckled quietly.

"Will this suffice? It is what I envisioned when I read Lord
Hoffemeyer's instructions." I was used to showing men my body.
I simply had to remind myself that Thomas was just another man.
Not the man who had broken my heart.

He walked over to me, his expression unreadable, and I felt him
tug on the fabric. I glanced over my shoulder as he arranged the
cloth to expose one of my legs. He tucked—perhaps with too
much care—the remaining cloth, smoothing it down over my
inner thigh.

"Are you quite finished?" My tone was droll.

He stepped back as if assessing his work.

"Turn a bit toward me. I think we need more of your breasts
exposed…for Lord Hoffemeyer, of course."

I gave him a brief smile, wondering if fifty percent was
enough.

He studied the effect.

"Just a tweak…" He reached out and, with his thumb and fore-
finger, tweaked the pink nub of my breast. It puckered instantly.

"There, I wanted a look of arousal."

I shook my head. "Of course you did," I muttered.

"Listen to me. Place one hand beneath you. You know, as though you are pleasuring yourself."

"I don't recall that being in the instructions, Thomas."

His eyes narrowed and his mouth lifted in a smirk.

"He and I spoke in vivid detail, trust me."

"Just how *vivid,* if you don't mind?" I asked, sliding my hand between my stomach and the couch, my fingers covering my triangle of soft curls.

"I need you to look aroused, Grace. And given the present situation, I find it awkward to help you achieve the look myself."

"What a gentleman. I'd quite forgotten."

He sighed and chewed the tip of his brush, looking deep in thought.

"Don't even think about touching me, Thomas," I warned.

"Well, then." He shrugged, walking back to his easel. "You have to achieve it as best you can. I need that look of being pleasured by your lover reflected in your eyes."

"But don't you have to sketch me first? Is how my eyes look all that important?"

"Are you telling me how I should do my job?" he sputtered. "For God's sake, passion, Grace, that expression of being satisfied. You do your job, I'll do mine."

Perhaps his innocent muse was causing poor Thomas more frustration than he realized. I lay there for a moment and watched him roll up his shirtsleeves, pick up his piece of charcoal and begin to sketch furiously. He did not look up. Pride and loathing warred inside of me. I wanted to treat him with the same blasé attitude that he was treating me with.

With a pronounced sigh of frustration, I flopped to my back and placed my hand between my thighs, massaging furiously, finding no pleasure whatsoever in the action.

"That is not working for you, Grace," Thomas interjected.

"Be quiet." I turned, pinning him with a frustrated look, took a deep breath and looked back at the ceiling. Focused now, I emitted a sigh that would have caused an astute cock to come to attention. Softly, I touched myself with gentle strokes, summoning a familiar smoky curl deep in my core. I rolled my palm over my breast, capturing a stiff nipple between my fingers. With each stroke, my concerns drifted away and the image of Thomas lavishing me with his tongue that rainy morning so long ago, emerged in my head. I heard the sound of my sighs in the silence and I remembered implicitly how he mastered my body, drawing me to the edge again and again, until I begged him to take me.

A soft moan escaped my lips as I thought of him on his knees, his arms wrapped around my legs, thrusting into me with fervent, slow determination. I remembered the look on his face, the emotion in his eyes as he stared down at me.

My hips rocked with the sensual image in my head. My breath caught and I grabbed the arm of the chair as I arched my back, plunging two fingers deep inside me.

I licked my lips as I turned and met Thomas's heated gaze. His hand was poised midair, his eyes filled with need. I wondered what he was thinking; if he, too, was remembering that day. I continued to roll my hips as my juices, warm and wet, spilled over my fingers. I swallowed and held my hand out. "I surmise this is *vivid* enough for you?" My gaze drifted down to the tented hood of his trousers. "Yes, I do believe it is," I said, and shifted to find my pose.

Chapter 5

THERE WERE DAYS I WANTED TO SCREAM. I WANTED to ask him what he saw in Helen that he did not see in me. But I would stop myself, bathed in my self-awareness of the answer. The distinctions were painfully clear. Helen represented everything innocent, unstained, not yet scarred by the world. I was the embodiment of exactly the opposite. When I first met Thomas, with his eccentric behavior, his healthy appetite for sex and his modern view of things, I never expected him to be the sort to put people in boxes. Not once, before the night at the opera, had I ever felt he judged me for my past, but he had made his true thoughts on that quite clear. Ironically, the notoriety I had achieved by modeling for the brotherhood had caused many of my former clients to shy away, afraid to be seen with me for what it might do to them socially. As long as I was a faceless, nameless whore, I was worth a romp, but now I had a sordid reputation and I could not go back to prostitution.

I'd been posing for Thomas off and on for several months, often wondering if he ever mentioned me to his new muse. The truth was, I wondered many things about them. Did they talk and laugh as we once had? Did they enjoy walks in the park together? Were they, too, lovers, as Thomas and I had been? Perhaps it was foolish to entertain these thoughts, as they only served to frustrate me more.

Still, all must not have been paradise in Thomas's world. He was moody, unsettled. One day he would be full of life, and the next pensive and withdrawn. Whatever was going on over at his studio was affecting him like a barometer. By good fortune, he no longer used me as a vehicle for his repressed sexual needs. This made me realize, with some sadness, that he was, or had been, bedding his new muse, and his mood swings were most likely a result of her compliance, or lack thereof.

It was an oppressive summer day. The air was thick with the stifling humidity of an approaching thunderstorm. The view beyond the hotel window was dismal, gray, a foreshadowing of impending rain. Thomas was in one of his moods. Sour faced, tired, unshaven. He looked as if he'd just rolled out of bed…alone. Either that or he was taking ill. I tried to stay out of his way.

An itch on my nose caused me to move, scratching it with the tip of my finger.

"Grace, do not move," he snapped.

We'd become like actors in a silent play, playing our parts, not touching, not connecting with each other. It was strange to see Thomas so void of passion. Regardless of how we'd parted those many months ago, I could not cast his welfare aside. My heart would simply not allow it. Deep down, I still cared for him.

His eyebrows pinched together in fierce concentration as he dabbed his brush on his palette.

"Thomas? Is there something weighing on you?"

"Don't ask," he muttered, adding more paint and then scowling at his choice.

"If you need someone to listen, Thomas. If it's about the academy—"

"I don't need to talk to anyone about anything. I don't *want* to talk about it. Do you understand, Grace?" He scraped off the blob of paint he'd been mixing and started over, his jaw set firm in determination.

I stared at the back of the canvas, noting the wooden framework that held it in place. It had more personality at present than did Thomas. The light outside was waning as the dark rain clouds rolled in. I'd posed enough for Thomas and the others to know that he'd either have to quit or light some lamps soon to continue.

"Are you at a point where I can move?" I asked. "I'll light the lamps if you wish."

He glanced up briefly. "Make it quick."

There was a measure of comfort in that he trusted me to know what needed to be done. If only he would trust me with other things.

I did not bother putting on my dressing gown as I moved in haste to light the kerosene lamps. I placed them where I thought the light would do most good, having decided Thomas would move them where he wanted.

I was hurrying back to the couch when he reached out and grabbed my wrist. I looked first at my arm, and then at Thomas. He had a far-off look on his face as he stared at the canvas.

"I've asked Helen to marry me, Grace."

Though I never expected to resume a relationship with Thomas, a cold spot formed in my stomach at the thought of him married. Why did I assume that we would always stay as we were? I stared at where his long fingers curled around my arm. His hands, capable, strong, were one of the first things I'd noticed about him. "Then I suppose congratulations are in order," I stated quietly.

"Grace." He looked up at me.

I glanced away immediately, my body tensing at the tone in his voice. "I'm quite sure the two of you will make a handsome couple and be desperately happy." I forced the words from my mouth though I did not believe them.

"There's more to it, Grace. I had to propose because…it was the right thing."

I eased from his grip. "The right thing? What do you mean?"

"She carries my child, Grace."

I grabbed the edge of the canvas and it slid off the easel, crashing to the floor. I watched in a blind stupor as he picked it up, righting it. My heart pounded against my chest and I found it difficult to breathe. I could barely see the floor before me as I found my dressing robe. My hands were shaking violently as I fought the silky fabric trying to find the *goddamn fucking* sleeve. At last, I punched my arm through the hole and pulled the robe around my nakedness, tying the belt at my waist with a resolute jerk. Still feeling exposed, I turned, at least now able to face him. "I think that you should go, Thomas. Go attend to your affairs, to your future bride and to your…child. I wish you all the best, truly." I held my back straight, forcing my knees not to buckle.

"You said you would listen," he remarked, dotting it with a sarcastic laugh.

I whirled on him then. "So I did. But I thought you were pouting over some asinine art critic, or maybe you'd missed out on the freshest scones this morning. For God's sake, I had no idea it would be *this!*"

He dropped his palette on the table and strode toward me, his eyes blazing. I noted how dark the circles were under his eyes. He grabbed my arms and shook me once. I stiffened under his stern glare.

"Do you think I want this? Good God, Grace. Me? A father? You know me better than anyone. Can you honestly see me expounding on life's virtue and offering discipline to a child? But what can I do? Jesus, Grace, what choice do I have?"

"Are you certain it is yours?" I asked, a spark of hope emerging in my mind.

"Fairly certain," he said, searching my eyes as if maybe I'd found an escape to his dilemma. He shook his head. "No, I am certain."

Though I did not wish to confirm his certainty by asking for details, I needed to know one thing. "Do you love her?" The warmth of his hands on my arms only increased the ache in my heart. He stared at me, looking for answers that I could not give. "Jesus, Grace, I don't even know that I'm capable of the kind of love she deserves."

His words, though unrealized by him, showed the enormous feeling, if not love, that he felt for her. A sharp pain stabbed my heart. "She has agreed to marry you, then?"

He nodded.

I bit my lip, forcing the words from my mouth. "You care deeply for her. I…can see it."

"But is that enough, Grace?" he asked. His eyes, always alive with passion, were filled with dread, uncertainty. "We have so little in common. She demands so much of me. The poor thing is so frail. She…*needs* me."

I shut my eyes to the softness in his voice as he talked of her. Perhaps there was a difference between loving someone and feeling a need to be there for them, but that was something Thomas would have to decide for himself, not something I could tell him now.

"You've already decided. You are bringing a child into this world, and that child will need you, as will its mother."

His face was pale, as if he might be sick. "I am not reliable in matters of the heart, Grace." His eyes turned pleadingly to mine.

"On that we agree," I said with a slight smile.

Those mesmerizing eyes looked at me, and I caught a glimpse of the man I had once called my friend.

"You were right, you know. I am a snob—or was. I have kicked myself every night since you climbed out of that carriage." The look in his eyes was contrite and I knew he was being sincere.

It seemed absurd to me that he would bother with such a confession now of all times, but for Thomas, it was like making restitution for his sins. "How very odd," I stated with a tilt of my head. "I have done exactly the same thing. You must be severely bruised by now." I raised an eyebrow.

His face, though drawn, managed a weary smile.

"Can you ever forgive me, Grace?" he asked, taking my hands in his.

How could I forgive that his new muse was living my dream? Then again, I had to be honest and ask myself whether his behavior would be any different if it was me carrying his child. Thomas was who he was, and I could not change that. Time would tell, but I doubted that even marriage would.

I reached up, cupping his face. I was not one to judge anyone's character. With all of his faults, Thomas was, deep down, a good man. "I already have, Thomas. Many times over." I studied his face. "But I have dearly missed our companionship."

He hugged me close, pressing his face into my shoulder.

"Dear Grace, your friendship means the world to me. It is my constant."

He kissed my cheek. My breath caught and my eyes drifted shut.

"You know me best, Grace. You have seen me at my worst—"

"Yes," I said quietly.

"And at my best," he said, easing me back to look at him. His eyes shimmered.

"Definitely." Already my body was reacting to his warm gaze.

"Be mine tonight, Grace. Let me share this one night with the woman who knows me best and loves me, anyway."

I should have said no. I should have sent him away. But he was right.

A rumble of thunder rattled the windowpanes. The ping of rain pelting the glass punctuated each moment that he stared at me, waiting for my answer. I undid the tie of my robe and dropped the garment at my feet. "Come with me, Thomas." I led him to the bed that the hotel staff had shoved, with the rest of the room's furniture, to the corner of the room. I lay on the bed waiting, watching as he peeled off his clothing and his firm body came into view.

He lay down, stretched out beside me on the bed, and I welcomed his mouth, as we sought solace for the wrongs we could not right, for a past we could not recapture. All we had was this moment, safe from the eye of the turbulent world around us—

this moment of his hands gliding over my skin, our bodies touching, soft flesh to hard muscle.

"You are my heart, Grace," he whispered against the small of my back. His hand caressed the sensitive valley between my thighs, stroking me until I was wet and writhing for him.

I rose on my knees, pressing my back to his chest, his hands gently caressing, squeezing my breasts. "Do not speak such things, Thomas. Passion is all I want tonight." I bowed forward, raising my hips in silent invitation.

His breath was hot, wafting over my back, his teeth nipping my bottom. A groan tore from my throat when he parted me, easing into me slowly, moving his hips with measured ease until our bodies fused entirely.

"I never want to lose you," he whispered, curling his body over mine, brushing my hair aside and kissing my neck.

My fingers fisted into the tangled linens, my teeth raking across my lower lip, tasting him on my tongue.

His rocked his hips, his flesh moving against my thighs, drawing me up quickly, and then he began to pump with deep, masterful strokes and I surrendered with my sighs, etching this moment in my mind.

We'd never used a sheath. I'd never had need to, as I could not bear children. At one time it was something that I'd fretted about. But it didn't matter now. He was going to have a child of his own to cherish, and his own family.

My climax ripped through my body at the same time his name tore from my throat, a viable sign of our joining, and, too, our parting.

Thomas uttered a guttural sound, teetering on his own release. He grabbed my hips and held me close, slamming into me once more, spilling his hot seed.

He kissed the back of my shoulder and drew me down beside him on the bed. For a time we lay together in silence. I did not want to speak. I wanted only to have his arm wrapped around me as it was, his fingers caressing the underside of my breast.

"Let me braid your hair once more."

He brushed my hair to the side and laid his cheek against my shoulder.

I smiled, though the feeling was bittersweet. I turned into his arms. "Perhaps later, Thomas. This time I want to look at you when I come."

He made love to me again and I fought the selfishness of wishing it was me and not Helen who, by her pregnancy, had managed to claim Thomas when I could not.

Later, I sat facing away from him, the bedsheets pulled over my legs as he braided my hair. I debated whether to bring up the subject of his child again, but thought that if I were to talk about it, it would just make it more real. "Have you thought of names, Thomas? I finally asked.

"I can't bring myself to do so, Grace. I have left that in Helen's hands." His bodiless voice answered from behind me. Lightning flashed through the window, bathing the room in a brilliant ghostlike wash.

"Perhaps I'll call her Grace," he said softly.

I whirled to face him. "You wouldn't dare. Promise me, Thomas. You promise me that you will never give that name to this child, or any others you may have."

"I'm sorry. I didn't mean to upset you." He kissed me gently.

I shook my head, contrite. "It's just that there are so many other wonderful names to bestow on a child."

He kissed my shoulder. "Perhaps, but none of them nearly as lovely as yours."

"Oh, for God's sake, Thomas. Stop it," I demanded.

"Stop? Stop what?"

"Stop putting thoughts in my head that I am dearer to you than I really am. We have known each other for too long and in truth, we have only used each other when one of us is lonely. Hasn't that been the way of it?"

"Grace, didn't you hear me? Weren't you listening when I said—"

"I know." My voice lowered as I pressed my hand to my mouth. "I know. There is no need to tiptoe around me. I will always care about you."

When there was no response, I turned to look at him, finding him staring at me with a puzzled expression. My hair, partially braided, hung loose in his palm.

"Is that what you think? Do you really think I've spoken these words to anyone else? Yes, we've both had our share of lovers—do not look away from me, Grace."

He came around the bed and knelt in front of me. "I swear to you that I have never had what we share, beyond the bed—this bond we have—with any other woman. And I fear, though I believe you already know, that I never will have. You have spoiled me, Grace, but I cannot change the way things are." He studied me. "And maybe if things were different, we might have never met."

Too raw was the notion that we were his ideal of the tragic Shakespearean lovers, destined never to be together. My view of things was clear and, for his own well-being, Thomas's view should be as clear. What good were his heartfelt confessions to me now? They would not keep me warm in a cold bed while he slept at Helen's side. "Perhaps, but we shall never know, shall we?" I leaned toward him, brushing his hair over his ear. "I will be nothing more than a dear memory in your old age."

He shook his head, grabbing my hand. "No, Grace, you are the only woman I have ever loved."

"Loved? Oh, dear God." I held up my hand. "If you care even just the tiniest bit for me, Thomas, you will not say another word. Just go…go now."

"But Grace…"

"I beg you, Thomas. Go."

"But the painting? No, you must understand—"

I pushed him away and scooted off the bed. His words raced after me like tangible things, nipping at my heels. "I'll speak to the baron about the painting. Perhaps someone else could—"

"That is *my* work," he thundered. "I will be the only one to finish it."

He followed close behind as I picked up his clothes that had scattered when he'd tossed them in the throes of passion. I spun on my heel and dropped the clothes in his arms. "Perhaps later, but not now, Thomas. I beg you, please leave."

He dressed slowly, eyeing me as I doused all the kerosene lamps, save one. He gathered his paint box and tools, and reached for the painting.

"Please leave it. It isn't dry anyway, and the rain will ruin it." I had pulled on my dressing gown as if the normalcy of it would somehow put things back to the way they were before.

"When will I see you again, Grace?" Thomas asked as he pulled on his coat. "I will need to finish the portrait in order for us both to receive our payment."

"I'll send word when I am ready. Goodbye, Thomas," I said quietly. "Please tell the desk clerk I'll be staying here tonight." He leaned forward to kiss me and I turned my head. If he didn't leave soon I would not be able to hold in the storm of tears that were about to be unleashed.

"Good night, Grace." He hesitated in the hall and turned, starting to speak. I closed the door gently and leaned against it. I squeezed my fists and gulped for air as the sobs crawled up my throat. I'd never hated my life more than at that moment. I hated my past, hated what I'd done, hated the choices I'd made.

I strode to the window, flipped open the latch and shoved it open against the torrent of rain and wind. The onslaught of water sprayed my skin, soaking my gown. Flashes of lightning, followed by loud crashes of thunder, drowned out the strangled sound of my anguished cries.

Four weeks had passed since I asked Thomas to leave. I was at the mercy of Lord Hoffemeyer's kindness in allowing me to stay on at the apartment, having convinced myself that eventually I would be able to muster the courage to face Thomas again. Until such time, I took advantage of Lord Hoffemeyer's accounts and bought clothes that I never thought I would wear. In addition, I'd heard from Watts that Thomas was selling off some of his paintings at public auctions. I asked him to keep me informed of where and when Thomas took in his paintings, but made him swear not to tell Thomas. I felt responsible for Thomas's losing out on his commission, as I hadn't yet contacted him about finishing the painting. I'd kept it, propping it on the library shelf, amongst the rest of Thomas's paintings that I'd purchased anonymously with Lord Hoffemeyer's money by sending Dobbs to the auctions.

"Dobbs has brought you another one, Grace."

Lord Hoffemeyer, in town only for a few hours, leaned the painting against his small writing desk. I stared at it, seeing the quality of Thomas's work diminish with each project. "Thank you." I placed a chaste kiss on Lord Hoffemeyer's rosy cheek. He grabbed my arm and his grip eased. "When do you think you'll see Thomas again…to finish my portrait? Don't you think the poor man has suffered enough?"

"I don't know what you mean, Lord Hoffemeyer." I pulled my arm away and gave him a side glance.

"I saw the way he looked at you that night way back at the opera, Grace. I could see how he felt about you."

I laughed. "Apparently, Lord Hoffemeyer, you haven't heard the news about Helen. She's going to have his child. I would guess they've married by now."

"What is apparent to me," he said, looking at the library walls that featured my private shrine to Thomas's paintings, "is that you still have feelings for him."

"It doesn't matter, does it?" I had considered that this obsession with his painting would drive me mad. Still, I held on to the thread that many of the paintings, though haphazardly done, portrayed a nude seated on a rose-colored couch, and that caused me to believe that he thought of me often.

"If you want something badly enough, my dear, you must keep

after it, no matter what it takes, no matter how long." Lord Hoffemeyer stood in front of me, his hand cupping my cheek as his dark eyes held mine. I wondered if he was talking about me or himself, but I could not bring myself to ask him. Instead, I eased away and held up the new painting, looking for a spot to hang it.

"I'll send Dobbs in to hang this." He looked around the room. "I'm not sure there is a spot left on the wall."

"I'll just do a bit of rearranging, then," I offered brightly. "How were the bids on this one. Did Dobbs say?" I stared at the blurred oil-painted image. It was another nude seated in a chair, looking over her shoulder. But the face was obscure, as was the background. "Perhaps you could take one of these home with you?" I offered, waving my hand at the numerous paintings.

"I would like to see the two of you reconciled. His workmanship has changed. I know you see it as well as I do, Grace. His reputation with the ton is weakening."

"They refuse to see his talent," I offered, holding the painting at arm's length.

"Yes, well, he isn't helping matters, writing his biting public exposés on London society and that scandalous poetry he calls art in the radical news sheet he's started up. What is it called…? *The Germ?* Even the name belittles his intent."

"They are jealous," I said in Thomas's defense. I'd heard rumors and seen a copy of the news sheet, too. In addition to the decline in the quality of his art, it seemed he was doing all he could to be as contradictory as possible.

"I don't need to tell you that his reputation for being a troublemaker is becoming public knowledge. People are refusing to buy his work."

"It's a small obstacle. People are fickle, milord. He just needs to find one good subject, and he will win the hearts of the critics again."

"He's never had them, my dear," Lord Hoffemeyer reminded me.

I put the painting down. "When must you return to Pomerania, Baron?"

"In a few days. Oh, I nearly forgot. A messenger was at the door when I arrived. I hope you don't mind that I took the message for you." He pulled out a folded piece of paper, sealed with Thomas's wax imprint.

I opened it and read Thomas's eloquent handwriting—a matter of particular pride with him.

Dear Grace,
I am in desperate need. The brotherhood grows restless with the academy's vicious attacks on my work. I need your calming influence on them, Grace. They listen to you. I cannot tolerate their bickering amongst themselves

And there is one more thing. I do not pretend that this is any easier to read than it is for me to ask it. Helen has grown near her time and she is of such a delicate constitution that she's been advised not to overdo things. I was wondering if I might impose on you—rather, beg your assistance—in this matter. You know that relations with my family barely exist and we have none with hers. I need someone to cook for us and clean my studio and, frankly, Grace, I would prefer Helen not touch my tools. She does not know them as you do. You needn't worry of me being underfoot. I plan to be away on the days that you'll be here, knowing how you feel about me.

You, of course, can simply toss this away and pretend you never received it, but I appeal to our long-standing friendship. I have no one else to turn to. I will await your word. My travels begin three days from Thursday. I hope for your favorable reply.
Yours in friendship (I hope!) and art,
Thomas

Chapter 6

THREE DAYS LATER, I FOUND MYSELF ON THE doorstep to Thomas's studio. I cautioned myself that I was playing a game I would never win. But if I could not have Thomas in any other way except as his housekeeper, then so be it. I'd allowed him into my heart that fateful rainy morning long ago and pitiful as it might have seemed to some who knew me, I think most knew of my true feelings for Thomas and therefore understood.

William answered the door, and I didn't have time to hide my surprise. "I had not expected to see you here, William. How are you?"

He ushered me inside. "It is good to see you, Grace. I'm well, but I am concerned about Helen. I cannot tell you how good it is to know there will be another woman at the house."

I smiled, taking off my hat and hanging it on one of the hooks in the hallway. "Women tend to get a bit out of sorts as their time draws near, William. I'm surprised you were not aware of that."

William looked back at me as we headed up the stairs. "I am indeed familiar with a woman's travails, but I thought women with child gained weight—Helen seems to grow thinner by the day. She is tired frequently and not eating well and I'm hopeful your cooking, excellent as I recall, will help to put some meat back on her bones."

Mrs. Rodin was young and impressed me just as I thought she would. She was frail-looking and kept to herself, often preferring to stay in her bedroom or read downstairs in the front parlor. She seemed intelligent but rather lost. I attributed it at first to her pregnancy, but later I noticed she behaved differently—more independently—when Thomas wasn't around than when he was.

I also noticed that the brothers did not stop by with the same frequency they used to, and when they did, Helen claimed to be indisposed. Perhaps most disconcerting, however, was the tension I felt between Helen and William. They seemed to tiptoe around each other whenever I was there.

Still, I did my job as was requested, and left the drama of Thomas's household to him. He was, as always when he put his mind to a task, absorbed in his new research. He'd leave early on the days I arrived and not return until I'd left the studio. In many ways, between the three of them, I felt as if I was cleaning house for a group of ghosts.

I did try to converse with Helen about her health. I tried pleasantly to ask how things were going, reassuring her that Thomas would come around when he was done with his research and he could focus again. Apparently, she did not like my meddling, as upon my next cleaning day, she asked to borrow my coach and driver for the day. Of course, I told her she could, but she did not tell me where she was going or why, and I did not ask, certain I would only succeed in agitating her again.

Several hours later, William ambled into the kitchen and leaned over the stove, inhaling the scent of the lamb stew I was cooking.

"That smells heavenly, Grace. Is it about ready?"

"It is ready now. Has Helen returned? She borrowed my coach and driver this morning."

William looked puzzled. "She didn't say where she was going?"

I shook my head. "I didn't think to ask. She is a grown woman, after all."

"Perhaps, but I don't like the idea of her traipsing about in her condition."

"William." I smiled, spooning a generous amount of stew into his bowl. "Women are stronger than most men think. I've known women who work the fields, have a child, and are back out in the field the next morning."

"Go on." He looked at me with disbelief as he took the bowl from my hand.

"It's true," I said, serving myself. "She probably needed the fresh air. It seems she has been sedentary at Thomas's request. Maybe she decided to go out and find something for the nursery." I sat down on one of the work stools in the kitchen. William pulled up another, propping one foot on the bottom rung as he held the bowl under his mouth.

It was nearly impossible to look at him and not see a younger version of Thomas. It seemed surreal to be sitting in Thomas's kitchen discussing his child with his brother, and it made me realize that my heart had not yet healed. I wondered if it ever would completely. I took a bite of my stew and looked to change the conversation. "Tell me what you are doing these days, William."

"I just returned from Florence recently. I was there to study the architecture and visit the Uffizi. It is quite remarkable. The ancient architecture and the parks inspired me. You should visit it one day. I think you would enjoy it, Grace."

I laughed quietly. "Perhaps, but for now, my inspiration is more confined to making sure Thomas doesn't run out of his Prussian blue."

William chuckled. "My brother can be quite particular about some things."

I sensed there was more that he wanted to say. "Thomas does have his way of doing things, doesn't he?"

"I don't wish to complain, Grace. He has been more than generous funding my studies as he does, encouraging my designs, discussing the possibilities of how I can use my skills. He has been most patient with me."

"He is a good man, your brother," I agreed.

He nodded, placed his empty bowl on the table and folded his hands on his lap. "It's how he treats Helen that I disapprove of." He shook his head. "I have no right to speak out against him, of course, but were she my wife, I would not leave her every day to go tromping in the woods in search of a background." He slapped the butcher's table beside him. "There, I've got that off my chest. And I would appreciate it if this stayed between us, Grace."

Little did he realize that I hadn't spoken to Thomas in many weeks, nor did I see that changing for the better anytime soon. "Your confidence is safe with me, William, but in his defense, doesn't he have to make a living as well as care for his family? You should know that research takes time. Look at your own situation. You're still gathering research in order to produce the one project that will make the world take notice."

He sighed and nodded. "You have been my brother's friend for some time, haven't you?"

"A few years, yes," I replied.

"Then you would say that you know him fairly well?"

I shrugged. "You are his brother. You know him better than anyone, I would think."

"No, I don't think so. There are times when I'm not sure that is true. He thinks differently than I do. Sometimes his choices, the things he says and the things he does—I don't agree with."

I eyed him as I took another bite of stew and wondered if we were still talking in generalities, or if he was referring to something or someone more specifically. I did not press the topic further, and once he finished eating, William thanked me for the stew, and went to his room.

Later, after I'd done some washing and strung a line across the end of the studio near the kitchen, William, freshly shaven and looking admittedly dashing, stuck his head in the studio door.

"I'm off, Grace, to meet some people for supper. Is there anything I can do for you before I leave?"

I glanced out the double doors to the balcony, realizing that the day was waning. It would be dark soon and Helen hadn't returned with my carriage. "I was going to ask if you might give me a lift home, but I wonder if one of us should stay until Helen returns."

I saw the look of struggle in William's eyes. "This meeting has been set up for several weeks. They are potential clients with an upholstery business and are interested in my designs. Perhaps I should cancel and reschedule." He rubbed his jaw.

"Not at all, William. I can stay on a while longer. She's bound to be home soon."

He wrote down the name of the hotel where his meeting was. "If you should need me. It is impossible to reach my brother."

I bade him good luck, stuffed the note in my pocket and finished with the wash. Sometime later, I sat down at the kitchen table with a cup of tea and, laying my head on my arm for just a moment, promptly drifted off to sleep.

I awoke in semidarkness. I walked to the balcony door and saw my carriage in the street below. Checking the bedroom, I found Helen sound asleep. Not wishing to disturb her, I eased the door shut and went on home.

I was exhausted from the rigorous cleaning I'd done that day. I'd asked myself more than once why I stayed on as I did. The plain truth was because I felt at home there. The brotherhood—Thomas, even William—trusted me and showed me that they appreciated my efforts. In the past, I'd delighted when they threw their impromptu get-togethers to celebrate even the smallest accomplishments. The wine flowed freely, they ate and talked until all hours on topics I've never understood, nor likely ever would. They referred to Thomas as the "old man," a name given to him due to his being in his mid-thirties, and he would laugh. But there'd been no such get-togethers since my return to the studio. I thought about what William had said about Thomas being gone so much at a time when his very fragile wife would no doubt appreciate his company. I would not say anything to Thomas, as I had given William my word. However, I had a feeling that a storm was brewing and that the young Mrs. Rodin might well be in the eye of it.

I poured my nightly glass of port and shuffled wearily across the high-polished hardwood floors of my little apartment. Lord Hoffemeyer had been most generous with me, and never asked anything from me in return. Of course, I had nothing to offer him except companionship when he was in town, and even then, he'd never placed me in a compromising position, or caused me to question his intent.

I slid open the pocket doors leading to the library and lit the oil lamps, placing them where the light would best illuminate my private Thomas Rodin collection. Taking my port, I sat down in the plush, overstuffed reading chair and released a tired sigh. I let my eyes scan the paintings, hung from the chair rail to the ceiling—side to side, top to bottom. I thought about Lord Hoffemeyer's comment last time he was in town, about how my feelings for Thomas hadn't changed. He seemed as bent on seeing us reconciled as I sometimes felt. It seemed that Lord Hoffemeyer and I were Thomas's only support. But it was a support sheathed in silence—the more I heard the critics badgering him, the more of his paintings I bought. I dreaded what it would do to Thomas's pride if he ever found out.

Overtired, I slept later than usual and, knowing I was not scheduled today to go to Thomas's, I took a leisurely bath and washed my hair. I had not been to the Cremorne in some time and I wanted to see how Deidre was getting on. I'd just finished a light supper when there was an urgent knock on my door. The knock issued again, and more fervent this time. I knew it wasn't Lord Hoffemeyer. He was on business in Germany until Saturday. "I'm coming," I called. The only other person who knew where I lived, besides Thomas, was Deidre.

I opened the door and Thomas swept by me in full stride, walking into the front room.

"Is he here?" he called from the other room.

"Is who—Lord Hoffemeyer? No, he doesn't stay here, Thomas. Our relationship isn't like that."

I followed him down the short hall and into the room, seeing him about to open the library doors. "I'll ask you kindly to stop this tirade and tell me what is going on."

He dropped his hands to his sides, still facing the door. "I thought perhaps you were in a hurry to get home to your wealthy companion yesterday."

His tone was surly, yet from what I could tell he hadn't been drinking. "Did you have a purpose in coming here, or did you just have a whim to insult someone, Thomas?"

He pushed his hands over his hair, clamping his head as if frustrated. "Have you got anything to drink, preferably something strong?"

I had, of course, his favorite port in the parlor. "Go sit down, I'll bring us something." I hurried back, decanter and glasses in hand. "What is troubling you?" I asked as I began to pour. "Have you been up all night?"

He nodded, rubbing his hand over his face. He looked at me then, as if he just realized where he was. I'd never seen a face so filled with loss. His eyes were rimmed with dark circles and they were red from crying. "Thomas, where have you been? What has happened?"

"Helen…lost…" He stumbled on his words, dropping his chin to his chest. "Grace, the baby is dead." His face crumpled in pain and he grabbed the filled glass, tossing it down his throat.

The decanter slipped from my grip and I caught it with my other hand. "Oh, God, no, Thomas." I eased down beside him on the floral couch. Everything around us was the picture of perfection and order—the colors, fabrics, pictures on the wall—and none of it belonged to either of us. *We* were the only familiar things to each other in the room.

He rubbed his eyes and his face looked drawn, years older than he really was.

"William found her on the floor by the bedroom door when he got home from his meeting. She'd already lost a lot of blood."

"Helen…good Lord, Thomas, what about Helen? Is she all right?"

He nodded. "She's going to be fine."

I shook my head, retracing my steps from the day before. "She asked to borrow my coach. Of course I told her yes. She didn't offer where she was going, how long she'd be gone. I didn't think to ask, Thomas. I told William to go on, I'd stay and wait for her. I must have dozed off, waiting, and when I woke up, she was home, sleeping soundly in her bed. I saw no signs that anything was amiss."

He stared at his hands clasped in his lap. "There is no way anyone could have prevented it, save perhaps Helen herself."

"What do you mean, Thomas?" I frowned at his words. "What woman can anticipate such a thing?"

"She fell while visiting her mother and refused medical attention, Grace."

His weary face turned to mine and I could see the questions in his eyes, but I had no answers.

"Is this my punishment, then? For not being good enough for her? Not being there when she needed me?"

"Thomas, you just said no one could have stopped this from happening. Not even you. Helen is young and most likely will be able to have more children."

His gaze shot to mine and he shook his head. The muscle of his jaw ticked as he stared at me, trying to get the words out of his mouth.

"They said it was a girl…she was stillborn. They wouldn't let Helen see her, but I asked to, I had to see her."

His breathing grew labored. The stoic expression on his face crumpling under the weight he carried inside of him.

"I had a daughter, Grace."

He fell toward me, his arms encircling my waist, and pressed his face into my lap. His anguish drew out in heart-wrenching deep sobs. I had no knowledge of how to console him, except to lay my head on his and cry with him. His shoulders shook, his tears expelling the pain until at last he quieted.

I rubbed his back.

"I can't go to the studio tonight, Grace. William is angry with me. I feel lost. Might I stay here?"

He sat up and brushed his cheeks, blew his nose on his handkerchief. "I can sleep on the couch."

I looked at how it fit barely the two of us. "There is a guest room down the hall. You can stay there if you like. Come on, let me show you where you can wash your face and then I'll bring you some tea."

"I would rather have port."

"I know, but I think I should bring you tea."

He nodded and paused at the door to a small room with a single bed. I'd never used it, but I wondered if Lord and Lady Hoffemeyer had a daughter. Thomas drew me close and hugged me tight, burying his face in my shoulder.

"Thank you, Grace."

I woke sometime during the night and found Thomas asleep in the reading chair in my bedroom. His long legs were stretched out before him, the blanket pulled up around his shoulders. I drifted back to sleep and, with the light of day, I awoke to find the blanket neatly folded on the chair and Thomas gone.

He sent a note two days later, asking if I would mind staying on and helping out until Helen was fully recuperated. I replied that I felt they needed their privacy at this time. I heard no more after that.

Lord Hoffemeyer's return was delayed for another three weeks due to pressing business, but he told me that he had very special plans for me when he returned next to London. In my letter response, I conveyed the news about Thomas and stated that he was slowly moving forward with his life, but I didn't feel he was ready yet to resume the portrait. Lord Hoffemeyer replied that he would make sure Thomas received an invitation to the gala he was bringing me to. It would be attended by important people and do Thomas good to get out again and socialize. I did not know what I'd done to deserve such kindness from Lord Hoffemeyer, but I was forever in his debt for how well he treated me and how much he supported Thomas.

Lord Hoffemeyer had bought me a beautiful gown, sheepishly admitting to having borrowed one of my dresses to take to the seamstress. He made sure that it would be ready for tonight. It was a deep royal blue, with sequins, satin and ribbons.

"It has never been worn and is the latest in Paris fashion," he said with a twinkle in his eye.

"It's breathtaking." I held it up to me and turned to face him. The cook looked on admiringly, holding Lord Hoffemeyer's coat and hat.

"Go, try it on, and let me see how it looks." He insisted as he sat on the settee in the parlor and waited.

The cook assisted me, drawing my corset ribbons so that my bust fit properly in the low-cut gown. I used a bustle, tying it at my waist, before slipping the gown over my head. It dipped off my shoulders, enhancing the plumped-up swell of my breasts. The cook fastened the hooks and I watched in the mirror as I was transformed into a creature of elegance. I wound my hair loose around my head, using long hairpins to secure it. I had only my worn boots to wear, but the gown covered them.

I looked in the mirror, pinching my cheeks, and gently raking my teeth across my lips to give them color. The last time I'd made an attempt to dazzle the London ton, it had been a disaster. I was determined that it would not happen again. I pressed my hands under my bust and shifted my breasts until they lay like a sumptuous satin-wrapped package. With a deep breath, but not too deep, I waltzed into the parlor.

"Oh, my dear, how exquisitely beautiful you look."

Lord Hoffemeyer stood and came over to me, bowing low. He took my hand and twirled me once, then brought my hand to his lips. With a look of satisfaction, he held my hand as he took me in from head to foot.

"You look good enough to eat," he said, leaning forward to place a lingering kiss on my cheek. "Yes, this suits you, Grace. You will be the envy of the ton tonight."

Chapter 7

London 1863

LORD HOFFEMEYER MADE SURE I FELT WELCOME at the gala. He introduced me to those he knew, praising my taste in art and my skill at dance. It was a thin veneer, we both knew, as I was nothing more than his occasional companion. I knew little about him and he knew very little about me. Still, with Thomas as a common denominator, it was a comfortable arrangement.

When I saw Thomas enter the ballroom, dressed in an elegant black tailcoat, white shirt and cravat, I excused myself.

"I'll be right back," I said, leaning down to Lord Hoffemeyer's ear.

He squeezed my hand. "Don't be too long. They are about to start the next set."

I wound my way through the crowd until I reached Thomas. I tapped his back with my fan and he turned, not recognizing me at first. He gave me a hospitable but entirely apathetic smile, which I suspected was making his face stiff by now. Then his eyes widened.

"Grace?"

"You are looking quite dapper this evening, Thomas," I said. "I wasn't aware that you owned proper evening attire."

He leaned toward me, the scent of his soap and sandalwood wafting across my nose.

"It's William's," he whispered. "A bit stuffy."

"That's because you only wear two frock coats, both designed over seventy years ago."

He grinned and offered a shrug. "It's good to see you, too, Grace. By the way, I wanted to thank you again for all your help at the studio."

I was glad that we were able to slip into such natural conversation. "How is Helen? Is she here?"

He grabbed two champagne glasses from a server who walked by. "She's visiting her family." He handed me a glass and gently touched his to mine. He looked around as he spoke. "So, are you here with Hoffemeyer?"

"Of course, why else would I be here?" The champagne was loosening my tongue.

"Has he said anything about his portrait?"

"No, he hasn't mentioned it," I replied. "I didn't think you'd be ready yet to return to it."

"Or was it that you weren't ready, Grace?"

He smiled and gave a young woman a nod as she passed by, looking demurely at him from beneath hooded lids.

"Perhaps you are ready," I muttered, taking a long swallow of my sparkling drink.

He turned his attention back on me. "You look stunning tonight, Grace."

"Thank you. It's nice of you to notice."

"About the portrait—" Thomas began, but Lord Hoffemeyer appeared at my side, interrupting him.

"There you are, you naughty girl. You promised me the next dance." He looked at Thomas and beamed. "And you've found Thomas, as well! I'm glad you decided to come tonight. There is something I wish to discuss with you, but it will have to wait. I must steal this woman from you."

Thomas's smile dissolved.

"Come, Grace. I have a few more people I'd like you to meet." Lord Hoffemeyer slipped his hand over my upper arm. I glanced back at Thomas as I was steered away from him.

"Milord, if you please," I said, keeping a smile on my face. I was beginning to tire of his domineering behavior.

"My apologies, Grace. I have been away more than a month and I wanted you all to myself this evening."

"To yourself?" I asked.

He smiled, the tops of his cheeks turning rosy. "Humor an old man, Grace. I want to look good among this crowd. I have a number of business associates here tonight—wealthy business associates."

"Of course," I replied. "I understand." It was the least I could do to pay him back for all he'd done for me. We danced the next set, which pleased him, but he plopped down on the first chair he could find afterward and wiped his brow.

"Are you well?" I asked, offering him a glass of punch from the nearby refreshment table. I caught the wandering eye of a young server, his gaze riveted to the front of my dress as he paused to offer canapés. I politely gave him a smile.

"Was that boy flirting with you, Grace? I'll have him taking his leave."

I recoiled in surprise. "You will do nothing of the sort or you may well have to address more than half the men you have introduced me to this evening. Had you not wanted anyone to notice, you should have bought me a gown with a higher neck."

"You're right." His eyes drifted to my exposed flesh. "And what a travesty that would be." He looked up at me sweetly. "You are radiant, my dear. Would you do me the honor of a turn in the garden?"

"Only if you promise to behave yourself." I tucked my arm through his. We stepped out onto the stone terrace edged by a low wall that shielded it from the garden walk below. Several tiers of

stone steps led to a maze of ornately trimmed hedges and dim
lanterns hung on posts. I held Lord Hoffemeyer's arm, enjoying
the view of the night sky above and the dimly lit gardens below.
The scent of fresh roses and dewy grass permeated the air. Small
private seating areas were situated off the main garden path, some
containing statues surrounded by benches, others with bubbling
fountains.

"Shall we sit a moment, Grace?" He offered me a seat on a
stone bench before he settled his large frame next to me.

"How is Lady Hoffemeyer?" I asked, shifting to face him so
that our bodies were not so close.

"It's about her that I wanted to speak with you."

"Certainly, milord. I hope she is not ill."

"No, nothing of the sort." He cleared his throat. "Grace, I've
been good to you, haven't I?" He placed his hand on my knee.

I moved my leg from beneath his grasp. "Indeed you have,
and Thomas was just commenting that he is ready to get back
to your portrait."

"It's not about the portrait." He turned to face me, taking me
by the shoulders. "I need you to now do something for me."

I frowned, searching his dark eyes, wondering what I had to
offer him.

"I need you to become Thomas's lover again."

"Lord Hoffemeyer, what are you saying?"

"Do not deny that you were once lovers. The look was unmistakable on both of your faces." His grip grew tighter.

"You're hurting me," I warned.

His fingers relaxed and he sighed.

"You're so beautiful, Grace, and your heart—"

He placed his hand over my breast.

"You would do anything now that I asked, wouldn't you, my
dear? If you knew it would help me?" His fingers squeezed my
breast and I jerked away, nearly falling off the bench. His hand
darted out, catching my arm and preventing my fall. I righted
myself and stood, stepping away from him.

"I don't know what's come over you, milord. Has your kindness been but a ruse to gain way into my drawers? You know what I am, why go to the trouble?"

His dark eyes shot to mine. "Would that have been all I needed to do?" He looked at me, puzzled. "Simply ask you?"

I stopped him with my hand, trying to clarify my swirling thoughts. "Wait, what about the portrait? What about hiring Thomas? What purpose was there in any of that if you only wanted me to have sex with you?" I felt as if someone had poured a bucket of ice water over me. In all the times I'd been solicited, none had felt as strange as this.

"Don't you see? I'm afraid I need you and Thomas together."

"What are you proposing? Thomas and I have not been together for well over a year. He is married and, I would like to think, happily so."

He brushed his fingers through his wiry gray mustache, a perplexed look on his face. "Yes, I realize that may be a problem."

He stood then and came to me, slipping his arms around my waist. "I have confidence that you can convince him, Grace. I have seen how he burns for you."

"And if I refuse?" I stated firmly, trying to extract myself from his arms.

"Listen to me, Grace." His grip around me tightened. "My wife has very definite tastes. She has wanted one thing since that night at the opera and has hounded me for well over a year for it. Trust me, my wife can be a very demanding woman," he whispered against my cheek.

Over his shoulder I saw the lights of the ballroom, heard the din of music as it filtered into the night. Here, in the dim shadows, no one could see us unless they knew where to look. I knew he could overpower me without a thought. "What is it that Lady Hoffemeyer wants, milord?" I asked, trying to figure out how to escape him.

"She merely wants a weekend of pleasure, Grace. At our estate in Pomerania. It would be very discreet, very tasteful. You'd have everything you desired."

"You want me to bed your wife, is that it?" I asked.

A low growl rumbled in his chest. "She wants the both of you—you and Thomas—to join us. I think, Grace, that you both will find my lovely wife can be most accommodating."

I had been oblivious to his intent. Now I knew that Lord and Lady Hoffemeyer were part of the elite who dabbled in the sex games of the affluent. What they did made street whores look like angels.

"I'm afraid, Lord Hoffemeyer, that I can't agree to—"

"Oh, no…no." He placed his finger gently to my lips and patted my cheek as if consoling an injured child.

I held my breath, seeing a side to him that I'd not seen before. His gentle manner was deceptive and I had a feeling to rile him would mean grave danger for me.

"You mustn't say you can't, no, no, you mustn't." He slid the pad of his thumb along my lower lip. "You see, Lady Hoffemeyer has been patiently waiting, and I confess that I, too, have been waiting as long to see you with her…and Thomas." He chuckled. "Well, Thomas already knows what she is like firsthand."

"You mean that she is a raving, sadistic lunatic?" Thomas walked out from behind a hedge. "I had a feeling that there might have been more to your hospitality, Lord Hoffemeyer. The nude painting was only an appetizer meant to entice us, am I correct?"

I stared at Thomas, feeling blindly stupid that I hadn't seen this before now.

"She has eccentric tastes, I admit—" Hoffemeyer shrugged "—but you seemed to enjoy yourself last time, Thomas."

"The only memory I have of that night, I carry right here where your wife started after me with a horsewhip." He pointed to a scar across his brow. I'd been told it was the result of nothing more than a childhood accident involving William. "Let her go, Hoffemeyer."

"Let's be reasonable, Thomas. I know that you and Grace can use the money. You have medical bills, I'm certain, and Grace, well, without me, Grace would be on the streets. Why not bring the portrait with you and you can finish it there?"

"I see your wife still keeps you on a short leash," Thomas remarked, slipping his hand in mine and easing me slowly away from Hoffemeyer's embrace.

Hoffemeyer slid his finger slowly around the inside of his collar, his eyes glittering as he grinned at Thomas. "The critics despise your work, Thomas. Your precious brotherhood will soon tire of that. I can offer you enough so that you'll never have to sell another painting if you don't want to. Think about it. One weekend—I promise to make it the height of pleasure for you both."

"We aren't interested in your proposition. Now if you'll excuse us—"

Torn from Thomas's grasp, I was hauled backward, stumbling against Lord Hoffemeyer's broad chest.

"I have invested far too much in this to come away empty-handed. And without Grace, there will be no one left to buy your paintings."

"Thomas, don't listen to him," I said, struggling against his firm grasp.

"She's the only reason you've still got a roof over your head—or rather, I am. Who do you think has funded her private Rodin collection?"

Thomas's teal gaze swerved to mine.

"Is this true, Grace?" he asked quietly.

I tried to wrench free from Lord Hoffemeyer, but his hold was too tight. "Yes, but—"

Thomas's fist sailed past my face, colliding with Hoffemeyer's nose. The impact sent the baron stumbling backward and he landed on his arse.

"You'll regret this, Rodin. Both of you will. I'll see your name is the laughingstock of the art world."

"You've not been keeping up, Hoffemeyer. I've already managed to achieve that honor."

"Thomas," I said, keeping an eye on Lord Hoffemeyer, who was nursing his nose. I hurried to Thomas's embrace.

Thomas smiled and took off his coat, placing it around my shoulders. "You've torn your dress," he soothed, cupping my cheek. "Are you all right?"

I nodded, but couldn't stop shaking. "About those paintings. I cherish each one and thought perhaps one day you might have your own gallery…."

"Those are my paintings. I bought every last one of them and I intend to destroy every one unless you change your mind," Lord Hoffemeyer bellowed as he scrambled to his feet.

"You actually talked this big oaf into buying my art at above-market price, so that you could keep my work?"

"I'm sorry, Thomas. I know this comes as a severe blow to your ego."

He grabbed my face, kissing me hard.

"You're bloody brilliant, Grace." He grinned and dissolved into laughter.

I felt a tug and was yanked again from Thomas.

Thomas released a tolerant sigh. "You are a stubborn man, Hoffemeyer." He bent down and retrieved a fallen tree branch, raising it above his head.

"No, Thomas, that's enough," I stated. "I won't see you put away for this. He is not worth it."

"Listen to your wench, Thomas. She has amazing wisdom for a woman of her profession."

Thomas's gaze slid to mine.

I balled my fist and brought it back hard on Lord Hoffemeyer's already injured nose. Blood spattered onto my glove, dotting my torn dress. I walked to Thomas, my head held high, as Lord Hoffemeyer nursed his likely broken nose.

"I'll have you brought up on charges, Rodin, and your whore will be out on the streets where I found her unless she agrees to go with me now."

I knew he meant what he said. Every ruthless word. Would one night of satisfying his request be worth not seeing Thomas thrown in jail? As for me, I knew how to live on the streets. I'd been doing that all my life. "If I go with him, it will be okay, Thomas."

Thomas rushed to my side. "No, Grace, I won't let you go. I've been at that woman's mercy and it is not pleasure."

I glanced at the baron. Blood showed on his teeth as he sneered at me. He knew what he was doing. He knew he could get what he wanted if he put Thomas at risk.

"We have no choice, Thomas," I said quietly.

"We don't?" He nodded toward the terrace, where a break in the dancing had brought several guests outside for air. He raised his voice loud enough to be heard by the crowd. "I'm afraid, Lord Hoffemeyer, you'll first have to explain Grace's torn dress to the ton."

I returned Thomas's smile.

"You think your pathetic low-life testimonials will stand up against my word? The truth is, I never wanted her, anyway," He pointed at Thomas and his voice boomed, "It was *you* that I wanted back in my bed!"

A collective gasp was emitted from the terrace.

Lord Hoffemeyer turned in surprise as several men rushed down the steps and captured him by his arms. "I want you off my property, you vagrant…you whore," he spit as they hauled him away.

Thomas took me back to the studio that night, offering me one of his old dress shirts to wear to bed.

He looked up at me as he poured us both a port. "Did you see Hoffemeyer's face? I think you broke his nose." He handed me a glass and settled into the chair across from me. I curled my feet under me and drew the afghan up around my lap. "We're fortunate there were witnesses on the veranda," I said, holding the glass between my hands.

"You don't think I could have taken him on?" He smiled.

I wanted to ask Thomas about his relations with the Hoffemeyers, but suspected it was a life experience he would sooner forget. "You're an artist, Thomas, not a fighter." I raised my glass to him. "Nonetheless, I salute you, my brave knight."

He touched his hand to his chest and nodded. His smile teased me, tempting me to walk over and snuggle in his lap. I switched topics. "What will become of him?"

Thomas sighed. "If they discover he's engaged in relations with other men here in London, he will be imprisoned. But a man like Hoffemeyer has many affluent connections, I'm sure."

"Can they arrest you, based on what Lord Hoffemeyer said?"

Thomas shook his head. "No, there is no proof and that was some time ago, in a different country. I was young, experimental, fearless. Hoffemeyer's in for a long night. Our men in blue may not be the most expedient, but they are most thorough."

I had few possessions back at the apartment, but with Hoffemeyer's threat to destroy Thomas's paintings, I wondered whether to go collect them tonight. "Perhaps I should go see to collecting my things from the apartment?" Thomas shook his head.

"It can wait until morning. I would rather know that you are here tonight, so I can keep my eye on you."

"I had no idea the penalty for buggery was so severe. What about Frank Woolner? Does anyone know his sexual preference?" I asked.

"I've known Frank a very long time, Grace. He's careful, and always has been, in his relations. We keep a close eye on each other." He sipped his port and looked into the fire. "None of us has really thought twice about Frank's preferences. That's the beauty of the brotherhood—age, gender, sexual persuasion—they don't matter. The brotherhood is only interested in a person's artistic passion."

I thought about how true it was that the brotherhood always seemed to rally around one another when the need arose, and I wondered, being left now without a place to lay my head, if I, too, would be watched out for? I could not—rather, would not—stay at the studio, not under the present circumstances, but it hadn't occurred to me that I might have help from the brothers.

Thomas held his glass between his hands and stared at me, his eyes softening, and the intensity of his gaze caused my bones to dissolve. "What are you thinking, Thomas?"

His mouth quirked. "I'd forgotten how utterly beautiful you are and how, if the circumstances were different right now, I would do my damnedest to get you into my bed." He tipped back his port and drained the glass.

I couldn't let that happen, no matter how much I wanted it. "Always the rogue, my Thomas," I said finally. "You can hardly take a breath without making a woman swoon, can you?"

He gave me a wicked grin. "Did I make you swoon that day, Grace? Here? Do you remember?"

I shifted in my chair, remembering the memory of his tongue and his head between my legs. I sighed and looked away.

"Did I, Grace?" he asked quietly.

He set his glass aside, dropped to the floor and came to me on his knees. He gently grabbed the collar of my shirt and drew my face to his, so close I could smell the port on his breath.

I forced myself to look in his eyes. "Why are you doing this, Thomas?"

"I just want you to remember when we were together. I want you to remember how good it was."

My lips burned to meet his, but I did not dare. I knew where it would lead.

"Why, Thomas? Why do you want me to remember?"

His eyes lowered to my mouth and back to meet my gaze.

"Because I can't forget," he said softly.

"Thomas?"

Thomas leaped to his feet and turned toward the entrance.

"Helen?"

"Surprise." She gave him a firm smile.

I stood and placed my glass on the mantel. It was time I should go.

"Oh, please don't feel you must leave on my account."

She was staring at Thomas but speaking to me.

The sound of the door slamming downstairs drew her attention away for a moment.

William bounded through the door of the studio, stopping short when he saw Helen. "Thomas, there was a bag downstairs, I thought perhaps Helen—"

"Hello, William," she said with a polite tone.

"Helen," he responded, darting a glance at Thomas and then me with barely a stitch on.

"Will, be a good man and go hold your carriage for me," I said, slanting the none-too-pleased Helen a look. "Your husband came to my rescue tonight, Helen. Don't be too hard on him." I looked at Thomas. "I'll get my clothes."

"Grace," Thomas said, "there's no need for you to leave, not after what you've been through."

"I'm fine, Thomas. I'm sure that you and Helen have a lot to discuss."

Helen followed me into the hallway and I was nearly run down by William flying up the stairs with Helen's bags. I wasted no time retrieving my things from the guest room, aware that Helen was marking every minute I remained in her house. Much to her discomfiture, Thomas walked me down to the carriage.

"You'll be all right?" he asked.

I leaned forward and gave him a peck on the cheek. "Thank you, Thomas. I think you're about to face someone far tougher than Lord Hoffemeyer."

He stood by the carriage, looking as though he wanted to say something, and then slammed the door, causing the horses to bolt forward.

Chapter 8

I'D PURPOSELY WAITED A DAY OR TWO FOR HELEN and Thomas to have some time to clear the air, before heading back to clean the studio. I met Thomas rushing out the door, head down, in a great hurry.

"Thomas?"

"Don't speak to me, Grace. Not now." He climbed in his carriage and didn't look back.

I spotted the bags at the top of the stairs. It didn't take much to figure out that Helen was leaving. I found her in the studio. She held a sketch of herself in her hand. "He won't miss one," I told her. "I have several that he doesn't even know about."

"It was too much responsibility for me, I think…being his muse." Helen looked at me. "May I ask you something?"

I shrugged.

"You've known Thomas for some time."

I shook my head. "Some days it seems like a lifetime, others, I am not sure I know him at all."

She nodded. "At what point did you know you loved him?"

I looked at her and laughed. *Love?* How could she possibly understand what I felt? I tugged out my hat pin and dropped my hat on the table. "You have a misguided notion, Helen."

"Do I?"

I regarded her, wondering if she blamed me for her and Thomas's problems. I realized then that she didn't understand him the way I did. "A man like Thomas has many models—many women he calls 'muse.' I was never your rival, nor were any of the other women who model for him. His mistress is the ever-changing, ever-demanding passionate affair he has with his art, his work." I could see she did not believe me by the look in her eyes.

"I have spent a lifetime in the company of men—many, many men. I see the same problem all over. Women struggle to compete with a man's passion, instead of allowing him the freedom to explore his mistress. The secret is being available when he grows tired of her and turns his eye your way."

"Is that enough for you, Grace?" she asked. "Don't you want more from someone than that?"

"To be utterly worshipped, treated like a goddess for a few moments with no strings, no false promises? Who would want more than that?" What I couldn't tell her is what it did to me to see someone I cared so deeply for become consumed by his notion of "the muse." "His muses," Thomas called them. They inspired him; he worshipped them entirely, believing that the mutual passion they shared somehow translated to his painting. I could have tried, but she wouldn't have understood.

William came in and kissed Helen on the temple. It surprised me that it took me so long to see how he felt for her. Still, knowing them for as long as I had, I knew the division this had to have caused and the pain both of them must be silently suffering. I could sense the tension in the house and hoped that time would heal them and allow them to be as close again.

"The carriage is ready. How about you?" he said.

"Yes, I'm ready. Goodbye, Grace."

He escorted her to the carriage and ran back upstairs for one last look around the studio.

"I came to say goodbye, Grace."

"You're all set, then?" I asked.

"Tell Thomas goodbye for me."

I smiled. "I will."

He studied me a moment.

"You knew, didn't you? How I felt about Helen?"

"I suspected it for some time, but I kept your confidence, William. Are the two of you going to be okay?" I asked.

He nodded. "I've loved Helen from the first day I met her, Grace. I just didn't know what to do about Thomas. I am his younger brother, but it seems I have spent my life taking care of him."

"I meant are you and Thomas going to be all right? I have no doubt that Helen is going to make you a fine wife. I just don't want you to forget your brother is a—"

"Yes, a good man. I know." He smiled and hugged me. "When do you suppose he'll wake up and see what a good woman you are?"

I smiled and looked down at my hands. "Thank you for that, William."

After he left, I brought a rug to the balcony to shake out the dirt. Helen and William's carriage was just pulling away. Down the road stood Thomas, dressed in his finest coat and top hat, talking to a dark-haired woman in a fancy black coach. *A new muse.*

"When indeed, William?" I said softly.

It was time for me to move on again. I suppose that by now I should have been more used to it. Perhaps the events of recent days had caused me to want to settle down more than ever, or perhaps Thomas had simply spoiled me for other men. I did not want to think that I would never find another man like him, and yet, part of me knew that to have a man like Thomas would be a constant bout of heartache. I was getting too old for such things. My body, not as youthful as it once was, longed for the security that came with having the same man's arm around you every night, a man who understood and accepted all the subtle changes that came with age, and found you beautiful anyway.

But I knew that it would not be long before Thomas had another muse in the studio, one more beautiful than the last, one that inspired his passion, would become smitten by his attention, perhaps entice him to marry again. I did not deceive myself into thinking that he and I had the type of relationship built to create a long-lasting commitment. We enjoyed each other's company as much precisely because there were no ties.

I'd spent the night back at the apartment, gathering my few belongings, and at dawn, the cook came to me with a note that had been delivered to the door.

Dearest Grace,

I heard through the rumor mill that you were looking for employment. I can't say that I'm sad about that beast you were keeping company with. I had my thoughts, but I kept them to myself. I mean, if I couldn't see any redeeming qualities in him, Grace, there weren't any, trust me, I'm just that good. As it happens I have need of a housekeeper—my third one this month just walked out on me without even benefit of a notice! It's a travesty, I tell you, finding good help these days! Can I help that I am perversely clean and demand more than an occasional shake of a rug to please me? I won't pretend, darling, to tell you that it would be easy to live with me, but I think we'd have a jolly good time getting on each other's nerves. What say you, Grace? Shall we make Thomas green with envy thinking that you maybe had changed me?

Awaiting your reply, Frank.

I took a deep breath and released a sigh of relief. "I'll have a note for Dobbs to deliver for me," I said to my cook.

The cook twisted her fingers as she looked at me. "Do you have something to say?"

"If I may speak freely?"

I nodded.

"Mr. Dobbs told me that they plan to release Lord Hoffemeyer no later than tomorrow morning. He has requested Dobbs meet him at the station as he plans to come here before he leaves for Germany, mum."

"Has the messenger left?" I asked.

"No, mum, he's waiting for a response."

I gave the boy my response and, within the hour, Frank was helping me load my things in the carriage. I asked the cook to stay in the kitchen, hoping that her warning was a sign of her camaraderie. As it was, though, I paced Frank's house both night and day for a full week. I never again heard from Lord Hoffemeyer and I hoped that Thomas hadn't either.

Frank and I fell into a comfortable arrangement, and we nurtured a friendship based on true companionship. Frank did most of the cooking, although he allowed me to do a thing or two in the kitchen. There was only one topic that we did not discuss and that was Thomas. Although he never spoke of it openly, I think he knew the feelings that I harbored deep inside for his friend.

After several days of sequestering myself at Frank's flat, I felt as if I couldn't breathe. I needed to get out, so I went down to the gardens to check in on Deidre.

It felt good to walk in the gardens again, although some things had changed. There didn't seem to be as many familiar faces. The theater troupe that once performed daily had disbanded. Poverty and illness had taken its toll on the populace.

There was a stiff breeze this evening along the river walk—a preview of colder weather to come. Men, women and children huddled near bonfires built along the old boardwalk, and tents made of blankets served as temporary shelter until the authorities moved the homeless along. I thought of how Deidre could have been among them by now, how it could have been me had Frank not taken me in. I knew Deidre wouldn't have minded taking me if I had nowhere to go, but I knew, too, that her position at the pub was her meal ticket and I wasn't going to take that from her.

I wrapped my shawl tighter around me, looking out across the Thames as the sun broke through the gray clouds, sending a brilliant shaft of light down the middle of the river. I lifted my hand, shading my eyes from the intense reflection. At the bottom of the embankment, I noted a man seated beside a tree. He had a small easel and seemed oblivious to anyone else as he painted.

I sauntered down and stood behind him, studying his work.

"I'm not doing portraits this week," he said, not looking up.

"I was just admiring your landscape." I said, looking over his shoulder. "Do you paint for a living?"

"Does it look like it?" His tone and expression were caustic.

I raised my eyebrows. "Well, you've certainly developed the attitude, at any rate."

He did not respond.

"You might consider a touch of cadmium red just there." I suggested, pointing to the spot.

He looked at me then, his pale gray eyes and scraggly beard making him look like a fierce, primal warrior. I could not place his dialect.

"Are you an artist?"

"Me? Good Lord, no! But I have done a bit of modeling, if you would like me to introduce you to some artists I know. I would be most willing to arrange it."

"Modeling, you say?" He continued to paint without looking at me.

"Your work is good. Perhaps if you were to tamp down that attitude of yours a bit and learn from a good mentor, you'd be exceptional."

"Now you're a critic?" he said.

"No, but I am a fair judge of talent. I believe you're good enough to perhaps get the Exhibition one day."

He snorted. "The Academy's Exhibition?" His brogue was thick—Scottish, if I were to hazard a guess.

"Where is it that you hail from?" I asked.

"Pembroke, Wales."

He stood then and wiped his hand on his shirt, then, and stuck his hand out to mine.

"Have you been in London long, then?"

"Nay, only a few weeks," he said. "I do portraits here and there. They bring in enough to keep me at one of the boardinghouses a few blocks down the road."

"Have you eaten?" I asked, fingering a bag carrying a few coins that I kept in the pocket of my skirt.

"Aye, miss, 'tis kind of you to ask."

"I'm sorry, I don't believe you stated your name."

"Oh!" He grinned sheepishly, removing a tattered tweed cap. "The name is Edward…Edward Rhys. I'm pleased to make your acquaintance."

"Is there an address that I might give my friend where he might reach you?"

He looked around and tugged the cap down over his unruly dark blond hair. The style itself gave a certain old-world manliness to his solemn looks. "When the weather is good. I'll be here in the gardens," he answered.

"Well, then, Mr. Rhys, I'll tell him to look for you here." I gave him a smile and a nod and turned to go back up the hill and make my way to the pub, hoping to have supper with Deidre if she was not too busy.

"Wait, lass!" he called after me. "You didn't tell me your name." He had a handsome smile that might well give Thomas a run for his money where his younger models were concerned.

"It's Grace."

"Aye, then, Grace. Good day to you until we meet again." The words gliding off his tongue warmed me like a fine brandy on a cold night.

"Grace!"

Startled, I turned my attention up the hill and saw Harriet, one of the barmaids from the pub, running toward me. Fear was etched on her young face and a cold feeling of dread gripped my stomach.

"It's Deidre, she's in the maze. She won't wake up."

I grabbed her hand. "Show me." I turned around and found Mr. Rhys staring at me. "I may need your help! Come quickly."

Deidre's face was chalk-white, her blank eyes ringed with a purplish hue. I dropped to her side and shook her shoulders, but she was limp as a rag doll.

"Grace." Mr. Rhys tried to pull me away, but I fought him off.

"Deidre! Can you hear me?" I shook her again.

"Grace." Mr. Rhys's voice was low, calming, a contrast to Harriett's uncontrolled sobbing behind us.

Mr. Rhys knelt by her, sweeping aside her collar to rest his fingers against her neck. It was then that I noticed the angry marks on her neck. Mr. Rhys placed his palm over her eyes, closing them. He took off his jacket and gently laid it over her.

"I'm going to get a constable, Grace. I must ask that you not touch her."

What seemed like hours passed before we were allowed to leave the gardens. When the authorities were satisfied with our stories, they said she'd be given a Christian burial in the poor man's cemetery, unless we could afford otherwise. None of us had the means to finance such an undertaking, so we watched them take her away on a cart.

Mr. Rhys offered to walk Harriet and me back to the pub, but I declined, needing to be by myself. Harriet went back to work, and I trudged up the familiar steps to my old room feeling as if I carried rocks on my shoulders.

The stench in the alleyway below hadn't changed as I pushed against the door, hunting for a lamp in the semidarkness and finding the tin of matchsticks to light it. I stood in the center of the small room. It did not look different, but it felt different. I closed the door, slid the latch into place and tucked a chair beneath the curved door handle. Tears welled in my eyes as I spotted Deidre's shawl. She must have gone out without it. I picked it up and hugged it to my chest as I lay down on the bed and cried myself to sleep.

The next morning I returned to Woolner's flat, sharing with him what had happened, and as I'd promised, I asked Frank to tell Thomas where he could find Mr. Rhys.

I pulled out the portrait of me Thomas had started, hoping to replace the image of Deidre's dying expression with another picture in my mind. Frank kept quiet for a time, then put the painting away as I stared at it.

"What are you doing?" I glanced up at him.

"Come to dinner at the studio, tonight, Grace. The boys would love to see you. It's been too long. Besides, Thomas says he wants us all together. He has a surprise. He asked for you to be there, specifically."

"He asked about me?" The smallest glimmer of hope lifted my heart.

"Well, he knew that you'd been staying here. I told him about your friend and he thought it would be good for you to join us."

Frank riffled through my sparse wardrobe. "I wish you'd kept some of those exquisite gowns, Grace. These things are so tattered." Frank tsked.

"I wanted no reminders of Hoffemeyer, Frank."

"Of course, sweeting. It's just that you looked like a queen in them. Here." He handed me my best gown. "Wear this. Thomas always loved you in this."

"Frank, Thomas has a new muse. What did you say her name was?"

"The bitch? I mean, Sara—the lovely young thing with raven-black hair and a heart to match. Mark my words, she'll be gone before spring." Frank smiled as he started to close the door. "Carriage arrives in the hour. Chop-chop, sweeting."

It was good to be among the core members of the brotherhood, the boys I'd known since Thomas and I met. Whenever they were together, the conversation was lively and it made you feel that—at least for a few moments—life made sense, if only in our world.

Our chairs were drawn in a circle so we could easily see each other when we spoke. I hadn't laughed in such a long time. Most of these men were at least ten years younger, but when we were together, it was as friends—without age, gender, or social status. We all anxiously tried to guess what Thomas's surprise would be. I hoped it would be inviting Mr. Rhys to be his protégé.

Frank had described Sara's physical beauty perfectly; as to her personality, I had yet to form an opinion. The real test would be how she acted when she was around Thomas. She did have a knack for taking a quiet gathering of friends and making it an affair to remember.

No wineglass went very long without someone pouring it full. She had prepared oysters on the half shell, tiny sandwiches cut in perfect triangles and bite-size cubes of cake, covered in a stiff icing she called *fondant*. It was the only thing that impressed Frank. For some reason, he had an issue with this muse, more than he had with Helen.

My first impression, beyond her raven locks and crystal blue eyes, was much the same as Frank's. "Ambitious, that one," he said. "Let's see if she's worth her salt."

He and Watts proceeded to place bets on whether they could goad her into admitting an interest in having her nipples pierced, as was all the rage at the clubs frequented by the affluent these days. I had my doubts if she would play along, but to my surprise, she did. In fact, she grew quite brazen, stating that she might well have it done if it were safe. At which point I challenged her good-naturedly, offering that I would have mine pierced if she would do the honors. Perhaps I felt challenged that she seemed so comfortable in Thomas's studio. I knew that she lived there and suspected that she and Thomas were lovers. He never had a muse who wasn't a lover. It was a relationship that Thomas understood perfectly, but the poor women he bedded never understood completely. Sara, I feared, was no different. Only time would tell whether I was right or wrong.

Putting a decided halt to our fun, Thomas entered the studio and told me in no uncertain terms that the critics didn't need another thing to toss at the brotherhood just now. He cupped my cheek and smiled, then turned to the rest of the group.

"Now, if my two favorite women are done with this nonsense, I suggest that if anything should be allowed to touch either of you lovely creatures it should be me." He gave us a charming grin and quickly moved to Sara, drawing her into his embrace, whispering something in her ear. She looked over his shoulder directly at me, her blue eyes challenging.

"Everyone, I'd like you to meet Mr. Edward Rhys, newest member of our little den of creativity."

I averted my eyes from hers, secretly blossoming inside with pride that Thomas valued my opinion of Edward Rhys. I was not living there, but my presence was of value.

Chapter 9

SEVERAL WEEKS LATER, FRANK AND I WERE HAVING dinner and I was telling him about my experiences with Lord Hoffemeyer. He hadn't heard the full story of what happened in the garden.

"But it's not turned you away from the idea of men altogether, has it, Grace?"

"Are you asking for yourself or a friend?" I teased. We both knew who he was alluding to.

He blushed and then narrowed his gaze on mine.

"You know what I mean, sweeting."

"If this is about Thomas again..." I shook my head. "I don't think you quite understand the relationship that Thomas and I share. We have an understanding, you see."

"So you say," Frank commented drily. "But I know my Thomas. Be patient, Grace. He'll come around."

I smiled and went on with my supper, refraining from engaging in an argument over which one of us knew Thomas best.

Frank's expression suddenly brightened. "I've got it! *You*—a fictionalized version, of course—are going to be my next submission to the brotherhood's newsletter. If Thomas wants to point out the pitfalls of our society, your story of that monster Hoffemeyer trying to blackmail you is just the ticket!"

"I feel fairly certain, Frank, that Thomas would prefer we put the incident behind us."

"You can help me, Grace. We'll stand this Hoffemeyer chap right on his nose, maybe slap him around a bit in the process." He wiggled his eyebrows, his grin full of wicked intent.

"Me? Help you with your writing?" I laughed.

"Think of it, Grace, you might be helping to teach other unsuspecting women to be wary of a wolf in sheep's clothing."

I thought a moment on that and nodded. "When do we start?"

It did not take long for Thomas to show up at Woolner's flat, and when he did he was bloody furious.

"What in Christ's name are you doing?" He tossed the manuscript we'd sent to him on the table and looked at me, his turquoise eyes ablaze.

I was in the process of setting the table for Frank and myself. "It's nice to see you, too, Thomas," I responded, and before he could answer, Frank appeared from the kitchen, carrying a pot of steaming potato soup with ham.

"Thomas! I see you finally accepted my invitation to drop by." Frank placed the pot on a folded towel. He glanced at the papers strewn on the table. "I see you received my submission. Can you stay for supper?"

My gaze swerved to Frank, silently asking him what the hell he was doing.

Frank shrugged and the corner of his mouth lifted in a slight smile. "He has to eat."

Thomas yanked out a chair and sat, and then his eyes rolled up to mine and he leaped to his feet, waiting until I slid into my chair. I hid my smile, absurdly delighted that even in his fury, he thought of the gentlemanly gesture. I tried not to read too much into his agitation, but the fact that he was here and staying for supper instead of being at home with his muse made me wonder if there was trouble brewing again on the home front.

"This article, Frank. It's about what happened to Grace."

Frank frowned. "As I am aware, Thomas, and for the record, it's some of my best work, don't you agree?"

Thomas picked up the papers and skimmed over the article. He shook his head. "It's far too dangerous. If Hoffemeyer saw this, or any of his power-hungry partners did, there would be hell to pay and Grace would be right in the midst of it."

"I gave my permission to write it, Thomas. At least perhaps someone else won't fall into the trap that I did."

"It's not wise." Thomas spoke slowly, steadying his voice.

I could see his point, and yet between what had happened to me and to Deidre, I wanted someone to know what an easy target for criminals women on the street were. "It's a growing problem, Thomas, one that, if it isn't addressed, will one day result in much greater tragedy."

"Perhaps, then, you could write of your affairs, Thomas," Frank challenged. "*That* would make for far more interesting reading." He rose from his chair in a huff and went into the kitchen.

"Did you have to tell him everything?" Thomas asked, tapping his fingers on the table.

"I told him the truth, Thomas. Isn't that what you've always preached to the brotherhood? Wasn't that the reason you started your news sheet?"

He raked his hand through his hair. It was then that I noticed the streak of silver near his temple. "You're right, I suppose." He rubbed his knuckle over his lips, deep in his thoughts. "I'll think about it, Grace." He looked at me, his eyes filled with sincerity. "I just don't want to see you hurt anymore."

I patted his hand, grateful for his concern. "And I don't want to see other women hurt. Do you?"

He frowned, and though I could see that he did not entirely agree on our method, he did agree with me. Changing the topic,

I tried to solicit a smile from him. "Is the new muse working out well?"

"Are you sleeping with Woolner?" he countered.

Beyond surprised by his remark, I dropped my spoon in my bowl. "*That* is a ridiculous notion, and further, it is none of your business even if you didn't already know that I am not Frank's type. Are *you* sleeping with Sara?" I asked, pinning him with a look that meant I was not about to be bullied.

He hesitated. "That's my affair and not what we're talking about," he shot back, folding his arms over his chest.

I chuckled and picked up my spoon to resume eating. We were at an impasse. I wasn't sure if it was me who had changed or Thomas, but something had occurred. I was tired of being his part-time lover. I'd had a taste of wealth and seen the dark side of the affluent. I'd seen the face of a dear friend murdered by God knows who and God knows why, because she'd had no choice but to do what she did to survive. I realized how easily it could have been me. Both incidents had forced me to face some harsh facts about myself. I was no longer content with letting life control me. I wanted to have more of a voice. I wanted to feel I had the same rights as other men and women.

He pushed from his chair, stuffing his hands in his pockets, and began to pace the dining room. "Things aren't going well at the studio," he said finally. I let him continue. "I'm having problems with Sara."

I didn't look at him and continued to eat in silence. Being his sounding board was also getting to be tiresome.

"Well? Don't you have something to say?" he asked.

"Didn't you just tell me that it was none of my affair?" I took a sip of my wine.

"That was before," he stated, walking to the other end of the table.

"Before what, exactly, Thomas?"

"Before I asked you for help, Grace. Christ, do I have to spell it out? I'm asking your opinion on how to handle this."

"Why do you want my opinion, Thomas?"

"Grace, next to William, you know me the best of anyone and you can see how I botched that."

"So you're trying *not* to botch this, is that what you're saying?"

"No, I feel that she shouldn't have any misconceptions that I'm going to marry her."

"Because you've slept with her?"

He held his hands out and shrugged.

"How noble of you," I stated drily. I wondered if Thomas had ever had the same concerns about me. My ire rankled knowing the thought had likely never crossed his mind. I was, after all, just a former streetwalker, not exactly the type of woman men clamored to marry.

"You say that like you don't care."

I pinned him with a stern look. "Perhaps because I don't."

He searched my face. "Truly, you don't give a damn who I sleep with?"

"What do you want from me, Thomas? Why do you need my blessing for every woman you've ever slept with?"

He sat back in his chair and studied me.

"That is a very good question, Grace, one that I shall ponder long and hard while I am in Rome over the holidays. Another reason I came by. I'm leaving tomorrow and wanted to ask if you would check in from time to time on the studio. Edward and Sara will be staying there over the holidays. Edward is working on a new project for exhibition."

"Thomas Rodin, what are you doing?" I narrowed my gaze. "You are purposely going off and leaving those two alone, aren't you?"

He grinned. "Grace, she's pushing me. You know how I am. I'm not marriage material. Now, Edward—" he pointed at me "—there's a man made for marriage."

"Thomas, people's hearts are not things to be toyed with."

He looked down at the table, then leaned forward and took my hand, rubbing his fingers over my knuckles.

"Trust me, Grace. There is a method to my madness."

"Oh, really?" I tugged at my hand and he held it tight. "I didn't think you needed to have a method."

"Woolner!" he yelled aloud, keeping his green-blue eyes on mine.

"What?" came the response from within the kitchen. "I'm working on the dessert."

"Do you need us for a while?" He leaned back in his chair and smiled, waiting for Woolner's response.

"Bloody hell, the damn thing deflated. What did you say, Thomas?"

"Make another, Woolner, we'll wait."

Thomas stood and drew me to my feet. I tried feebly to tug away, but, what the hell, the truth was I needed him tonight.

He scooped me over his shoulder and smacked my bum.

"Has the thought occurred to you that I might not want to go to bed with you?" I asked.

"No, I could see it in your eyes. I know how you are, Grace, when you get mad at me. It's a cover-up for being aroused."

"You pompous bastard," I said, squirming on his shoulder.

"Do you deny it?" he asked, his hand sliding beneath my skirts to caress my calf.

"You're incorrigible." I shut my eyes, fighting the wicked thoughts developing in my mind.

"I love it when you're mad at me, Grace."

"Get to the bedroom, Thomas," I stated through my ragged breathing.

"What is going on?" Frank appeared at the breezeway between the dining room and kitchen. "Where are you two…oh, Jupiter's balls." He turned around. "I'll be in the kitchen."

All of my noble thoughts of changing my ways, of wanting more stability went right out the window as Thomas dropped my feet to the floor and reached back, slamming the door with his hand. He shrugged from his jacket, slipped off his cravat and started to unbutton his shirt.

I knew I was going to regret this later, but it had been so long. "Your divorce is final, then, with Helen?"

His fingers stilled and he looked at me. "Yes, Grace."

He was leaving tomorrow, and in all likelihood he would return from Rome with yet another muse. Oh, God, what was wrong with me? As always, it seemed, we found ourselves connecting for a brief interlude of passion, a few moments of sanity in a chaotic world, before fate repelled us apart. How long could I keep doing this to myself?

There was an odd familiarity to going to bed with Thomas. It was comfortable, it felt right and if I was deluding myself, then I confess to happily doing so. I lifted my hair, turning my back so he could unfasten the buttons of my dress. With each turn, his knuckles brushed lightly over my back, increasing my anticipation. My dress slid over my shoulders and he placed tender kisses where my flesh was exposed. Unhurried, he turned me in his arms, holding my face as he teased my lips, sampling, coaxing. His kisses were slow and his tongue gently demanding. I surrendered after the first moment his mouth touched mine, giving myself to him freely.

We kissed, urging one another on, teasing, satisfying, giving and taking in equal amounts. There was no need to speak, we'd said everything before. His mouth caressed my throat as he lifted my chemise over my head and tossed it aside, then held my breasts, laving the tight buds with his teeth and tongue.

The restrictions of our clothing fell away, and each kiss, each caress, fueled the slow heat building between us. He knew the places to touch, knew how to bring a gasp or a sigh from me.

Since the night he told me he was going to marry Helen, I had promised myself not to let Thomas have more of me than my body. Then along came Sara and now she, too, seemed but a whim. I had to ask myself, what did that make me? *The one he kept coming back to.*

Thomas drew me onto his lap, wrapping me in his embrace, offering me the passion of the flesh he knew so well. I was content, safe in his arms, my body joined with his, our mouths tender one minute, frenzied the next.

"Grace," he said quietly.

His hands caressed my lower back, pulling my body close. I rested my forehead to his, feeling a delicious possessiveness that I didn't want to spoil.

"Let's not talk, Thomas," I replied, rolling my hips to remind him of why we were here. I held his neck and bowed backward. His hand glided with soft reverence over my breasts.

"Sweet God, Grace," he whispered. "Why is it always like this for us?"

My body grew tight, molten desire consuming me. "No regrets, remember, Thomas?" I said, bringing myself upright to face him. I ran the tip of my finger over his tempting mouth. "You are strikingly handsome, Mr. Rodin. Are you aware of that?" I whispered.

He slid his hand around my neck and drew me into a fiery kiss. "Come to Rome with me, Grace. We could explore the sights, make love every night, drink good wine. It would be glorious."

"You'll be busy with the boys." My breath caught as his mouth left mine and moved to my shoulder. His hands caressed my body, knowing just where to touch, how to touch me.

"I won't ask you twice, Grace." He planted nibbling kisses along my jaw, beneath the sensitive spot below my ear. His fingers slipped between us, teasing where his body joined mine. My body trembled on the edge of my release. His hard gaze, filled with lust, held mine. "Don't ask me, Thomas. Don't make me deny you."

I cupped his unshaven face and kissed him, sensing his frustration, and slowly gave way to his desire. He flopped back on the bed, his hands covering my breasts as I rode him furiously.

"Yes, Grace," he hissed, his hips bucking as he thrust upward deep into my core. *"Yes, my love."*

I did not let the words linger in my brain. I gave them no time to touch my heart. My climax overtook me in a blinding rush, causing me to scream his name out loud. His eyes, glittering with lust, never left mine as he drove into me, spilling his seed.

He pulled me to his side and tucked me beneath his arm. "Stay with me tonight, Grace."

"You're in my bed." I smiled, sliding my hand over the sheen of his firm stomach.

"Then ask me to stay."

I fought the urge to ask him why he wanted me to go with him, now—at the last minute—instead of asking me when his plans were made.

"I don't think that's a good idea. Not tonight."

He looked at me in surprise. "Aren't you going to miss me?"

"Did I say that?" I tugged the hair on his chest.

"Ow, wench." He frowned, but mischief sparkled in his eyes.

"Moody rake," I tossed back.

"I am not moody."

"Oh, please." I rose on my elbow and looked down at him. "Concede at least to that, Thomas. There is no doubt you are, on occasion, unbearably moody."

"It is, I suppose, a creative hazard."

"Which you have elevated to an art form," I teased, offering him a grin.

He turned onto his side and I wished there was a way that I could have captured the expression on his face. I saw in his glittering green-blue eyes delight that I had not seen for a long time. It made my heart swell with unwarranted pride that I might have something to do with it.

"Come with me to Rome," he said again, teasing me with a kiss.

"Thomas, you said you would not ask me twice."

"I lied." He grinned. "Please Grace, think of the fun we'd have."

I was afraid if I went with him that whatever we'd created here might end forever there. I had to leave him *wanting* to come back...hopefully, to me. "I'm sorry, Thomas. I can't."

He looked flustered. "Why not? What's keeping you here?"

You. Us. "I just can't go," I stated flatly.

He swung his feet to the floor and sat with his back to me. I reached over to trace his lower spine. He stood up.

"I don't understand."

I don't understand it myself, Thomas. "I don't know how to explain it." I pushed from the bed and put my arms around his back. "I will be here when you get home."

I sensed the tension in his body dissolve and he pulled me into his embrace. We stood holding each other until a knock sounded on the door.

"Cake's done," Woolner hollered through the closed door.

Thomas's laugh rumbled against my cheek.

"Happy Christmas, Thomas," I said quietly, pressing my ear to his chest, memorizing the beat of his heart.

"Happy Christmas, Grace."

Chapter 10

FRANK WENT NORTH TO SEE HIS FAMILY OVER THE holidays, graciously inviting me along. He did not feel that I should spend the holidays alone, watching over both his apartment and the studio.

He kissed my forehead and eyed me. "Are you certain you don't want to come meet my family? God knows my mother would be pleased if I brought a woman home."

"Thank you, Frank, but I told Thomas I'd keep an eye on the studio."

"And what else are you planning to do with your time?" His eyes did not mask his curiosity.

"Well, I won't be pining away after Thomas, if that is your meaning."

"Good girl. He's a scallywag, Grace. Honestly, I don't know what you see in him."

"I thought you were the one who told me to be patient with him?"

"That was before he left you and went to Rome," Frank huffed.

I hadn't told Frank that Thomas wanted me to go with him. I had my reasons and it was better to let things play out as fate saw fit.

"Let it go, Frank. It's Christmas," I said. I had plans to pull out the painting of me that Thomas had nearly finished and see what needed to be done to complete it. I didn't want any negative thoughts muddying that process.

"You're right, sweeting." He hugged me. "I'll be back in a week, unless things get excruciatingly boring! Happy Christmas, darling."

As it was, Frank did return earlier than expected and we spent New Year's Eve on the town celebrating in true Frank Woolner style. On more than one occasion since the holidays, I'd gone by the studio, finding it undisturbed and void of either Sara or Edward. Though I found it a bit strange, I thought little of it. Perhaps Thomas's plan was working and Edward and Sara were spending more time with each other away from the studio, or perhaps she'd changed her mind and gone back home.

The weeks passed and before I knew it, it was nearly the end of January. Frank and I had received only one letter from Thomas since he'd left. My trips to the studio had grown less frequent as I spent more time studying and soliciting Frank's help with touching up Thomas's painting of me.

"You have a keen eye," Frank stated, looking over my shoulder as I dabbed light on the high point of my shoulder. I'd been careful not to change the foundation of the painting.

"Do you think he'll appreciate that I've tried to finish it?" I asked, glancing up at Frank.

"Oh, heavens, he'll have a fit, but after he looks at it—really looks at it—I don't see how he could possibly be angry." Frank kissed the top of my head. "What do you plan to do with it?"

"I haven't given it much thought. Just show it to Thomas and see what he says."

"Hmm," Frank patted my shoulder. "I'll get us some tea."

Watts stopped in unannounced while Frank and I enjoyed our afternoon tea and a new recipe for biscuits that he'd brought back from his family's cook. Watts's amber eyes glittered with keen interest as he helped himself to a biscuit and spread it with orange marmalade. "So, I assume the two of you have heard about Edward and Sara?"

I finished swallowing my tea. "Um…no. We haven't seen anyone from the brotherhood recently. What happened?"

"Seems they were married in Wales over Christmas."

I stared at him. "Married?" I repeated to make sure I'd heard him correctly. "That is awfully sudden, isn't it?" That explained why no one had been around when I went to the studio.

Watts waved his biscuit at me. "Not to my way of thinking. I saw how that woman eyed him the first night Thomas brought him to the studio.

"Have you heard from Thomas?" I asked. "Does he know?"

Watts shook his head. "I haven't had a chance to go by and see him yet. He just asked me to see to it that the next issue of *The Germ* gets out."

"You mean he's back from Rome?" The news startled me and my gaze swerved to Frank, who seemed to be studying his teacup intently.

Watts glanced from me to Frank. "He got back about a week ago. I thought you knew. When I saw Frank the other day, I told him—" He clamped his mouth shut, realizing the tension he'd unintentionally created.

"Frank?" I asked. "Did you know he was back? Why didn't you tell me?"

Frank stabbed Watts with a furious look and sighed, turning his attention to me. "I thought…hell, I hoped that he would have contacted you himself by now, sweeting."

I sat back and dropped my biscuit on my plate, no longer having an appetite. Why should things be any different? "Well, you know our Thomas. He's probably deep into a new project." *Or has a new muse.* "But what about Edward and Sara? Did they stay in Wales?"

Watts perked up, happy to have the topic steered away from me. "Here's the strange part. They've been living in the farmhouse that Thomas owned. The one he was saving for a communal brotherhood studio, someday. Guess that's no longer the case," he stated, popping the last bit of his biscuit into his mouth. He licked his fingers and rose, taking a sip of tea to wash down his food. "I've got to run. Just came by to pick up your article, Frank."

Frank went to his desk, found his script and handed it to Watts.

"Let me know what you two hear about Thomas," Watts said.

Frank walked him to the door and had a sheepish look on his face when he returned to the dining room.

"I'm sorry, sweeting," he said softly.

"Thomas's acreage? Why would he give that up…and to Edward?"

Frank shrugged. "The studio was his and William's dream. I think after what happened between him and Will, his heart wasn't in it anymore. Edward was his protégé and has nothing. Maybe he decided to give it to Edward out of charity, or he just didn't care. I don't know any better than you why Thomas makes the choices he does."

"You're probably right, Frank, and I would be wise to stay out of it and mind my own business, right? But I'm concerned why he wouldn't have contacted any of the people closest to him."

Frank considered my words. "You know how the critics have been riding him. Thomas doesn't respond well to criticism."

"I want to go check on him. Will you come with me?"

"Let me clean this up and we'll head over to the studio straight away."

The pungent stench of stale liquor hit Frank and me when I opened the door.

"Thomas?" I called, easing the door fully open. The door brushed an empty bottle of port, sending it rolling across the wood floor, smacking the wall.

"Oh, dear," Frank muttered under his breath.

We found Thomas seated at his writing desk. Hundreds of

pieces of wadded pieces of paper were flung around the room. His cupboard storing his port hung open and it was empty, the bottles strewn about the room with used glasses perched next to them.

"Ah, there you are! My last two friends in all of London and quite possibly the planet." Thomas tried to stand, but his boot caught on the table leg and he fell back in his chair with a rousing thud.

"It's a bit early for port, isn't it?" I moved about the room, gathering up the bottles. Frank took a trash receptacle and silently began picking up the garbage scattered around the room.

"Don't start with me, Grace. God knows I don't need another woman harping on me, telling me what I should and shouldn't do."

I continued to carry used dishes to the kitchen, stopping long enough to put on a kettle for some strong tea. "You have me mixed up with your critics, Thomas," I said.

"Oh, no, Grace. The critics, now *there* is another matter entirely. I'm talking about my muses, Grace."

I glanced at Frank, who just shook his head.

"They're all the same. Luring me to them like sultry sirens." He grabbed at the air as if mimicking being pulled in. "Their beautiful smiles, porcelain faces, swanlike necks...sucking me under until I surrender to their passion."

"Good God," Frank muttered, tossing another paper wad in the trash.

"Then, bam!" He smacked his fist to the table, bringing my head up. I exchanged looks with Frank.

"I'm suddenly not around enough, or doing more of this, not enough of that. 'Take me here, Thomas. Let's stay in, Thomas. Isn't it too early for port, Thomas?'" he bellowed, swerving his bleary-eyed face to mine.

"You are nasty when you're drunk," I stated calmly.

He lifted his hand and looked at Frank. "You see? I cannot please them. What is a man to do, Woolner?"

"Help me get him to the kitchen," I said, taking Thomas under the arm.

"You needn't worry, Grace. I have sucked the place dry. There is nothing more for me to drink and I have absolutely no money to buy more. Oh!" He gave me a sardonic grin. "And no one will buy my paintings."

Frank and I escorted him, listening to his jabbering all the way to the kitchen sink. I started the pump and got a steady stream of cold water rushing from the spout. "Put him under."

I suspect the Pope in Rome heard his colorful testimony. He still had a lot of fight left in him. Frank held him as best he could and I shoved his head under the water.

Thomas's hands flailed, his words gurgling as he tried to speak.

"It won't do any good to cuss, Thomas, we can't understand you," Frank advised.

Thomas slammed his palms against the sink. "Enough!"

Frank and I walked him to his chair in front of the fireplace. As I set to the task of getting Thomas to remove his sodden clothes, Frank built a warm fire. I grabbed a throw from across the back of a chair and tucked it around his naked shoulders.

"Drink this." I shoved a cup of strong tea into his hands.

"Hair of the dog?" he asked, raising his bloodshot eyes to mine.

"Straight strong tea, Thomas."

"Do you want to talk about what happened that made you do this to yourself?" I asked, sitting down across from him.

"I'm going to go see if I can drum up something for him to eat," Frank offered.

Thomas stared at me. Only one other time had I seen him look as bad as he did now.

"My father died while I was in Rome. I didn't know about it until I got home."

"I'm sorry, Thomas."

"I haven't been in touch with my parents for years. William was always the one who kept us connected, and well, now...I haven't heard from him in so long." He paused to stare at his teacup.

"I came home and found a note from Sara, telling me that she and Edward had gotten married. They came by the studio a few days later to gather their things. Edward didn't know where they would stay and I understood them not wanting to stay here, so in a moment of weakness, perhaps pride—" he shrugged "—I told them they could have the cottage. They might as well. What good is it to me anymore?"

I nodded, not wanting to ask the question pressing my heart. I summoned my courage, needing to know. "This was more than you expected, wasn't it?" I asked.

Thomas's hair, dripping wet, was matted to his head. I rose, took the towel from his shoulders and began to rub it over his head, drying his hair.

"I don't know, Grace. I thought I knew what I was doing. The truth is I don't know how to live without my muse." He laughed quietly.

Which one, Thomas? I thought, staring blindly into the fire. I realized then, that until today he'd never called me his "muse." Had our relationship gone beyond that of a master and his muse? Did he consider me more of a confidant, a friend, or simply a set of comforting arms when he could not appease or be appeased by his "muses"?

"You'll find another muse, Thomas, and you'll begin to paint again," I said.

It was not long before I had moved back in with Thomas, taking care of him as I'd always done. He went in and out of his moods, drinking less, but still drinking to get through them. He'd started writing poetry with Frank's guidance and tried his hand with a few short stories. But the critics were ruthless, calling his style "lascivious and novice." In a desperate attempt to show the academy he was still viable, he produced a painting that the committee called "the desperate ravings of a man who has never quite made the level of his peers who graduated from the academy." He was growing more discouraged and I, right along with him.

I came home one day, after I'd peddled a couple of Thomas's original works on the street and gotten enough money to pay for some food, to find him in the studio, stuffing his clothes into a bag. "Where are you going?"

He glanced up. "Oh, Grace, I'm glad you're here. I received an invitation from Edward to take an extended visit to the country. He says the hills are awash with color and they have a garden that is in full bloom. He feels that it will be good for me, perhaps inspire me to pick up a brush."

He turned to me and held my shoulders. "I know this is sudden, but Edward needs me now. He's heading to India on research and would feel better if Sara was looked after while he was away."

"Why doesn't she come here?" I asked.

"Because the country and the fresh air is not *here,* Grace." He smiled snapping his bag shut. "It's *there.*"

"And what about me?" I asked, tipping my head.

"You're not alone here. You have Woolner and the rest of the chaps. I know you're in good hands."

It was at that point that I realized, I think much as William had, that I was going to have to step away from Thomas's shadow. I was going to have to give up caring for him, and either he would fall flat on his face or he would find another to take my place, as I had taken William's.

"I'm going to tell you something, Thomas, and it may change the course of our friendship, but I need to say it just the same."

He stood, jiggling his bag beneath his hand.

"It not about whether or not you have a muse, is it, Thomas?"

He shook his head. "Grace, if you have a point, please get straight to it. I have a carriage waiting."

"It's the thrill of the hunt, I think. You aren't inspired by *the muse.* You're inspired by the challenge of what you think you cannot obtain and are, in the process, Thomas, blinded to what you already have."

"If this is about Sara, Grace, she is a happily married woman. I am doing this as a favor to a friend while he is on a research trip. Nothing more." He kissed my cheek and gave me a puzzled look. "I swear I don't know where you get these ideas. My hope is that a few weeks in the country will serve to inspire my painting again. Don't let Frank near the kitchen. He's liable to burn down my house!"

A few weeks later, I was not surprised when I came out from the kitchen with a cup of tea and found Edward standing in the studio, his back toward me, looking down at a portrait of Sara.

"Edward?"

"Hello, Grace," he said, not turning around.

"Thomas is still out at the farm." I set the tray with my tea on Thomas's writing desk.

"Yes, I know, I just came from there." He laid the painting down and faced me. His face was drawn. He looked haggard.

I held the teapot up in silent offering and he waved it away as he grabbed a chair and drew it to the opposite side of the desk.

"I came for your advice, Grace."

"I think we're going to need something stronger," I said, going to Thomas's special cabinet. Fortunately, he'd spared two bottles of fine Scotch whiskey from his previous tirades. I selected a bottle and grabbed two glasses, pouring a finger in each. I slid one across the desk to Edward and held up mine in a silent toast.

"What happened?" I braced myself, both mentally and emotionally, for what was my greatest fear—that Thomas and Sara had somehow rekindled their relationship and they wanted to make it a permanent arrangement.

"I feel that I can speak frankly with you." His burr was thick. "In view of your...well, your profession."

I sighed and tipped the glass back, swallowing the contents whole. My eyes watered as the heat seared my throat. I poured myself another glass and Edward quickly downed his portion, slamming it on the desk for me to refill. This, I had a feeling, wasn't easy for him. "Go on, Edward, I've been expecting this," I stated with a heavy sigh. I leaned back in my chair and held the glass to the light, eyeing the amber color, wondering how much of it would obliterate Thomas from my mind.

"I love my wife, Grace." Edward stared at the table, playing the rounded edge of his glass along the tabletop. "I am willing to do whatever it takes to make her happy."

"You're a good man," I said, my thoughts growing pleasantly hazy. *But you are no match for the likes of Thomas Rodin.* "If you don't mind me asking, why would you go away and invite Thomas to stay there?"

He shook his head. "I suppose there were many reasons. I knew they shared a past. I wanted her to be happy and maybe part of me needed to know if she was over him."

I nodded, understanding his logic.

"I came home early to tell her how I'd missed her, how much I loved her, and I found the two of them in the library." His gaze met mine. "She was sitting on his lap, bare as the day she was born."

"And Thomas?" I wanted to close my eyes to shut out the image, but curiosity held my gaze to Edward's.

"Fully clothed."

I uttered a quiet sigh of relief. "What happened next?" I took a sip of my whiskey this time, needing to understand what it was that Edward needed from me. A friend to listen? To bed me in retaliation? "Did you quarrel with Sara?"

Edward shook his head. "Nay, Grace. You need to understand, things had not been good between us." He looked away for a moment and then back to me. "I'm not exactly the type of man to do what I did, but for her I would do anything. Christ, Grace, it had been ages since I'd seen that beautiful look on her face. I was mesmerized, watching the two of them for a moment before they knew I was there. So lost in her pleasure—"

"I understand," I interrupted, not needing to hear a detailed description. "What happened, then?"

"I pleasured her with my tongue," he remarked, tipping back his glass and taking a healthy swallow.

As the image of the three of them leaped into my mind, I downed the second glass without a thought. At that moment, I had never been more envious of another woman in my entire life. "So—" I coughed "—the three of you...?" I left it open-ended, unable to bring myself to suggest what I thought came next.

"Nay, 'twas no more than drawing a screaming climax from her," he stated blatantly.

I stared at him in silence. *What should I say? Well done?*

"I came here because you seem to know Thomas."

I laughed aloud at that. "It seems that everyone, including Thomas, thinks this is true, but I do not pretend to understand him, Edward. I'm sorry if that's why you came, but I cannot help you."

"I came to ask you if Thomas is the type of man who would be selfless enough to share a woman with another man."

"You mean you're thinking of asking him to live there, with you?"

"Aye, if it's what Sara wants, I will manage," he said, tipping his glass to his throat and emptying it. He shook his head as the whiskey found its mark.

"What about what you want, Edward?" I asked. The Scotch had given me just enough courage to speak my mind openly.

He frowned as he poured more liquor in his glass and held the bottle up to me. I shook my head. I needed to keep my thinking straight.

"I want to make a good life for Sara. I want to have a family with lots of wee bairns running around. I want to make her happy, and then I'll be happy."

"And she knows this?"

"I've not had the chance to tell her just yet."

"Did she tell you that she had feelings for Thomas?"

"Nay, not recently, though I know they were once lovers when she was here," Edward said.

"It seems, Edward, that you and I have a similar problem. You want your wife back and I want Thomas."

"You and Thomas? I had no idea. I'm sorry, Grace, this must have been hard for you to hear."

I waved his apology away. "I have lived through worse things, and truthfully, Edward, what I feel for Thomas, I fear, may be one-sided."

"I'm sorry for Thomas, that he is too thickheaded to see what jewel lies within his grasp."

My eyes watered and I swallowed the lump in my throat. "I thank you for that, Edward, but you came here to ask my advice. And I would advise you to go to your wife and not only tell her how you feel about her, but show her and keep showing her every day. Include her in everything, and together build that life you want so badly."

"And what about Thomas?" he asked, pushing from his chair, a new determination lighting his eyes.

"Let Thomas figure things out on his own. It's about time he did."

Edward captured me in a fierce hug, lifting my feet off the floor.

"Oh, gracious," came Frank's startled voice from the doorway.

Edward set my feet to the floor. "Edward was just leaving, and Frank, I need your help with something."

"My thanks to you, Grace." Edward took my hand and kissed it, nodding to Frank as he left the studio.

I went to the double balcony doors and watched Edward climb into his carriage. I had a feeling that Sara would not be able to resist the determination and adoration of her husband, and it would not be long before Thomas returned to the studio. Frank's voice brought me out from my thoughts.

"I trust you're going to explain every sordid detail of what just happened."

I had packed all of my worldly belongings in a single trunk. With Frank's help, I'd sent the painting to the academy for determination for entry into next Spring Exhibition. Frank had encouraged me to sign my name, but I insisted Thomas's should be on it. Finally, Frank took the brush from me and signed *PBR—G & T.*

"There," he said. "Pre-Raphaelite Brotherhood—Grace and Thomas. Surely the old man won't find fault with that!"

I had also asked him to book me passage on the next steamer to America.

Frank handed me the portfolio with the one-way ticket inside. "Are you sure about this, Grace?" he asked.

I gave him a wobbly smile. "I trust I won't need it, Frank. But I hope you understand my reason for doing this. I will gladly repay you once I am employed."

"God help us, let's pray our Thomas has a brain in that head of his." Frank hugged me and sniffed, looking away.

A few days later, a messenger delivered two envelopes to the studio. Nervously, I tore open the one bearing Thomas's handwriting.

Dearest Grace,
I would forever be in your debt if you would kindly send a carriage for me at the cottage house. Will explain when I see you.
Yours,
Thomas

The other note, stamped with the seal of the Royal Academy, I tucked in my pocket. I grabbed my wrap and pulled it up around my neck to ward off the unusual chill in the air. Then, I summoned a suitable coach to be sure we were covered in the event of a downpour.

The carriage jostled through the streets, leaving the brick cobblestone and stench of the Thames, easing into a gentle rocking motion with the soft dirt beneath the wheels. I watched blindly out the window, wondering what was to become of Edward and Sara, wondering if seeing the love between the two of them, if seeing their commitment to make their marriage work, would spark something inside of Thomas. It was, after all, the second time he'd lost a muse to another man.

Still, I had to be realistic. Thomas could as easily respond the same as he always had, expecting me to be there for him until he found another muse to pursue.

As difficult a decision as it was, I knew if he had not changed, I would have no choice but to leave him; either that, or forever remain a ghost in his life. I would never have any real substance. He asked me once if I didn't deserve better. I had finally realized that I did.

Thomas was standing outside on the circular rock path leading to the front door of the cottage. A white mist hovered over the quiet pasture beyond the house. It was an idyllic setting for a young couple to raise a family, as I prayed would be the case for Edward and Sara. Still, I felt sad for Thomas, knowing how he would miss his walks along the rolling hillsides.

The coach shimmied to a stop and Thomas's smile was tight, unreadable, as he handed his bags to the coach driver. I pressed my face close to the window, studying the cottage with its sloping roof and ivy crawling up the trellis to the windows above. A movement in one of the second-floor windows caught my eye, and I saw Sara standing there, wrapped, it looked as if in a sheet, her hand pressed to the glass. Behind her, Edward came into view, pulling her into his embrace.

I scooted away from the door to make room for Thomas to get in. I laid my bag purposely on the seat beside me.

"Good morning, Grace." He settled himself across from me and smiled as if being picked up from such liaisons was a normal event.

"Good morning, Thomas. I trust your visit to the country was pleasant?"

He leaned forward and gave me a peck on the cheek. "Of course, fresh country air is always invigorating."

A chuckle escaped my throat. "How are Edward and Sara?"

He shoved open the window, slipped his hand out and slapped

the side of the carriage. His eyes scanned the view beyond the window. "Fine," he said, as the carriage jerked forward. "They're going to be fine."

He turned to me then. "It was good of you to come, Grace. You didn't have to, you know."

"I know, Thomas. I wanted to," I replied, avoiding his steady gaze by looking out my window. A few seconds of silence passed and I heard him sigh. "What is it?" I asked, giving him a side glance.

He shrugged, his hands clasped between his knees. "Just thinking."

"About what?"

"Us. Here we are. Together again. Neither of us seems able to stay in a relationship for very long."

"Speak for yourself," I stated softly. "Besides, I thought you'd already decided that you weren't the type to settle down."

"Do you think people like us can ever find true happiness?" he asked.

I thought about it a moment and looked at him. "I suppose it depends on your definition of happiness. I mean, what is happiness after all, but being in the company of good friends and able to pursue your passion?"

He regarded me intently. "You know me well."

"I should think so after all this time, but frankly, Thomas, there are days when I don't feel I know who you are at all." I swung my gaze back outside and thought of the ticket in my bag, unable to imagine leaving London, leaving him. I was grateful for the friends we shared, for having seen the passion of his art fulfilled. But what, then, was *my* passion?

"Grace?"

"My mind was wandering, sorry." I looked at him and, though I noted he was aging, he was still as fit and handsome as the day we met. That seemed a lifetime ago. The question of my passion continued to niggle at my brain.

"What is it, Thomas? You have that gleam in your eye. The one that makes me think you'd like to undress me."

A slow, wicked grin curled up the side of his delectable mouth. The shadow of his unshaven face made him look more roguish than ever. Without contest, he was a breathtaking man. I realized then what made my body hum, what caused my heart to race— what made me believe that *anything* was possible. My passion— my deepest desire and dream—was *Thomas*.

He crooked his dark eyebrow. A gesture so small, and yet it unraveled my heart.

"I will want more from you this time, Thomas. I grow too old to continue playing these games."

He lifted an errant strand of hair from my forehead and brushed it back from my face. His featherlight touch traced the contours of my cheek, drifting over the pearl buttons on the front of my dress.

"You are still as beautiful as the day we met, Grace." He hesitated, searching my eyes.

"And you are as much of a rogue now as then," I added. "Handsome and charming as ever." I covered his hand, which was resting on my lap, and summoned the courage to look into his eyes. "But I do not wish to corral you, Thomas. I enjoy, far too much for my own good, I fear, your unbridled zeal—your passion."

His mouth quirked into a crooked smile, but his eyes narrowed. "Leaving no room for you to find your own passion. Isn't that what you're trying to say?"

My eyes tingled with unshed tears. I turned my face to the window.

"I truly have neglected you, haven't I?"

He raised my hand, pressing his lips to the back of it. I glanced at his untamed curls beginning to pepper with silver. "Do not patronize me, Thomas. I am not one of your new girls, easily charmed."

"Aren't you?" he teased, turning my wrist to kiss the sensitive flesh on the inside. "I felt your pulse quicken, just now."

My gaze bored into his, furious that he could manipulate my desire with such little effort. My whole life had revolved around men, what *they* required. I was only just beginning to understand what it was that *I* needed. I slipped my hand from his.

"Grace, I'm not sure I know if I am any good at…relationships. Affairs, yes, but…"

I offered him a dubious look.

"Yes, I have a reputation. I am aware of that."

He looked at the floor, his hands clasped.

"So, the idea of being content with one woman in your bed for a lifetime doesn't appeal to you? You enjoy the variety, is that what you're trying to say?" I stared out the window.

His callused fingers touched my chin, turning my face to his. He leaned forward, paused, then gave me a soft, chaste kiss. I kept my eyes shut, absorbing the truth of the point he'd evaded. There would likely be more muses and I could either choose to be his mistress, or not.

"I was wrong, Grace, in my belief of what passion is. I have been reckless."

I nodded and opened my eyes. "You have that reputation, as well."

He frowned and sighed deeply. "I always thought passion was something to be achieved. Grace, I will be honest, I do not regret my past."

"Nor do I judge you for your past, any more than you judge me."

He pressed his fingers to my mouth. "Let me finish, please."

I nodded.

"I do not regret my past, *except* for not having spent more of it in your company."

I bit my lip, my eyes welling.

"I saw how Sara looked at Edward. How desire ignited the spark between them, but it is love that keeps the fire burning. That's what you tried to tell me the day I left to come here, wasn't it? You were asking me to see that love was standing right in front of me. A love I was too blinded by my misguided emotion to see."

"You are slightly dim in that regard." I offered a wobbly smile, tears streaking down my cheeks.

He shook his head, blinking as he sniffed and looked back at me. "I am. God help me, perhaps a knock on the head would have helped."

"I doubt it would have been enough," I replied.

"All I have ever done has been fueled by my passion. What else do I know, Grace? I have spent my life's work searching for the perfect element to appease the critics. Somewhere along the way, the quest became my obsession. But when Edward returned to tell me that he'd do whatever Sara wanted to make her happy, I saw the depth of his love for her."

I nodded. "I know. Edward came to me and told me he'd do whatever she wanted, even if that meant sharing her with you."

"She didn't want me, Grace. She only needed attention. Once Edward realized that, *he* became the only thing she wanted."

"And what about you, Thomas? What is it you want?" I asked.

He leaned forward, drying my tears with his thumb before placing a tender kiss on my forehead, my cheek and then my lips. His mouth hovered over mine.

"What I desire more than my next breath is to spend the rest of my days making a life with you," he whispered against my mouth. "I don't deserve you." He pressed his cheek to mine and I leaned against him, praying this was not a dream.

"There is something you need to know first, Thomas, if we are to share our life together." I pulled the note with the academy's seal from my pocket.

He blinked, taking the envelope, and turned it over in his hand. "I don't understand."

"You will. Open it."

He moved my bag and came to sit at my side. Offering me a glance, he slid open the note. After reading it through, he looked at me with a puzzled expression. "It's about the nude, it's been accepted for the Spring Exhibition. But, it wasn't finished."

"Perhaps some of your skill has rubbed off on a most unlikely student," I offered with a shrug.

He chuckled and it grew into the rich laughter that I'd not heard in a very long time.

"You're not angry that they accepted, then?" I asked.

He folded the note and tucked it in his breast pocket. "Not in the least, but it would appear that I am *your* willing and loyal protégé—in life, love *and* art."

"You seem teachable," I teased.

"Then teach me, Grace. Be my mentor, my lover, my companion." He traced his knuckle under my jaw.

"Is that all?" I challenged, determined to have it all.

He kissed me softly. "And be my wife."

I savored his mouth on mine. "Perhaps you should draw the shade, Mr. Rodin. It is a long ride home."

He grinned, leaning past me to close the fringed shades. "What now?" His eyes glittered with desire.

"Undress me, Thomas." I took his hand in mine. "And make it last a lifetime."

★ ★ ★ ★ ★

ACKNOWLEDGMENTS

I'd like to thank my editor, Lara Hyde, and the rest of the Spice team at Harlequin, who encourage me to explore outside of the box in my writing. I have grown immensely as a writer under their guidance. I would also like to thank Renee Bernard for her friendship, help with Victorian culture and sharing resources. To Amy and Genella, for the numerous read-throughs, changes and suggestions—you guys rock! To Jo C., my port in the storm who is great at perspective issues. And finally, to Daniel Gabriel Rossetti, the Pre-Raphaelite Brotherhood and their muses—one and all—who by their unconventionality inspired not only this book, but also my view in believing in one's passion.

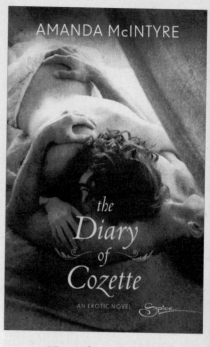

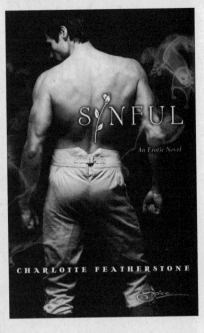

naughty bits 2, the highly anticipated sequel to the successful debut volume from the editors of Spice Briefs, delivers nine new unapologetically raunchy and romantic tales that promise to spark the libido. In this collection of first-rate short erotic literature, lusty selections by such provocative authors as Megan Hart, Lillian Feisty, Saskia Walker and Portia Da Costa will pique, tease and satisfy any appetite, and prove that good things do come in small packages.

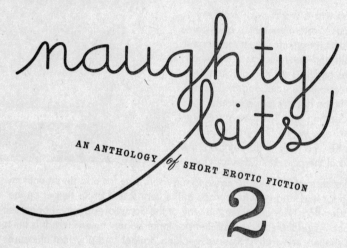

naughty bits

AN ANTHOLOGY *of* SHORT EROTIC FICTION

2

on sale now wherever books are sold!

Since launching in 2007, Spice Briefs has become the hot eBook destination for the sauciest erotic fiction on the Web. *Want more of what we've got?*
Visit www.SpiceBriefs.com.

Spice

www.Spice-Books.com

SV60541TR